SHADOWS IN THE FIRE

SHADOWS IN THE FIRE

GRAY BASNIGHT

FIVE STAR
A part of Gale, Cengage Learning

GALE
CENGAGE Learning

Farmington Hills, Mich • San Francisco • New York • Waterville, Maine
Meriden, Conn • Mason, Ohio • Chicago

GALE
CENGAGE Learning®

Five Star™ Publishing, a part of Cengage Learning, Inc.

LIBRARY OF CONGRESS CATALOGING-IN-PUBLICATION DATA

Basnight, Gray, 1953–
    Shadows in the fire / Gray Basnight. — First edition.
      pages ; cm
    ISBN 978-1-4328-2989-6 (hardcover) — ISBN 1-4328-2989-0
(hardcover) — ISBN 978-1-4328-2982-7 (ebook) — ISBN 1-4328-
2982-3 (ebook)
    1. African American girls—Virginia—Richmond—Fiction. 2.
Slavery—Virginia—Richmond—History—19th century—Fiction.
3. United States—History—Civil War, 1861–1865—Fiction. I. Title.
PS3602.A8467S43 2015
813'.6—dc23   2014041553

First Edition. First Printing: April 2015
Find us on Facebook– https://www.facebook.com/FiveStarCengage
Visit our website– http://www.gale.cengage.com/fivestar/
Contact Five Star™ Publishing at FiveStar@cengage.com

Printed in the United States of America
1 2 3 4 5 6 7 19 18 17 16 15

Dedicated to the belief that an American Slave Memorial rightfully belongs on Richmond's Monument Avenue in remembrance, honor, and apology.

"Thank God I have lived to see this! I want to see Richmond."

—President Abraham Lincoln,
meeting with General Ulysses S. Grant
at City Point, Virginia, April 2, 1865

"Well, well, the old ape is here."

—White Richmonder viewing Lincoln, April 4, 1865

"Bress de Lord, dere is de great messiah! Glory, hallelujah!"

—Richmond slave viewing Lincoln, April 4, 1865

CONTENTS

★ ★ ★ ★ ★

BEFORE THE WAR

★ ★ ★ ★ ★

CHAPTER ONE:
MISS FRANCINE PEGRAM

I steal time every dawn to wonder about my mother. I did not know her, but after I awaken each morning with the sun, I always take a moment upon my bucky-board bed in the pantry to wonder where she is and how she fares. Sometimes there is some knowledge about where people go, some little piece of news, like Miss Ben-Vicki who got sold off to a farm family in Bowling Green. That was all we knew. Even though we never heard from her again, it was something. And we were glad to have it.

Not so with my mother. For my mother, there was nothing. But when I take time before rising to begin my labors, I wonder where she is. I wonder what she looks like and if I may favor her. The only knowledge I have is her name. She was called Miss Avery-Ann Pettigrew. And like me, she was a slave, which means she cast no shadow just as I cast no shadow. That is because a slave *is* a shadow, a mere dark reflection of its owner's godly glow. Like all shadows, the owner sees us plain when he wishes, but takes no notice when not inclined to cast a downward gaze. And when we get sent away or sold off, there is nothing left behind.

I have many names. To all masters and mistresses, military men, citizens of the merchant class, and all others with the freedom to come and go as they please in Richmond, I am, simply, "girl." That's what they call me when they believe they are being decent, or at the very least, not mean in spirit. When not being decent, or when being outright indecent—it is "pick-aninny," or "negress," or "nigger-girl."

Missus and Master Pegram sometimes call me "pantry rat," a pet name they consider a clever kindness. They even have a song about it, which amuses them whenever they deliver it in their seesaw manner, which sounds more like chicken-chortle than music. They gave me the name because I sleep in the kitchen pantry and, I suppose, because I am skinny and move fast and quiet as I go about my labors of cooking, cleaning, stitching, fetching water, and—the one I look forward to—running errands in the grand city of Richmond.

Extra Pettigrew calls me "Missy Fran." I like that best—not because he too is a slave or because I prefer that to my proper name, but because I know he likes me when he says it. And sometimes it makes him smile his big smile.

Some refer to me as house servant or kitchen maid, though I am younger in years than others who live in fine homes and deliver those same labors. But older and more experienced slaves are expensive, so—times being what they are—Master and Missus make do with me.

There is one name for me that is common to all. It is what my mother named me, it is what Missus Ruth and Master Maxcy Pegram call me most usually all the time, and it is how my fellow slaves and all white men and women of Richmond know me. That name is Francine.

CHAPTER TWO:
MISS FRANCINE PEGRAM

I was sold over the back fence of the Spotswood Hotel when I wasn't yet one year old. After that, my name changed over from Francine Pettigrew to Francine Pegram. Extra was present and remembers the barter. He tells me Master Pettigrew handed me over—just plunked me down into the waiting arms of Master and Missus Pegram "for cause," as the saying goes, which I believe means for nothing.

Slaves are not normally sold for nothing, but I was different—I was a bargain on both ends of the barter:

For Master Pettigrew, the owner of the Spotswood Hotel, which lay at the northwest corner behind the Pegram backyard, it was an expense removed from his business ledger.

For Master Pegram, it was occupation for his wife's troubled mind—occupation that he hoped would meet her motherly needs and quiet her ways.

For Missus Pegram, my arrival measured as a promissory note of future cook, maid, seamstress and a thoroughly clean house.

As to my fulfillment of the barter, it broke differently for each of the three. For Master Pettigrew, the deal was a good hand-wash from the get-go. I made that happen simply by being handed off to another, like my mother was handed off. Though it took time, I vouchsafed the final measure of the barter by learning nearly everything there is to know about scrubbing down and fixing up. But the middle part of the bargain, the part about helping Master Pegram by calming Missus Pegram's ways, well—those results have been mixed. It has been a house haunted by Missus Pegram's worries as far back as memories take me. In the early years, Master Pegram took care of her, returning her to their bed when she commenced pacing the floor at night, talking aloud and sometimes raving about devils and specters and bad men and something she called the "evil smile" that floated outside the house.

It scared me when she took on with the oddness. She would go several weeks without a spell, then it would come over her without warning and I would be awakened in the night upon my bucky-board bed, where I could hear her footfall pacing the floor above me as she loudly whispered with great fear. Next she would speak normal to persons not present, then she'd change over to crazy raving with all manner of profane utterings that I never once heard her speak in polite company. Frequently she bounded back and forth in the upstairs corridor like a galloping pony. I could hear the hard pounding of her feet on the oaken boards as she raced from the front window overlooking Ninth Street, to the back window overlooking the backyard and the Spotswood slave-quarters beyond the fence and the big oak tree.

"Damn you . . . oh, damn you, you damnable man!" she chanted on the lap to the front. Then, "Damn you . . . oh, damn you, you damnable man" she chanted on the return lap to the rear window. Sometimes she'd throw in something about "oh, my darling Jasper," which always led to a bout of weeping.

Listening from my bucky-board, I always pictured her naked feet flapping up and down with the deformity she possessed. Directly beside the little toe of her left foot, there was a protrusion that looked like a sixth toe, an even littler little toe being born. It even had its own tiny toenail. Just like her oddness of the mind, that toe always scared me, making me think it may be the devil's signature.

On those nights when she took to galloping in the upstairs corridor, it could take Master Pegram most of the night to calm her down and get her back to bed. In the early years, he never did ask for my help. Neither did either of them ever mention it to me, or to each other that I knew of. I understood it to be a secret added on at the bottom of the Lord's list of "thou shalt nots" and one that I must never dare mention. But that changed when the war labors were set to commence—and he did finally speak about her behaviors to me in a shy manner.

Just about the time Master Pegram was called off to perform his engineer duties for long stretches of time, he pulled me aside and advised me that Missus Pegram's safekeeping was to be added to my house labors while he was away. He called her spells her "dark haunts."

"But don't worry," he said, "she'll come 'round. Just make sure she gets back to her bed and stays there. Bring her water during the nights and breakfast in the mornings. But don't worry, those dark haunts will end. She'll come round, she always does."

Knowing this to be one of the three reasons I was handed over the back fence "for cause," I feared failing him—and spoke of it to Extra.

"Oh, poosh, Missy Fran," Extra said to me. "It ain't nothin."

"You sure?"

"Sure I'm sure," he said.

"And that little toe?"

"Oddness of the body don't make people take on crazy."

"You sure?"

"Missy Fran," Extra said, "birth defacements ain't got nuthin' to do with the devil, if that's the way you thinking." He was right, of course. That is what I was thinking.

"I hope not."

"Ain't nobody perfect. Master Pettigrew got a big ole blotch of skin on his chest that's ruby-red and purple too. I see it when I help with his bath. It right odd looking. Sometimes I think it look like a firestorm in the night sky."

"It don't worry you?"

"At first. Not no more. And there a slave boy I work with at Gallego Mill—he's got these funny-looking, big ole ears that poke out like giant handles on a mixin' bowl." Extra pushed his ears out with both hands to show me what the boy looked like. "His ears near 'bout big as my hands, and they fold the wrong way, like God put his head on backwards."

"But Missus has devil spells—she sees people that float. She takes on about dead babies and such."

"That too, Missy Fran. Sometimes the oddness ain't on the body. Sometimes it on the mind. You know Cussin' Sally-Martha at the Spotswood. She ain't right in the head. And you know Riverjames at the Shockoe House. He almost fifty, but most of the time, he act like a child—like he younger than you. Poor ole Riverjames is big and strong, but he ain't got no understanding about nothin'."

Chapter Three:
Miss Francine Pegram

Just as I did not know my mother, so it was with my daddy. I asked Missus Pegram about it once and understood very quickly that it was yet another privacy too tender to be spoken on. So I let it be.

It was Master Pegram that later brought up the subject of my relations. Once, when the missus left the two of us alone in the house, which was a rare event, he departed his evening cigar, bourbon glass, and newspaper to speak to me in the kitchen. It was then he presented me with my pocket knife. At first, I conjured he had indulged too deeply in the bourbon bottle, as he did from time to time, and was talking nonsense. But then he made it clear that he meant what he was saying.

"You take good care of it, Miss Francine," he said. He spoke in a kind but discomfited voice that reminded me of the time he shyly advised me how to address the dark haunts of the missus. "It belonged to your granddaddy. It was in his pocket the day he died." I swelled with happiness and pride.

"How did my granddaddy die?" I asked. Master Pegram looked away. Then looked at one of the pots I was tending.

"What's that you're making for our dinner?" he asked.

"That one's black-eyed peas with bacon."

"Well, that's fine. And what's that?"

"That one's boiled cabbage. It got some bacon too."

"Oh, fine. Yes, that's just fine," he said, pretending to smile as he turned to go back to his cigar, bourbon glass, and newspaper. I should not have done it, but I did.

"Master Pegram, sah," I said, stopping him in the corridor.

"Yes, Miss Francine?"

"How did my granddaddy die?"

He answered without looking in my direction. He did not even look back into the kitchen; he just stared forward into the corridor. "He was a train man," he said in soft, slow words. "He was working on the Danville line when a large wagon laden with rails tipped over and rolled down a hill. He was crushed."

I was a stunned child. I looked at the knife. It was small, a one-blade knife inlaid with a rich dark wood. A crack ran straight across a narrow vein in the wood but it was not deep enough to dislodge the inlay. At that moment, when I first beheld the gift, my only connection with any blood ancestor—it felt wonderfully heavy in my hand, a great treasure that I vowed to guard with care.

CHAPTER FOUR:
EXTRA PETTIGREW

The night Missy Fran was born in the out-quarters of the Spotswood Hotel, I got sent away. I won't but four year old, and I wanted to see it happen. I wanted to watch Miss Avery-Ann Pettigrew to see how babies come. But they wouldn't let me. They sent me to the hotel kitchen for the whole night, where I slept on the floor by the big iron stove. The slave quarters had been the site of birthing before. I was born there myself. But when Missy Fran came, Miss Ben-Vickie and ole Miss Edna sent me away with two other boys. When I complained, Miss Ben-Vickie slapped me a good pop upside the face.

Next day I met Missy Fran for the first time. She was tiny, just a tiny little thing—but she looked straight on at me, like she could really see me, like she was sizing me up. Miss Ben-Vickie noted how her eyes were light brown in color and could fix good on a thing when she looked at it.

"That's not the way of babies," she said. "Most babies just working at gettin' over the pains o'birthin', just like the momma working at gettin' over it. It hard for 'em both. It hard for baby just like it hard for momma."

Miss Ben-Vickie knew about babies. She helped slave mommas going back to before the Spotswood was built—even my own momma, who died of the consumption when I still a baby.

"That girl born under the sign of the fox," Miss Ben-Vickie said. "All animals got stars. Ole fox got one too. Ole fox not

21

'round much. You watch dat baby. You watch," she said. "Dat baby a fox baby."

But Master Mills P. Pettigrew don't believe in star signs. He only believe in money and the Spotswood Hotel, which he owns along with everything in it—including me, Missy Fran, her momma, and all the other slaves in the kitchen, out-yard, and stable. Not long after Missy Fran come into the world, Master Pettigrew sold Missy Fran's momma at auction in Odd Fellows Hall on Mayo Street. The buyer didn't want no baby in the deal, 'cause he just wanted a nigger whore-woman, what they call a fine negress concubine. That's what Missy Fran's momma was. Miss Avery-Ann Pettigrew was the private concubine to Master Pettigrew. Two other slave girls got share-whored out in the early years. Master Pettigrew called them a sideline to his hotel business. Sometimes, just like our fine chicken suppers in the dining room, those two girls were the very reason why some men would book a visit at the Spotswood. But Miss Avery-Ann never got share-whored, except to one other man that I knew about.

Before Missy Fran's momma got sold off, the baby was taken away from her and that's when I stepped up to help Miss Ben-Vickie and ole Edna who taught me how. I won't but four, but I made certain she was kept in clean unders. And I stole extra milk from the kitchen.

Master Pettigrew was not happy about having a baby around and gave us a hard warning about falling behind in the hotel work. He always ran everybody hard, even the two Irish girls who worked the dining room and lived in a first-floor hotel room on the back side. And he liked to talk to everyone in another language that he called dead Latin.

"Neehill-add-neehill," was his favorite saying. He'd recite it to everyone. "I am a businessman. And in business you get nothing for nothing." Another one started out "Ergo sum . . ."

and went on with a long line of tiny words that he said equaled in meaning to say, "I am a businessman, this hotel is a business, we are all in business." In our own regular language, he was attached to saying, with a frequency, "Business is to the Confederacy as Jesus is to the church."

His favorite slave was Old Caesar, a rheumatoid former field hand who had grown useless to the Spotswood's contracted potato and greens farmer. He was old and not very able in body, but he proved lively and able as the hotel's doorman. In his dead Latin, Master Pettigrew called him "seena-qua-none." And I once heard him tell Old Caesar how much he loved him by naming him as an "obeisant asset at the baptizing bienvenue of the Spotswood lobby."

Such a mouthful of good words did not come often, which made some slaves not care much for Old Caesar—because when Master Pettigrew finished praising him, there weren't any kind words left over for anyone else. But I liked Caesar fine. I pretty much like all the slaves in Master Pettigrew's hotel family, even Cussin' Sally-Martha.

And Master Pettigrew fretted plenty about us having a new baby to look after. Not long before Missy Fran was plunked over the back fence to the Pegrams, he came to the fire pit in the out-yard at nighttime in warm weather while we was having our corncobs and cabbage and made us all stand up to listen to what he got to say. That was something he did from time to time because interrupting our dinner and making us stand let us know it was important and we had best listen good. On this particular visit, he sermonized with his "neehill-add-neehill," and he laid down the usual rules about work and not wasting time on a new baby, warning that failure would mean loss of dinner, a beating, getting hired out to do farm work, or even being sold off for good.

I remember this sermon in particular 'cause I was bold. I

asked a question. I asked him if he know'd where Missy Fran's momma was sold off to. Well, he didn't like being asked nuthin' by a five-year-old boy.

"Extra, what do you see coming and going in this hotel?"

"Men, sah."

"What kind of men?" he asked.

" 'Potent men, sah."

"That's right," he said, "important men. Businessmen. Men with money. Men in tobacco and cotton. Men in government and the military."

"Seem like more coming every day, sah."

"That's right," he said stepping away from me. "And I must finance improvements. Businesses must grow bigger as business grows bigger. I know ya'll don't understand that, but that's the way it is. Neehill-add-neehill, nothing for nothing."

"It's already five floor tall, sah," I said. "One of the biggest in all Richmond."

"There are ways to grow other than just growing larger," he told me. "Upkeep and physical improvement is another way, Extra."

"Yes-sah."

He leaned down to my face and spoke with a quiet meanness, his lips near 'bout touching my eyes. "What do you mean—'yes-sah?' "

"I mean—yes-sah."

"You mean you understand what I am saying?"

"Yes-sah."

"Say it back to me, then. What did I say?"

"You said you goan make things better."

Still leaning down on me, I could see he looked surprised, like he was figuring hard on something having to do with me and I wondered if I was going to get a pop. The truth is—I *did* know what he was telling us. I knew because I saw it happen. I saw what happened after Miss Francine's concubine momma got sold off. Master Pettigrew used that money to cover the hotel lobby and stairwell with a fine dark wood that had what they called dovetail grooving. After that, there came a fancy double-seat privy in the outyard, which was for hotel guests only—naturally.

But I knew something else too. I knew something happened that night at the fire pit. I didn't know what exactly. But I felt it. I felt it in the way Master Pettigrew spoke at me and saw it in the way he looked at me. I even got the odd idea that maybe he was a touch pleased with me for saying what I said.

"That's right," he finally said in a plain manner, standing up straight and *without* popping me. "Extra's right," he said to the others, "we are going to make things better 'round here." Then he turned and walked back into the hotel, leaving some of 'em at the fire pit nodding favors at me for speaking up, which made me feel good.

After that, I tried to keep my caring for Missy Fran a secret. But Master Pettigrew did eventually catch on. I was over five year old when it happened. He jerked me by the arm, pulling me into his office directly behind the hotel lobby.

"Extra," he say, "I am missing various assorted kitchen stock. Do you know anything on this?" he asked me.

Well, if it had been chickens and ham, or potatoes and cabbage, I could have said "no." I could have said, "No, sah, I don't know nuthin'." After all, babies don't eat chickens and ham. But it was not chickens and ham that went missing. It was milk and oatmeal, and cornmeal used for hotel baking, and cooking, and such.

I delayed too long in making an answer, so he popped me good 'n' hard upside my noggin. That got me to talking: "I is feeding Missy Fran, sah," I confessed. He didn't say nothing. He just looked at me. "She sho is a hungry chile," I added, hop-

25

ing that would settle the matter without more fuss just the way my speakin' up settled it that night at the fire pit. But this time my trick did not work. I got another good hard pop.

The next day I stood aside under the limbs of the big oak tree near the out-quarters, where I'd been shucking corn to be served at evening supper in the dining room, and watched as Master Pettigrew handed the baby over to the arms of Mistress Pegram. The men shook hands. Then the Pegrams walked into their home through the rear door with their new baby while Master Pettigrew went back to the hotel office and I went back to shucking corn. It made me sad, but I knew Missy Fran be better off in that big house.

CHAPTER FIVE:
EXTRA PETTIGREW

I missed caring for Missy Fran, but I was happy for her to be given over to a fine house. Yet I was worried too. We all knew Mistress Pegram had strange ways. From the early days, I heard talk that she lost all her babies before their birthin' time came. But she did have a real baby once. I know 'cause ole Miss Edna was on hand to help with the birthin' in the early years and spoke about it dying of the chest croup after two months o'livin'. Miss Edna says that's when the strangeness commenced.

Later, when Missy Fran was older, she asked me 'bout it bunches o'times. I always did what I figured best—which was to say it's not the devil that made Mistress Pegram take on with crazy ways. Telling her anything else would only stir a hot pot. That's why I never told her about Mistress Pegram birthin' a real baby in the early years.

'Course, ole Edna would have given her different counsel. Sometimes at night, in warm weather when we was sleeping in the hotel out-quarters and all the Pegrams' windows were open, we could hear Mistress Pegram ranting about God and the devil and babies and dead folks. On and on she went, sometimes for hours.

"Uhh-huh-h-h, ole man Scamp paying her a visit tonight," ole Edna would moan from her blanket by the fire. "Yes-sah-h-h. He gonna yank her good this time."

While it was happening, we'd all just lay quiet—privately hoping ole man Scamp would not spread his visitation from the

Pegram house to all of us sleeping in the Spotswood out-quarters.

It was on a hot night like that one that I first decided to someday tell Missy Fran all the truths I knew of her life. I planned to tell her someday that Mistress Pegram once had a real baby that died—and that was when she commenced takin' on with strange behaviors. And I planned to tell her that Mistress Pegram's oddness was likely worsened by her knowing what I knew, that Mister Pegram was allowed privileges as a partner of the flesh with Miss Avery-Ann in her groundfloor room on the back of the hotel. My master allowed it in those early years as barter for Mister Pegram steering military men to the Spotswood instead of the Ballard, which was an even bigger hotel. And once, when Master Pettigrew was away tending to family matters in Winchester, Mister Pegram was invited to spend long hours in that backroom. It was then, I heard others say, that Miss Francine was beget, as they say in the Bible.

When the war started, Missy Fran was too young for me to tell her that her new master, Mister Maxcy Pegram, was her daddy and that she was half white. At that time I was twelve, so I understood about things like whoring, and dead babies, and barter deals for babies, and such. But at eight year old, she was too young and didn't understand nothing about things like that.

★ ★ ★ ★ ★

THE WAR

★ ★ ★ ★ ★

★ ★ ★ ★ ★

The War

★ ★ ★ ★ ★

Chapter Six:
Miss Francine Pegram

For me, the war changed nothing and everything.

It changed nothing because I kept at my house labors as shadow to the missus. It changed everything because its unkind business altered all Richmond in such mighty ways as it brought episodes of hunger and hardship, which only worsened with each passing month like a cruel fever.

Early on, there were grand parades of Butternut boys. That's what I called them right from the start. Missus Pegram called them "our lads," or "our fine young men," and other such names. Master Pegram called them "our brave Confederate army," or "the courageous men in gray." I just called them "Butternut." That's the color of their uniforms—stained gray by the kernel of the butternut. After time, the gray dye mostly fades to a fair brown, but when that cotton muslin is pulled from the washtub, the butternut makes it the smooth color of smoke rising from a pure fire of pinewood.

Sometimes their parades in fresh butternut gray marched right past our house on Ninth Street, going up the hill, past the Great House of Government and on to war in the north; sometimes they marched down that same hill, across the river and on to war in the south.

On Sunday afternoons, smaller groups of young men wearing newly dyed butternut cotton and toting plenty of musket rifles on full display over their shoulders would parade back and forth without any particular direction in mind as their shiny drums boomed and clattered out dandy tunes of war rally that made people feel good.

That did not last long.

First, the parades stopped. Except for the Butternut guarding the Great House of Government, most went off and did not come back. Older men ran the stores, which Missus called "the shop-class," while other men, who always appeared mousy to me, ran the offices of government. That only left the slave men. And it was slave men who did most all the work in the city. As for the mistresses, they mostly stayed home except for churchgoing and shopping duties.

Even with fewer mouths to feed in Richmond, food grew scarce. Master Pegram saw that coming. The first year he made us plant a backyard garden. Missus Pegram could not foresee the need, citing all variety of shops, markets, and merchants.

"If the war shuts one store, why, there are many others," she said.

"And what if the war shuts them all?" he asked.

"Oh, poosh, General Lee will not allow all our shops to close down. Why, we would starve," she protested.

I believe her objection was based on worry over how a backyard garden might appear to her society circle. But Master Pegram was right. Meat disappeared first, followed by milk and cheese, then bread. Missus Pegram and I tended the garden as best we could. But the sour dirt being what it was—our vegetables did poorly. The cabbage was mostly lost. The potatoes were malformed, tiny things. But we ate them anyway. We did have a goodly harvest of small cucumbers and several batches of decent greens.

Early on, Master General Lee himself came into our Ninth Street parlor. I served him coffee while he sat on the red settee much prized by my missus. For the balance, I held perch upon my servant's chair in the hallway while he studied piles of unrolled engineering maps that Master Pegram placed before him. He asked lots of questions about highway conditions and such and asked Master Pegram if he would join the cause to devote his services as repairman upon the Confederacy's roads and bridges. From the hallway where I sat, it sounded like Master Pegram bust two buttons on his suit jacket as his chest swelled so big with pride before he could answer that, yes, he certainly would offer his services.

As he departed, Master General Lee nodded at me. It was then that I noticed that he had the tiniest feet of any man alive. It made me smile on the inside to see it. I declare, his shoes were smaller in size than my own.

Afterward, Master Pegram was flush with a happiness that I had never before seen in his manner. It was almost as though he'd received a blessing of the rapture in church, or been into his bourbon bottle, which he had not. He went on and on about men I did not know, men that he cited as being in possession of "blazing greatness." He spoke of someone named Alexander and someone named Caesar, who certainly was not the Old Caesar I know who stands at the Spotswood's main entryway around the corner on Main Street.

It was about a year after the parlor visitation by Mister General Lee that the newspapers began bringing big change to our lives. After the Butternut and Yankee went hard at each other in some town or near some creek, there would follow long columns in the newspapers listing the names of all the dead boys. That would bring on lamenting rounds of wailing and woe as bountiful death visited many homes. Many mistresses were taken to their bed over husbands and sons fallen in battle. The study of names was a regular event in the lives of the mistresses, oft repeated and restudied during afternoon socials.

"So-and-so was killed in such-and-such town . . . I declare . . . is that so-and-so boy from Manchester . . . I declare . . .

Oh, Miss So-and-So must be prostrate with grief . . . I declare
. . . Oh, Mistress So-and-So who lives on Grace Street has now
lost both husband and son . . . I do declare."

Sometimes their "declares" were followed by fits of boo-
hooing when the dead boy was known to Missus Pegram or one
of the many mistresses in her circle. A sure way to fire up a fit
of weeping was the sight of shoes on display upon the footpath.
During shopping outings, we would sometimes come upon a
fine pair of Sunday shoes, looking truly lonesome, placed in
front of this house or that—a sad signal that a man, whether
husband or brother or son, had been named in one of the newspaper columns as being among the dead. Shoes were in short
supply. So the mistress of the house would place the dead man's
shoes near the footpath. If they were the proper size, any passing mister, or even a servant boy, might avail himself.

As our contract with hunger worsened, the mistresses' objections grew louder. They whooped and wailed in the parlor after
each Sunday service as I served coffee and what few hard
candies we had remaining.

"Something must be done," said the plump Mistress Bartow.
"Why, the bakers are delivering everything they make to our
armies. Our courageous boys are important to be certain; of
course we must feed them. But we need to eat as well."

"There are calls for civil action," said Mistress Garland. "I
believe it our duty to heed the call."

"It's true," avowed Mistress Bartow. "We need bread too. It's
only natural. And when it is available, why—the prices! Lord-a-
mighty, Mister Bee wants eighteen dollars for a pound of bacon.
And flour! He's selling flour at eight hundred dollars a barrel!"
She wailed it so loud I wanted to put my fingers in my ears.

"Mister Perrin is no longer baking at all for the city," said
Mistress Garland. "All his loaves are going straight to the
Fredericksburg Station for shipment to General Lee." It was the

only time I could recall that General Lee's name was mentioned without long, drawn-out praise using words like "glorious" and "gallant."

As usual, their flow of grievances converged to punish mostly one man—Mister President Davis, who Missus Pegram said, "is ruining our affairs."

"Nothing but a damned politician," Mistress Garland called him. "Nothing more than that—except, maybe, the perfect fool."

"He certainly is more than that. He's a mongoloid idiot," Mistress Bartow barked in her deep voice, the fat under her arms quivering as she shook her finger in the air. "General Lee is not aware of our situation and he must be informed. Why, he would not allow the homefront to go hungry if he knew how pinched we all are." None of them mentioned to her that she may be served tolerably well by losing some poundage from her considerable girth, though I guessed more than one held such thoughts in their heads at that moment.

With time, hunger made their talk turn to action. The newspapers called it "the Bread Riot."

My recollection is that it started as a street parade of mistresses walking easy on Grace Street, gathering excitement as they arrived at the various buildings of government. Their purpose was to urge the bakers of Richmond to leave some loaves on their shelves—instead of shipping them all to the Butternut.

But their strategies were not well received. It got ugly. The mistresses behaved in an unexpected manner. The window of Mister Perrin's bakeshop was broken. Sentries dislodged them from the streets. Some mistresses were even carted off, hoisted away like no more than a box of freight, and more than a few ended the day being knocked about and in full possession of the sores and bruises to prove it. It was an ugly outcome that appeared to me to blindside the mistresses.

Afterward, they were much changed.

"We are in battle to boot," Mistress Garland said the next day, her voice trembling, set to bust with tears. "What difference if we are shot by Yankee minie-ball, beaten dead by our own security brigades, or taken by starvation while sitting upon our very bedstead?"

The episode led Mistress Bartow to cuss Mister President Davis with even less hindrance. "Mississippi malefactor," she called him. "Why, that man dared throw money at our feet to convince us to give up and go home. What we need is bread—not money."

"Ruby Branch was pushed to the street," vented Mistress Garland in a voice brittle with high-sounding emotion. "They knocked her right down into the mud. And after all she's done for the war effort. Why, she has volunteered near about every Sunday on Chimborazo Hill."

My missus, too, was changed by the episode. Months later, the very subject of it set her to grinding her jaw and sending her thoughts into another place that made me fear a spell of oddness loomed on the horizon. Typically, she did not participate in the various cuss-rounds heaped at Mister President Davis. But upon the whole unkind matter of the bread brawl, she volunteered only enough breath to speak her mind in clear pronunciation by naming the man a "noodle."

CHAPTER SEVEN:
MISS FRANCINE PEGRAM

Despite getting roughed up in the Bread Riot, the mistresses still felt a need to fuss over the Butternut.

I accompanied Missus Pegram on many occasions when she visited Chimborazo Hospital with the others as part of their works of kindnesses to wave the flag and pet the wounded. They would meet in St. Paul's lobby after Sunday services to assemble flower bundles. They cut strips of blue ribbon, which they used to bundle up and tie the bouquets—caterwauling all the while.

"Oh, Ruth, I am so sorry I cannot accompany you this morning to Chimborazo."

"Oh, Marion, do say hello to your husband for me. I know you are so glad he is safely returned home."

"Oh, Margaret, I declare, thank you so much for bringing these lilies. They are so lovely. I just know our brave, wounded lads will enjoy them."

"Oh, Marion, how did you get such colorful daisies this year?"

"Oh, Ruth . . ."

"Oh, Margaret . . ."

"Oh, Loretta . . ."

"Oh, Marion . . . I declare . . . I declare . . . I declare."

Afterward—and in full crinoline petticoat—they would carry their baskets brimming with flower bunches to Chimborazo, with me among the servants in tow to do the carrying. I struggled to hold my basket aloft in the crook of both arms as we paraded through the wards. Each long building had a single aisle lined with beds on both sides, occupied by wounded men whose bodies were absent arms and legs, struggling in all the throes of life, death, and everything in between. Some of them looked out with eyes that appeared to peep from another world. Some lay quiet. Some cried.

On the right it was "Bless you, son," as Missus Pegram laid a flower bunch on each soldier's pillow. On the left it was "Get well soon," from Mistress Mouton as she placed the flower bunch in their hands, if they had hands. Sometimes they changed over to saying, "Thank you for serving, soldier," "The Confederacy thanks you, soldier," and sometimes "The South loves you, sir," but mostly they stuck with "Bless you" and "Get well."

We ushered along from ward building to ward building, parading down each aisle, handing out spring blossoms. The flowers were mostly peach-colored daisies with one small lily in each bundle; buttercup and honeysuckle got added in to make them appear more plentiful than they really were. I was grateful for each gift of blossoms passed along—for it meant my load grew gradually lighter.

As war labors dragged on, Master Pegram was away for longer stretches. That was fine for me, because it allowed more time for my secret nighttime reading lessons with Missus. Reading was the only good thing about the war for me. By the fourth year, I could read Grimms' on my own. Missus Pegram once praised me for learning so much reading so quick. Then she seemed to take back the praise by calling it "understandable" and "to be expected." I wondered what she meant but there was no more remark on it.

In time, I understood that she too enjoyed our reading lessons. For her, they offered good distraction from the devil's enterprise. The longer I stood behind her in her upstairs bedroom, brushing her long hair and reading the primer and other materials over her shoulder, the less time she would be on her own and the less likely it was that she would slip into a spell. Like me, she was afraid of the spells that made her rave about devils and bad men and something called "the evil smile" that floated outside the house.

Of course, the reading lessons were not really secret. Master Pegram knew of them but did not object, because he knew that they distracted from her inner worries. Even so, whenever Master was home there were no lessons, and after I turned twelve years of age, Missus laid down a new rule: whenever Master was home, I was not allowed upstairs—ever. The way it was presented to me, I understood it to be a rule that behooved me to obey. And I added it to the bottom of the Lord's list of "thou shalt nots."

A few days after I was forbidden to go upstairs whenever Master was present, he came home for a visit that lasted nearly four days, one of his longest in over a year. The war was not going well and Missus Pegram's list of worries grew to include fear of reading her husband's name among the long lists of dead boys that appeared in the newspapers after a battle.

"They're saying the Yankees have us in a tight box," she warned her husband that night. "You be careful you don't stumble upon one of these roaring battles between here and that awful Washington City." He dismissed her with a silly rhyme—which he recited so many times over bourbon that night, both me and Missus grew weary of it:

Lee needs my brain for Yankee killing,
Not my aim which ain't worth a shilling.

"You take care about that," she snapped back at last. "The Confederacy doesn't have many engineers and I have only one.

39

You take care that some Yankee sharpshooter doesn't get you in his sights."

"Oh, poosh," he said, trying to sound amusing, which he did not because he had more bourbon than usual. "If the Yankees got any sharpshooters at all, they're keeping 'em under lock and key in Cincinnati, or some other place."

I always liked the word "Cincinnati." It sounded like a place that must be special because of the music you could declare while drawing out the saying of it.

It was only after that four-day visit by Master Pegram that I came to have some understanding of why I was not allowed upstairs whenever he was home. I have been told a number of times that I am fair of face. Missus Pegram never said it. But Master Pegram did once or twice. And right after that four-day visit, there came a Butternut boarder who stayed in the upstairs guest room who took on with me some, admiring my eyes, which he called tawny-tan, and praising me with fancy words when Missus was out of hearing range, which was seldom. But Missus must have known somehow what he was getting at, so that boarder did not stay long. And when other boarders came, she kept a tight watch on their movements. Different servant men said things too, calling me handsome or eyeing me over with the goat face.

The uptake of it all let me know early on that I needed to make plans. It was Extra I had my eye on. Even in the early years before the war, I knew he was special. I settled upon him for good when I heard about a beating incident with Master Pettigrew, who was not easy-handed when he laid into slaves. If any hotel guest complained about a slave, that slave earned great heapings of disfavors from Master Pettigrew. Even the Irish girls working the dining hall were denied supper if they forgot to call anyone "sir" or "ma'am." And Jules, the mute errand-boy, was loaned out to a farmer in need of fieldhands for a full month just for taking too long with one particular errand.

That hotel owner was hard on man-slaves—but because of the importance of kitchen labors—he was even harder on women-slaves. Poorly prepared meals could earn threats of being sold off farther south. Letting the meat in the meat house soil with fly-eggs would earn loss of supper for a week. The worst punishments were reserved for the most unwelcome deeds: stealing or getting sassy with a guest. For those violations, Master Pettigrew was known to be generous with the back of his hand and even, on occasion, his wide swinging forearm capped like a club with the clamped-down knuckles of his big fist.

Polly Ramseur felt his hand more than once. She had a manner that seemed not to recall upshot of her own conduct—or perhaps she could not master the various urges buried in her choler. Not three days after she was backhanded for scooping extra bacon lard into the servant's soup pot, a chicken turned up missing. It was that incident that showed me that Extra's heart was plumb.

"There was six chickens taken to the out-yard that day," Extra vowed. "I know 'cause I delivered 'em to Master Pettigrew. He inspected 'em and counted 'em good, then he passed 'em over to Polly at the pit-fire for cooking. When the service platter was returned to the kitchen, the chickens was all cooked and cut. The meat was all removed and towered up in a big ole pile."

"Then how'd Master Pettigrew know a chicken was missing?" I asked.

"Missy Fran," Extra said, "that dead-Latin talking man don't ever miss a trick. He took that big ole pile of chicken meat and dumped it on the kitchen countertop. Then he took to digging. He put the meat in one pile and the bones in the other. Then, from the pile of bones, he pulled out every leg bone. Then he lined up the leg bones in a tidy row. Then he counted 'em. Ten. There was ten leg bones. So he turns to me and says 'Extra, how many leg bones ought there be in six chickens?' So, I told him.

" 'Twelve, sah,' I said.

" 'Twelve,' he says back at me.

" 'Yes-sah,' I said. 'Twelve. Twice as many as was chickens in the first place.'

" 'That's right,' he says. Then he says, 'Extra, how many leg bones you see in that tidy row?' So I told him.

"Ten, sah.

" 'That's right,' he says. 'Ten.' 'Twas then I knew poor ole Polly was in for hard times."

"She stole and ate a whole chicken?" I asked.

"Reckon so."

"After getting beat for putting bacon fat in her soup?"

"I reckon, Missy Fran."

"Polly should have put all the bones back in that big pile after eating the chicken."

"I thought o' that too. But poor ole Polly ain't that smart."

"Extra, where'd you get that goose egg," I asked, eyeing a swollen spot around his left eye. I looked closely and knew it would get even bigger and turn purple with time.

"Master Pettigrew," he answered.

"Extra! You took Polly's beating?"

"I did, Missy Fran."

"Why?"

"Well, Master Pettigrew took on about 'how I suppose to serve chicken stew with only five chickens,' and 'how I suppose to make chicken soup with the bones of only five chickens,' and 'how I suppose to pay for six chickens when I got only five.' On and on he went, working in some of his dead Latin too. And I knew poor ole Polly was in for a bad way. So I just swallowed good, and I said 'Master, sah, 'twas me that ate that chicken. I ate it after working hard all that day totin' liquor barrels from Danville Station and I was hungry.' "

"He walloped you?"

"Sure did. It took him by surprise. He stared hard at me like maybe he think I was lying. I wondered if he knew I was trying to help poor ole Polly avoid a whupping. But then he stepped back, swung his arm wide, and just slammed down on my noggin good 'n hard."

"You still hurt, Extra?"

"Not much. I'll be fine. Missy Fran, I'm glad you're not with the hotel no more. You're in a better place with the Pegrams. I know it's not like the big ole marble mansion-houses on Franklin Street and west on Grace Street, and I know Mistress Pegram take on with odd ways. But it's a real house. And you learn to read. You in a real house and you better off than the hotel."

"Did Polly learn you helped her?"

"I never told her. But she knows. I reckon ole Edna or Cussin' Sally-Martha told her."

"They saw you get walloped?"

"Uh-huh. Well, ole Edna just heard it 'cause she's mostly blind you know. But Cussin' Sally-Martha saw it good. They were both in the kitchen at the time."

"What did Polly do with the missing bones after eating that chicken?"

"Dunno. Reckon she just tossed 'em in the pit-fire."

That sealed it for me. I loved him and wanted him to be my husband. Time and the war proved me correct. Of all servants, Extra was the most clever. His state as a "for hire" man allowed him to make some headway on his own. He worked a variety of labors and knew how to make his way beyond porter chores that required little more than toting and fetching.

Early in the war he learned how to work with tools. By the end of the war, he could build and repair, lay brick and mortar, drive horse and carriage of any size, and take care of black-smithing duties too. Most important—he knew tobacco. He worked with tobacco from field to warehouse and from there to its sale for chewing and smoking. I could not conjure him possessing any destiny other than clever endurance.

Never being one to plot my ways in secret, I told him my thoughts straight out. There had been nearly four years of war already and we were all so worn down and tired by it all that we could not imagine it getting any worse. During an evening trip to the Pegram privy, which sat at the backyard corner near the Spotswood slave quarters, I saw him in the out-yard. There, during one of our back-fence get-togethers, I asked him what he thought of my idea. He did not answer right away. But when he finally did—I was pleased.

"It work fine for me," he said. "I care for you as a baby. It be fine to care for you when you a woman too."

"So it's settled?"

"We talk more when you a woman," he said.

"When will that be?" I asked, leaning over the fence and wanting a kiss to seal our bond.

"Soon enough," he said without kissing me. "You still a child now."

Chapter Eight:
Extra Pettigrew

The war brung big changes for me. It meant opportunity. I got to do more than hotel porter work and I was able to better myself. They allowed it 'cause all the white men was off at war, so we got bonded out, as they called it—hired off to the tobacco house and the cotton mill. Some of us even got sent to the Tredegar iron manufactory.

And I got to go at large—to walk about on my own. It's good to walk like a real man on the streets of Richmond without stopping to answer as to why I am out and about without a master. As always, I bore a paper from Master Pettigrew allowing me out—as bonded property—but people got so caught up with news of General Lee they mostly stopped stopping me.

Sometimes I pretended I was one of 'em. I'd walk down Main, Grace, or Franklin Street and fall in behind their shadows, thinking that I too am like them, a salesman, arms merchant, or stock market man. Old Caesar told me some of the new arrivals are called "factors" and "factotums." I didn't know what kind of work a factor or factotum does, but on the day he told me about it, I walked among them thinking, I too am a factor, and I too am trotting off to my place of factotum business in some fancy office high up in one of the many tall buildings east of the Spotswood.

As for real work, the big tobacco houses is best—mostly loading and unloading hogshead barrels, which is hard work done mainly in the hot season.

One time, when wagons was in short supply, and a farmer brung a big crop to market by boat, they stretched us out from the James River down below, all the way up the hill to the warehouses in the business part of town. We took the loads straight onto our backs from the boat, then walked it up the hill from Canal Street—all the way up to Grace Street. I thought at that time, if the Lord is looking down upon Richmond on this day—he may mistake us all for a parade of ants toting bread crumbs back to the nest.

But there was more to it than just toting tobacco. Over time, I learned how to cure it in the smoke room until it was fine and dark. And I got taught how to dip the leaves in spices or sugar to make sweet plugs flavored with licorice or rum.

We stole too. As the war dragged on, they were looking less and less. So we stole more and more. Tobacco is good tender. We sell it to make some little monies, gamble it, barter it, or just smoke it. They don't miss it. It's not like stealing from Master Pettigrew, who counts every potato. There's just so much tobacco, always coming in and going out. Sometimes at the end of the day, they even give us some—floor sweepings mixed with dirt, but that's still tobacco.

And there's always some merchant man willing and waiting to offer thus-and-so barter to any slave who shows up at the back door of his shop with a ripe bundle of bright leaf tucked under his coat. Of course, they had law-rules to punish 'em for taking barter from a slave or even a free black—but when people lose what they have, they get mad and mostly don't care no more about what the rules tell 'em they supposed to do.

Chapter Nine:
Extra Pettigrew

I knew Chimborazo.

Master Pettigrew bonded me out to that place for two whole months in the war's third year when the nurses and surgeon doctors ran low on Johnny boy porters to help in the wards. Me and Riverjames Cleburne, who I knew from the Shockoe Tobacco House, got sent over to empty out chamber pots, scrub down sickness, and stoke the furnaces with fire logs and chopped-off legs.

That whole time we slept on a heap of rags we saved and piled up in the crawlspace under Building Forty-One, which had protection from wind and cold, being in the middle and surrounded by other buildings as it was, near the very top of Chimborazo Hill. From there, we could hear the moans of aching Johnny boys coming down through the flooring at night, making for little sleep. So we mostly just laid on our rags, smoking our stolen rolled-up tobacco, dozing off and on—and listening to the suffering of them men as they lay in their beds above us wailing with war pain.

Slave girls assigned to Chimborazo sometimes got barter offers from wounded Butternut in return for pleasure favors. When no ward nurses or surgeon doctors was around, the soldiers mostly got what they bartered for—slave girls not having much in the way of monies or knickknacks like the doodad filled with face powder I saw a girl named Miss Loretta accept in the exchange with a man who got his right leg chopped off at the hip.

It was on this account that Riverjames got in trouble. A rebel officer with no feet and bloody wrappings around his middle saw that Riverjames owned a pouch of fine tobacco and he wanted some of it. But Riverjames—being a former fieldhand, unable to talk good and behaving mostly like a little child even though he was more than three times my own age—saw the ways of the girls and thought that he too could barter for some doodad in exchange for his tobacco. The baffled officer looked out from his poor, sunk-in eyes.

"You see my legs?" he asked.

"Ya-ya-yas-sah, I see 'em," said Riverjames in his sputtering, bouncing way of talking like a man-child, leaning close over the officer's soiled bedding.

"What do you see at the end of my legs?"

"Ah se-se-see you ain't got no feet."

"That's right. And here?" he asked, making a gesture to the bloody wrappings around his middle."

"Ya-ya-yes-sah."

"What you think that is?"

"Innards gah-gah-got shot," Riverjames said.

"That's right. I got hit at Sharpsburg. You ever hear of that?"

"N-n-no-sah."

"Well, I have. That's where a Napoleon twelve-pounder popped my guts with grapeshot. You know about that?"

"N-n-no-sah."

"That's right—you don't." He tapped the bandages wrapping his middle. "I lost some of the guts that was in there, and my gizzard and my giblets too."

"Ah is right so-so-sorry, sah."

"That's right. You are sorry."

"Ye-ye-yes-sah."

"You are sorry. And you are a dumb darkie."

"Ye-ye-yes-sah."

"A big ole, thick-neck, stuttering, dumb-ass, dim-wit, darkie."

"Ye-ye-yes-sah."

"And what am I?"

"Wah-wah-white man, sah. Rah-rah-rebel officer." The soldier nodded approval and let his head rest back on his pillow—soiled yellow and brown.

"Very commendable." They locked onto each others' eyes as Riverjames leaned over that officer's broke body, his rolling neck and shoulders in constant motion. I was worried about the exchange, but did not meddle. "Indeed, you did well, boy, very commendable," he muttered again, composing himself.

"Tha-tha-thank you, sah."

"Now that we got our relations all worked out good—hand me that tobacco pouch."

The tussle that followed was not much of a tussle. It was pretty much a tussle of one. The soldier was so consumed by a spell of anger that he couldn't stop thrashing about when River-james snatched the tobacco pouch from his reach. I swear that Johnny Reb did remind me of a little baby the way he simply didn't care no more about nothing except crying. His thrashing turned into clawing and crawling; then his clawing and crawling turned into moaning; then his moaning turned into a collapsed heap of bleeding on the floor. He made such a noisy fuss that a drunken surgeon-doctor and two scruffy, tired-looking soldiers came running—arriving just as the outraged officer gave up the ghost after dragging himself down the aisle almost three bed-lengths away in pursuit of Riverjames, who mostly just backed away and made his own less noisy objections about "tha-tha-this be my-my own tobacky."

The drunk surgeon-doctor did not seem to care that the offi-cer had died—but he did care about the soiled bedding and bloody mess that lay scattered about so badly it appeared to be the work of several men. For that, he blamed Riverjames. He seized a board that lay inclined in a corner, previously used to brace broken limbs—swung it over his left shoulder and slammed it forward squarely onto Riverjames' right ear. The big slave barely flinched at the blow, but his ear did commence running with a generous amount of blood. He was mostly just confused about what was happening—and why, which made me feel right sorry for him. Before departing the ward, the surgeon-doctor pitched the board back into the corner where he found it and gestured to the two soldiers, who beat Riverjames with the butts of their musket-rifles, using more spark in the act than their sad appearance seemed to possess.

Riverjames never did fall down, but he did unintentionally oblige the two exhausted soldiers by sitting on an empty bedside, allowing them to raise their musket-rifles only half as high—so the butts could find their target about his head, neck, and chest with less effort.

Afterward, I sent Riverjames to lie in our bed of rags under Building Forty-One. I cleaned up the ungodly mess on the floor wrought by the dead officer's thrashing. Then I did the work of two slaves for the remainder of that day.

It was during those long work days in the wards of Chimborazo that I first heard talk of the war nearing an end. The wounded Johnnies spoke of hearing about a last-ditch plan to put slave men in Johnny pants, teaching us to shoot and sending us up against the Yankees in big numbers. They called it "nigger army" and "wall o'niggers."

Truth be told, I would not object to learning real soldier work. The nearest I came to soldiering was helping to dig what they called Roman defense trench-lines at the city ramparts. In the early years, I thought highly of the Johnny boys' dapper look and had a private fancy I too would be handsome in Butternut gray. I was particular fond of the drummers when they paraded about on the grounds of the Great House of Government. And I was keen on learning how to use a musket-rifle, which was something they never allowed any of us near.

But when talk about "nigger army" got passed through town, it was met with loud dead-Latin objections from Master Pettigrew. He ranted on about "mea" and "vita" and "dominium." He took to citing "the fourth commandment," which he said prevented the Great House of Government from coming into his home and taking his slaves. That confused me because I understood "thou shalt not steal" to be further on down the list of "shalt nots." Even so, I gathered the meaning. Like the others, I was an investment. But more than the other slaves, I was also a goodly roll of revenue from my bonded-out labors, which he did not want put to an end by seeing me killed somewhere up north in one of those congregations of butchery we kept hearing about with regularity. But anyway, it never did happen. They did not put us in Johnny pants and no one knew if it ever was a real strategy being hatched by Mister General Lee or just idle talk of a last-ditch hope that spread like fire.

There came another signal of war's end, which I heard from a slave who worked uptown at the Ballard Hotel, which was bigger and a lot fancier than the Spotswood. He advised me that three Irish girls showed up to work in the Ballard's fine dining hall, which ended his own white-jacket waiter work and the little tip monies he got to keep. His master sent him back to being a stable boy. But worse—he said he heard talk of many Irish men coming soon to take other jobs from bonded-out slaves in the tobacco warehouses, cotton mills, and even the Tredegar manufactory.

That news worried me bad. I knew it meant going back to the old days of doing nothing but toting and fetching. When I told Missy Fran, she smartly said we needed to work together, needed to pool our labors to get through everything still set to come. I wasn't sure what to say when she made it known she was talking about us getting married. She was only a girl. But she was the most handsome and smartest girl I knew—and she could read. So I said yes. I told her it would be fine with me— someday.

Later, I bragged about my plans to marry Missy Fran and was surprised to find that ole Miss Edna did not care for the idea. But I stood my ground—I told her I was my own man and I planned to take Missy Fran as my wife when Missy Fran became a full woman. That's when she slapped me. It was a good hard pop, same as she gave me the night Missy Fran was born in the out-quarters.

I didn't question her for it. I just took it. By that time, ole Edna was mostly blind and I figured she just mad 'cause Missy Fran still a girl. I was sixteen. But at twelve year of age, Missy Fran was still just a girl.

★ ★ ★ ★ ★

The Fire:
Day One
SUNDAY, APRIL 2, 1865

★ ★ ★ ★ ★

Chapter Ten:
Miss Francine Pegram

The first day marking great change in the world began with a distant thunder in the night. It was some type of cannon boom.

I could not guess how close the cannonball landed. It may have dropped from the sky near the river, or a few blocks east among the many tobacco warehouses. Wherever it landed, it made a wave of explosive rumble and was close enough that it shook my bucky-board bed. It was not an upheaval—but it was a new shock added upon many other particulars, the sum of them serving me notice, and I was scared.

The time was not even near sunrise. It was still very dark and I had been fretting with the dog dream. It's always the same dream, the same dog. He is tall with a big head, swayed back ears, thick neck, and muscular hips—all of him coated over with a moist fur that shimmers, even in darkness. He is sitting lightly upon his rump directly before me, head thrust forward, powerful rear legs ready to spring, and, worst of all, he is snarling, teeth on display, dark eyes fixed ready and steady upon me.

In a way—the dream is a trick of the mind. I know it is not really about the dog wanting to attack me and bloody me. Rather, it is about my tolerance for his presence, and how far my tolerance may carry me. The trick is—I must not move. Any shift, even the slightest movement of expression or alteration of manner would invite quick attack. Thus, I always pursue my only option: I pose with hardened stillness and pretend I neither notice the beast nor care about his presence.

I have always been afraid of big dogs. That may be why they visit me as demons in the night. I have heard it said that we are haunted by that which frightens us most. So it is with me.

There is never a true conclusion to the dream. I never outsmart the beast and he never springs forward to rip the veins of my neck. Without variation, at some stage in the face-off, I become unable to deny my fearful state for a moment longer; my tolerance fades and I make ready to shriek and run. But instead of doing either, I burst awake with a great venting relief that there is really no dog at all but only the welcome darkness.

That morning was different. The distant cannon boom rattled the house just as the big dog's loins appeared to give the slightest hoist, making ready to pounce at me. I did awaken, as always. But I did so as my bucky-board gave a shaking rock, and the whole thing sent me into a shrieking terror. I shot from my bucky-board bed, ran from the kitchen pantry, through the darkened kitchen, the dining hall, the parlor, and into the entryway, screaming with every flying step.

I stopped silent before the front door, mid-panic, to listen. The house felt oddly silent. Except for the slow ticks of the Thomas clock on the parlor mantle—there was nothing. The furniture cast faint shadows from the clouded glow of a quarter moon.

Then, from a distance came a strange noise—kind of a "WHOOMP" noise. It sounded like a great underground sucking of air. A moment later, another cannon boom slammed somewhere in the city, causing another wave of rattling that made the glass in the parlor's main window clatter with objection.

This second boom renewed my fears and set me to shrieking again. I did another loop through the rooms of the house. I waved my arms and screamed about bullets, bombs, battles, and Yankees. Had I not been more frightened of whatever was happening outside, than the consequences of it upon the inside, I would have raced past the front door and gone fleeing up Ninth Street like a child chased by hornets.

Fearing the house to be on the very brink of explosion and collapse, I cried out for mercy with what few words I could form: "Oh, Lord Jesus . . . save us . . . it's the Yankees . . . oh, Jesus . . . oh, Lord . . . save us . . . oh, Jesus, Jesus, Jesus . . . the Yankees, Yankees, Yankees!"

I was about to commence my third loop of the house when I heard vague entreaties drowned by my own screams.

"Stop that," the voice demanded. "Stop that at once."

I halted once more in the entryway. Again, the house fell into silence. The voice did not come from the porch; no one had arrived at the door. Again, there was the tock-tock-tock of the Thomas clock on the mantle. And again, there was nothing else. I feared there would come another sucking WHOOMP-noise followed by a third booming rattle. I listened intently, but there was none. Then the silence was broken.

"Miss Francine! Stop that!"

It was the voice of Missus Pegram. I turned and looked up. She stood upon the stairway landing, peering down hard, directly at me with big anger in her wrathful eyes. "Listen to me when I speak to you, child!"

"Oh, Missus Pegram," I whined.

"Stop that right now!" she interrupted.

"Oh, Missus Pegram, it's the Yankees," I cried, looking up at her. "They're sending cannonballs to our side of the river! To Richmond! They're coming." Then something else occurred. My eyes turned into spigots. Tears burst from them and I drew out every word with trembling lips.

"Miss Francine! I said stop that right now!"

I could tell from her manner that she was more than merely angry with me for being frightened. She was frightened too. I could hear it in her voice, bleeding past her words of anger. She leaned forward over the railing, gripping it with both hands, the toes of her bare feet curled past the landing, clutching the edge revealing the deformed little toe of her left foot. She wore her cotton nightdress, which hadn't been properly washed in weeks. It hung loosely on her gaunt frame, revealing much of her limp, generous bosom underneath. Her great beehive of gray-brown hair, normally parted neatly down the middle, was unkempt, partly tucked away and partly hanging at the sides.

"Oh, Missus Pegram!" I trembled.

"You quit that running 'round, I said!"

Her commanding voice quivered with fear even as it intoned genuine irritation at my running wild.

"But the Yankees," I cried in protest.

"Never mind! You hush up and quit that! Get the oil lamp and go to the cellar. I will be there directly."

Her instruction shut me up quick. Even in daylight I hated and feared the cellar. Now, in the darkness—and with war labors growing near—it was a thought I could not accept with much tolerance. Even though I stopped crying out, I still trembled. I did not move toward the cellar.

"Miss Francine! Stop that whimpering."

She leaned farther over the railing. Her hands and toes gripped more tightly. "Do as I instruct. I will be there directly." This time she spoke with a small tone of reassurance. She turned and strode back to her bedroom, her naked feet making their familiar flapping sound upon the oaken boards. "And get your dress," she said, from deep in the upstairs corridor.

Only then did I discover that I was naked except for my unders. If I had really bolted past the front door as I was inclined to do, I would have been running up the Ninth Street hill nearly in my full natural.

I did as she instructed. Still in a panic, I ran back to the kitchen pantry just as hard as I raced from it moments earlier. That little room, properly used for food storage, doubled as my bedroom. Master Pegram long ago named it "Francine's boudoir," a saying that amused him greatly every time he spoke the words. It held all my possessions. There was my gingham dress, hanging loosely on a peg over the stepping-stool where I left it the night before. My blanket was an unfolded mess upon the bucky-board. Below that, lay my "brokens," as we called them, a pair of decent leather shoes given me by the Mistress Bartow, whose daughter outgrew them years earlier. I possessed a second dress, identical in every way to the first, which lay folded on a pantry shelf. There was also one change of unders and one pair of socks.

On a regular morning, I would take proper time to fold my blanket, then remove the bucky-board from its perch upon the two barrels and lean it behind the pantry door. That was a regular morning duty that turned "Francine's boudoir" back into a proper kitchen pantry. I would then use the stepping-stool to don my brokens and lace them up, good and tight.

But there was nothing regular about the start of this day, the time being some vague part of night. I held my breath during the portion of a moment it took me to don my gingham dress. It had one deep pocket that held my most cherished possession, the pocket knife with a cracked handle that belonged to my granddaddy. I did take time to reach into the pocket as I did every morning, looking for the reassuring feel of the metal. It was still there. I left my brokens where they sat and raced from the pantry without tending to other regular duties. In the parlor, I took the oil lamp and the tinderbox from the side-table drawer.

Next would come the dreaded cellar. I took some comfort that there had been no follow-up WHOOMPING-booms, or rattling objections from the windows. Yet my insides still had a full, shivering whimper and now my fears of the cellar made them worse.

The cellar door lay at the end of the corridor under the staircase. I approached it slowly. A loose floorboard in the hallway emitted a bird squeak. From the corridor, I could hear Missus Pegram in her upstairs bedroom. Her door was open and I knew she was tending to her chamber-pot needs ahead of joining me. I too needed a visit to the privy, but under the present conditions, I paid no heed.

The cellar door was made of three long, heavy boards, probably hickory, and were not polished or finely hewn like the pine doors that closed off every other room of the house. It had one latch, which I unhooked; the grip handle required a long, steady pull. Once opened, a rush of cold air flowed over me and kept going past me into the corridor. I wondered if Missus Pegram would feel the chill when it arrived upstairs and, not wanting her more upset by additional events, hoped she would not.

At first, I stood back, staying clear of the opening. When nothing happened, I eased closer with a caution. I could see the great darkness commence near the sixth step, precisely halfway down. Beyond that, that moon blanched nothing. There were not even the outlines of shadows. It was pitch. It looked like the darkness that surrounds the dog's eyes in my nighttime fears.

I took the first five steps with care, then paused. The sixth step, where the total gloom began, was like a drop-off into deep, black water. Taking care with the oil lamp, I balanced and felt for the solid lumber of step number six. I wondered if creatures swimming in the depths would rise up to welcome the arrival of my ankle with their teeth.

Although I feared it mightily, I knew the cellar well. Missus Pegram used it for storage to keep our provisions cool in summer. She frequently sent me down to retrieve yams and greens and the like, an errand I always performed quickly, even when aided by the little bit of daylight provided by the crack in the shutter doors leading to the backyard or the light that fell from the corridor on the main floor.

One corner of the cellar held Master Pegram's old horse-riding leather goods, rendered useless because we had no horse. We hadn't possessed one since the early months of the war, when Almond Eyes was turned over to the Butternut in the middle of the summer. But they didn't want his old saddlery and gathered horse leathers, which was worn out even then, so now it serves only as cellar flotsam. I do not know if Almond Eyes was sold, donated, or otherwise taken as a Butternut demand—the latter being something named as "official requisition," a development much suffered by some families who possessed many horses or other items in want by the army.

An old sword in a fancy silver sheath hung on a nail over the horse leathers and was draped with a filigree of spider cob. I recall hearing it named as the sword of Master Pegram's daddy or granddaddy, used in some other war of the past. Leaning in a nearby corner was a long gun, also used by the Pegram ancestors in that past war. It was a rusty, majestic looking old musket that Missus Pegram labeled as "useless."

Another corner of the cellar held barrels, pails, bins, trunks, and crates filled with bric, items put away for store that Missus Pegram huffed about from time to time. The contents belonged mostly to Master Pegram's forebears and she called it all a "useless memorial to antiquity."

Besides the darkness, there was another cause for my fear of the cellar. During my journeys there, I would sometimes disturb a resident that called the dungeon his home. It was a great rat, long and lissome, with a wickedly arched back. As I am want to give everything a name, I called the varmint Ole Mister Rat. I once came upon him eating Almond Eyes' old saddle as though it were a special feast. He was gnawing hard and ravenous upon the underside, where I figured the leather to be soft. On that day, he did not see me early on as usual. I stalked my way to the yam barrel like a ghost, without sound. When I pried open the lid, it gave a harsh squeak, surprising him; he charged from under the saddle, squealing at me and running about like a mad devil from the underworld. It scared me so bad I didn't even cry out. I just watched him race from corner to corner, eyeing me hard with every step. He was scared too. At one point during his fit he went to the stone wall opposite the yam crate, where he stood on his rear legs and stretched his front claws up on the wall, as high as they would go. He appeared set to scale straight up the side of the cellar wall. Then he glanced back at me and thought better of it, opting instead to disappear inside his hidey-hole somewhere within the "memorial to antiquity." I wondered then if maybe Ole Mister Rat might really be a Missus, with babies to protect.

From step number six, I eased further down into the darkness. Seven, eight, nine. The darkness rose to my waist. Ten, eleven, twelve. I was swallowed by the cellar. The dirt floor was damp; I gripped it with my naked toes as I stopped to listen. Any sound of clicking might be Ole Mister Rat's claws scurrying to escape my arrival. There was nothing. I looked to the opposite side, where four short steps lead up to the backyard cellar entrance, but the crack between the shutter doors was not visible. With only a quarter moon in a cloudy night sky, nothing shown through. I waited. After a pause, I could barely make out the dimmest of a thin, blanched line of shadowy light emerging between the doors.

I toed my way toward the middle of the south wall, where two sturdy old potato bins waited. A satisfactory height for sitting, they were placed there for war shelter purposes, but thus far had never been necessary to take safe harbors. I put the lamp on a smaller bin nearby.

For the first time since bolting from my bucky-board, I took a good long breath. I was pleased there were no signs of Ole Mister Rat. If he had been squeaking and scurrying about it would have made my privy needs all the worse for me. Maybe he too heard the odd WHOOMPING-booms and house rattles and decided this would be a fine night to stay curled up inside his hidey-hole.

The upstairs door creaked. "Miss Francine! Are you down there?"

"Yes'm."

"I told you to fetch the oil lamp."

"Yes'm, I got it."

"Lord, child! Light that lamp! Why do you think I told you to fetch it?!"

"Yes'm."

In the darkness, I withdrew a wooden match from the tinderbox and scraped it sharply on the rough side-plank of the potato bin, then quickly lifted the glass and touched it to the wick. The cellar flickered to life. The outline of every bin, pail, and barrel suddenly appeared in the shadows. The saddle and assorted items of horse leathery piled in their corner looked to me like a large nest, filled with great numbers of tunnels and pathways that would delight small creatures. The sword hung over the saddle, dipping at an angle from its nail as though pointing a warning to some spot behind the stirrups. Now that I could see the saddle, I smelled it too. The odor was not the rich aroma of nicely oiled leather. It was musty and unkempt and bore the stains of water ruin where the cellar flooded from time to time. I strained my eyes in the lamp's glow, studying the various openings in the leathery pile, but there were no signs of either whiskers or the quick flicking of Ole Mister Rat's tail poking from any of the many hidey-holes.

"Lord, child. Did you descend these steps in the dark? And carrying the lamp to boot!" Missus Pegram was heaving loud disfavors at me as she clomped heavily down each step in her bare feet. "I declare child, why do you think I told you to fetch that lamp? It was so you could find your way!"

It was fear of a collapsing house that made me lose good sense, fear that gripped me still; yet I knew better than to make any effort to halt the missus when she was possessed of homily.

"Yes'm," I said.

"If you had tripped and broken the lamp, then where would we be?"

"Yes'm."

"I declare! I have tried to show you how to think for yourself. Teach you reading. Let you take some privilege. Then you go traipsing about dark cellar stairs and with an unlighted oil lamp in your very hands, as though abandoned of all reason. I declare!"

"Yes'm." She settled upon the empty potato bin next to me. I understood that the homily was masking her own heavy state of worry.

"I declare, Francine. Try to use better sense."

"Yes'm. I'm sorry, ma'am." My expression of true regret earned me a brisk pat on the leg.

"All right," she said dismissing me, "we're here now." Her tone let me know the volley of laments had concluded. She had dressed hastily in her worn-out blue calico, once a fine day dress, but had not bothered with petticoats.

Her hair was clipped up, but stringy portions still hung loosely behind her neck. I considered rising to tend to it but thought better, knowing it would not sit well. She was more worried about the WHOOMPING-booms than she was displeased with me or concerned about her appearance. I knew that, because she had pattered down the steps without slippers, exposing her deformed left foot in the lamplight—a clear message to let her unkempt hair go. It was not a good time for primping.

"Oh Lordy, look at this sorry mess," she said, surveying the various piles of empty crates, bins, and barrels. "I told Maxcy I wanted a proper kitchen cellar. How can a woman make do with that upstairs kitchen of mine and this dilapidated mess down here." She sighed unhappily. Her jaw tightened down, gnawing upon itself. She commenced working her teeth together, a sign that she was tilting toward angry thoughts. "And look at that pile of leather. I declare, why does Maxcy insist on keeping a saddle down here when we no longer possess a horse." I wondered if she knew that Ole Mister Rat lived under that saddle.

"Missus . . ."

"Now don't start that again!"

"But, Missus . . ."

"Francine! Hush! We are safe here. Everything will be fine." Her lips trembled. She fought against a burst of tears, which surprised me.

"Yes'm," I said, also with lips atremble as I caught her renewed worries.

"Now, Francine—" She made a downward sweeping gesture at me with her left hand. The message of it was clear. She did not want us both to spend the remainder of the night wailing upon a potato bin in the darkened cellar. It was not something she wished to add to her repertoire of war tricks.

"We'll just stay here until we're certain it's safe. That's all. We'll be fine. You'll see."

"Yes'm." The lamp flickered.

"How much oil do we have Francine?"

"About one hour's worth, ma'am."

"Is there more in the drum?"

"No, ma'am. This is the last."

"All right. We'll see about bartering for more from Mister Bee in the morning."

"Yes'm."

"What about that Johnnycake?"

"No more, ma'am. We ate the last of it early last week."

"All right. We'll see about that too. Maybe Mister Bee will have some yams as well. The Lord will provide, Miss Francine. When Daddy returns today or tomorrow he will surely bring something." She sometimes called Master Pegram "Daddy," even though they had no children. "We have plenty of water and we have . . ." Then her words trailed off—I knew she was going to say we have "a fine house," but if a WHOOMPING-boom landed on it there would be no more house—". . . and we have more to be grateful for than many others. So don't worry. Daddy will be home soon enough." Her words displayed effort to reassure me, but I knew she was mostly reassuring herself.

I knew too that if Master Pegram brought anything home it would be little more than hardtack, the same cracker the Butternut lived on during their war labors. I disliked it, but always choked it down anyway. It filled my belly, allowing me to take my mind off my hunger for a few hours. Johnnycake wasn't much better but did have some flavor, particularly when I made it.

Sensing the timing more satisfactory, I weighed in.

"Was that the Yankees, ma'am?"

She pulled a handkerchief rag from between her bosoms and dabbed at her neck. "I believe it was. Yankee artillery probably," she said, distracted, without looking at me. "Aiming for Trede-gar most likely. Our foundry is a rich target for those cowards."

"Does that mean they're close?"

"I believe they're north of Richmond. Maybe east, according to the papers."

"Where is General Lee?"

"Why, he's south at Petersburg, Miss Francine. You know that." I did know that. But I didn't like the sound of it. If there were Yankees to the north and east of Richmond and General Lee was to the south, it seemed to me the city could be in for new tricks. I was mindful that the day just past was Saturday— the first of the month—a day for April fooling, an unhappy link to commotions that worried me greatly.

"They coming here?" I asked, pleased that she was talking with me and no longer heaving disfavors.

"Well they certainly want to, don't they? But don't you worry. Richmond will not fall as long as General Lee is in the field." Her face stiffened with pride, as all the women in Missus Pegram's social world did when speaking of General Lee, dressing up his name with words like "brave" and "fine" and "gentle- man." Plump Mistress Bartow always called him "our gallant Sir General Lee," drawing out the words to such a length that I could near about refill her with a complete coffee cup before she finished saying it.

"Of course," Missus Pegram went on, finding her courage, "those sore-backs will eventually have to come out of their holes in the ground down there in Petersburg, won't they? Or they'll be forced out. In mid-spring most likely. Either way, when the time comes, he will defeat them for good." She enjoyed saying the words "for good," hammering them out like drum taps.

"What about the others?"

"What others?"

"The Yankees you said were north and east?"

She finished her distracted dabbing with the handkerchief rag and tucked it back into her bosom with some annoyance. "Well, not everyone under arms is at Petersburg. Richmond has defenders aplenty. Our ramparts are well manned. Now stop that worrying and hush up!"

"Yes'm."

We both fell silent. I pondered the time. There was still no indication of light spilling from the crack between the double doors leading to the backyard. It was half past the two o'clock I guessed, maybe three.

After a few minutes, Missus leaned back against the cellar's stone wall and fell asleep in an upright position on the potato bin. I listened hard for more WHOOMPING-booms coming from outside, but there were none. I listened for scratchy noises coming from under the horse leathers. That too was quiet. The shadows of saddle leathers, bins, and barrels had a mysterious orange glow caused by the oil lamp. With us and the lamplight invading his world, I conjured that Ole Mister Rat preferred not to move about. Perhaps he thought about us the same way we thought of the Yankees. They were all around Richmond and practicing to destroy our house. Maybe he too was in a state of fear, hiding in his deepest hidey-hole, worrying about the meaning of us settling down upon empty potato bins in front of his own house at this odd time of night.

Missus Pegram's lips puffed lightly as she made soft snoring noises. One edge of her dried-out lips twisted open, revealing her tooth that stuck out sideways. She was private about that tooth. I knew it was the reason she smiled only with tightly gripped lips, so it would not be put on wide display for all to observe. I studied it in the spotty hue of the lamplight just before the oil gave out. It was ugly with yellow, and stuck out at an angle like an awning over a window.

CHAPTER ELEVEN:
MISS FRANCINE PEGRAM

I always awaken with the sun—and that morning was no different, even though the sun consisted of nothing more than a thin, bright crack of light beaming from the gap between the cellar's backyard shutter doors. Smaller arrows of light spilled from above the door's wooden planks. The one long slit of light cast a beam onto the stone wall near Missus Pegram and me.

She remained asleep in a fitful manner, leaning against the stone wall, slumped into an unhappy heap. Her elbows were jammed together at her waist. Her face turned to one side. Should she incline her head one tiny bit further with her lips still puffing rhythmically with sleep, she would be lapping at the surface of a moist, gray stone.

Instead of waking her, something in the half-light got my attention. The narrow beam of sunlight caught a daddy longlegs perched on the small bin where stood the oil lamp, now empty of oil. He cautiously dabbed at the thin streak of light with one of his legs as if determining whether it might pose some danger.

Unlike my sentiments about dogs, I am accustomed to all manner of spiders and bugs. For the most part, I pay them no mind, except for the yellow jackets of summer. But some bugs I fancy—and among them, the daddy longlegs is my favorite. It has always been a marvel to me. Those long and skinny legs support a little gray, egg-shaped creature that can dip or rise as it sees fit. They are not quick, but they can move fast when they want to. And when they want to move slowly, they certainly can do that too.

I leaned forward for a closer look in the dim light—wondering if there might be others. I stretched to look behind the lamp and the sides of the bin, but I saw no others scaling the wooden planks or traveling nearby upon the cellar's dirt floor. That disappointed me. In summer, I have seen whole armies of daddy longlegs gathered so thickly they made a blanket-covering upon a tree trunk or the privy wall, and they moved like birds in a great flock. Perhaps, I conjured, this was the first of the season— the very first daddy longlegs of the coming spring and summer! I liked that idea because it meant the season's lead bug had allowed me to spot it.

"Stop squirming!"

Missus Pegram rolled forward from her cramped heap, moaning softly. Her mouth appeared misshapen, as though her dry lips were mismatched. Her defaced tooth protruded sharply from the side. When she commenced pulling and tucking at her hair, a small white head-bug scurried for cover from her middle part-line. After pulling the beehive to some order, she withdrew her handkerchief rag from her bosoms to wipe her face.

"Good morning, Missus," I said. She made no response. It was not a good morning. She was very discomfited by the manner we had spent the last few hours. But there had been no additional WHOOMPING-booms and no more rattles. So at the very least, the day would begin without the shock of destruction we feared had come to Richmond and perhaps even to our house at number 212 Ninth Street.

"Will Master Pegram return today, Missus?"

She paused briefly in her primping. "Perhaps, now that the rains have stopped," she mumbled. "Or tomorrow." She wrapped a piece of the handkerchief rag around one finger, rubbed it on her tongue, then dabbed the moistened end at the corners of her eyes. My need to walk the privy path was great.

"Ma'am, I haven't been outdoors for a while." Unfazed she continued primping, cleaning her eyes. Then, after a moment, she spoke.

"Very well," she said. "I think the danger has passed for now. Francine, go into the yard through the cellar doors yonder. Then fetch fresh water for my basin. I'll open the back door when I go up. And don't lollygag! I want to attend services this morning. Afterward we shall pay a shopping visit to Mister Bee's."

"Yes, ma'am," I said, pleased to hear it. I glanced at the little bin. The daddy longlegs was gone.

Departing my seat on the potato bin, I ascended the small flight of rickety wooden steps and unlatched the shutter doors. The glare of morning sunlight was harsh and hurt my eyes. I squinted, stepping into the yard as nimbly as I could, balancing my need for haste with the sudden need to shield my eyes from blinding light.

The backyard was not very large and most of it occupied by our worthless garden—now growing only weeds, as this was April. I held both hands over my eyes and walked the muddy path to the privy. Inside I opened the small window and peered past the low hanging limbs of the giant oak tree, over the rickety fence and into the Spotswood out-yard beyond where stood the hotel's slave quarters where I was born.

All was quiet there. I hoped to see Extra—but he was not about. Neither was Cussin' Sally-Martha, Polly Ramseur, ole Miss Edna, or any of the others. The pit-fire had become a boiling ditch of wet ash, flooded out by the last stretch of rainy days. There was not even the usual bunch of dogs and cats sniffing about—which they especially did when there were no servants in attendance to chase them off. I conjured that dogs probably knew they risked being cooked on the pit if they showed themselves to have a sniff at it.

Outside, while pumping water for Missus, my eyes fully adjusted and I saw it was a grand day. I felt the sun bearing the first hint of spring warmth. The sky was sharp blue, with a few bright, puffy white clouds floating past. On the ground, scattered loblollies dotted the backyard, left by our recent storminess and forcing me to take care not to slush into them with my naked toes.

Missus Pegram made a dash to the privy while I worked the gooseneck pump handle and hauled the bucket upstairs to her bedroom wash basin. I poured a large portion into the washbowl, a smaller portion into the hand bowl and the balance into the chamber bowl, which made it easier to empty with one toss when the time came. I laid out the best towel of the uncleaned lot next to the basin. It was not fresh, but neither was it soiled, having been used only lightly since our last major wash effort in the fall.

There was nothing fresh in Missus Pegram's armoire. I could not recall which dress she last wore to services. Fresh or no, putting out a repeat would earn me another round of disfavors. Sunday attire required the widest possible sequence of dresses. I stood before the open doors, studying the options presented by the disordered mess. In earlier years, Missus Pegram's clothing was a marvel of fine apparel, orderly arranged. All her hats lined up like little soldiers along the upper shelving. The countertop of a bureau held cups of fancy clips, belts, ties, and what-nots; its drawers were filled with selections of chemise and stockings and bodices. The many dresses, petticoats, and crinolines, always very clean, were hung in order of use: house, daydress, evening, church.

Now, nothing was proper.

A mess of dresses and personals that had gone overlong without a good cleaning lay piled upon the armoire's floor. The row of hats was missing several of its members. One hat, I knew, had been crushed by accident. Another was bartered for a small supply of lotion and soap at Mister Morgan's Notions & Hardware Shop. But that did not explain the others. I counted five open spaces on the hat shelf. It was unlikely that Missus Pegram bartered them without my knowing of it. For the last few years, since shortly after the start of the war business, she seldom left the house without me. Perhaps, I conjured, Master Pegram had taken the best hats for some exchange of goods.

There had been no lye-detergent since October. In January, we scrubbed two dresses on the washboard and used the last of her hand soap, but now they too were beyond good cleanliness. Making a gamble, I laid out the fancy dark gray cotton with puff sleeves and black trim. It was a good churchgoing dress because it cinched up her bosom proper, all the way to the neck, with a broach. I sprinkled a dash of perfume on it. Then I laid out a full round of crinolines, the most soiled for going on first, the least for last.

Before finishing, there came a clopping din of horses in the street, which I judged by the sound to be a half dozen riders, but it caused me no distraction. Noisy movement of Butternut was familiar to all Richmond. Early on, when large groups marched from the city, the various mistresses gathered on stoop and pathway to wave and cheer. It was a custom that diminished over time. At first, the war business meant going without men. Over time, it grew to mean going without soap, then meat, then bread, and finally the whole thing just wore down the will of the mistresses to take to the streets and cheer for "the cause," as it was called.

It was Missus Pegram's voice that drew me to the upstairs window. Having emerged from the privy, she was standing near the easeway handing out her usual round of "good mornings" and "God bless you gentlemen" to the Butternut on horseback who had pulled to a stop directly in front of the house—drawn by the water trough across the street at the Basin Bottom Livery. They responded to her with a round of equally usual nods and short tips of their hats.

I watched them. They were a pack of beat-down weary-looking soldiers wet with sweat, which I took to mean they had been riding hard for several hours. Their horses, even more weary, slobbered at the mouth and their rump hides oozed with milky lather. One horse, the shortest, not much taller than a pony, leaned so far to one side it appeared to me he would tip over. I have seen horses adjust to relieve their pain one leg at a time, but never two legs at once the way this foaming, suffering creature did.

The Butternut, too, were grateful for a pause; their chests heaved with long, satisfactory movement. They scratched. They wiped their faces and adjusted cloak and jacket. One soldier dismounted to tend a twisted harness. They took turns walking their horses to the water trough at the Basin Bottom Livery, where the animals replenished their exhausted bodies.

During her exchange of morning pleasantries, Missus Pegram edged closer to the curb. She concentrated on one rider in particular, who reined his horse close to our yard's edge. From the upstairs window, I could only hear a patchwork of words, but I knew she was fishing for war news and maybe hopeful to hear news about the possibility of food deliveries. I could easily make out the usual round of "I declares" and a few "Oh my Lords."

The nature of the Butternut's voice was softer than Missus Pegram's and did not rise to the window with much clarity. I did hear Missus speak the word "artillery" and knew she was inquiring about the WHOOMPING-booms that sent us both running to the cellar during the night.

After a moment Missus Pegram's carriage altered. The man

on horseback said something that changed her manner from casual civility, sending her backbone straight up into what I knew to be a bearing of dutiful obedience.

"Certainly, sir," I heard her say.

In one quick move she turned and looked up—dead-on— into my eyes. Sometimes it frightened me that Missus Pegram was like God in her ability to know where I was, what I was doing, sometimes even what I was thinking. In this case, I could only conjure she knew the sound of voices from the street would set me to listen in at the second-floor front window to satisfy my curiosity.

"Miss Francine, come to the front yard," she said, an instruction firmly accompanied by a gesture. Before departing the window, I noticed that every rider taking a rest on Ninth Street was looking up at me.

They all awaited me like guests at the dinner table ready for turkey dinner. "Yes'm?" I said, arriving at Missus Pegram's side in the front yard.

"Miss Francine, the Major would like fresh water for his men and a wagon of wounded soldiers soon to arrive from Petersburg."

"Yes'm," I said. "Yessah," I said to the one she called "the Major." He was riding a large bay, the biggest of the group, whose mouth oozed with a cloud of white foam. The noise of the wagon led by a double team at full trot rattled loudly to the south, just about one block away.

"That's very kind of you, ma'am," the Major said to Missus Pegram. He made a casual gesture to another on horseback, a bedraggled-looking man with glittery green eyes who saw the instruction and promptly dismounted. All of them were holding a gaze upon me. Their drawn, tired faces seemed to find some amusement in my dutiful arrival in the front yard. One of them handed me a crooked grin.

"You might need some assistance, Li'l Miss," the Major said to me. "Lieutenant Dunnovant here will help." I struggled with discomfort, hoping for some new development that would remove all their smiling eyes from me.

"It's our pleasure, Major," Missus Pegram sang out. "Water is something we have in abundance. Miss Francine, show Lieutenant Dunnovant the way to our backyard well."

"Yes'm."

The Major made another, bigger gesture, this time to the approaching wagon driver, who lurched the team to a stop under the drooping limbs of the sycamore tree, the only tree in front of the Pegram house. The two left wheels drew to a halt in thick loblollies created by the three days of rain.

With the wagon came a sudden assault of foul odor. The large bed of the dray was filled with wounded men, bringing on the odor of sickness and filth. Missus Pegram withdrew her handkerchief and put it to her nostrils. Then, fearing it to be an act of incivility, quickly removed it. She scurried ahead of the wagon to speak further with the Major, who politely obliged her sensibilities by reining his horse a few steps to the north.

The dismounted man with the green eyes walked to the rear of the wagon.

"Fresh water! Canteens to the rear," he announced. He stretched to receive the containers from among the nest of miserable creatures who lay in various manner of torment. Their arms waved aloft bearing water containers, looking like a field of limp corn stalks, some of them adorned with nasty bandages coated over with foul yellow sickness and with blood of all colors from wet red to dried black.

The green-eyed man took only the containers, ignoring the cups which some waving hands held up. One container had a strap that snagged under the backside of a wounded man. Lieutenant Dunnovant gave it a hard tug, causing the soldier to moan with agony as it snapped free.

I watched the sadness from yard's edge at mid-wagon, where the nearest wounded man seemed to take notice of me. He lay on his right side, his upper body leaning over the railing. I could not see the nature of his injuries but understood them to be horrible. His scratched and bloodied face twisted into a nightmare image of pain—his wavy brown hair was clotted over with blood and filth. The sight of him sent a chill of fright down the back of my neck, yet I could not remove my eyes from a study of him. His lips and mouth pushed forward into a pucker, working in and out like a fish straining to maintain life after being pulled from the lake. A limp, black tongue poked from the middle of the strained opening.

I pitied him sorely and stepped forward. The black center of his afflicted eyes widened when I moved, which I took to be a sign of appreciation. 'Twas then, two short steps closer, that I could see over the edge of the wagon railing.

With the help of Jesus, never will I see such a thing again. The floor of the wagon bed was awash in filth. Men lay atop other men. Some were naked save for layers of caked dirt and blood. Many had missing hands, arms, and feet. One man's eyeball bulged from his face, hanging to a level with his nostrils, dangling by a web of sinew. And I could see too the full view and nature of the wounded man that I took notice of. He had no legs. But that was not the worst of it. He did not appear to be in possession of a middle. The place where a man wears a belt around his trousers was missing; his body stopped shallow, somewhere down there amid the foul-smelling brew of blood and filth that washed about upon the wagon bed. How he remained alive was a mystery that frightened me too much to ponder. I feared I might retch my stomach right there in the yard.

"Ready, Li'l Miss?" The green-eyed man stood holding an

armfull of containers; those with attached straps were swung over his shoulder. "Lead the way, Li'l Miss."

I stepped away from the wagon with chills. My guts had loosened. I suddenly had need to visit the privy again.

"Dis way, sah."

I spoke to him the way Extra warned that I must. "Don't let 'em know you know better ways," he advised. "Don't let 'em know you can read, 'speshly not the Butternut."

Crossing the yard, I could hear Missus talking with the Major as they walked together, leading his horse to the water trough. She wagged on about Mistress Lee, telling him she was indisposed and had not been to church for some time.

"Well now, I'm sorry to hear that," the Major said several times during her recounting of the situation. Visitors to Richmond always asked after Mistress Lee. It was a natural thing to do. And they were always sorry to hear that she was not well. "I'm real sorry," he said. "I'm just real sorry to hear that."

At the easeway I paused to let the soldier walk ahead of me, which he did, the containers dangling noisily behind him. It was then I realized that he too possessed so foul an odor that I could hardly stand the short walk behind him without pinching my nostrils. He did not appear wounded, and his Butternut outfit, while dirty, was not overly befouled. Yet he smelled of the same loathsome odor of blood and filth and death as those in that wagon laden with torment.

"Sight of them boys worrying you, Li'l Miss?" he asked casually while I strode behind him. It was as though he knew my thoughts. I did not answer. "They are a sorry bunch, that's certain enough," he said. In the backyard I pointed to the well spigot and took a step in the direction of the privy.

"Scoose me, sah," I said.

"Go ahead, Li'l Miss," he nodded at the privy. I knew he watched me walk the privy path because the containers did not resume their jangling noise until the door closed behind me. Inside, I gave vent to stomach sickness. The sight of the man with only half a body had set me to such shock and chills it loosened my insides, making me wretch good and hard, even though I had eaten nothing for two days or more. I was grateful Missus Pegram remained in front, wagging on about the latest war news—not present to see me leave the soldier on his own. She would not approve of that. I heard the squeak of the well arm commence pumping, followed by the flush of water. I glanced again at the Spotswood out-yard. It was still abandoned.

When I rejoined Lieutenant Dunnovant, he had already filled several containers which I reassembled on the well platform in orderly fashion. Some were made of tin, some of wood. He eye-balled me hard while he pumped the gooseneck handle. 'Twas then he commenced taking on with me.

"You mighty purty, Li'l Miss," he said. I did not look straight on at him. He worried me some, but I knew the matter would not be overly burdensome because our timely return was expected by the Major, Missus Pegram, and the wagon of torment. I judged him to be smart. His green eyes shown like gems; I wondered if, with such a pair of eyes, he could see in the darkness the way dogs and varmints of the night can see. His light-brown beard was scraggly, with spots of naked, smooth skin on both cheeks. He was of moderate height, thin, angular, strong.

"You got yoursef a man yet, Li'l Miss?" he asked. I stole a glance at the hotel yard, wondering, hoping Extra might suddenly be there—watching. But there was no one. "One of ya'll with such fine looks must surely have a man by now."

"Would you like me take aholt some o'the containers, sah?"

"Yes, Li'l Miss. That'll make it go quicker." I stepped up to the well platform and kneeled before the spigot with a wooden container. He pumped slowly while I carefully held it under the flow so the full rush of water poured directly into the chamber. I could feel him working me over with the eyes of the goat. For a while there was silence. As each container filled, I capped it and placed it next to the others.

"I say, you had yourself a man yet?" This time he asked the question with a different tone. It was not a mean tone. But it was without the false friendliness that he milked upon the first asking. I didn't know what to say, but understood I was required to speak.

"Yessah. Nosah." It wasn't intended. The words simply came that way. I glanced again at the hotel yard. Still no movement. Not that Extra could have done anything had he been watching, but the sight of him may have forced this foul-smelling man to change his manner.

"Yes-sir-no-sir. Well now," he said, returning to his false tone of friendship. "What kind of answer is that? I got me a 'yes' and I got me a 'no.' " He pumped the well handle in silence for a moment, working upon me with his green goat-eyes. " 'Course—now I contemplate it, that's a good answer. Matter of fact, maybe that's the best answer of all. And that means you smart enough to know the best answer, don't it? Are you smart, Li'l Miss?" He waited for me to answer, but I did not.

"I say, ain't you smart enough to know the best answer, Li'l Miss?" I glanced in his direction but quickly glanced back to the container without looking into his goat-eyes. At that moment I lost my grip on the container and the sound of splashing water offered a good excuse to be distracted from his question.

"Well, no matter," he said, letting it go. Each time he pumped the gooseneck there was a squeak on the down-stroke followed by a rush of water. His gaze continued to work hard on me so I kept my own eyes down. I could see he wore the boots of a horseman. They were made of good cow leather, darkened over with age and filth. He worked the spigot arm.

Squeeeek—swooosh; squeeeek—swooosh.

I struggled to hold my breath. He smelled so foul I feared my stomach may wretch yet again right there on the well platform.

"You care to use our privy, sah?" I asked, knowing it to be an invitation Missus always made to visitors and hoping it to be a useful distraction. He looked away to consider it in the opposite corner of the yard.

"Why does it lean over like that?" he asked.

"Oak tree, sah," I said.

"Eh?"

"You see that oak tree, sah? On the other side?"

"Mm-mmm."

"There's a powerful big root growing under. It lifting the privy to one side."

"Oh, yeah," he said.

"Missus Pegram want it fixed. But Master Pegram like it. He call it the 'Leaning Privy of Pegram.' " That made a serious smile come over him.

"Is 'at a fact?" he said, giving a tiny laugh. Then he renewed his study of me.

Squeeeek—swooosh; squeeeek—swooosh.

"Where is that master now, Li'l Miss?"

"Away doin' war work. He a engineer, sah."

"Is 'at right?"

"Yea-sah."

"Engineer, huh?"

"Yes-sah. He help wid the roads, rails, 'n highways and such."

"Uh-huh."

"Yea-sah. He meet regular wid Mister President Davis and wid Mister Genrul Lee too."

"Is 'at right?"

"Yea-sah. One time Genrul Lee hisself come into parlor. They talk 'bout bridges and such."

"Well, well. My, my."

"Yea-sah."

"Right here in the parlor of this house?"

"Yea-sah!"

"Is 'at right?"

"Oh yea-sah. We made coffee for 'em."

"Well, well. Is 'at right? Ole Marse Robert himself, eh?"

"Yea-sah."

"Whatchu think of him Li'l Miss?"

"He handsome, sah."

"Is at right?"

"Yes-sah. He got teeny-weeny feet. And he comb his hair over to cover his top baldness."

"Is 'at right?"

"Yes-sah."

Squeeek—swooosh; squeeek—swooosh.

He paused pumping only when a container filled, which I carefully capped and placed among the pile, then uncapped an empty one to make it ready under the spout. The ones without caps or corks I balanced upright in the pile. A few were leather sacks that looked like bloated bellies when I laid them out, roiling back and forth with a gurgling wave.

"Yes, ma'am. Like I say, you sure is mighty purty, Li'l Miss." My uncertainty did not let up.

"Thank ya, sah," I said, hoping it to be a safe response.

"How old are you?"

"Dunno, sah. Twelve."

"Twelve. So maybe you got yourself a man and maybe you don't got a man. Uh, uh, uh," he snorted in a singsong manner. I struggled for a response that might distract him. He was not overly impressed with my story about Mister General Lee. That was odd. Most everyone would stop fast to hear any recollection about the grand general.

"Dem men gonna die, sah?" I wondered why I had not thought of it before. It succeeded. His tone changed for the better.

"Them boys in the wagon are worrying you, ain't they, Li'l Miss?"

"They mighty sorry, sah."

"You are right about that, Li'l Miss." He shook his head in agreement and sucked his teeth. "They are the sorriest of the sorriest. Chimborazo will be their last stop most likely, if they make it that far. And that's a fact."

"Where dem men do war-work, suh?"

"Petersburg, Li'l Miss. Uhh-huh-h-h. We all late of Petersburg." He removed his steady gaze from me and the goat eyes faded.

"Dat's where Genrul Lee is," I said.

He looked south, into the morning sky. "Sure 'nuff, Li'l Miss. He's there all right. He's there along with what's left of the whole Army of Virginia."

"Why ya'll come to Richmond now? Just to bring de wounded to Chimborazo?" The green eyes darted at me—but with a different purpose. They took on airs of suspicion.

"Well, now. You really are a smart one, Li'l Miss. You think maybe we got some business other than toting wounded do you?"

I hesitated. "Maybe so, sah."

"Well, maybe you are right. Maybe we got other business. Now you know, Li'l Miss—the nature of business belongs to those that got to tend to it. Ain't that right? But if you learn other folks' business, then you know what they up to. Don'cha?" He vigorously pumped the well handle.

Squeeek—swoosh; squeeek—swooosh.

"Therein lay the crowning secret of all triumph since the great Caesar. Keepin' your own business and gettin' the business of others. Keepin' and gettin'. Gettin' and keepin'." He paused. He stopped pumping the gooseneck and looked at me.

"Wha'chu think of that, Li'l Smart Miss? Ain't that the supreme cipher of victory?"

I could not conjure his meaning. I feared he was hinting of a fight to come, a fight in downtown Richmond. That was a big worry for everyone. We all fretted hard that the Yankees and the Butternut would bring their war-labors right onto the streets, destroying everything and sending us all fleeing.

"Everybody worried we nex, sah. 'Fraid ya'll come here for the nex big fight." He eased up a bit.

"That why you wanna know why we comin' up Ninth Street this morning?"

"Yes-sah."

"Well, I can settle that for you. The fight for Richmond ain't never been in Richmond. Has it?"

"No-sah."

"That's right. And it ain't never gonna be, either." He seemed to speak with certain knowledge, and I was pleased to hear it.

"What happen nex, sah?"

"Well, now, Li'l Miss. I reckon the next event will make itself known soon enough." His look took on a mixed manner. If there is a word to name it, I do not know it. He was sad, angry, and worried all in one distracted countenance. He again looked beyond the gooseneck into the sky; then he looked beyond the sky into some place that only he could see. "Yes, ma'am, Li'l Miss," he said slowly. "I fear it will not be long now."

When the final container was filled I made a fuss over some busy work to avoid further exchange with him. I took a rag from the platform and wiped down the containers in a business-like manner. Then I selected a number of containers that came with attached straps and hoisted them over my shoulders. He also took a number with straps; we shared the burden of the toting of containers without straps—balancing them in our arms. He walked ahead of me on the return trip. I was grateful the breeze in the easeway flowed toward Ninth Street, lessening the wake of his foul odor.

By now Missus Pegram and the Major were well acquainted. He had dismounted while another Butternut walked his horse to the livery trough. From the easeway, I heard her pronounce his surname. "Major Anderson, I certainly hope Maxcy can be of assistance," she said, calling Master Pegram by his Christian name.

"If his First Engineers are tending the Danville rails that'll help," the Major said. "Supplies need to get through. The Yankees are dug in mighty deep down Petersburg way." We emerged from the easeway and crossed the front yard.

"Well now, that's fine, just fine," praised the Major.

He and Missus stood side by side. He eyed us, both laden like mules with newly filled water containers. The green-eyed man returned to the rear of the wagon to serve the containers to the field of limp, bloody, and bandaged arms that reached out to receive them. Then he took my load from me in an official manner without any hint of his goat-eyed performance at the well pump. Not wanting to view the wounded men up close again, I kept my gaze downward. Even without looking straight on, I could see that a couple of wounded men assisted those unable to hold a container by pouring water onto heads and faces. One man without hands sat like a helpless baby bird in a nest of straw—his bloody, cracked mouth opened wide to receive the gift of water.

"That's fine, just fine," said the Major, watching us, "yes, ma'am, mighty fine indeed." He tipped his hat to Missus Pegram. I scurried to her side as soon as I could. "Thank you, ma'am, for allowing my wounded to have their canteens filled."

"You are certainly welcome, Major Anderson! I have enjoyed

our talk. I will convey your sentiments to Mistress Lee the very next time I see her." The Major's horse was returned to him, and he mounted up.

"Thank you kindly, ma'am. Her well-being is mighty important to us all." He tugged the reins hard, startling the horse, which gave a kick with its rear legs. It maneuvered sideways from the curb.

"God bless you, Major!" Missus pronounced with an overly wide smile that quivered a little on the lower lip. He tipped his hat a second time then spurred the giant, tired horse into a sudden canter. The hooves made a racket and the wagon too lurched into noisy motion. The green-eyed man had remounted his own horse and paid no notice of me or Missus Pegram as he departed, which pleased me. Had he handed over a final goat-eyed face toward me it would not have set well with Missus Pegram, who would be certain to notice it. I conjured he knew that, too.

The sudden movement of the wagon sent up a fresh chorus of moans from the suffering men crowded in the rear. Several of those able to drink from their newly filled containers lost their grip, spilling water and sending containers tumbling from their bandaged hands. The man with half a body still leaned from the wagon, his armpits locked atop the railing's edge; both arms protruded stiffly, but his lips no longer puckered like a fish. His ashen-purple face bent to one side. I knew he was gone. He had died while I was filling water containers and Missus Pegram traded social talk with the Major. No one else appeared to notice. The torment of his companions was deep and held no allowance for them to take note of the suffering of others, or whether anyone's suffering had concluded. The sight of his countenance, now fixed in death, sent yet another chill down my neck. Before I could think about it more, I was interrupted by Missus Pegram, who put her arm around me and pulled me back toward the house.

"Lord, child!" she said, drawing out the words in a low-toned cry after the wagon departed. "Oh, me-e-e." She struggled to get into the house before she burst into full public display. "Oh, me-e-e . . . oh, me-e-e," she wailed quietly at me. "Oh, Lord have mercy!"

She had seen more than I understood. The way her body touched mine told me that I was required to help her navigate the yard and front steps. Once inside and the door closed, she barely landed upon the fancy red settee before boiling over into great sobs. She bled loudly with cries of woe and worry. I fetched a rag from the kitchen. In between her sobbing, I could make out a handful of laments—among them, "those poor boys," and "our brave boys," and "our sons of the Confederacy," and so forth. When she had cried it out fully and recovered sufficiently to speak she looked straight at me.

"Miss Francine," she began. "I have spent many afternoons lending hand and heart on Chimborazo Hill. But of all the miseries to be observed there among our brave boys with missing limbs and sad demeanor, I have never witnessed such misery." She sat upon the fancy red settee, her knees together tight and shoulders stooped, her body leaning into me as though she wished to climb inside my eyes and take safe harbor there.

"Oh, Lord. It was so fresh, so, so recent. I declare! Major Anderson said those boys were wounded in battle during the night. Just hours ago! I declare! The war is going to arrive on our front stoop by tomorrow." Her eyes bulged and widened. "The major talked like it was near 'bout over at Petersburg. Oh me . . . oh me . . . oh me. And the odor! Oh, so foul. It was horrible. Just horrible." And with that she buried her face into her knees and commenced another round of great sobbing. She took on so, her back arched and her shoulders heaved in and out.

The performance came as a great surprise and pulled me from my own shock delivered by the wagon of torment. I feared it would be followed by one of her "dark haunts" that laid her up in bed for a week.

Indeed—after the second round of tears passed, Missus Pegram was taken by a fit of pattering about the house in her odd way. She walked from room to room, grinding her jaw together and sometimes talking out loud in ways that made no sense. She would enter a room without purpose and come out of it addled, as though her reason for going there proved unsatisfactory and irritating. Twice she went back outside to see if there might be passing riders bearing more news. But there was nothing.

Distracted to a panic, she sat at the side table before the great window and quickly wrote out a pass, which she handed to me along with a coin, and hastily sent me to the lobby of the Spotswood Hotel to purchase the latest newspaper.

The way things stood, I knew not to tarry. Under usual circumstance, I would take my time during a newspaper run up the Ninth Street hill. I would "good day" and "fine afternoon" to any mistress or mister I passed on Ninth Street or around the corner on Main. And once inside the hotel, I might even lollygag with this one or that one looking to lose some time if Master Pettigrew was not around.

There would be none of that this morning.

Once outside the house, I read the pass:

April, 1865,
Be advised to allow passage.
    The colored girl bearing this pass is my property.
    Francine Pegram is 12 years, 5', 90 lbs.

Ruth Pegram
212 Ninth Street, Richmond

CHAPTER TWELVE:
MISS FRANCINE PEGRAM

She had failed to note the precise date, which may have been intentional. That would make the pass good for the entire month.

I folded the small paper with care and pushed it under my treasured knife inside the pocket of my gingham dress, where the knife's weight would guard against loss. The sun had strengthened since I departed the cellar; it was just beginning to remove the chill from the morning air. Mindful of my duty, I did not lollygag. I tucked my head into my chest and commenced a swift pace for the half-block walk up the hill to Main and the full block west to the corner at Eighth Street.

Old Caesar, Master Pettigrew's door servant, held his usual perch near the front. He was the oldest manservant at the Spotswood and had a great protruding middle, yet he moved with more nimbleness than a man gifted with skinny youth. Even in the summer heat, Old Caesar could bounce up and down the Spotswood steps with a full load of satchels in each hand, grip carriage door handles and help misters and mistresses in and out of all doors with an ease that looked like a fine dance.

On this morning he sat on a tall, skinny stool that held only half his backsides, requiring him to sit at an angle that looked uncomfortable but likely aided him when it came time to heave over to the quick labor of hoisting satchels and holding doors. I ascended the porch, keeping aside from the entranceway should any guest come or go, thus requiring Old Caesar to tend to his door or satchel duties.

"Gud monin', Miss Francine," he whispered, giving me a smile of friendship. "Ya'll in search of a newspaper?"

"Good morning, Caesar. Yes. Did it arrive this morning?"

"Sho did, but dey all gone. Sold like hot cakes on a cole day. Lordy, everbody worried—looking for war news." He shook his head and leaned down to speak as though telling a secret. "Seem like somethin' up. Somethin' 'potent maybe." From his half-bottom perch, he watched the lobby through a porch window, ready to move should a hotel guest exit.

"Caeser, have you seen Extra this morning?"

"Sho did. He told me early this morning that Mastah Pettigrew got him bonded out to Butternut all week. He left right quick."

"Bonded to the Butternut? What do you suppose it's all about?"

"Don't know, Miss Francine. Mistah Pettigrew, he say— 'Caesar, you mind de comin's and go'ins good, and let me know of any oddness that pass.' I says 'yes-sah, yes-sah.' But I can't figure it out. I don't know what oddness to be lookin' for. It's all purty much business like usual. 'Course, sometime business like usual can be right odd itself, so I just don't know. But I'm keepin' up de watch anyway."

I thought of telling him about the riders and the wagon of wounded and the power it held over me and Missus Pegram, but thought better of it. Extra warned me that if Old Caesar learns your business, it'll soon be other folks' business, too.

"Caesar, all the newspapers are sold already?"

"Sho 'nuff. Just like hot cakes on a cole day."

"Ain't nary a one left?"

A wide grin came over his face. "Now, Miss Francine, sho did take ya'll a long time to ask." He opened the lid on a basket which I knew to contain a scarf and a horse brush. "Ya'll know

I can't forget ya, Miss Francine." He withdrew a newspaper from the basket and handed it to me. "And give your missus my regard."

"Thank you, Caesar."

"No'm. You keep it," he said when I offered the twenty-five-cent coin. "I saved de baker dozen extra for you. So the money won't be missed. Let me know if deres any oddity in de news, so's I can pass it on."

"Thank you, Caesar."

I gave the pages a quick study on the return walk, looking for long lists of names. If there had been another big war contest where Yankee and Butternut went hard at each other in some country town—that would be a familiar event which might put an end to Missus Pegram's worries and explain Old Caesar's job of looking for "oddness." But there were no long columns detailing the names of dead boys.

Missus was on the fancy red settee in the parlor, much calmed when I returned. Her hair was now brushed and properly parted. She took the newspaper and proceeded to spend a long chunk of time studying it. I placed the coin on the table then sat on a guest chair near the main window where I could keep a watch on her and also on travelers coming and going up and down the Ninth Street hill.

Another wagon of wounded men lurched north from the river. Riders stopped at the Basin Bottom Livery across Ninth Street in search of fresh animals, but there were none to be had. The stalls had been empty for months. They watered their horses, then traveled on just as the wagon riders had done earlier that morning.

After a while, Missus Pegram profaned quietly at some piece of news. So absorbed was she in her reading that she was unaware of having spoken at all, let alone heave a profanity. Her jaw was set on edge; she ground her teeth slowly. That affirmed for me that Richmond was in a bad way. I worried that the next set-to might be near commencement and the next long list of names to follow would chronicle those fallen in the battle of Ninth Street.

The parlor brightened as the morning sun spilled in through the main window. Missus Pegram was proud of her parlor. It contained the finest furniture of the house. The fancy red settee, like all the treasures of the house, was from France. There were a number of straight-back chairs that would be moved to the dining room for crowded dinners, though there hadn't been any of those for more than two years. There was a fancy green sitting chair named for Queen Anne and two end tables with fancy carved legs. On the wall over the red settee there hung four framed pictures depicting scenes in Paris, which is in France. They were perfectly arranged so the space between them formed a cross. Missus once named the pictures to me but I cannot recall the details. One portrayed a great church, another showed boats on a river, and the third was a wide avenue with many buggies and carriages and masters and mistresses happily strolling along the pathway with fine parasols and colorful hats. The fourth picture in the arrangement portrayed a rotund dandy wearing fur robes being served morning coffee by many fine ladies.

Anything from France was a matter of pride for Missus Pegram. Her bedroom vanity and matching bench had arched legs that curved, which she called "country French." And our finest dishware, from Mister Gregg's Metropolitan Novelty Store, was blue in color and trimmed in fancy gold with words that read "Made in France" on the back of each plate. It all made me conjure that most everything from France must be fancy and ugly all at the same time, for that is the way it always appeared to me.

Sitting beside Missus Pegram on the fancy red settee was

something not from France. It was a doll. We called it the "China-head doll" because the head, according to Missus Pegram, was made of fine, delicate glass all the way from distant China. The doll wore a proper girl's Sunday dress with full crinolines and perfectly polished black leather shoes, each attached around the ankle with a tiny, perfectly formed little buckle. Her soft, yellow hair appeared natural and grew from under a red hat. She had rosy cheeks and skin blanched so white it rivaled fresh snow. Her eyes were painted a bright blue and sparkled with life.

The Thomas clock on the mantel rang eight times. I was desperate with hunger and hoped that after her paper reading, Missus Pegram would announce an outing in search of bread or potatoes.

Outside, a mongrel dog with ribs on full display walked briskly down the Ninth Street hill as though he had an appointment to keep near the river. Jules, the mute Spotswood streetrunner, emerged from the Basin Bottom Livery and whistled for the dog to come. The dog looked toward the sound but quickly looked away again, paying no obedience, keeping to his hasty pace. Thus ignored, Jules turned and ambled unhappily back inside the livery, where he lived when not running errands in service to the guests in Master Pettigrew's hotel. I knew he was hungry too and I felt badly for him, but I was glad he did not catch the mongrel. Even though I fear dogs, I was glad to see that old creature pass up the opportunity to become Jules's breakfast.

Missus Pegram folded the newspaper and put it aside. She placed an elbow on the sloping arm of the fancy red settee and rested her forehead in the palm of her hand. She breathed calmly for a good long while and I do believe she said her prayers. Then, after a short time, she returned to normal as if emerging from a cloud.

"Well, Miss Francine," she said. "Don't you think it's time?"

"Yes, ma'am," I said jumping from my chair, thinking she meant it was time to barter-shop for food. My pained stomach was sorely empty. I wanted warm baked potatoes but would have settled for cold Johnnycake.

"Very well, let's finish with Sunday dress," she said. My face must have signaled disappointment. "Now don't pout, Miss Francine. We'll shop directly after services. I'll wear the black cotton hat with the gray dress you have already laid out. Mister Gordon said he had received some inquiry for more recent French millinery from Savannah. That hat should barter well for our dinner."

"Yes, ma'am," I said. Mister Gordon operated the Lady's Fashion Emporium on Grace Street, where I was not only admitted but welcomed as a servant to help Missus Pegram change clothing in the purchase of various crinolines and dresses.

Having already washed while I was buying the newspaper, she took less time than usual. She undressed, powdered, and re-dressed with a distraction. Only once did she narrow down on me with a disfavor for tying her bodice improperly. Afterward, she donned only the second and third crinolines, the least soiled of the three I had laid out. After dressing, she took a blue ribbon from her vanity drawer and tied my hair behind my head.

"Do you still have that pass I wrote out for you this morning?" she asked.

"Yes, ma'am."

"Very well then."

We hastened from the house before I had time to don my brokens. She moved so quickly to maneuver the front steps, I scarce had time to lift her hems. During the walk up the Ninth Street hill her lips moved—making words, though she was not speaking aloud. I took it to be just another sign that we were in a bad way and the day would not end well for us. It also meant she had not truly emerged from the cloud of worry that commenced with the WHOOMPING-boom noises of the night.

I toted her parasol as I trailed behind during the walk up the hill to St. Paul's. Before reaching the side of the church, she took the parasol from me for the final few steps.

There were a few soldiers at loiter on the side of the church near the servant's bench, on guard duty but seeming very relaxed as they held their musket-rifles loosely, which pleased me. I conjured that if there was going to be a set-to in the streets of Richmond, they would likely not be gathering in so casual a manner. We passed them, exchanging a round of "Good morning, gentlemen" and "Good day, sirs," which was followed by a polite round of "Morning, ma'am," spoken by each of the Butternut.

Near the corner another soldier stood a little more formally. One of the mistress ladies was running her lips at him real good, handing out a full round of "thank you's," all smiles and praise for his service to the glorious cause. It was Mistress Hatton, who had the biggest bosom of them all, which she did occasionally put on view—but never on Sunday morning. On this morning, she had her bosom thoroughly covered up and clamped down, just as did Missus Pegram in her dark gray dress. She saw us coming and quickly concluded her speech to the soldier, joining up with us. Then Mistress Winder joined up too and the three of them took to wagging their tongues.

Whenever the women greeted each other in those circumstances, the name "Mistress Lee" was always the first to be mentioned. That morning was no different. "She won't be attending this morning," Mistress Winder said. "She's still under the weather, you know." The names to be discussed after "Mistress Lee" usually lined up with regularity: General Lee, Mistress Davis, Mister President Davis, the war, the Yankees, that horrible General Grant, and finally Richmond itself, which always got named as noisy, dirty, crowded, and filled up with such riff-raff, pickpockets, and scoundrel types from all over. The three of them paraded up the steps "oh-my-Lord-ing" and "goodness-gracious-ing" at each other as they entered St. Paul's.

I stayed at loiter a short while, waiting to see if I would be needed further, but Missus Pegram never looked back. There were other women taking on with the soldiers, and after a while, they too fell in wagging their tongues over Mistress Lee as they all ascended the steps and entered the house of worship.

I returned to the bench on the side of the church along Ninth Street, my usual position when Missus attended Sunday services. Servants were allowed inside St. Paul's but only on the upper level. That was always a puzzling rule to me because it seemed the upper-level seats were superior in every way.

Extra agreed. Master Pettigrew did not attend service very often—but when he did, Extra accompanied him. Extra called the upper level "better hearing and better seeing, too." And there were other bonuses. "From up there you got a full view on who's sleeping, who's got the 'Messenger' tucked inside the hymn book, and who's playing dots-and-boxes," he said. "Plus you ain't got to fight past fancy feather hats to view His Excellency when he gets to waving and pointing and carrying on."

I wondered why they didn't switch it around and put the servants downstairs. With the masters and mistresses in the upper gallery, they could enjoy the superior view as well as keep a watch on the servants. But such an idea never seemed to be to their way of thinking.

Either way—upstairs or down—I never attended St. Paul's Sunday services on the inside. Missus said I was too young. I thought maybe she did not want to leave me alone with all those other slave boys.

"When you're older," she always said. "Not just yet, when

you're older."

Extra had his own thoughts about it.

"She worried you'll get hold of a hymn book and commence singin' and readin' and readin' and singin'," he said. "Then everybody will know you can read. Won't be hard for 'em to figure how you come to learn. Missus Pegram—she worried how folks will look at it."

The preacher was a short man, puffed up with a pride of bearing like no Butternut officer I ever saw. He walked in a way that made his body seem a thing apart, like he was two people— one possessed of powerful invisible spirit, the other possessed of visible body bullied into fancy display of service by the unseen spirit.

His head appeared to be a block of square stone with a face of real flesh emblazoned upon it as if put there by God himself. If that was so, I could not help but wonder that God accomplished the job with a touch of humor, because he endowed the man with not one string of hair, excepting a patch of bushy curliness that grew on the back of his neck and peeked out from around the front of each ear. On some Sundays it did appear he oiled up those two little protrusions, making them bounce with fanciness.

His name too was fancy, tacked on with a long list of ornamental titles. He was called His Eminence Most Excellent Doctor Charles Minnigerode. He had the loudest voice you could imagine and always made certain he could be heard on the outside of St. Paul's as well as inside. With his voice, a partially opened window was good enough. On very cold mornings he would crack the window come sermon time, then shut it tight afterward so as not to freeze out the worshippers on the inside. I wondered if he made those adjustments for me, knowing I was on my bench. It was a vanity I queried Missus about.

"Oh, poosh," she said. "He's just hoping to rattle the ears of some passing Catholic." I did not know what that meant. A second query was met with a brief answer.

"The cathedral," she said unhappily under her breath, "St. Peter's." I knew there was another church directly across Grace Street. On hot Sundays in July, the doors and windows of both churches would be flung wide, making Grace Street recipient to a noisy pageant of competing singing and praying. Come sermon time, the ministers seemed to enter a battle for who could preach loudest. His Eminence Most Excellent Doctor always won.

I settled onto my bench, where other servants waited at loiter as usual, and the singing started. I did not recognize the first hymn, which was not unusual. It told of a man named Zachariah, blessed by the God of Israel, who visited and redeemed his people. I frequently wondered why so much about Sunday services was about gods other than Jesus and people other than Jesus' people.

There were prayers followed by another hymn on the proper subject of churchgoing. It contained the chorus, "Holy, holy, holy Lord Jesus." It went on with "you calm our fears" followed by lots more "holy, holy, holy."

During that hymn I caught sight of the oddest man I have ever laid vision to. He walked alone up the Ninth Street hill with a wooden satchel strapped around his shoulders. His head was overly large for his body. His face seemed burned a deep red and was dented with large pock scars on his cheeks. A curtain of oily brown and gray hair hung to his shoulders from three sides of his great head, which was bald on top.

As he came closer, I could see that his large, round eyes held no color at all—but only black centers swollen so big they were surrounded only by white. His nose and mouth were moist with ooze and he frequently dabbed at them with a soiled handkerchief, which he kept at the ready, dangling from one tiny hand.

The other servants gawked as he passed, turning to watch him, some with their jaws hanging loose at the sight. He took no notice of their mooning and finished his labored struggle up the hill, fighting for his wind as he wiped his mouth and nose. Not far from me, he approached a servant minding a buggy hitched to an old riding pony.

"Boy," he called out. The servant stood from his seat in the wagon's step well. I could tell he worried about being approached by someone who looked more like a jack-o'-lantern than a true white man. "How long since services began?" he asked.

"Service, sah?" the servant repeated, staring at the man's face.

"Yes. When did it begin?"

"I dunno sah. Not too long. Dey only on de second song."

"Second song?" He turned and gazed the length of St. Paul's from one end to the other with his black eyes. He looked up at the spire, then down at the waiting crowd consisting mostly of slaves attending horses and bored Butternut soldiers.

"Yes-sah. Dis number two."

"How many songs are there typically?" the man asked, turning back to the slave, who could not fathom the meaning of the man or his questions.

"How many songs, sah?"

"Yes. I want to know how long before the women come out?"

"I dunno about songs, sah. But all you gotta do is wait 'til they drink and eat Jesus. They all be out after that."

The jack-o'-lantern grunted and walked away, wheezing and dabbing at his nose. One Butternut sentry eyed the odd man cautiously, but made no movement toward him. I was watching him turn west in front of St. Paul's as another voice startled me.

"That sho is a pretty ribbon ya'll got in your hair this morning." It was Extra! He stood directly beside me, tall and lean, handsome and smiling down at me. The sight of him drove away all fears and even pains of hunger.

"Extra!" I cried.

"Yes, ma'am," he said, putting his teeth on wide display.

"Oh, Extra."

"Sho is," he said. He stood directly between me and a spot of sun glimmering between clouds, lending a moment of blinding radiance. I put up my hand to shield my eyes. "I say that sho is a pretty ribbon," he repeated.

"Never mind ribbons," I chided. "Sit down. I saw Old Caesar this morning. He says you're bonded to the Butternut all week." He sat next to me on the servant's bench.

"Caesar got it right, Missy Fran. Colonel Sam Gist his name."

"Is he in services now?"

"Sho is. Gettin' morning prayer ahead o'rampart inspection."

"You been called to war work?"

"Dunno Miss Francine. It may just be work on the rails. I hear the Yankees got all rails outside town torn to bits. Maybe I just spend a week workin' on the rails. Ramparts need work, too. Drewey's Bluff maybe. Lots of digging."

"Extra, Missus Pegram is real upset."

"What she frettin' over?"

"Petersburg, I think. Is your colonel-man headed that way?"

"Dunno fer certain, Missy Fran, but she got plenty right to fret over Petersburg. I heard Colonel Gist talking. He say it getting worse. He say they all livin' in holes—both Billies and Johnnies. He say they livin' like rats and something gotta change soon. Uhn, uhn, uhn," he said, looking down and shaking his head, "that Petersburg just sound like a sad ole mess. Missy Fran, I dunno, but this morning Master Pettigrew says maybe the whole thing gonna bust loose. Maybe they fear the Yankees set to invade us. That's why they puttin' me on digging at the ramparts. They gatherin' up as many as they can for that."

"Don't Master Pettigrew want you back at the hotel?"

"No, Missy. Not yet. Ain't got 'nuff paying customers in town for him to keep me on as a porter. He lookin' to barter me as much as he can. Ain't nobody but the women doing what little work is at de hotel right now. Tobacco houses and flour mills don't need nobody no more neither—maybe not 'til hot weather set in." He kept a steady watch on a tall bay at idle near the curb.

"Is that your colonel-man's horse?"

"Yes, it is. And them boys be from the farms." He nodded at a wagon drawn to a stop near an alleyway on the other side of Ninth Street, halfway down the block, led by a single team of sorry-looking mules. The wagon bed was filled with more than a dozen men. I knew with a quick look they were field slaves. "I'll be going with them," he said.

They sat on the floor of the wagon, looking like spent cattle headed for the meat-packer. Their heads spun this way and that, eyeballing everything that came and went as though they had never been on a city street before.

"Extra, they're a mess," I said. "Who's going to work the farms come spring if they put all the land labor to war work?"

"Dunno. Right now, they need to tend to ramparts and rails. They ain't 'nuff Johnnies left for the fighting and the laboring, too. Reckon they'll worry 'bout plantin' time when plantin' time come. Dunno for certain. I'm thinking I'll be going below Manchester. Dunno how far. Deep Bottom maybe. Drewey's Bluff. Colonel Gist tell me I'll be in charge o'them boys over yonder. As a bonded man, I gotta make sure the field hands do proper work."

"If Petersburg is that bad—and they send you there—you thinking about running?"

"No. Ain't no need, Miss Francine. Way I read Colonel Gist

and Master Pettigrew, things set to change." He kept his watch on the big bay and the farm slaves in the wagon. "Anyway, I don't think they plannin' on sendin' us further'n the ramparts."

"What if there's fighting?"

"Don't worry, Missy Fran. Mister Pettigrew don't wanna lose me. If he lose me, he lose lots o'money. I heard Colonel Gist talking with Sergeant Paxton. He say he doubt that could happen now with all the attention going to Petersburg."

We talked at length during services, catching up on other events. He had spent most of March bonded to the Seabrooks and Shockoe tobacco warehouses. As part of his duties he'd traveled all the way to Danville, Dinwiddie, and even Roanoke Rapids to bring feed and seed from city warehouse to farm.

"You've been to Roanoke Rapids?" I jumped in, knowing Master Pegram owned a farm there with his half-brother, which Missus planned as their last resort getaway.

"Sho have."

"So you know how to get there?"

"Sho do. It just over the state line. After Richmond, the towns worth noting go Petersburg, Jarratt, Emporia, and then Roanoke Rapids."

"You know Master Pegram owns a farm there with his half-brother."

"Yes, Missy. You told me. They grow tobacco."

"I heard Missus saying we may get away there if the Yankees come to Richmond."

"That be good. But Pegram's ain't got no more horse and buggy."

"Even so—what about Petersburg?"

"You gotta go around that. We did last week. We went way around. Gave it wide birth. Went all the way to Powhatan before turning south. Took most the day and part of the night, too."

After a while the sermon started. His Eminence Most Excellent worked up slow, as always, with his singsong manner, talking low, then talking hard, then low, then hard—leading up to the part where he shouted, pointed, and waved his arms about redemption and rejoicing. I always enjoyed the sound of it, even when I did not understand the meaning of the words. This morning was such a morning. The sermon was about people with lots of *z*'s and *x*'s in their names. They came and went to places with mountains and desert. There were red horses and black horses, chariots and angels. Some went north and some south. And all the while God spoke to this one and that one, giving and taking, taking and giving. Whenever God spoke he always started with the word "behold." It's a good word. The way His Eminence Most Excellent pronounced it—it summoned me to attention every time, which, I conjured, is why God said it so much.

"He going good now," Extra said as we listened.

"He sure is."

"Way he talking about people of different lands fighting and praying, it sound almost like the Billy and Johnny."

A change in tone always signaled the end of the sermon. His Eminence Most Excellent slowed his pace, commencing a quieter pitch but with menacing temper. This day, the hushed tone signal arrived with warnings of nations at war with Jerusalem, houses plundered, women ravished. I hoped he was not making predictions about Richmond.

"You leaving right after church?"

"Sure am. Colonel say he got to make a stop at Danville depot. Gotta pick up or drop off something for the late morning train, then we off to inspect ramparts."

"How long will that take?"

"Dunno. Bunch o'days I reckon."

I told him about the wagon of wounded I witnessed earlier that morning. Extra was generous with kind words, saying he too had viewed sorely wounded men at Chimborazo and knew it to be a hard experience.

It was he who brought up our future plans.

"I'm doing good as a bonded man," he said, "at least for now. Maybe that will keep up for a while. Depending on how this all work out, maybe we can live in town after we get married. Maybe the Pegrams will let you live at the Spotswood. If not, at least you'll be close by."

It was too many "maybes," but I didn't want to spoil it—not with Extra about to ride out of town. My hope was that Extra and me could end up at Daddy's Little Farm in Roanoke Rapids.

That Sunday was Communion day. After the sermon, His Eminence Most Excellent commenced oaths over the bread and wine, a show delivered in a fancy language all its own. It was during that portion of the service when a show of another kind kicked up. A Butternut rider hastily crossed Ninth Street from the buildings of government to the east. He reigned in his horse, handed over the tack to a valet at loiter, and rushed into St. Paul's. We wondered what it meant, but it did not take long to learn the purpose.

First, the rider emerged. He returned to his horse and rode off without any haste at all. Then another man emerged and briskly strode down the St. Paul's steps.

"Lordy, Missy Fran. Oh, lordy me. Look at that." Extra leaned in to speak to me so only I could hear.

"What is it, Extra?"

"Lordy, Missy Fran. That Mister President Davis." I recognized him, too. He had silky gray hair and a tuft of short chin whiskers that came straight down, looking silly, like they had sprouted overnight by accident.

"He's leaving services in the middle?" I asked.

"Sho 'nuff is. He leaving during the part about drinking the blood o' Jesus."

"Extra, that's the most important part."

"Sho is. That's the part where they get salvation." He paused to study the backsides of Mister President Davis strolling up Ninth Street. "Lordy, Missy Fran. That rider was a messenger. Whatever it's about, it's 'nuff to draw the president out—right in the middle o' the most important part."

Extra could not read and did not talk as good as some, but he was smart. He knew what was happening just as it was happening.

Necks craned at the event. Every servant at loiter and Butternut on duty watched Mister President Davis walk to the corner at Ninth and Grace Streets. No one understood its meaning, but everyone seemed to sense it foretold something important. I noted he was not in a hurry. His Sunday suit coat did not flap as he walked, but hung steady behind him. He was perfectly alone, his head tucked down as though thinking, or maybe worrying about something that weighed heavy. On the other side of Ninth Street he walked north, toward his Great White House beyond Broad Street.

"Unh, unh, unnhh," Extra said, shaking his head as Mister President Davis was lost to everyone's sight. He looked down between his knees. "Lordy, Lord. Unh, unh, unh!"

"Extra, what does it mean?"

"Ah dunno, but I'm guessing all officers will be movin' right quick."

"Moving where? To do what?"

"Dunno, Missy Fran. Maybe moving just for sake o' moving. Sometimes they gotta look right busy too, just for sake o' lookin busy, just like we gotta do sometimes to keep from gettin' a beatin'."

"Extra, that message was important."

"Uh-huh. It was that, Missy Fran. It was that."

Inside St. Paul's, His Eminence Most Excellent stumbled over the remaining oaths of bread and wine. It was something that never happened before and it made me wonder what else was taking place in the prayer pews. It was not long before an answer arrived. There were more departures. At first, they were only Butternut.

The quickest among them turned south and came straight past my servant's bench. He was a stout, important-looking Butternut with streaming long curls of red hair and bushy red sideburns; fancy gold braiding adorned both sleeves of his stiff tunic, which was dappled with mud and with all the carved wood buttons tightly cinched to the collar. Extra saw him coming, gave a start, and moved quickly toward the big bay. I knew that meant he was Colonel Gist, the man Extra was bonded to for the next group of days. Without speaking a word he walked straight to the horse, took the reins from Extra, mounted up, and rode off in a haste. Another Butternut, less important looking, with undone buttons and jacket flaps hanging loosely, spoke gruff words to Extra, then gestured for him to follow. They both set off across Ninth Street to the wagon filled with broke-down field slaves.

"Come to the house when you're finished," I called out as forcefully as I dared, hoping my words would earn only Extra's attention. He turned and gave me his wonderful smile.

"Don't fret, Missy Fran. I be over directly," he said.

Before turning away he put the end of one finger to his lips, as though kissing it. When his hand fell away, it revealed a great smile, wide with confidence. I saw it as a promise of his love for me. He was a true man. He was my man to be. And he was tall and glorious in the morning sun.

The Butternut with the flapping jacket mounted the buckboard beside Extra, who gee'd the sorry-looking mule team. The wagon lurched from the alleyway onto Ninth Street and turned north, with the field slaves bouncing unhappily in the back, looking dirty, beat down, and bewildered.

Other Butternut withdrew. Some went for horses, others walked with haste to the buildings of government. There followed a scurry of a few hasty feet as the departures widened to some regular worshippers.

His Excellency was not happy with the interrupting scurry and he let the remaining worshippers know it. He did not say it outright, but changed up his tone, heaping disfavor with the pitch of his voice upon those displaying uncivil manner. I conjure he must have made a gesture, or bore down hard with stoned-carved eyes upon those nervous worshippers angling in their pews to get at the aisle and then scoot to the door. That stopped the floodtide. His tone returned to a mostly normal manner. A short time afterward, His Excellency concluded the service with the briefest prayer I ever heard him deliver. It was followed with a sharp chorus of grateful "Amens."

The normal course of events was for plenty of lingering smiles and handshaking after services. His Excellency usually perched on the steps handing out "good mornings" and "God bless you's" to anyone who wanted to receive one. They returned his greetings with "oh what a lovely sermon" or "my goodness that was a wonderful service, Doctor." There was none of that this morning. Things were much changed from the usual. The sudden departure of Mister President Davis was an ingredient that altered the recipe. Those who departed early feared its meaning. Those who remained may have feared it even more.

Their manner called to mind the story of all the animals coming off Noah's great boat—the worshippers emerged from St. Paul's looking about, appearing worried over where their ship had landed. They descended the steps with uncertainty as they peeked out, making certain it was a familiar world and safe to proceed. They examined the Butternut soldiers and servants at loiter, all of whom returned their gaze with idle curiosity. Some handshakes were delivered. I did hear a few "good mornings" and one or two "God bless you's," but without the usual vigor. His Eminence Most Excellent must have remained inside, for I did not see him. After a moment, the pace picked up. The remaining "God bless you's" were delivered with tight-faced grins as they all dashed for horse, buggy, and footpath as though everyone suddenly had to go to the privy.

CHAPTER THIRTEEN:
MISS FRANCINE PEGRAM

The next event landed with a shock as sure as if it had been another rattling WHOOMP-boom. Missus Pegram passed me in a tight state. She strode past without speaking, gripping the parasol so firmly the ruffles lost their shape. I fell in behind. On the way down Ninth Street she handed out a tight smile or two at fellow worshippers then picked up the pace going down the hill so that we got home in half the usual time. Seeing that we would not be bartering for dinner did not sit well with my hunger pains.

Back inside, she let flow her symptoms. She wrung her hands and pattered about with distraction from parlor to hallway to kitchen and back to parlor. She went to the Thomas clock time after time as if each new minute were an hour that would bring about forebodings.

I sat quietly on my hallway slave's chair watching her perform her own version of the same display I had put on after racing from my bucky-board before the start of day. She had barely recovered from the ugly sight of the wagon of torment only to have her fears return during church—the very place she had gone for salvation from worry. As always when in these states, she would talk aloud. This time around there were only snippets of words: "please," "oh, God," "Gen'l Lee," "it can't be," "if only Stonewall was alive," "Maxcy, where are you?" Her curses were the most understandable of her mutterings: "That damn coward Jefferson Davis," "that damn Jew Benjamin," and "that damn drunkard Ulysses Grant."

On one of her loops she stopped in front of me, looking down with a pair of hardened eyes and a fixed jaw set on edge. It was a look I had never seen before. She didn't say anything, but just stood there with poison in her eyes, thinking thoughts I am glad she did not speak aloud. I looked back, slack and scared. I can never know the true nature of her mind at that moment, yet am confident that my own safety was not among her tightly gripped worries.

Her pattering was interrupted by a series of sharp thud-noises on the front stoop followed by a giant "thrummp." The sounds pulled my missus from her inner distractions and thankfully removed her mean-eyed fix from me.

She ran to the parlor window and leaned at an angle to peep onto the stoop. At the sight of it, she let out a "whoa" holler and hurried to open the door, with me trailing behind.

It was Mistress Bartow lying flat out on her side, her hand still gripping a heavy satchel bulging with goods. Her head must have been leaning upon the door, because when Missus Pegram flung it open, her head plopped to the floor, making one final thud. The sight and sound of it alarmed us both—but I declare I can't help but report it did also look comical.

She was a big woman, the largest of Missus Pegram's social venue. Everywhere that Missus Pegram is bony with graying skin, Mistress Bartow is plush with rosy flesh. All during the war, when so many of them reduced in size because of hunger and limited provisions, Mistress Bartow only seemed to grow larger.

There she was, spread across the porch boards. Her generous bosom was pressed so hard by the weight of her body, I thought she was going to pop out in public. Her legs were spread, one foot poked in the air, and her dress near-about wrapped the entire front stoop like a crinoline canopy.

Missus Pegram set about "oh-no-ing" and "oh-my-goodness-ing" as we both worked to roll Mistress Bartow over and set her upright. That done, we each took an elbow to get her inside as she "oh-my-Lorded" and "oh-for-heavens-saked" all the way to the nearest chair, which happened to be the fancy green one named for Queen Anne.

I fetched the satchel from the porch. It was heavy, and I could lift it only enough to hoist it past the doorway then drag it to the hall near my servant's chair. I could tell from the feel that it was mostly clothing, but one side bulged in the shape of a large fry-pan.

Missus Pegram fanned Mistress Bartow with her skirts while I trotted off swift to the kitchen on instruction to fetch a cup of water from the pitcher. She wasn't really hurt. She seemed none the worse for her thrump-tumble on the porch, and the thud-noise her head made when it bumped the threshold was no more than a spot of aggravation to her overly powdered and rouged-up face. Yet she was much disturbed by the whole event and continued to raise a fuss. I patted her hand while she sipped water. Then came more trouble. She tried to "oh, my lordy" at the same time she took a sip of water, which delivered liquid to the wrong place, making her commence coughing and thrashing about like a crazy woman. That set Missus Pegram to once again lifting her skirts to fan her, while I gave one of her shoulder bones a round of gentle pats, the way I had seen others do whenever anyone got to choking at the dinner table.

It took a while, but once Mistress Bartow settled down, she paid no mind to the entire spectacle. She just set right into an excited rush of words about the news.

"Oh, Ruth," she said to Missus Pegram, between her final hacks of coughing. "It's horrible—oh, what are we to do." She thrashed some more, puckering her plump ruby lips sharply to hack out the last round of coughing from her throat. "Oh,

Ruth," she whined several more times, then she started to cry.

It all added up to make my missus impatient.

"Lord, Helen," she said to Mistress Bartow in a tone completely overlooking that her guest had just about fallen into the house then coughed herself into seizure. "What is it, Helen? Oh, Lord, what has happened?"

"Ruth! This morning in church! I've been told that was a message direct from General Lee!" What little facial color was left in my missus drained off. "Oh, Lord, Ruth, they're saying that . . . oh, Lord, have mercy!"

Missus Pegram narrowed down. "They're saying what?" She spoke in a voice that let Missus Bartow know it would be best if she answered-up properly.

"They're saying the city is to be evacuated. I packed a grip. But I don't know where to go. With my husband and daughter long dead, I have no one." Missus stepped back to consider the news. The tightness in her face fell away. Her eyes widened. Her lips parted. A fearful silence followed while she held her gaze upon her friend.

It is true that Mistress Bartow was alone. She was widowed early on. I never knew her husband, who died young of one thing or another. But I did know her daughter Evelyn, who succumbed to the croup during the first year of the war. Indeed, it was from Evelyn that I had inherited my prize brokens.

"Helen," Missus said, finally breaking the quiet, speaking dismissively. "Even if you had family, there's nowhere to flee."

"We must, Ruth."

"Oh, poosh," she said. "General Lee will not leave us without defense. Besides, Maxcy will not be home until tomorrow or maybe Tuesday. I must wait for him."

"Oh, Ruth," she panted, "we must! There is no choice in the matter." She gulped for air to deliver the next message. "Ruth, President Davis has already departed. The Yankees! The Yankees! They're right outside the Richmond lines. The ramparts will surely fall. Ruth, I fear we are already left defenseless . . . why . . . we'll be all be raped and murdered by freed-up niggers and liquored-up Yankees if we don't run." She broke off into a heap of tears. A mighty wash came from her eyes, making tracks through the face powder applied that morning for St. Paul services.

"The president has left Richmond?" my missus asked, her eyes again narrowing.

"Oh, Ruth, some are saying he's simply taken to his heels. Just run off!" She barely managed to speak the words between heaving sobs.

Missus Pegram set her teeth and chin down tight as she eye-balled hard at Mistress Bartow, much the way she had done to me just moments earlier. I could see a string of curses in her—even though she was too shocked to give them voice.

In between Mistress Bartow's blubbers she "oh, lordied" and blew her nose, then "I declared" and blew her nose some more until she wore out her own lace-edged handkerchief, which required me to fetch a stiff kitchen rag—which was not appropriate for the job, but under the circumstances there was not much else to offer and neither of them objected.

A groundswell of restless noise rose from the street, interrupting the boiling Bartow tears with a sharp report—a kind of "popping" sound of the type that tries the nerves when men are at war. It stopped Mistress Bartow's tears fast and we all moved to the parlor window.

It was not what we feared. There were no Butternut about, or Yankees, or even anyone with a musket-rifle at all. There was only a two-wheel wagon heavily laden with an assortment of odd bags and crates, pulled by a single old carthorse that stopped dead still in the middle of Ninth Street, where it was making a stubborn objection to the weight of the wagon load. A man in the wagon balanced atop the pile with one leg braced on the cart rim, the other atop the very uppermost crate as he reached down, digging into the mixed heap. Standing nearby were three children and two women, one of them a white-haired collection of bones stooped with age. They all looked on dumbly at the street drama.

The man withdrew an old saddle and tossed it to the street, causing a second noise, similar but not as loud as the first. The saddle landed next to a pile of shovels tied together. The old nag turned her head to study the saddle but did not seem impressed. The man in the cart called out a one-word inquiry to the horse. It sounded like "EYAH?" When there was no response, he braced his position and again dug into the carted store of goods.

"Oh, Lord, have mercy," Mistress Bartow whined loudly. "It's the Garnetts!"

"What in the world?" Missus Pegram said staring, moving only her lips as she spoke with all teeth locked together.

"Oh, Ruth, that is the entire Garnett family. Why, that old woman is Mary-Jean Garnett's mother who came to live with them from Port Royal. She's not well enough to travel."

"Where do they think they're going? They won't make it across the river in that condition." Missus Pegram stared from the parlor window; her jaw remained set hard and she spoke in an oddly calm voice, all her words in even, measured tones, which worried me.

Mister Garnett seized upon a medium-sized cask that sent Mistress Garnett waving and shouting objections, but he paid her no mind and tossed it onto Ninth Street, where it broke open sending up puffs of yellow powder. The carthorse remained immovable. Mister Garnett tossed another crate, which smashed open revealing a collection of iron cooking pots. Next came a large satchel, most likely containing clothing or bedding. It landed flat on its side with a great plop, stirring up a twirl of Ninth Street dust, which mixed with the yellow powder from the demolished cask.

The carthorse studied the latest jetsam, gave an unfriendly nod, then commenced straining at the yoke without being whipped. Mister Garnett hopped from the cart, picked up Mistress Mary-Jean Garnett's white-haired mother by the shoulders and plunked her down in a standing position at the rear edge of the cart, then he ran to the front where he took the old nag's reins. The others commenced walking alongside, looking just as beat down and unhappy as the cart-horse. The old mother stood in the rear of the cart, gripping one railing edge with both hands, head down, legs spread apart for balance. She looked old and thin and frail and thoroughly incapable of riding even half a block in such a condition, yet she held her grip solid, bouncing in that ramshackle old cart until they all disappeared from our view.

"What is that?" Mistress Bartow asked.

"Meal," my missus answered calmly.

"Oh, my Lord," Mistress Bartow whined with objection. We were all stunned by the sight. Meal. Real cornmeal! It was a kitchen store we had not enjoyed in any quantity for many months. The three of us stood at the parlor window watching the heap of rich blessing left scattered upon Ninth Street dirt. Clouds of ghostly bright yellow hung close to the ground, moving slowly about, looking like a low-hanging morning fog. I stared at the little mountain of powder with hunger and conjured running to the street with a scoop. Missus Pegram and Mistress Bartow were likely indulging in the same thoughts. None of us acted quickly enough.

Another vehicle moved south. This time it was a riding carriage pulled by a large tawny at full gallop, driven by an excited man who whipped the horse and called out loud curses that we could easily hear in the parlor. He profaned the Lord and the Yankees both. Without regard for consequence, hooves and wheels trampled the flotsam in Ninth Street, slamming into the discarded crates and casks, and bounced high off the overstuffed satchel. None of it slowed the horse; the carriage kept its race to the south, quickly departing our view. The wheels also plowed the pile of precious cornmeal, sending fast currents of yellow clouds swirling into the air and speeding down Ninth Street as though chasing the carriage that just disturbed it. I watched it swirl and spin and slowly settle back into yellow fog, a treasure lost.

After we had been standing silent for a while, it was Mistress Bartow who spoke, though it was nothing we had not heard previously.

"Oh, my Lord," she said. "What in the world!" She said it just as more people in a mad haste passed south. There were men trotting on horseback and sprinting on foot. Two mistresses in full dress crinolines toting parasols passed south, bent at the waist, holding their hems, running as fast as their cinched-up feet would carry them. A wagon pulled by twin mules carried a crowd of men huddled in the load bed, making me recall both the wagon of torment headed for Chimborazo and the wagon of field hands headed for ramparts work with Extra. These passengers were neither wounded nor field hands; they were all white men, mostly attired in proper coat and hat, workers in one of the offices of government, I conjured. I couldn't see their faces. None of them looked about like the field hands did, with a mix of fear and curiosity. They just sat, obedient and hangdog.

Mistress Bartow commenced crying again.

"Oh, Ruth! Everyone is running." Waters recommenced—bursting from every vent in her face. Her arms thrashed about as she made her laments. Missus Pegram ignored her this second time around.

"Yes," said Missus Pegram, staring at the spectacle, still speaking in a dead calm, so stony it raised bumps on my neck.

"Where is everybody going?" Mistress Bartow blubbered.

"They don't know. They're not going anywhere," my missus said. "They're just scared of the Yankees."

"Well, so am I," Mistress Bartow whined, barely audible in a high-pitched voice that squeaked like Ole Mister Rat.

We must have been an amusing sight to the Lord. There we were—Missus Pegram, Mistress Bartow, and me, a twelve-year-old slave girl—standing at the Ninth Street window watching the world go past, a trio of feeble spectators at a festival of dread. Mistress Bartow stood in place, wailing and thrashing. Missus Pegram, I conjured, was doing the same on the inside, but outside she was pulled together so tight I wondered if she mayn't have trouble fully unlocking everything when the time came. As for me—I was scared of the Yankees because everybody else was scared of the Yankees; but I was also scared that Missus Pegram was about to commence seeing devils and men that float in the air.

"Helen, where's the army?" Missus Pegram said after a while.

"Huh?" Mistress Bartow's dumbfounded response was all she could manage between blubbers.

"The army, Helen. Soldiers. Confederate forces stationed in the city. Where are the soldiers?"

"Well, I'm afraid I don't know. Loretta Garland and Ruby Branch told me that damn Jeff Davis departed the city. I returned to my apartment room to pack a grip and came straight here. I'm afraid that's all the news I gathered."

"What are the others doing?"

"Beg pardon?"

"Helen, the other single women who live in the Franklin Building of Lady's Residences. Your neighbors. What are they doing?"

"Why, I'm afraid I didn't ask any of 'em."

"Very well, then. We need more information. So let's get more," Missus announced with confidence. "Francine, get my parasol. Helen, blow your nose, we're going back to church."

We got as far as Ninth and Franklin Street when Missus Pegram received all the news she required. Several blocks to the east, we could see the traffic passing south. Twelfth, Thirteenth, and Fourteenth Streets were choked with Butternut headed for the river crossing at Mayo Bridge. They were not running, but marching at a brisk pace: wagons, carts, mules, dogs, horses, cannon, and soldiers. Soldiers, soldiers, soldiers, bunches of lines of them, walking in a manner that set up a noisy rhythm to their pace so loud I wondered why we had not heard it from the parlor.

"Oh, Ruth, there's your answer," Mistress Bartow said, gawking at the parade in the distance. She was set to recommence her wailing in public, but Missus Pegram cut her short.

"Helen, you stop that right now," she said sharply. And Mistress Bartow did.

We resumed our walk up the Ninth Street hill toward St. Paul's, passing more discarded property. Between Main and Franklin we encountered a business desk and chair left in the middle of the narrow footpath. A writing tablet still rested on the surface, as well as a pile of loose paper weighted down by a small iron statue of a bird dog, his nose and leg lifted in point. It was a comical sight, appearing as though the chair's occupant would return any moment to resume his work.

Missus Pegram's locked jaw twitched with a grinding motion as we walked around it.

Several groups of mistresses and a few old men gathered on the St. Paul's steps. Mistress Bartow and Missus Pegram fell in with them, talking excitedly, weeping, "Oh-my-Lording," "I-declaring," asking questions, receiving answers, gesturing toward the buildings of government where we could witness more But-ternut exiting, moving south and falling in with the march to the River James.

Their talk labored on a few topics. Everyone wondered from which direction the Yankees would invade and which direction would be the best for refugeeing so as to avoid them.

Another topic they hammered was Mister President Davis. They cursed him for leaving Richmond and for failing to provide a plan for them. The women put their lace handkerchiefs to their mouths and, in hushed voices, called him "coward" or "scoundrel." Such behavior was not new, but I had never before heard them profane Mister President Davis on the St. Paul's steps.

Staying in Richmond was another topic of their hasty talk. "Persisting" they called it. And the idea of being a "persister" led naturally to a great number of "oh, naws" and much profan-ing upon the Yankees: "Oh, naw . . . the Yankees will kill us all . . . oh, naw, the women won't be safe . . . oh, naw, the whiskey . . . oh, naw, the niggers . . . oh, naw, oh, naw, oh, naw."

I stood aside, watching and listening. I looked for His Eminence Most Excellent Doctor Charles Minningerode, but he was nowhere to be seen. Similar gatherings of Catholics were taking place in front of the cathedral across Grace Street. To the west, Mister Morgan nailed boards to the front of his Notions & Hardware Shop. Farther down in the same block, Mister Gordon did the same to the Lady's Fashion Emporium. To the east, the parade of Butternut trickled down to almost nothing. In the time it took us to walk up the Ninth Street hill and spend a few minutes "oh-nawing" in front of St. Paul's, the soldiers had nearly completed their evacuation.

Mistress Bartow and my missus were summoned to a larger gathering that included Mistress Winder a few steps up. Taking no interest in hearing anymore "oh, naws," I lagged behind, missing the particulars of their talk. I looked for Extra, wondering if these developments altered his bonded work upon the ramparts.

The jack-o'-lantern man made a brief reappearance on the other side of Grace Street. I caught sight of him waddling from the west as quickly as his squat legs could carry him, his wooden satchel strapped over his shoulder and bouncing on his rear quarters with every tottering step. From a block away, he eyed first the crowd at St. Paul's then the crowd at the cathedral. Although the crowd of Catholics was smaller, it was closer and he moved toward it—then ambled his way into it as he held up a bill of announcement in his tiny hands.

Mistresses and a few masters moved excitably from one little knotted gathering in front of St. Paul's to another in quest of trustworthy information. Knowing my own fate was bound to hers, I kept a steady watch on Missus Pegram—and in doing so, kept particular heed to the grinding of her tightly locked jaw. It showed no measure of loosening. That altered a little when Mistress and Mister Winder joined up with her. Her eyes brightened and I conjured that a plan would soon be hatched.

The Winders were older than the Pegrams. Mistress Winder was not a handsome woman. Everything about her was small, except her nostrils—great flared openings shaped like boats that offered a view straight up both channels. She wore too much pink face powder and had a bosom so flat I wondered if all her dresses required cinching-up by a tailor to make them fit proper.

Neither of them had family ties to war labors, which made them unusual. There was not a son, brother, or even a nephew they could talk of that wore a uniform of any kind. That was a kinship Missus Pegram enjoyed, as she too had no children and liked the respite from afternoon teas weighed heavily with great woe over sons and brothers lost to the cause. When Missus Pegram could have social time alone with Mistress Winder, the talk avoided news of who was wearing black or where they had done a round of parlor sitting in honor of some dead boy. Instead, their talk dwelled on some new pink evening dress seen in the window at Mister Gordon's Lady's Fashion Emporium, or they happily recalled memories of Savannah, where Mistress Winder was raised and where Missus Pegram spent two years in a formal girls' school. There was also abundant talk over their courting days, when missus spoke of "sassy boys" who tried to kiss her under the low-hanging limbs of the green apple tree in Bon Air, where everyone went for holiday relief from the heavy waves of Richmond's summer heat.

As for Mister Winder, he was a rich man who owned a carriage company on Broad Street. The two of them lived in a large house with marble columns on Main Street several blocks to the west and owned many servants who dressed in the best finery. "Oh, he got started as a lowly wheelwright," Mistress Winder was quick to say to anyone making winks and nods upon the subject of their wealth.

It wasn't long after joining the crowd of Catholics that the jack-o'-lantern man ambled his way across Grace Street to the larger crowd of Episcopalians at St. Paul's. His big, round, red face was so marked up with holes that I could hardly gaze upon it when he passed by me—looking like it had been used as a target for revolver practice. His swollen nose oozed with croup sickness.

After a brief pause eyeing the crowd, he weighed in—holding up his bill of announcement. He did not talk, but only held the bill for all to see, especially the mistresses. When he turned toward me, I could see its words:

Jewel Merchant
Buy/Sell
Call at Spotswood, rm. 415

Before he could work his way to the Pegram, Bartow, Winder knot halfway up the St. Paul's steps, they all separated and descended with excitement. The Winders departed to the west. Missus Pegram and Mistress Bartow moved together in the opposite direction toward me. The sudden burst from their clutch of worry resembled a sort of child's game, as though they were all running to commence a round of hide-and-seek. At the sight of it, I knew a plan had been hatched.

"C'mon, Francine," was all Missus said.

She led the way, her skinny legs moving so fast they nearly broke into a gallop. At such a pace, Mistress Bartow would normally have made objection, yet she did not pronounce a single complaint. She tucked her elbows in and trod along second in line, toting her girth with agility, her great bosoms heaving and bouncing with each step.

We again navigated the abandoned desk and chair between Franklin and Main. More debris had been scattered since we passed a short time earlier, including a tin washtub filled with clothing, but we paid it no mind.

In the house, Mistress Bartow required a rest on the Queen Anne chair to get her breath, while I went upstairs to help Missus Pegram hastily pack a satchel of her own. She said little to me. There was just an occasional "none of that," or "just the one," in reference to various items of toilet and clothing. It was a woman's satchel that opened at the top, made of heavy wool, the sides decorated with fancy embroidered flowers.

Once we finished packing and cinched it shut, Missus Pegram told me to sit on the vanity bench, which I did. She closed the door, then pushed the slop jar with her foot to maneuver it from its position where I last had tucked it under the bed. She removed the lid, raised her hems, plucked down her unders, and squatted over the bowl, holding a grip to the rear bedpost with one hand for balance.

"Francine," she began while relieving herself, "the Winders are coming by with a four-seater in a few minutes. Cyrus and Marion have nowhere to go outside of Richmond and we have no wagon or horse of any kind. So we shall pool our resources. I have invited them to be our guests at Daddy's Little Farm. When General Lee resolves this matter we shall all return."

"Yes'm," I said, pleased. I wondered how I could let Extra know that I was bound for Daddy's Little Farm at Roanoke Rapids. Perhaps I could leave a message with Old Caesar.

"One of her servants will drive the team, a trained horseman. I believe his name is Compson. It may take a while to arrive safely at Roanoke Rapids, as we shall have to do a roundabout west of Petersburg."

"Yes'm," I said again. I did not know Compson. Being rich, the Winders had a number of servants both inside and out.

"Daddy's Little Farm isn't much. There's just a small house, little more than shelter. Of course, it is shelter we require in this storm, so we must make do. With Daddy's half-brother present we shall be very cramped. The Winders are unaccustomed to hardship, so we shall rely on Compson for assistance. Barring delays or misfortune we should arrive by nightfall."

"Yes'm," I said a third time. Then, "I'll fetch my other gingham and put on my brokens," I said.

"That won't be necessary, Francine," she said in a plain tone. "You are to stay here." My face must have revealed fast surprise; she was prepared with a quick response. "Now, Francine," she began, "there is nothing to fret about. We will face inconvenience while you reside here in comfort. And it is only one night alone for you. Daddy is due back tomorrow. Now, Francine, listen carefully. When Maxcy arrives you must tell him that I have departed with the Winders for Daddy's Little Farm. Mister Winder is leaving a horse and buggy in his stable for him to join us there tomorrow night. Do you understand, Francine?"

My lips quivered. I was set to burst into tears.

"Now, Francine, you stop that! I cannot tend to Helen's wailing and yours, too. It's too much. Do you hear? This is a good plan. It is a very difficult day and this is the best I can manage. We shall all be fine. But you must let Master Pegram know we are evacuating to Daddy's Little Farm. Do you understand?"

"But the Yankees . . ." I objected.

"Francine," she said, locking her teeth together, "listen to me, child—Daddy Pegram needs to know where I have gone and by what means. Without mail delivery, we will have no means of correspondence and I need your help with this, honey."

The only other times Missus Pegram ever called me "honey" was during evenings when Master Pegram was away and she taught me to read while I brushed out her hair, practicing my letters over her shoulder.

"Besides," she went on, "the Yankees will make no objection to you. They will even take kindly to you, most likely, even though you don't fully understand that."

"Yes'm," I said, this time mumbling the words with a grudge, knowing that if I told her otherwise it would risk a wallop.

She finished her toilet, hoisted her unders, let fall her hems, replaced the chamber pot lid, then toed the jar back into position under the bed. She gestured for me to rise and sat at the vanity to apply fresh powder and fragrance.

"Just stay inside, Francine. Mind me, child, and you shall be fine. Do not answer the door for anyone. The Yankees shan't bother you a'tall."

I had another "yes'm" set upon my lips but did not speak it. It just stayed inside my throat, refusing to come out. She did not notice that I failed to respond with obedience. She seemed to forget my presence altogether. With her jaw set tight, she studied her image in the mirror and pulled a long breath from her chest. It reminded me of the way a man takes a full glass of bourbon all in one gulp. She hastily finished her vanity work, tucked additional handkerchiefs, all of them dirty, into her reticule, and rushed from the room in full distraction. I followed behind, descending one step at a time, the woolen satchel hoisted to my chest with both arms.

Mistress Bartow was not on the Queen Anne where we left her. During our absence she had lugged her satchel from the hallway to the front pathway, where she stood waiting for the Winders' wagon.

"Francine, carry my grip to the front and join Helen. I'm going to write a note for Daddy. I'll be out directly."

"Yes'm," I said.

Outside, I plunked Missus Pegram's satchel in the yard next to Mistress Bartow's larger tote just as the Winders' four-seater arrived, led by an unusually vigorous team of handsome muddy-whites. They were driven by a thick-set, broad-shouldered slave man with a serious-looking face and square jaw. Everything about Compson Winder appeared clean and perfectly crisp, an oddity after four years of war—an oddity even for the footman of a rich factory owner. He wore polished black high-top riding boots, clean gray jodhpurs, a clean white shirt with a collar covered by a fancy red vest, and a fine black top hat, all without a spot of mud. Even the wagon appeared new, with smooth black leather seats. It made me remember the olden days when Missus Pegram's crinolines were perfectly crisp and all the horses were well fed, stout, and fresh.

Missus arrived at the street as Compson hoisted both satchels with ease to one side of the carriage floor, then helped Missus Pegram and Mistress Bartow to their seats. Mistress Bartow's weight gave the carriage a bouncing heave when she plunked down, and I knew that Compson had deliberately seated her opposite the satchels for balance. The two of them sat opposite Mister and Mistress Winder, who had exchanged their Sunday clothes for more proper riding attire.

"Francine, you be sure to give Daddy the note I left in the parlor," Mistress Pegram called out. "And finish the rest of that Johnnycake." She followed up with a clinched smile and a gesture with her eyes indicating I should not loiter at the street but quickly return to the house. She knew, of course, there was no Johnnycake to be had. I conjured she pretended otherwise to make matters appear better to the Winders.

I turned and obediently trotted up the short walkway, climbed the stoop, crossed the porch, entered the house, closed the door behind me, and went to the parlor window to watch their departure. Mistresses Winder and Bartow had their handkerchiefs at the ready to block dust from their nostrils. Missus Pegram dug one of hers from her reticule. The only one who noticed me observing from the window was Compson, who made no clear expression but in whose eyes I thought I saw a great worry—though I could not conjure if they reflected thoughts of me, himself, his passengers, or of the journey to come.

Compson gee'd and lashed the reins once. The muddy-whites lurched with obedience into a quick trot and the wagon moved south toward Canal Street, Byrd Street, the James River, and the smaller city of Manchester beyond.

CHAPTER FOURTEEN:
MISS FRANCINE PEGRAM

It wasn't until they all departed—and I stood before the parlor window watching the late morning skies filter closer into afternoon—that I understood the full meaning of it.

I was alone.

Nothing like it had ever happened.

Richmond was becoming something other than Richmond and I had been left perfectly alone to watch it all take place from a two-story clapboard house at number 212 Ninth Street that was filled with fancy things, doodads, books and furniture from France—and me: a girl, pickaninny, slave, negress, pantry rat, nigger-girl.

The sun was just commencing to cast shorter shadows, marking the approach of midday. Everything was the same, but different: the rosy-cheeked China-head doll with her blanched skin more delicate than a baby's, perched happily upon the fancy red settee, her wide blue eyes sparkling at me with happy sentiment; the Thomas clock on the mantel tocked out its familiar message of passing time; and the green Queen Anne chair with curved legs sat opposite, flanked by twin side tables. Everything was normal, yet nothing was.

'Twas then I noticed the folded writing paper on one of the fancy side tables. I opened it and read:

Daddy,
That damnable Jeff Davis has finally done us in. I have evacu-

ated to the farm with Helen and the Winders. With my leader-
ship and their able horseman Compson, I anticipate arrival
shortly after nightfall. A horse and buggy await you in the
Winders' stable on Main St.
Make immediate effort to join us at the farm upon your safe
return to Richmond where Francine awaits.

— Ruth

I refolded the paper and replaced it on the side table.

I was scared, just as when the day began with WHOOMPING-booms and the dog dream—events that now seemed far in the past. I did not know what I should do first, but I knew I was starving—and before I could do anything about that, I must first overcome my fears.

There was no food in the kitchen and I knew it, yet that is where my feet took me. In the pantry I decided against donning my brokens or changing into my other gingham. That could wait for the return of Master Pegram and our own reconnoiter to Daddy's Little Farm at Roanoke Rapids.

I performed my usual morning duties, never before delayed so late in the day. I cleaned up a small pile of yellow straw-tack fallen to the floor under my bucky-board, the issue of a rent in the seam of my blanket. The woolen wrapper was once the "extra throw" for the Pegrams on the coldest nights, which I had folded into threes, stuffed with straw and stitched up to make it serve as both mattress and blanket.

The tack was dry and easy to clean up. I fingered it back into the seam rent, stored the blanket on a pantry shelf, hoisted the bucky-board from atop the two empty apple barrels, and put it behind the pantry door.

Afterward, I conjured it to be an unnecessary task as the missus wouldn't be about for the rest of the day or the next day, either. If Master Pegram returned, he would certainly have no need to enter the pantry as there was no food on the shelves.

There hadn't been any stores of pantry-kept foods for many months.

I wondered when the days might return when the barrels were filled with apples or pecans and the various bins, baskets, and shelves were laden with coffee, onions, greens, and piles of turnip and tuber. In those earlier days, I fancied the pantry the best room in the house for sleeping, especially on baking day. On baking day, I slept inside a great aromatic cloud of fresh bread.

I pulled the main drapes over the Ninth Street window and stepped to one side to peek out in secret. People were going and coming in both directions, and I could not figure if there was any way to understand a purpose for those who moved up Ninth Street to the north, as opposed to those who moved down it to the south.

The sky grew more clear as the three days of rain receded further into memory. It was growing warmer, and perhaps it was even the warmest day of the year thus far, which bore hint of an early spring. The wagon ruts of Ninth Street were slowly drying the mud, turning it back into dirt.

Some people out front were so distracted in their minds they spoke aloud to themselves. One man in a churchgoing suit paused in front of the house and did little more than look straight up, directly into the sunlight. He reminded me of the way a lizard suns himself on a fence post. At first I thought he was praying but he did not remove his hat.

A mistress in full petticoats crossed back and forth across the loblolly muck of Ninth Street several times, unable to make up her mind which side to be on. When she passed close by the window I could see in her face that she was not of a mind to arrive anywhere at all, but was only deep in worry and shock. Others appeared the same, their faces turned inward to thoughts haunted with great burden.

I was set to feel sorry for myself but did not have long to kindle my sympathies. A noise commenced, like a slow thunder in the distance—a kind of distant drumbeat: brum-brum-brum-brum. I was afraid it might be the war about to set up business right in front of the house. It also grabbed attentions of the odd ones on the street, pulling them from their inner toils and making them all turn north and stare. They did not run. They just stood dumb, looking at the source of the rising noise. That eased me a bit. I figured it must not be the arrival of Yankee fighting with Butternut, at least not yet. Anyway, there were no sounds of musket shots or WHOOMPING-booms either.

The thunder grew louder: *brum-brum-brum.* Gradually the dumb ones in the street moved aside and took to the narrow footpaths, ignoring what muck puddles remained to soil their foot leather. All heads craned like birds in a tree watching out at some peculiar assembly.

Brum-brum-brum.

A rattling noise behind me in the parlor made me turn around. The four pictures of Paris, France, were snapping and bouncing against the wall with each noise. The upper right picture, the one of the big fancy church, turned slightly crooked.

Then came the main window itself. The glass shook in the frame, vibrating like a pot at boil.

Brum-brum-brum.

The Thomas clock too felt it and responded with very slight but regular chimes.

Brum-brum-brum.

Finally, the cause of the noise passed the house. It was Butternut. The Johnnies. Hundreds and hundreds of them. They were lined up in rows as they marched south down Ninth Street.

The parade included wagons of every shape, horses, mules, and mongrel dogs. There was even a pair of sad old milk cows struggling to keep up, clopping along with drooping heads, their skin sagging so low it almost scraped the wagon ruts, demonstrating just how plump they had once been.

The men and boys were mixed in appearance. Some were worn and ragged with uniforms appearing more like reworked burlap sacks than real trousers, and most were a collection of bones inside those sacks. The ones with weapons shouldered them proper; those without muskets let their arms swing free. The oldest were old men. The youngest were just boys: some looked even younger than me, and one of them had a drum that he played, but I could barely hear the sound of his "rat-a-tat-tat, rat-a-tat-tat" as it was mostly drowned out by the *brum-brumming* of the marchers' feet.

When the full migration was present in front of the house, it took to shaking so it made me wonder if the boards would hold together. The *brum*-chant sent clouds of dust rising and twirling all around the men and around everything else too as they marched south toward the bridge that would take them across the river and to Manchester beyond.

The very last creature in the parade was an old mongrel dog who didn't really follow straight on, but somehow seemed to walk sideways, like maybe he didn't want to go with the others and was looking for someone at the curb to call out to him so he could remain behind. But no one summoned him, so he just waddled on sideways with his long tongue hanging limp.

The house rattles hushed after the Butternut passed and the spectators edged onto the street again. They snapped from their inner worries and commenced talking loudly about what it all meant. From the parlor I could hear them giving voice to their gooseflesh.

"They're from the northern defense."

"What? The outer defense?"

"Yes, ma'am. They're retreating through the city! That's the last of 'em."

"The northern defenses, too? The ramparts?"

"Yes, ma'am, even the ramparts. It's total evacuation! First the city troops, now the outer lines are passing through."

"Richmond is defenseless?"

"Yes, ma'am. That's the last of 'em. We are defenseless."

"What are we to do? Why, Lord-a-mighty, the Yankees will just walk easy-as-you-please, right into the city!"

Women cried as the men said it. Some hid their faces in handkerchiefs. One mistress waved her arms, wailing and boo-hooing, carrying on as though attending a funeral. Some men followed with displays of coarse incivility. They cussed even more than I heard earlier on the St. Paul steps:

"That coward Davis deserves to hang."

"I'd like to relieve him of his privates and drag him down Main Street."

"Where's Judah Benjamin, that no-good Jew?"

"He done run off, too."

"This is his doing."

"Goddam," came the response.

"Goddam 'em all," came another.

No woman present raised a voice of objection, which I took as a sign that things were very much changed. When men shout curses in public and mistresses fail to show disapproval—it is clear that something peculiar has occurred.

After a while, both the cussing and wailing slowed and they all looked about, dumb with worry and fear. That's when the leave-taking commenced. It was as though a horn sounded and everyone knew what to do. Within seconds the street was clear for the first time since morning.

The last cuss word was barked by a white-faced fat man who, having uttered his final opinion upon the state of the world, turned and hastened south with a wobble so brisk it would have been a full-out gallop had he been a man of lesser poundage.

Chapter Fifteen:
Miss Francine Pegram

I took the sudden departure of all street spectators to be a sign that I, too, should take care of some necessaries. I turned my back to the window. The four pictures of Paris, France, hung cockeyed, jarred by the *brum-brum* rattle of the Butternut march. There was a small crack in the wall above the fancy red settee that caused a dusting of brittles to fall across one of its arms. The China-head doll remained perched at the opposite arm, untouched by the wall dust and unmoved by the clatter. Everything else seemed proper. The Thomas clock labored on like nothing had happened. Then, as if responding to my study of it, the internal workings whirred, making ready to announce the time. It rang out twelve times. By the conclusion of the twelfth chime, I had made my plan and commenced performing it.

I knew the cellar contained nothing to eat, as I knew the kitchen did not. Just the same, my hunger led me to the rough hickory door under the stairway.

Making certain Ole Mister Rat heard me coming, I decided to shout or sing some words from gospel or hymnal that I had committed to memory. But the only words I could conjure at the moment were Missus Pegram's singsong about me. So it was that which I delivered to the cellar, with each step spoken in time with the words so I could recite the full verse two complete times before landing upon step number twelve and the cool dirt floor of the cellar:

Oh, my little pantry rat,

Black as an Egyptian cat.

Nappy, no-account housemaid,

So I think I'll make a trade.

That's my little pantry rat.

Missus used the song for her social circle whenever hints were made that I was more to the household than servant. It was Mistress Garland who nailed the sore spot the hardest during tea one Sunday:

"I declare, Ruth," she said with a mean chuckle, "that little Ethiopian domestic is attached to your skirts like you're her momma." Missus dismissed the remark by reciting the pantry-rat song but I knew she did not care for the reference. And I was not surprised when Mistress Garland was not invited to tea again.

The song worked. When my toes plopped onto the dirt floor there were no sounds of scrape or scurry in the distance, which eased my worries of facing an unhappy encounter.

I quickly set about prying barrel lids and peeking through cracks in bins. It did not take long to settle the matter. There was not a single crumb left to eat in the cellar. Mindful that I should not challenge my luck with Ole Mister Rat by overextending my visit, I bounded a hasty return to the main corridor, three steps at a time.

I rechecked all the various bins and baskets in the kitchen and pantry with a peek or a shake to settle all doubts that nothing edible had been overlooked. I secured the locks on both the front and back doors. I raced upstairs three steps at a time to retrieve the one box I had never opened, though I could not conjure it could hold anything to eat. First, I pulled every curtain closed, taking care to lap one drapery edge over the other so no movement could be observed. The upstairs hallway window had see-through cotton curtains so I let that go as it was.

In the main bedroom, a gossamer of body talc lay sprinkled across Missus Pegram's vanity, the result of her final and hasty primping of her face before departure. The fine odor of powder mixed with the smell of the unemptied chamber pot under the bed. The edges of the pot glistened with wet from the last usage and a puddle remained to one side on the floorboards. When Mistress Pegram was in full petticoats she always left a puddle. I contemplated leaving it, but couldn't. With a hand rag that hung beside the vanity basin I mopped the puddle and cleaned the edges of the pot.

For a moment I stood at her bedside pondering the room. It had an odd sense of change. Everything in it was the same, yet different. Beside the vanity table there was Missus Pegram's cozy chair, used for dressing and where she sat in the evenings working me on my reading while I combed her hair. Two pictures hung on the side wall that I never understood. Both portrayed a flock of naked babies romping among the clouds with cheerful spirit. They had pink, round faces, plump bottoms, and floated like humming birds with feathery white wings. I figured them to be in heaven, which always puzzled me because it meant they had died while still babies and I could not conjure why Missus Pegram would display pictures of such sadness in her private bedroom. Once, while at cleaning labors with my dust rag, Missus Pegram advised me to take care with the pictures—calling them "cherubs." That only confused me further so I decided those pictures, too, must be from France.

Her bedding was framed by a grand piece of fine maple wood with four towers rising from each corner, all of it carved over with fancy images of ivy leaves and rice. Those carvings were always difficult to clean and required extra care with my rag. The bedding needed cleaning, but was still soft with feather pillows, cotton sheets, warm woolen blankets, and a delicately knitted top-spread of bleached-white cotton with fancy embroidered edging that required extra wash-care.

"Always take good care with that bedding, Miss Francine—it's Georgia cotton stitched in Charleston," she would say in her singsong manner when it came time to put the washtubs at boil.

A dark woolen blanket, folded three times, always lay across the foot of Missus Pegram's bed. On the colder nights, she and Master Pegram could reach down and pull it atop themselves for extra warmth to get through the colder hours without struggle against the chill.

On each side of the bed was a table, each with a single drawer and a cabinet beneath. I never bothered with Master Pegram's side of the bed. But I knew about Missus Pegram's side. In her drawer was an extra brush, a Bible, and a handkerchief. I imagined them to be things a lady requires while in bed. If she awakened during the night she could light a candle, brush her hair, blow her nose, and commence studying Jesus, though I never actually saw her doing any of that while in bed.

It was the cabinet below the drawer that beckoned at me. I knew it to house a wooden box, a mysterious coffer that gripped me with curiosity. Circumstances being what they were, my curiosity won me over. I opened the cabinet door in Missus Pegram's table and removed the box. I took the last candle of the house from her marble vanity basin, which required a firm tug because it was half consumed and the wax had spilled past the brass holder, sticking to the surface. I placed the box and candle atop the woolen blanket then toted the whole collection downstairs to the kitchen table.

Out back, I ventured one last sojourn to the privy. Afterward, standing at the fence, I gave a long crane of my neck at the Spotswood outbuildings. Everything there looked just as abandoned as the inside of the Pegram house. It was normal, yet not normal—like the unsettled quiet before a hard storm. The out-yard and hotel, too, looked like a bell had sounded and everybody just ran off—slaves, Irish girls, and all guests—leaving their business where it lay. From the ground floor to floor number five, there was no movement at any window. In the yard, wash tubs weren't even stacked up, but sat unsteady over the fire rocks where they were last used, some still filled with dirty wash water; cotton linens put on the line that morning were left to droop at their corners into muddy loblollies; the black pot that made stew three times a week lay knocked over at the fire pit; the cellar doors were closed but unlatched; and against the back wall, where in the early years there ran several stacked cords of chopped wood, there was now nothing but scattered bark and a few limbs of cedar kindling. If Extra's Master Pettigrew saw any of it there would be trouble. But then, trouble would be normal and this day was anything but normal. So I didn't know what to make of it.

I jumped the fence at the corner post and went to the out-quarters window to peek into the place where I was born and spent my first year of life. There was no one. The blankets lay scattered but there was no man, woman, or child to be seen in hiding. Where are they all, I wondered? Where was ole Miss Edna, Cussin' Sally-Martha, Polly Ramseur, Old Caesar, and Jules the mute runner-boy?

I conjured going farther. I thought of going to the hotel through the kitchen door, where I might be able to beg a piece of bread. The servants were most likely in the hotel cellar, where the doors are closed but unlatched. But in the end I decided against it. Such a request for bread might not go well with their idea of what is a favor and what is not a favor. Except for Extra and ole Miss Edna, they mostly haven't had much kindness for me since I got handed over "for cause."

Back inside the Pegrams' two-story clapboard house, I took a small piece of writing paper from a table drawer in the parlor, folded it into a small wedge, and gently inserted it under the rear of the Thomas clock to make it lopsided. The swinging pendulum slowed to a stop; the tocking fell silent. The hands read twenty past the twelve o'clock. I conjured that would make the house look abandoned along with the rest of Richmond should anyone, Yankees or otherwise, come poking around, peeking through windows, or worse.

I set up camp at the kitchen table. If needed for the night, there was half a candle and six matches in the tinderbox, which I set aside where they could not get wet or broken.

My stomach growled. I ignored it. The longer it took Master Pegram to return, the greater the need for food would become, but I had no solution. I was grateful that my curiosity about Missus Pegram's private coffer gave me some distraction from my hunger. It was about the length of one of Master Pettigrew's cigar boxes and twice as tall. I placed it center table and looked at its finely hewn wood, which smelled rich, like none I could identify. It was neither hickory nor pine, and of all the varieties of oak I knew, not one held such sweet aroma. It smelled of wet cinnamon and lamp oil. I wondered if France had special trees whose wood was much coveted for the making of bedside treasure chests. It had a small latch of tarnished silver on the front and two equally darkened hinges to the rear.

My stomach growled again, sending a hard pinch at me. I made my decision and fixed it in my mind to go ahead and commit the trick, since it was the only bin, box, or barrel in the entire house I had not peeped into in the past half hour. I pulled it close, pried up the latch, and opened the lid.

Inside was an assortment of items:

Two keys. Tied by a string. I had never seen them before and knew from appearance they would fit neither the front nor back door latches.

Game cards. The stack held together with a ribbon. Each bore the image of a city that I felt certain was Paris, France—the resemblance to the parlor pictures being strong.

Money. One Confederate bill worth fifty cents, which bore the image of the man I knew to be Mister President Davis, although it was not a very good likeness. In large writing across the image was the signature of the man in ink, the likely reason Missus kept this particular bill.

One even smaller box. Made of tin, labeled with brightly painted words: "Dr. Power's French Prevention." Inside were several little dark sacks that could stretch out in a way that gave me some amusement when they snapped back into place, stinging my fingers.

I conjured a notion of what personal use they must have. Once, when Mistress Bartow had more than her usual dose from the port bottle she commenced a woeful tongue-lashing at all slaves, calling them a variety of mean names because they made so many babies so early in life. Using a jumble of ugly language, she called for handing out "French gloves" to all servants.

"Lord-a-mighty," she wailed, "let's just hand out French gloves to all of 'em before there's so many they just take over the whole world!"

"Oh, Helen, hush up," Missus Pegram said.

"Why, Ruth, it's the truth. They're like dogs in the street. It's all they want to do. I declare, sometimes I think that's all they know how to do!" Her speech was met with shy amusement by the other mistresses who nodded approval and disapproval at the same time. I tucked the stretchy socks back inside the tin, which closed with a clever "snap."

Hand fan. Attached to a flat stick. It was made of paperboard and embossed with the words I recognized from my Bible lessons as David's Song, number twenty-three:

> The Lord is my shepherd, I shall not want;
>> he makes me lie down in green pastures.
> He leads me beside the still waters; he restores
>> my soul.
> He leads me in paths of righteousness for his
>> name's sake.
>
> Even though I walk through the valley of the
>> shadow of death,
>> I fear no evil; for thou art with me; thy rod
>> and thy staff, they comfort me.
>
> Thou preparest a table before me in the presence
>> of my enemies;
>> thou annointest my head with oil, my cup
>> overflows,
> Surely goodness and mercy shall follow me all
>> the days of my life;
>> and I shall dwell in the house of the Lord
>> forever.

The words appeared atop an image of an old man in a white robe, angry, with burning blue eyes and flowing white beard. He appeared ready to bust with bitter fury, cocking one arm over his head; with the other, he pointed one long, bony finger to the side at some unhappy place not pictured. He looked to me like Mister President Davis, maybe a hundred years on. I compared the paperboard image to the one on the Confederate bill and found the likeness to be valid. I fanned myself too while doing so, though it was not of much use for that purpose.

Official papers. Several had names of banks with rows of numbers. Some had little pictures at the top of the pages that I recognized. There was the Great House of Government, and a few blocks north, Byrd and Shockoe Tobacco Warehouses. Several of the papers had the Butternut crisscross flag. One had a shady green apple tree.

I recognized my name on one of the pages. "Francine Pegram" had been scribbled onto a line that began with something about what "all men know." It was dated 1853 and I took it to be a paper pertaining to my "for cause" delivery over the back fence as a baby.

I knew it to be a violation, but I took the paper with my name scribbled upon it, creased it to fold several times, then tucked it away to join my pocket knife and street pass.

Picture plate. It was one of the old tin-types, small and faded in shades of brown, picturing a baby, only a few weeks old, perched on the fancy red settee in the exact position where I have always known the China-head doll to rest.

The baby wore a great ruffled collar that curled about his neck, looking very uncomfortable. I do not know how to explain my knowledge of this—but I do know it with surety. The baby in the picture is dead. Its eyelids were partially closed and what portion of its eyes were visible glared with the dumb gaze of blank death. The writing on the back was in the hand of my missus:

Jasper Garner Pegram
June, 1848

So Missus had a baby after all!

The little boy looked frail with smallness. I knew the baby had died in the house because the picture-taking business had been brought into parlor from one of the shops on Main Street. I wondered where it was buried and why no mention had ever been made.

The box held one final item:

> Muslin wrapping. Bleached with oily stains, the muslin concealed an item of some heaviness. I held it aloft, then tugged at a corner of the cloth making it unfurl like a spool of thread until the cloth fell away, delivering its contents with a plop onto the table.

At first I was uncertain about the dried, shadowy object that tumbled out. It was a hardened, fleshy mass. It looked like an overly large shank of pork, improperly cooked, poorly smoked, and half devoured. It had been thoroughly gnawed on one side. An angled tooth print was deeply engraved at the top, disclosing the presence of Missus Pegram's jaw upon the thing. The size and weight of it required both hands to turn it over for closer study.

I understood immediately why me and Missus were allowed to spend the previous night in the cellar without objection. It was Ole Mister Rat. His shrunken face stared up at me in sad disapproval. I felt badly for him. His dangerous quickness and squealing voice would no longer rule over the tunnels burrowed amid Almond Eyes' various horse leathers in the memorial to antiquity.

When did Missus Pegram capture him? Maybe while I pumped and toted water. Perhaps she clobbered him with the shovel during the winter when he charged at full-screech in protest of her passing presence. She was less worried about him than I. And however she managed the task, I knew she did it with little fear. As for cooking, she likely boiled him after gutting the innards.

On the tabletop, within the muslin wrapping, lay a small batch of fly eggs—wiggling with objection at my disturbance of the meat wrapping. I looked for evidence of vermin on the meat, but saw none. Even so, the smell of Ole Mister Rat held a foulness that my nostrils harshly rejected, sending a strong message to my stomach. There was also an odor of leather and oil that combined with the nastiness.

That concluded my study of contents held by Missus Pegram's private coffer.

With the exception of the one document—and Ole Mister Rat, whose body I tossed to the floor along with his fly-egg-laced wrapping—I returned everything, closed the lid, and slid the latch neatly back into place. I dwelled upon the image of Missus Pegram at her bedside with the box, consumed with nervous secrecy, worried I might observe her examining the contents. It was that nervousness that had filled me with curious meddle. Now my curiosity was satisfied—a baby! Dead within weeks of birth!

There were new sounds outside that I did not recognize. I listened to them with wariness as I gulped a ladle of water. The cool liquid felt good going down inside my body—until it got to my empty stomach, where it sloshed with a gurgle noise.

A slanting line of warm sunlight peeped halfway up the kitchen wall, a line that I knew would slowly climb to the ceiling, then disappear with the arriving dark. The lazy part of the day would soon approach, the part when Missus Pegram would sit on one of the fancy parlor chairs reading her Bible to me until she drifted into sleep. She could sit upright, close her eyes, and just go right into a heavy nap. In that position, her lips always puffed out a little with each slumbering exhale. Sometimes I would do the same, following her into a quiet afternoon slumber, especially during the reading of chapters where I could not fathom a word of meaning—the Samuels, the Kings, the Chronicles, and so on. I could never reap any profit from the words sewn into those portions of the Good Book.

The distant street noises remained a distraction, making me uneasy. I needed to figure on some action in the event Master Pegram did not return soon. A long delay would mean starvation. I studied the possibilities.

Taking to the streets bore risk, which I could not measure. Mister Bee at the Grace Street Dry Goods & Grocer never spoke unkindly to me. Once he even awarded me a sucking candy while performing my errands. It had a sweet lemon taste that I let slowly melt on my tongue during the walk home behind Missus. If he were still open for business—he would be the only one to allow me to make trade arrangements. If I could get them, I could make a pound of dried beans go a long way.

I leaned over my perch to study the boiled body of Ole Mister Rat on the floor. From my chair I could see the mark of Missus Pegram's protruding side tooth upon his flank. That puzzled me. How often did she unroll her secret treasure for a bite? Once each night? Each morning? When she unfurled it, did she take one bite only? I had no answers. I could not picture her doing such a thing at all. War or no war, concealing cooked rat in a bedside box was not a behavior of any Richmond mistress I could conjure.

I took another ladle of water. Again it sloshed in my stomach with the sound of a rolling wave on the river as it bumps against the wharf stones.

Rat was on the menu more than once for the Spotswood servants. I once heard ole Edna boast about liking it, even naming it as good as squirrel meat. I doubted she would feel that way about fouled rat meat wrapped in nasty fly eggs.

I leaned over again to look at him. He did appear somewhat

like boiled squirrel.

Getting through another day and night without something to eat was an unkind challenge. I knew what I had to do. I held by breath. I grit my teeth. I held my breath again. Finally, I reached down and picked up the dried body of Ole Mister Rat. Without dwelling upon it, I pinched my nostrils with one hand and raised his flank to my mouth with the other. I ripped loose a small bite of hard, sour meat, which I chewed fast and swallowed. Then I spun it around and did the same thing on the other side. Then I did it again, and again, and again.

The taste fouled my throat even before I removed my clinched fingers from my nose. My stomach no longer sloshed like a river wave. Instead, it flooded with sourness. I opened my mouth wide and breathed deep and hard, sending air down my throat, hoping to stop the rising tide of sickness and send the rotten taste away at the same time. I knew I needed to keep the meat down, needed to let my body take from it what nourishment could be taken.

I drank another ladle of water, a small one, letting it slowly glide down my throat in a thin streamlet. I inhaled deeply again, trying to prevent my stomach from rejecting the meat. My belly rose out, looking plump as it received the tonic of water and air. That's the belly of a mother-to-be I thought, letting it ease back into position with an exhaling pucker, making me skinny again. In that way, alternating water with air, the tide of sickness gradually subsided.

I changed rooms. The parlor was a place I was not allowed to occupy without the company of Missus Pegram, except when I was working at the cleaning labors. Even then, she held a close loiter upon me. Now, with the curtains pulled shut, it was nearly dark in the best room of the house save a sharp light that peeped stubbornly from the drape edges. It was oddly silent without the rhythmic tock of the Thomas clock.

I settled upon the fancy red settee next to the China-head doll and imitated the hands-in-the-lap manner of that shiny-faced little mistress. I straightened the hem of my gingham to match the lace trim of her creamy, full-length dress. Instead of bloomers and polite, shiny black parlor shoes protruding from my hemline, I had only my bony ankles poking out and my naked feet still showing dirty evidence of morning travels to the pump, privy, and twice to St. Paul's.

We sat like partners watching a show. I stole a sidelong glance at her tiny lips and puffy cheeks, rosy with swollen goodness, her hair the color of sunshine tucked neatly behind her ears, and her blue sparkling eyes. Her eyes remained fixed, staring straight ahead to the pulled curtains with an eternal confidence that nothing would ever change and that nothing mattered except her own honorable perch upon the fancy red settee.

I felt my own hair, which hung loosely in strands at the back. My cheeks were neither puffy nor rosy and I suspected my brown eyes, no matter how light in color, never sparkled.

The longer I sat there, the more I noticed the afternoon shadows commencing their slow crawl across the furniture, falling to the floor corners, then steadily making gains, climbing the wall before disappearing.

Just stay inside, Francine. The Yankees shan't bother you a'tall.

That had been Missus Pegram's instruction. I couldn't imagine them not bothering me. They were the principal subject of dread during all socials. Plump Mistress Bartow could be relied upon to rail against them the most and the loudest, especially when the port bottle was upon the table. She was never at a loss with her tongue.

"Milk-livered," she called them. That would change over to "sorebacks," and then—after a glass of port—"damned blue-belly dogs." The drunker she got, the louder she became. "What do they know of our ways?" she barked. "Our business is none of theirs! Our ways are our ways!"

Once she got going, it was hard for her to stop. After several glasses of port she swore even more loudly. "Yankees are all mongrels anyway. From the vulgar classes up north! No purity a'tall. Bred from Europe's trash. Just a bunch of damned inbred mongrels."

General Grant was the worst Yankee of them all. When they got hold of him they near-about never let go. They cursed him as "that drunkard," "that damned butcher," "vulgar," "sloppy" and on and on they went about whiskey and cruelty, frequently naming him as "useless." And before they finished with him they typically had a round of ugly words for his home state of Ohio, too.

Mistress Bartow's Yankee speeches were usually greeted with an approving round of closed-mouth "hmm-hmms" and "uh-huhs" from the other mistresses as they contemplated what card to play or chewed upon a molasses candy. Only when she turned to the mechanics of the breeding process did they commence bashful giggles and a rotation of "Oh, Helen," "Hush up, Helen," and "I declare, Helen."

CHAPTER SIXTEEN:
MISS FRANCINE PEGRAM

I am sick.

The meat of Ole Mister Rat has made me ill. Sitting next to the China-head doll politely propped up beside me on the fancy red settee, I drifted into a fitful sleep. I dreamed of the great black dog, of my mother, and of Compson looking at me before he gee'd the horse team toward Roanoke Rapids. I awoke with each dream, sweating with illness.

I passed the remainder of the day's fading light in this stiff, proper position, feeling ill and slumbering on and off and on again. Whenever I fancied an odd noise, or whenever a cry of alarm from the street rose to a pitch that pulled me from my rest, I would look around with caution. Each time the China-head doll was unfazed. With each sidelong glance I delivered to her, the light on her face grew dimmer and more ghostly right along with the passing of the day.

In that way, day changed to night and more feverish visions invaded my sleep. I dreamed of witnessing a light show made from glowing rays of sunlight. Great flares of illumination cast upon the wall as though between rapidly moving clouds, turning the newly arrived night back into day for brief moments.

One flash spilled from the edges of the closed drapes, crept over the floor, clamored up the wall and onto the ceiling, where it fluttered about in shades of copper and brass, looking like a preening bird shaking its feathers. Then it was gone. It shut down like a door slammed, cutting it off, making the parlor dark again.

Another flash peeped under the edge of the drape and slowly crawled across the floor, right up to the edge of my feet dangling over the settee. It fluttered a moment, then shut down just as fast as the previous light did.

I dreamed the China-head doll could move her head and speak. She smiled politely.

"Jesus loves you, Miss Francine," she said, sitting next to me, her blush white cheeks glowing with goodness.

"Thank you, ma'am."

"Oh, you needn't call me 'ma'am.' "

"But you are white."

"Oh no, not really."

"What are you then?"

"You know, silly."

"I do?"

"Certainly."

"Won't you tell me?"

"Oh, Miss Francine. You already know—I am a doll-baby."

She cocked her head and smiled even wider. This dream also frightened and awakened me. Was I having a spell? Would I too see evil smiles that float? Then, after returning to my fitful slumbers, I dreamed of her again. I saw her rise from the fancy red settee and walk to the drape, where she peeped out at the world. From there she turned and spoke again.

"Come and see, Miss Francine."

"I'm afraid," I said.

"Do not be afraid—for your father loves you."

"My father is dead. Grandfather, too."

"No, silly, I am speaking of God. It is the Lord, our father in heaven that I speak of. It is He who loves you." The China-face doll put both hands on her hips. "Besides, Miss Francine, your daddy is not dead. Did he not give you his own father's pocket knife?"

"I . . . I . . . I do have a fine pocket knife." It was all I could manage in response.

"Very well, then," she said. "Oh, Miss Francine, do come to the window and see."

"See what? What is there?"

"You already know."

"No, I don't."

"Yes, you do, silly."

"Well, what is it?"

"Why, it is fire," the doll-baby said in a plain manner.

I bolted awake, my gingham sodden with the sweat of fever. The China-head doll sat next to me, her sparkling blue eyes wide open even as she lay flopped over on the armrest, where I must have knocked her with my elbow. I sat her upright and straightened the lace hem of her dress to make it proper again.

Fire!

The word awakened me into full caution. I slid to the edge of the fancy red settee and studied the parlor. It was peaceful. The walls were wrapped in layers of light-gray shadows; the floors were the colors of night. Various rumblings continued outside, but the inside remained silent and dark. I had no way to determine the time. The Thomas clock held at twenty past the twelve o'clock, the minute I stopped its tocking earlier in the day.

A light flashed from drape's edge just as it did in my dreams. I eased off the settee and walked carefully to peek from the window.

At first it was unclear what I was seeing. It was dark and bright at the same time. And it moved! Just a few blocks to the east I could see smoke arching to the sky. Under the smoke, glowing flames moved every which way, including, it seemed—

towards me!

Without thinking of consequence, I stepped forward and yanked wide the drapes.

Fire! Fire everywhere!

Fire was burning down whole blocks to the east, where I knew the tobacco warehouses stood. Fire was blazing forth from the windows of tall buildings of government, where important men in fancy suits did their banking, their trade work, and made plans for the business of war. Fire was gnawing at the street level, too. It was easy to see that Shockoe warehouse, Seabrooks warehouse and the Gallego flour mill were aflame. I knew at a glance that Mister Little's House for Single Men on Twelfth Street and the Feed & Seed Store on Eleventh were already gone.

The next sight put to mind of one of my stories from Grimms'. A dozen dogs fled the fiery streets. With tongues flapping, necks straining against necks, flanks bumping flanks, they ran west, racing from a fiery death. The last among them was a furry creature whose rump was aglow, a billowing orange torch sending smoky spires trailing behind. The poor beast stopped twice to lick and nose at the singeing flames, only to quickly give up the effort and resume racing off each time; his rear legs looked as though they were trying to overtake his front legs.

With the drapery pulled wide, the parlor seemed nearly as bright as daytime and coated over with a devilish glow. To the northeast, a tall building on Main Street collapsed upon itself, creating a feeble rumble that seemed not to match the event. Should not the fall of a great building make a great noise? It was followed by a slow-moving quiver that made all the windows rattle, passing through the house as a morning shiver passes through the body.

Shortly after, a new oddity ambled into sight. It was a lanky man fleeing south directly in front of the house while burdened about the arms with a multitude of sacks. With every third step he poked his worried face from behind the sacks to cast a wary glance backward, making him quicken his already jerky stride, though no one pursued him.

I watched like a cat in the window. His actions appeared thoroughly unconnected to the fires. During one backward glance, he stumped his toe on a stone and dropped a sack, which landed with a solid plop, sending up a puffy cloud of Ninth Street gossamer. Unconcerned, he adjusted his burden with a hoist and continued his nervous retreat south, disappearing from view as he put distance between himself and the cause of his worry that lay somewhere behind him.

Another man followed, entering from the east on Main Street directly from the blazes. He too was burdened with a heavy load—a barrel, which he bore upon his back, making him walk stooped over like a cripple-back man. He limped steadily across Ninth Street to the west, until he too departed my range, leaving the street empty again.

I could smell the fires as they churned in the distance, eating at downtown Richmond. The smoke heaved in swirls, a clear token for miles that great harm was being done. I wondered if the evacuated Butternut could see it, and if that would bring them racing back to save the city.

Ninth Street did not remain vacant for long. Before I saw the next set of odd ones, I could hear their ballyhoo rising to the north, like shouts of cheers at a parade and accompanied by the braying of horses, followed by a great rending screech of wood and a smashing of glass.

There followed a clatter of scraping noises as a team of mules emerged from Main Street straining west, dragging behind them a portion of a wall and window frame attached to their necks by rope. I recognized it as the entranceway of a store on Main Street known formally as Smith and Smith Home Furnishments. I had never been inside but had many times studied the window contents while waiting for Missus Pegram to return from her strolling look-see at the store's variety of stock. That window displayed a multitude of fancy knick-knacks and doo-dads from New Orleans, Savannah, Charleston, and Paris, France. There were small cabinets for teacups, music boxes, golden andirons, and silver statues of plump, naked babies like the cherubs hanging on Missus Pegram's bedroom wall. There were delicate fans of silk that she told me came all the way from China. During afternoon socials, the mistresses frequently cooed over the latest fancy items they had seen there, naming it as the "import shop."

Now that very import shop window was being dragged west down Main Street by a galloping mule team. Afterward came a steady parade of more odd ones with arms full of bounty clearly pillaged from deep inside it. From the parlor window I could see them emerging from Main; some turned south, some north, and some continued on west, fleeing across Ninth Street.

Different ones toted different bounty. A large woman held a fancy chair aloft, which she carried by the armrests. On the seat of the chair rested a colorful serving bowl that would easily break should it slide off the seat cushion. She waddled west as fast as she could manage, holding the chair tilted to an angle to keep the bowl safe.

Others followed. A man whose face I could not see ran west on the double quick toting a large mirror in a golden frame that covered his entire body. As he crossed Ninth Street, for one quick moment the mirror caught the image of fire to the east and sent a blinding flash straight into my eyes.

Two more excited men ran south directly past the house, each one carrying a bundle of items too large to manage. Despite their grim-looking dirty attire, their faces were happy, displaying broad, gleeful smiles. Their collective bounty included an assortment of glassware—they had urns and bedpans tucked under their arms, while their fingers clung to a variety of small oil lamps. One of them let slip a tall urn holding several brightly colored parasols, which promptly smashed upon impact. He paused to study the mess and cursed, which set the other one to a hearty laugh. It was not possible for either of them to retrieve the parasols as all arms, hands, and fingers were fully occupied. They scurried on as more odd ones came up behind.

The parade of merry thieves went on for some time. Foolishly, I remained gawking at them longer than I should have. I marveled at the clever way they figured new ways to cultivate their business. Some industrious men employed wheel carts, rolling away heavier loads of bounty with ease. The risk of more plentiful banditry also meant greater loss should the cart tip over—but that meant nothing to them, as they only cursed any mishap, regained the balance of their various loads, and rolled forward with a stacked cargo of three boxes instead of four. Had there been wagons with teams of horses, they likely would have put them to use as well.

One man quite fat in the belly even employed a billy goat. I had never before seen a goat in the city—at least, not a live one. This goat being led by a fat-belly man bore a half a dozen hams hanging over its sides, making it appear a small white mule-beast, fully packed for field labor. The man had a near empty bottle of whiskey in one hand and another full bottle at the ready, tucked under the other arm. Unlike others, he showed no concern of being observed. Both he and his goat kept an easy amble despite being pursued by a ravenous cloud of flies. He swilled a drink of whiskey, then swatted the goat to keep it moving, which made the animal's neck bell ring out. Then he spit, scratched, cursed the flies, and swatted the goat again.

Watching him—I was shocked back into my own unpleasant circumstances. It happened so quick it was difficult at first to understand the threat being posed. One of the strings holding a pig leg over the goat's back unraveled—sending the attached ham to Ninth Street dirt in a slow, drawn-out slump. Hearing the sound, the thief halted his goat a few steps beyond the castoff ham and looked back at it. Too drunk to take action, he only stared forlornly—the victim of a cruel fate depriving him of one portion of his stolen treasure.

The moment did not last long. As though he felt my study of him, he casually turned and looked straight into the parlor and right into my eyes! At first the glance was easygoing. There was no meanness in the exchange. Then my insides seized up.

I was discovered! I went cold with fear.

He seemed uncertain about what he was seeing. He squinted, raised his eyebrows, and bore down hard on me, studying me as best he could manage through besotted eyes. We held a fixed gaze for what seemed an immeasurable length of time. Finally, he broke off to glance back at the ham, still at rest upon the street. When he returned to look again into the parlor, which I am certain he did, I was not there.

I spun and dropped to a sitting position on the floor. I pressed my head against the wall conjuring my best action, depending on what trick the fat-belly man might try to play on me. I listened to see if I could hear him in the yard, on the steps, on the porch. So far—nothing.

All doors were locked. If I needed to move on the quick, I would have to get through the hallway and kitchen, to the back door, unlock it, and flee past the garden before he could get to me. Considering his state of drunken slosh, I reckoned it should be easily done before he could break the front door window and open the latch.

Sitting on the floor, I straightened my legs for comfort. The glassy eyes of the China-head doll stared at me. An orange glow illumined the parlor walls. I waited for the sound of the goat's bell to resume. The absence of it had me deadened with fear as I held my station on the floorboards just below the window ledge.

A shattering of glass rang out, so close I conjured it to come from a house nearby. It was followed by voices arguing and cursing so closely I could hear their words plainly:

"T'aint so," said one.

" 'Tis too," said the other.

"The shops is one thing. Thas enough!"

"C'mon, damn you."

"Naw. T'aint right. Nuh-uh. T'aint right, I tell you!"

"Ain't no difference, you sorry-ass slacker. Donchu know there ain't no honor among thieves—you dumb Alabama bastard."

"Oh, yeah it is! Not the houses. I ain't gonna. I just ain't gonna. Besides the ones who skeedaddled done took their gold and such with 'em."

"In these houses? Look in there. They got more than they can carry. You really is a sorry-ass man. How'd you ever find your way out of Alabama, anyway?"

Their quarrel was likely coming from the Stafford house, two doors north on Ninth Street. Not everyone had cleared out ahead of the Yankees. But I did not know if the Stafford house or any other nearby houses sheltered hidden occupants like myself.

I pictured the two thieves standing before the broken parlor window of the Stafford house as they squabbled over expansion of their business from public shop to private house. They were certainly unaware that I was listening. And they were probably unaware they were being observed by a fat-belly drunk man in the street leading a goat laden with a year's worth of ham. If they reconnoitered and robbed the man of his hams it would likely be more profitable for them than their currently contemplated business. But that was not to be. In all the ugly business of plunder I witnessed, I never did see one thief rob another.

"Aw'ight, damn you! If not here—where?"

"Let's head on up to Grace Street."

"Was you mated by a woman and a jackass? You musta been! We just come from up there you Alabama cross-breed. T'aint nuthing left. If it ain't burned out good, it's good and robbed already."

"Naw-huh. Not all of it."

"What ain't? Go on. Tell me you broke-off turd. Tell me what ain't been robbed yet already."

"West. West on Grace Street, the part that ain't got on fire yet. There's stores down there. Maybe the pickings is better."

"Aw'ight," came the grunted resignation after a pause.

In the end, I said a private word of gratitude to them both, because their sideshow proved a distraction of benefit. Shortly after their departure, the goat hooves commenced a song that delivered happy relief. First came a single chime of the animal's neck bell, then a double chime, and finally it rang out with hardiness—telling me that the fat-belly drunk man was also taking his leave in the company of his goat. I waited until the bell chimes faded before altering my station. Once they were completely gone, I crawled along the floor to the edge of the drapes where I could ease up and peek onto the street with secrecy.

Nothing!

For that moment, there was not a single person to be seen on Ninth Street. Like a bird in flight, I sprang for the draw cord and yanked the drapes closed, shutting out the glare of fire and once again returning the parlor to the moving shadows of orange glow.

Peeking again from the drape's edge, I could see Ninth Street had become spotted with the droppings of thieves moving in haste. Some of the orphaned goods I could recognize by the light of the churning fires now just one block away, some I could not. There were smashed china bowls and broken crockery. A box of hat feathers spilled open, sending downy colors of the rainbow flying every which way. A sack of eyeglasses was found to be useless, tossed aside, its contents spilled out and trampled by feet, hooves, and wheels. There were multiple bins, crates, and bulging sacks of burlap lying about, left where they fell from a cart or dropped by some overburdened thief.

I could not identify the nature of most of the droppings, but there was one bit of treasure left among the shadows that tugged at me. It was the curved body of that medium-large ham delivered to Ninth Street by that fat-belly drunk man and his goat. It was the solution to my hunger. A quick errand in the night—and the kitchen would be alive with the smell of bacon. The real riddle, of course, was how to retrieve it.

I kept a steady peek. The thieves came and went, respectful of each other and thoroughly unhindered by the fires to the east. The sound of breaking glass rang out in the distance with regularity. I conjured waiting until daylight. It would likely mean fewer odd ones to worry me, for I doubted they would carry on with their ugly business in the sunshine. But it also posed a greater risk of being discovered. And it posed a greater risk that someone else would retrieve the ham ahead of me.

So it was settled. If I must become a thief, then I must become a thief in the night.

Chapter Seventeen:
Miss Francine Pegram

It did not seem so while performing the task, but in true time, the job went quickly. I kneeled to all fours to stay good and clear of the doorway window, which had no drapes to pull. I crept past the foyer and into the hallway. I worked my way around my hallway service chair, where the floorboard delivered its usual bird squeak. The ghosts of orange glowered at me overhead, watching me from their positions on the walls and growing more excited as I moved. Once around the corner, beyond the hallway corridor, I stood up.

My options were—cellar or back door. For reasons I cannot fully relate, I chose the cellar. That Ole Mister Rat would not be there was a plain truth. His boiled, mostly eaten dead body lay that very moment upon the kitchen floor. That put one fear to rest. But I believe I may have selected departure from the house through the cellar because that passageway somehow held the manner of secrecy that lined up neatly with my intended actions.

Thinking ahead, I unlocked the back door should I require a quick return. Then, at half descent on the cellar steps, I paused to listen for any scratchy sounds moving about, a warning from any of Ole Mister Rat's relatives—who might not only object to my arrival in the cellar, but happily take vengeance upon me for eating the balance of him earlier in the afternoon.

There was nothing.

At stairwell bottom I worked my eyes and head at angles to

observe outlines of shadows. I edged along the dirt floor, making my way to the steps, and opened the shutter doors.

Standing half-emerged, I noted the world was directly opposite in appearance from the last time I departed. The previous morning my eyes required adjustment to the blinding sun. Now they required adjustment to the night and the odd glow of redness in the sky.

A distant rumbling, followed by a noisy shaking of the entire house, let me know that another building had collapsed. That did not sit well with someone else. Just as I feared, there were relatives of Ole Mister Rat living under Almond Eyes' horse leathers. Perhaps it was Ole Missus Rat. Just as the rattling shiver passed through the house and silence returned—there came a woeful, full-throated squeal from the cellar behind me. It was a great scream, loud and harsh, and it filled up the air with anger and fear. The sound of that warning from the only other occupant of the house was all I required to make me jump past all other worries. I did not want Ole Missus Rat taking her vengeance upon me for eating her husband, even if it was not I who captured, killed, and cooked him. The darkness, the cellar, the fires, the odd ones outside were all quickly cast off. I departed the cellar, letting the double shutter doors slam behind me, and ran into the glowing night under a sky streaked over with vast furrows of red and black smolder.

In two moments' time I was past the easeway and squatting behind the scraggly sycamore tree, whose trunk was not wide enough to cover me so I held steady like a lizard in the sun, squatting, my chin upon my knee waiting to see if my arrival ruffled anyone's attention. There was nothing. No one roused to a state of alarm, or even idle interest. I held my position.

Half a block to the south, a trio of drunken odd ones passed a bottle of whiskey among them. They had lost interest in thievery and bickered loudly over the timing of the Yankees' arrival. Silhouetted against the fires, they were a sore-looking group, as unsightly as I had ever seen, with great rents in their britches exposing grievously dirty flesh. Beneath the filth of their tatters, I could barely make out the Butternut color of their uniforms.

"They'll be on Grace Street by morning," said one of them.

"Oh paw-crap! Tomorrow noon," barked the second, angrily dismissing the first.

"Oh paw-crap on you," said the third. "You both got mongoloid brains. Why, the Yankees is already here!" he slurred—shrugging without a worry and gesturing toward the fires as if the flames proved his assertion.

The other two cussed him in response. One sucked hard on his nostrils and hacked up a chunk of croup, then spit it into the dirt, drawing the attention of the others and making them quiet down just long enough to watch it land with a splatter. They passed the whiskey bottle among them and resumed cussing.

Closer by, I could see the ham. It lay where it fell, wrapped tight in a brown canvas sack, slick with ooze from the oils inside. Nearby was a leather satchel, partly crushed, its sides crumpled in upon itself, looking as though it had been trampled under wheel and foot. From my perch behind the sycamore I could better see all the droppings, make out their shape, and note their nature. I could tell that a wooden crate came from a smithy shop because a broken rim spilled forth a small portion of its contents of horseshoes.

I was ready.

Holding to my squat position like a daddy longlegs, I darted into the street. Taking a breath and keeping my legs bent low, I ran along the nearest wagon rut, hoisted the ham to my breast, then turned and arrived back at the sycamore carrying the treasure.

I crouched behind the tree. There was no worrisome alteration of movement, no posture of alarm was made, no one came running, arms waving, shouting, "Stop, thief . . . you there, girl . . . pickanniny . . . negress . . , hold up . . . where is your mistress?"

The absence of outcry emboldened me. I was grateful for safe delivery and for the bounty of newly found treasure without making disturbance to the thieves. And the street remained littered with easy pickings.

I laid the ham gently between my feet, letting the oily canvas slide from my forearms to balance on the protruding sycamore roots. Then I made a second dash. On return, I clutched a paper sack and the partially crushed leather satchel.

I grew more bold in the minutes that followed, scurrying several more times onto Ninth Street to make capital of those droppings that could be fetched without raising alarm. Then came a surprise that could have been my undoing. The space behind the sycamore became an unnatural pile, a very noticeable mound of transferred goods. In my prideful cleverness, I had not calculated upon that. Once realized, I moved fast to fix the error. After transferring the bounty one armload at a time behind the sycamore, I rapidly transferred it again to the rear of the house, one armload at a time. That done, it was a handy job for me to fetch everything into the kitchen—this time, by way of the back door to avoid Ole Missus Rat.

Once accomplished, I hurried back to the parlor windows to study the street. There was nothing new and I was glad to see that Ninth Street remained littered over with abandoned goods.

The nearest fires choked off the tall flames and were now a series of smoldering furnaces; glowing red-hot brick peeked through the piles where the buildings had collapsed upon themselves. It made me wonder if the devil was a block away on Tenth Street, busily working at his labors, poking up holes of hellfire into downtown Richmond.

A few blocks south, the naked wall of one tall building stubbornly remained standing while the other three had dropped into ruin. The windows of that one wall framed the smoky sky in a ghostly checkerboard. Overhead, the rising smoke blew south in a hundred shades of gray, where the first hint of morning light was posting notice of its planned arrival. Watching that bashful glow beyond the rising smoke, I fancied the sun would rise more slowly. Once it got a full survey of the ghostly domain that just one day prior was the complete and wonderful city of Richmond, it would surely hesitate to drive the night away.

Chapter Eighteen:
Extra Pettigrew

I rose before the sun that morning. I peed on a root of the old oak tree while looking up at the Pegram house, which appeared curled up and asleep like an old dog in the corner.

While keeping quiet as always, I washed my face and neck with a bucket of water drawn from the well in the out-yard and left the balance of it beside the pump for the other slaves who would follow. One wash bucket per morning for everyone. That was Master Pettigrew's rule. "Oonays-per-deez," he called it in his dead Latin, "waste not, want not."

As usual, I began my regular morning duties in the hotel kitchen, loading the big iron stove with wood, which I set aflame to make things ready for ole Miss Edna to begin cooking what breakfast could be offered the guests, which, come the bustle of morning, the Irish girls would serve in the dining room. Mostly, it would be only warmed-over chicken water with a few beans. Still rubbing sandy sleep from my eyes, I leaned against the counter in the darkness until the water pot boiled. When it did, I prepared a small tin of coffee for Master Pettigrew and took it to his first-floor room near the reception desk.

He rose with a grunt, scratching at the blotch of ruby red skin on his chest. He peed in his chamber pot while passing a goodly volley of gas; then he sweetened the coffee tin with a spoonful of honey, which he kept hidden in the drawer next to his bed. Sitting in his dressing chair he slowly sipped the coffee while I laid out his trousers and white shirt that had been washed just the week before. I was making ready to tote his chamber pot to the servant's privy for emptying when he stopped me.

"Never mind that," he said in a sleepy voice. "Go to room four-twelve and waken Colonel Gist. I've bonded you to him all week."

"Am I done with the Shockoe warehouse, sah?"

He sipped his hot coffee before answering. "Yes, for now. They may require you again next week. For this week your horse and wagon skills are required by the military on the outskirts."

"Yessah."

"You may be gone all week. Colonel Gist will pay you directly when you're finished. Come back here immediately with the money when he does. Do you hear?"

"Yessah."

"Now, listen to me. If Colonel Gist gets killed, your bond is concluded. You understand? In that eventuality, you come back here immediately. If he dies, don't let 'em usurp you further. Come right back to me. You hear?"

"Yessah."

"All right. Go on. Vado . . . opus," he said, slurping down a big chug of coffee. "Get to work." He was speaking the dead Latin, but he was not shouting or being mean, so I ventured to ask about something that bothered me.

"Sah," I said, "there was more cannon fire during the night. You thinkin' there's gonna be fightin' in Richmond?"

"I heard the artillery too," he said quietly, in a way that made me worry, especially if he was worried about the same thing as me. "It is getting closer, isn't it?" He rubbed the ruby blotch again. "We could be nearing the end 'round here. Things could be fixin' to change. But don't you worry. You'll be fine. If it happens, you just keep low. None of 'em will bring their fight to

165

you. You hear?"

"Yessah."

"You just tell 'em you're my property. Tell 'em you're the property of the Spotswood Hotel. Don't none of the officers want to get on my wrong side. If they do, they know they risk not getting a room, breakfast, or a recommendation at the whorehouses."

"Yessah."

"All right now, Extra," he said. "Vado."

I knew Colonel Gist. He was a red-headed dandy who worked the Richmond ramparts when I won't toting him to the whorehouses. When I arrived at room 412, he was already awake and using candlelight by the bureau mirror to brush his fine long hair, sideburns, and beard. He had a tiny little set of scissors that he used to clip all protruding hairs, to make his red locks look perfectly smooth. Without bothering to look at me, he told me to set out on foot for Danville Station on Fourteenth Street and that he would meet me there on horseback.

So I did. I commenced walking through the city in the Sunday morning darkness. It was the first time I ever walked that much at night. Danville Station was west then south, to the foot of the Mayo Bridge. I didn't want to risk gettin' stopped by any master mister, or Johnny officer, so I just stuck to the roadsides and didn't bother lookin' in no windows or eyeballing any of the white whorewomen who eyeballed me.

After a while, I got to indulging in one of my fancies. This time, I was not a factor or factotum businessman, but a Johnny officer. I got stripes and doodads on my collar and shoulders, I thought. That makes me important. And as a messenger bearing correspondence from the ramparts to Master Bobby Lee himself, that made my passage even more important. I got to pass through all Richmond in the night, to deliver my letters straight to Master Lee's own hand. Anybody stop me—they find big trouble.

By the time I arrived, the sun was up and Colonel Gist was waiting for me on the train platform.

"Stand easy, boy. We got a while to wait."

"We waitin' on a train, sah?" I asked. I knew it would be more than an hour before the first train of the day arrived, and even then it might be late. Sometimes they never came at all.

"That's one thing we're waiting on," he blurted, quick with impatience like a hornet handing out a warning buzz. That told me he didn't like explaining his business to me, so I asked no more questions. After about an hour, a wagon lurched to a halt near our loiter on the walkway platform. Lord have mercy it was a sad sight. It was a dilapidated heap of a wagon pulled by a sorry-looking mule team so beat down it looked to me like they were both set to drop down dead at any moment. In the wagon bed the mules hauled a large group of field slaves with so little room they were all scrunched up, with their knees pulled to their chests. The driver saluted Colonel Gist.

"Good morning, sir."

"Good morning, Sergeant. This the best you could do?"

"Yessir. The mule team and wagon ain't much. But the niggers are big and able."

"All right Sergeant Paxton. Stand easy. We're waiting on the first train before heading out."

"Yes, sir," Sergeant Paxton called out to the colonel. He turned to the field hands scrunched up in the wagon bed. "You boys can get out and stretch your legs a while. But stay together. Don't be wandering off. If you got to piss or shit, go behind that shed down the track aways. But come straight back here. Ya'll hear?"

"Yessah," some of them mumbled as they slowly eased off the rear of the wagon and looked about at Danville Station—and at me with curiosity.

"Who's the city nigger?" Sergeant Paxton asked, meaning me.

"Bonded for the week. Got some skill handling wagons. We'll put him to minding the field niggers where they're most needed."

It was another hour before the train arrived. A Johnny messenger dismounted and trotted straight up to Colonel Gist, plunking a bundle of papers wrapped with a string into his hands. He looked nothing like the way I imagined myself to look when dreaming to be a messenger walking through Richmond in the dark. This man had no fancy doodads on his collar. He was a skinny private with clothing almost as dirty as the field hands in the wagon. And he couldn't have been much older than me.

"Good morning, sir," the messenger said, saluting Colonel Gist. "For President Davis, sir." The colonel pushed his red hair from his shoulder as he took the bundle.

"Very good private. Any trouble on the trip?"

"No sir, Colonel. We left Danville promptly. No Yankees along the way."

Less than a minute later I was sitting beside Sergeant Paxton on the buckboard riding back into downtown Richmond. We all trailed behind Colonel Gist on his big bay gelding as he brushed his red hair, riding easy to the Great White House of Mister President Davis at Twelfth and Clay Streets. The scrunched-up field hands bounced in the back, and the more Colonel Gist brushed, the more Sergeant Paxton cursed him under his breath.

"Gawd damn," he grumbled. "Gaw-oh-awd damn."

The guard at the Great White House admitted the colonel and the paper bundle immediately. A short while later a house servant wearing a white vest and a fine bow tie came to the wagon.

"Ya'll can rest a while," he said. "Colonel Gist will be joining

President Davis at worship services this morning. He says to tell you the journey to the ramparts will recommence after worship." That's when he eyed the field hands. "If ya'll require water there's a barrel in the stable for the coloreds."

Chapter Nineteen:
Extra Pettigrew

Later that morning, I was awful to glad see Missy Fran outside the church. She looked pretty and I wanted to stay with her and lose more time. But after seeing Mister President Davis bolt from services and cut a beeline up Ninth Street—I knew there would be no more of that. I tried to make the wagon keep up with Colonel Gist, but I lost him in traffic. The last I saw of him, he was at full canter in the mud, bounding past the Great House of Government at Twelfth and Bank Streets, his fancy red hair bouncing on his shoulders. Sergeant Paxton made it plain he did not care for the way things were going.

"Gawd damn if I'm going to follow that red-headed prig with a boatload o'niggers. Not when Gawd damn Jeff Davis is on the run."

"Where we supposed to go, sah?" I asked.

"Back to Danville Station so Gist can drop Davis' response orders, then on to Gawd damn Drewry's Bluff across the river." He said it all like a barking dog who couldn't be bothered with me or my questions. "After that, only Jesus knows where, and Jesus ain't talking to nobody in this hellacious hullabaloo." I lurched the wagon through mud and traffic in the direction of the Danville depot. After one block more, he stopped me.

"Whoa, boy. Pull it up here," he demanded. I stopped the wagon. He climbed down and walked away without saying word one. He just walked into the street, thick with Johnnies, all of them moving with haste as though something important was happening—but nobody seemed to know exactly what.

"What about Colonel Gist?" I called out. Sergeant Paxton stopped amid the disorder and turned around.

"What about him? That fop cares more 'bout his dandy red curls than his duty. I don't like nothing 'bout the Yankees. I'd kill 'em all if I could. But I ain't gonna take one of their minie balls just 'cause he gotta stop to comb his locks every Gawd damn hour. Gawd damn war's over and we all know it." He stood in the street, shouting and thumping his chest with his thumb. "I'm done. And I'm gonna go ride as many Irish and nigger girls as I got money for."

"What I do now?" I called out. He did not answer. "What I do with these boys?" I asked. He stopped and turned again.

"Listen, boy—take 'em all to Danville depot. Put a stamp on their nigger heads and mail 'em to that nigger lover Lincoln."

That was all he said. He walked off down Bank Street and turned into Byrd Alley, where a board hung overhead that I knew bore the word "Screamersville."

I drove the old wagon loaded with field slaves back to the Danville depot. There was one hissing train parked at the platform and great numbers of government men and Johnnies rushing about, filling it up with office cabinets and boxes— boxes that appeared to contain little more than piles of papers.

I thought of boarding the train and walking up and down the aisle looking for Colonel Gist, but there were no other slaves on board that I could see—so I decided against it. Instead, I drove the wagon as far down the tracks as I could, looking in the windows for his fancy red hair. One man in a government suit poked his head out a window and yelled at me.

"Hey, boy, where you think you're going?" he demanded.

"Just looking for de mastah, sah," I replied. "He a colonel."

"Well, you go on home. We got enough madness 'round here. And take them sorry-ass field niggers with you. Go on, get outta here."

"Yes-sah," I said, not looking to pose any argument. The wagon could go no further anyway, so I turned back. I parked the wagon out of the pathway of Johnny-boy bustle, crossed over to the other side of the train, and walked on foot along the entire length of it still searching each window for signs of Colonel Gist, but I could not find him.

I returned to the wagon and sat quietly with the field hands as we all watched the train come to life. It hissed, smoked, and spewed as the wheels cranked and chugged, pulling all seven cars to the southwest toward Danville. For the first time, the field hands spoke.

"Whachu gon do?" asked one of them after the train departed.

"Wha hap'n nex?" another wanted to know.

"We gonna be sent back?"

"Can't we'all stay," another asked with a sad voice. "Can't we stay in ole Rishomon?" he pleaded. "Things fixing to change over."

"Yeah, things gonna change."

"Yeah, we wants to see it happ'n."

It was Sergeant Paxton who had rounded them up. But now that he'd abandoned them for Screamersville whore-town, I didn't know what to do with them. And with Colonel Gist missing—I didn't know what to do with myself, either.

"Where ya'll from?" I asked.

"Farm," said one.

"Ole man Bookbinder plantation," said another.

"Where's that?" I asked.

"Mathews," came the answer, "on de middle neck."

"Yas-sah, we crabbin' in de crab season and farmin' in de farm season."

"Dey took us from Bookbinder," said one. "They call it 'war demand.' He near 'bout dead nohow."

"Who's nearly dead?"

"Ole man Bookbinder."

"He on de dead bed when we got rek-sissioned over to dat Johnny boy what run off sayin' de war wuz ovah."

"Dat Johnny boy got de smiles nah," said one sitting scrunched up in the very back of the wagon, almost laughing.

"Yes-sah, he look to have him a good ole time," said another. "He got him a big ole smile on de face right 'bout nah." That made several of them nod and laugh.

"How ya'll know about all that?" I asked.

"Dat easy," he answered.

"We'all know 'bout dat." said another in smiling agreement.

I too knew of Screamersville. Most everybody in Richmond did—men and women alike. There were many whore-joints: Lumpkins Alley, Locust Alley, the Thompson brothel, the house behind Duval's Drug Store where naked white women sat in the window. In the early years, when Master Pettigrew dabbled in the whore business, I learned that white men liked having their way with a black woman. But Master Pettigrew stopped that part of his hotel offerings before the war got started, when he sold off his two whore-women.

"Why this town has more harlots than Paris and New Orleans put together," he would say, whenever a guest made inquiry. "Ress-uh-ress. Vyatikus-uh-vyatikus. I have a business to run. Whoring is a sideline I got run out of by the competition. That's the way of free enterprise. You go to Screamersville," he told 'em. "My boy Extra will cart you over. And be sure to mention my name—you'll get real fine service if you do," he would say with a big wink.

Screamersville was the biggest and best-known whore-town in all Richmond. It lay concealed in the middle of the block just east of the Great House of Government. It was a wide-open ease-way at the end of Byrd Alley—a big ole open-air enterprise when weather was good; when weather was bad the whore business moved into the back doors and cellars of all the surrounding buildings. Folks who entered the fronts of those same buildings to shop for dry goods or do office work mostly seemed to pretend they had no idea of the goings-on taking place out the back doors of those very same buildings.

Its business grew during the war. Men of government and business and Johnny officers who stayed at the Spotswood visited so often that Master Pettigrew had me running the buckboard back and forth on a regular schedule—twice a day—afternoon and evening.

"Ya'll forget 'bout all that," I said to the field hands.

"Can't we stay?" the first one asked again. "Like dat Johnny boy, dat Sergeant Paxton. He wanna stay, so he gonna stay."

"Yea. We doan wanna hed back to de middle neck. Not yet noways. Ole man Bookbinder dead by now noways." The others looked at me, nodding their heads—hoping for the best and mumbling about wanting to be in Richmond 'cause they all sense big changes coming.

"Ya'll can't go to Screamersville," I told 'em. "That's for white men."

"We know dat," one said.

"Dere's other places what tend to us."

"Yea, we know other places to visit."

"Yea, we just wanna stay in ole Rishomon, 'cause things fixin' to change."

I pulled the wagon around and drove it back downtown, where I let them out. They each thanked me and called me "sir" as they walked away down Main Street in their filthy field trousers with their heads bobbing in all directions, happy to be let go but looking like lost children.

Chapter Twenty:
Extra Pettigrew

After I let the field hands go, I didn't know what to do with the wagon and mule-team that did not belong to me. I thought of Father Washington who, as a boy, spoke honestly of depriving his own daddy of a cherry tree. But even if I fed and watered those two ole mules, I knew they couldn't make the full-day trip back to the Middle Neck. So I drove to the Shockoe House, where a free black who worked the sugar trade gave me four dollar total in Yankee money for mules and dray, which made a tidy add-on to my tobacco pouch and what useless Confed coins I possessed.

I sat down on an empty hogshead by the loading dock to watch and think a while. At all angles the streets filled with businessmen and military men, white citizens mostly—but slaves, too. They all moved like there was a time limit—like the great flood was coming our way and they were all heading for Noah's great boat to escape. Wondering about that, I kept a watch to the south, but could see no dark waters rising up from the James River.

Then the Johnny boys commenced marching south, and thinking to lose some time, I walked a ways with 'em. I followed 'em down to Bloody Run Street at Mayo Bridge, where their number was so great they clogged the entrance, requiring an officer to stand on a wagon and call out rules for who had to wait and who got to cross over.

There was a fine drummer boy who switched his song while

they stood immobile. When marching, his drumming sang out as "rat-a-tat, rat-a-tat, rat-a-tat-tat-tat." While waiting it changed over to "whirrr-tat, whirrr-tat, whirrr-tat." He was a small boy, maybe ten year old with hair so white it looked the color of sunshine at noontime. A nearby tall Johnny Reb with some stripes on his shoulders saw me eyeing 'em over and took objection.

"Whatchu lookin' at, darkie?" he asked. He was a scraggly soldier, who I thought to pretend not to hear, but he wouldn't let me get away with it. "Hey, boy, I say whatchu lookin' at?"

"Nuttin', sah. I just lookin', sah."

"Lookin' at what?"

"Well, just lookin' at ya'll leaving, sah."

"Well, you go on. We got 'nuff watchers."

"Yes-sah," I said, turning away.

"Hey, boy," he called back, "when the Yankees get in town, tell 'em we refugeed northwest."

"Yes-sah," I said, nodding.

"To Shenandoah. Tell 'em that's where we headed. Northwest, back to the valley." I nodded again.

"Yes-sah."

"And ya'll behave while we gone. Ya hear? Stay out of the houses. And keep your nigger hands off the white women."

Still playing, the drummer boy turned to look at me with his tired and hungry face. His whiter than white hair hung down in his eyes as he kept up the at-wait song: whirrr-tat, whirr-tat, whirr-tat.

"Yes-sah," I said, turning to walk back up the hill, back into downtown Richmond.

While heading back uptown I took some tardy notice of a passing wagon. I almost missed it. But after it passed, I saw it being led by a fine team of healthy speckled whites such as had not been seen on the streets of Richmond in many months. It was driven by a dandy house servant in a bright red vest-coat. The whole thing stood out like a bright decoration in the darkness.

It was then I took notice of something else.

Among the passengers in the wagon was a woman that looked like Mistress Pegram, Missy Fran's own missus. I couldn't be certain. I had only a quick look as the wagon maneuvered into position to cross over at the Mayo Bridge. I recognized no one else in the buggy, which was as equally fine as the horses. That made no sense. If it was she, where was Master Pegram? And where was Missy Fran?

Not having any answers, and being in need of answers, I quickly turned to walk toward the house on Ninth Street.

From the old stable across the street, I could see that the curtain was pulled tight on the Pegram house. Everything about it was dark and quiet. I knew no one was inside. Mister Pegram is an important man, an engineer who works for the Johnnies, once hosted Mister General Lee himself in the parlor, and has that farm in Roanoke Rapids. Looking at that shut-down house—I knew he had come and evacuated them all to that farm. That's what everybody was doing—leaving. Anybody who could leave—left.

But I needed to make certain.

After looking to see that no white folks or Johnnies at loiter were watching me, I quickly ventured to the front door and gave it three hard knocks before stepping away. I stepped back to the yard just in case Mister or Mistress Pegram were inside. That way, they'd be less unhappy about answering a call from me than if I were standing on their porch as though I were a welcome neighbor or the dairy man.

As I figured, there came no answer. I was set to walk 'round back even though that was close to the Spotswood. If Master Pettigrew saw me losing time, lollygagging around town instead of laboring on the ramparts with Colonel Gist and Sergeant Paxton, it would mean a hard beating.

But thankfully, I didn't have to risk it. 'Twas then I saw Cussin' Sally-Martha in tow behind one of the two Irish girls who served tables in the Spotswood dining room. They were hurrying west on Main Street, back to the Spotswood, with Sally-Martha toting a small clutch-bag that appeared filled with nothing much. I knew they had been out and about in search of whatever foods could be bought or bartered. I was reluctant to stop 'em. Sally-Martha ain't never liked me much. But that won't odd. She didn't like nobody much. But I knew I had to speak to her.

"Pardon me, ma'am," I said to the young Irish girl. "Sally-Martha, can you tell me please—have you seen Missy Fran?" They stopped and stared at me. But neither one spoke. "Now, Miss Sally-Martha," I said with a little more tone to my manner, "I need to know if you've seen Missy Fran."

Still, there was no answer. The two Irish girls mostly stuck to themselves without saying much at all to the slaves working at the Spotswood. They were said to be sisters. And the younger one, thirteen or maybe fourteen years of age, with off-white hair and baby-blush skin near 'bout all over her neck and face, was the one that spoke up to help me.

"Sally-Martha, answer Extra," she instructed. Well, Cussin' Sally-Martha didn't like that none, but she did what she was told. She pushed out her lips and wrinkled her nose and commenced tossing a round of ill heaping at me.

"Naw, yo fool, yo goddam fool. I ain't seen de damn girl what you sure hell ain't gone marry. And I ain't seen de damn girl what you sure as fool-hell think you gone marry, either. I ain't seen either one o'dem damn happy house niggers. Watchu doin' wandering 'round here anyway . . ."

"That's enough," the Irish girl interrupted. "Extra, we can't

tarry. We have to get back. Mister Pettigrew has sent all the coloreds to the cellar and told what guests we have to stay in their
room. He's even got the shotgun on display, sitting atop the
reception desk. As soon as we get back from our barter-
shopping, he plans to lock down the hotel from trouble for the
day and coming night."

"Yes, ma'am," I said. "Is there anything left in town for
barter?" I asked.

"No. We only got a little milk and a bit of rice. That'll help
stretch our offerings for the guests 'til better delivery comes
through."

I thanked her, nodded at Cussin' Sally-Martha, and headed
off back to the Shockoe Tobacco House, grateful to have met
up with them because it saved me from getting caught by Master
Pettigrew. I didn't have anywhere in particular to go, but I did
not want to be sent to the cellar with the others.

As for Missy Fran, well, if she was not at the house, she must
have refugeed with the Pegrams. That was good. It meant she
would avoid the fighting, should there be any in Richmond.
And while on the Pegram family farm in Roanoke Rapids, she'd
likely have more to eat. There might even be livestock.

That made me think of the milk that Irish girl said they were
able to secure on their outing. I was hungry. And I sure would
enjoy a big ole glass of milk.

Chapter Twenty-One:
Extra Pettigrew

It was on the trip back into the business part of town that I saw the madness commence. I was supposed to head straight back to Master Pettigrew, but I was so taken by the oddity of everything that I disobeyed.

Men with torches rushed into Van Gronin's tobacco warehouse. In front of the Shockoe House on Cary Street, men smashed liquor crates on the street.

"Yo there—boy!" a white man almost as tall as me called out. "Come ovah here."

"Yes-sah?"

"What're you doing?"

"Was headin' for ramparts work with Colonel Gist, sah," I explained, "but everybody done refugeed outta town."

"Come with me," he said.

We entered Shockoe House, where some Johnny boys who had not evacuated stood uneasy. They called the tall man a "commissary agent" and took his orders to set the torch to the tobacco—perfectly good tobacco, some piled high on pallets, some still curing in their hogshead barrels.

"There's a wagon load of liquor outside. Take the barrels out to the streets, pour the liquor on 'em—then light 'em. We ain't leaving nothing for the Yankees," he said.

"Yes, sir—yes, sir—yes, sir," they all said in obedient response, ready to get on with the job like men who had somewhere else to be.

"Yes-sah," I said joining in.

I don't know how long I labored helping set fire to tobacco and pouring liquor onto the streets. I only know I spent a good chunk of that afternoon and well into evening helping the Johnnies and the commissary agent put the torch to the goods dragged from the Dibrell, Mayo, and Shockoe warehouses. Plenty of cotton also got destroyed.

Aside from us slaves, I understood tobacco to be the most valuable chattel in the city—and they didn't want the Yankees to get it. And I understood also, being afraid for the honor of white women, they didn't want the Yankees or the slaves getting drunk on a storehouse of stolen liquor. But I naturally understood something else, too. I understood it to be madness. I had never seen anything like it. And I was scared of what it all meant.

When the commissary agent won't looking, the Johnny boys stuffed their pockets with tobacco and set aside bottles of liquor for themselves.

"Wha 'boutch you, boy?" one said to me after awhile.

"Sah?"

"You want some o'this goddam liquor, boy?"

"I is fine, sah," I said.

"Well go ahead. We can't steal it all," he said.

"Might as well," the other one said. "It's a shame. Just a damn shame. That's what it is. There's thousands o'good white men starving in Petersburg and we're pouring out liquor and giving it away to the niggers. Just a goddam shame," he said.

And so I joined in. I stuffed my pockets with tobacco and set aside a bottle of fine bourbon by hiding it under the loading ramp.

It was nightfall before my work with the commissaries concluded and the fires began to spread beyond the tobacco piles in the streets and beyond the tobacco warehouses. First it spread to the nearby stores, then the stables filled with feed hay, then the flames leapt across streets to lap at the tall buildings where factors and factotums conduct their business.

After having labored to help set the fires, I had no mind to be ordered to work putting out the fires, so I hurried back to the Shockoe House to retrieve my concealed bourbon bottle. I found a hiding position inside a feed shed at the foot of Shockoe Slip, where I sat down and sipped my bourbon and watched as everyone who remained in Richmond scurried about like ants when their anthill gets wiped away.

As the fires spread in the warehouse district, things started to get hot in my shed. So I escaped to the high ground of the Great House of Government and passed the balance of Sunday evening under the nearby big statue of Father Washington. I laid up in the bushes happily getting drunk on my stolen bourbon while watching as more commissary men toted piles of rebel money and crates of papers onto the Great House grounds.

Sometime during the night, I saw Riverjames Cleburne meandering along with a bulky burlap bag slung over his shoulder and I called to him. He heard me from the other side of the Father Washington statue and looked in my direction, but did not move or call back, and I knew he was worried about who—or what—was calling him by name. So I decided to have some fun. Hiding in the bushes, I summoned him again in a loud whisper.

"Riverjames, c'mon up. Up hea, to the bushes."

He slowly walked toward the line of shrubbery behind the big statue where I lay concealed, his big ole sweaty head bobbing and his shoulders bouncing as he took one careful step at a time. When he got about halfway, he stopped short—leaning in with caution, his noggin thrust forward like a tortoise head poking from the shell.

"Mistah Ba-ba-bush—is you talkin' to me?"

"Yes-sah, Riverjames," I said. "I is talkin' to you." He fell back several hurried steps, his eyes popping and his tortoise head bobbing in and out as though he couldn't decide whether to draw in or stay out.

"Mistah Bush—wha-wha-why you pick me?"

"I pick you 'cause you is a good man," I said, playing God.

"Mistah Ba-Ba-Bush—ain't ya-ya-you 'spose to be afire?"

"Not this time. We already got enough fire 'round here."

He inched closer. "Mistah Bush—watchu wa-wa-want wid ma-ma-me?" With a belly full of fine bourbon I could barely keep up the joke without busting into full-blown guffaws.

"Riverjames," I whispered, "I want you to lead my people to Israel."

"Sah?"

"You heard me. I want you to lead all the freed-up darkies across the river waters to the holy land of emancipated and proclamated promise o'freedom. I wantchu to be my Moses."

"Sah?" he said again, his bulging eyes growing bigger.

"Come closer to me, Riverjames."

"Yes-sah." He stepped forward with caution until he was just a few feet from me.

"Whatchu got in that bag?" I asked.

"To-to-tobacky, sah. I got lots of it. I pa-pa-plan to gift the Yankee when they come to town. I plan to say thankee to de Yankee."

"Tobacco?"

"Yes-sah. I got cha-cha-chew tobacky, pipe-tobacky, and cigar-tobacky. I got 'em all. Ya'll care fo-fo-for a cigar?"

"Do you think the Lord our God would smoke a cigar?" I said, as though displeased.

"I do-do-don't know, sah? Is you really God?" I did not answer. After a while he became worried. "Sah?" he asked, his head bobbing. "Is you still there? I is sa-sa-sorry 'bout offering ya'll a cigar, Mistah Ba-Ba-Bush." Still, I did not respond. He inched closer until his face was only inches from mine in the darkness and I knew the time had come. I thrust my own head from the shrubbery until we nearly touched noses.

"Why if it ain't ole Riverjames!" I barked with a big drunken grin, giving up the joke.

Well—he was so surprised he commenced jumping and dancing and rocking and laughing all the while he was trying to form words but couldn't manage to make any sound except giggle laughter. I did the same. I rolled from the bushes, laid on my back, and we both howled with delight at the stars blinking down from the night sky.

When the fun wore off, I offered him some bourbon, which he refused. He offered me a cigar, which I took, and we both lay under the legs of Father Washington's giant horse, watching the fires slowly burn their way up the hill toward us. After a while, we climbed up the steps of the statue pedestal to lie upon the very top step, right at the horse's feet, directly under Father Washington, where we had a better view. I sipped my bourbon and we both puffed fine cigars while looking down at the flames as they destroyed everything between us and the river.

Concealed there like a bug in a board crack, I let the madness and the thievery and the fires and the night pass me by.

CHAPTER TWENTY-TWO:
COMPSON WINDER

Hell and damn; and damn and hell.

The day got ugly when they came home from church. Master Winder barked some dog orders at me to hitch up the best team to the best traveling wagon; then they both went racing through the house like time itself was on fire.

I was worried about my wife. I did not want to leave her. There was no room for her in the wagon, and when she made voice to join us, Master Winder yelled at her too in the dog voice, giving order that she stay in our room by the stable and keep the door locked. But it won't the Yankees that bothered me. Privately, we welcomed 'em. It foretold the end of the war, and their arrival meant nothing but change for us, which we anticipated would be good change, change for the better. So I should have been fine about it all. But I wasn't. I couldn't say exactly what worried me. There was fear of fighting in the streets. But there was more, too. There was something else not right about it, something that made me think this would end badly. If that were the case, I knew my job was to make certain the badness didn't take me with it.

All during the war, Master and Mistress Winder never got into much of a fit. Being rich, they had little to fret. And having no sons, they never felt the visitation of death at their door. Yet now—now the mistress moved faster than I thought her able and she wept the whole time, sending floods of blubber from her scooped-out nostrils while she flew about packing their bag and hiding their best valuables in nooks and crannies.

After I loaded up Mistress Pegram and that plump Mistress Bartow down below the Ninth Street hill, I thought of asking Master if I could send that Pegram slave girl uptown to join my wife. She looked me over with the same empty upset face as my wife when I left her in the stable. I should have asked him permission. But I didn't. I had three women in the wagon and all of 'em were in varying stages of the weeping-fears at having some Yankee knock 'em to the ground and pull down their petticoats. The way they all looked out at the world from those bulging bug-eyes you'd think every Yankee man headin' our way already had his pants off and his cock pointing skyward, at the ready for any Richmond mistress they could pounce upon. So I didn't ask. I just gee'd the team and drove to the Mayo Bridge, where we got delayed by all the others refugeeing farther south, including what was left of the Johnny boys.

Once across the James, things clogged up more. The muddy roads were not yet dry from our week of rain and all the soldiers and skeedaddling white folks just made 'em worse. Master Winder made the decision to hold to the main road and brave our chances straight through Petersburg, 'stead of detouring. The lesser-traveled roads might be easier but a roundabout, he said, would make the journey even longer.

Some of the soldiers we passed were a misery and their odor required the mistresses to put their handkerchiefs to their noses to avoid the stink. The sentiments I saw whirling in their dead-man eyes held things I did not care to think of—things I knew included seizing and killing and cooking and eating our horses. A lot of 'em begged handouts of food and water, which, the situation being what it was, Master Winder gestured for me to pass 'em by and keep the team moving as fast as I could, allowing for traffic and mud.

When we finally did make some clearance from the passing

assemblies, Mistress Winder withdrew dried fruit and the plump Mistress Bartow unwrapped a quantity of hardtack, and they all had a hasty dinner while I kept the wagon moving as fast as I could.

After many hours, we were barely south of Manchester when a captain ordered us to a halt and slowly walked his starving horse around the Winder wagon and twin horse team, appearing not to believe his eyes. He told Master Winder he must requisition the horses for military use and did not pay any mind at the protests which followed about us being made helpless without means to carry on our evacuation. He would have done it, too, had not a major come by to overrule him, which allowed us to scurry away like people shamed by good fortune.

After that, the skin-and-bones Mistress Pegram asked the Winders if they minded her using what remained of the day's fading light to read her Bible, and Mistress Winder asked her to read aloud, so she did—mostly Job:

> Haggard from want and hunger,
> they roamed the parched land
> in desolate wasteland at night.

I know my Bible. And I well know Job. But at that particular moment, I couldn't help but think of another book. I was listening to Job, but I was thinking of Exodus:

> I am the Lord thy God,
> which have delivered thee
> from the house of bondage.

Night was falling as we drew nigh to Colonial Heights. The lights of Petersburg could be seen on the hill in the distance surrounded by clouds of smoke rising from the battlefield beyond. They all stared hard at the site, making 'em look to me like a wagon full of dumb orphan children.

That's when things changed and I knew I had been right in worrying about the trip.

A crater made by an artillery shell blocked the road. While I slowed to maneuver the team around it, they all got to see what it contained, which made the three women recommence their wailing and bug-eye fears. It was horrible. It upset me, too. That still-smoldering pit contained parts of men and parts of horses all mixed up in a jumble. The explosion that killed them must have occurred recently, as the deep puddle of blood made a clogged tub of liquid darkness that the ground could not absorb.

Then men afoot came running. At first, it looked like they were fleeing battle. But when they grew near to the wagon, they called for me to stop and we all knew they too wanted to take our horses. I made the decision myself without direction from Master Winder. I gee'd the team hard to a full trot, turned the wagon, and we departed the main road. With the sounds of musket and artillery fire behind, I skirted Petersburg by heading west.

Soon after, the mistresses sang my praises for it. "Thank you, Compson," they said, "you're a fine horseman," and "I declare, you did the right thing, Compson."

Darkness came fast after that. Passing locals asked after news of Richmond, which Master Winder summed up in one word: "evacuation." And we began meeting up with white folks heading in the opposite direction. They had been Richmond refugees, but were abandoning their flight to the south as being more than they bargained for, so they were turning back north. One broke-down old farmer by the roadside heard our conversations and offered the use of his barn for the night after making his own inquiry for what news we had. Master Winder let the mistresses make that decision and they said they preferred sleeping in a barn to carrying on with the journey by night. So we pulled onto his private land and unloaded in the darkness.

The barn was overgrown with weeds and befouled with bat droppings, but that didn't bother me because I slept outside with the horses. After making a bed in the hay for Master and Mistress Winder with the horse blankets, I reconnoitered to a patch of soft grass where I could hear the plump Mistress Bartow inside, snoring the night away.

CHAPTER TWENTY-THREE:
PRESIDENT ABRAHAM LINCOLN

It was as fine a day as I have ever dreamed of having.

I had been more than a week at City Point, Virginia, with Mary and my youngest son, Tad. It was there, in full view of the James River and the mouth of the Appomattox, in the hospitality of Lieutenant General Grant and his kindly wife, Julia, that word came that Richmond was evacuated of all armed defenses. There followed a raucous burst of cheers. I can report that hats did fly. There was nothing but glowing smiles alighting the countenances of every man gathered and dedicated to the work of saving this nation.

When I gave order that my staff make ready for the boat journey up the James River to the shores of the rebellion's heart, it met with a round of unanimous, albeit benevolent, objections. It is true—this was not a journey for which anyone prepared. And it is true, it is Richmond, a city laden with manifest danger. But I held to my order nonetheless and advised my adjutants to make haste with all necessary arrangements. I gave them the balance of the evening and all of Monday, April third, to make preparations.

★ ★ ★ ★ ★

THE FIRE:
DAY TWO

MONDAY, APRIL 3, 1865

★ ★ ★ ★ ★

Chapter Twenty-Four:
Miss Francine Pegram

I placed some of my bounty on the kitchen table and dropped the rest on the floor around my chair. Three bundles were easy to figure: the ham, of course; an open crate containing two great glass jugs of whiskey; and there was a large eggshell, the largest I had ever seen—painted with bright colors of red, green, and specks of gold. I don't know why I took it. It posed no use. I eyeballed it with each dash to the street and came to fancy it. On the last trip, I scooped it covetously into my arms and concealed it behind the sycamore.

My hunger came first.

After retrieving the sharpest knife from Missus Pegram's cutlery bowl, I placed the ham directly before me in an open space on the crowded tabletop and carefully rolled back the canvas covering. The meat was cooked fine, and the smoky aroma invaded me, setting my lips and whole body to eagerness. I must have appeared like the ravenous dog about to receive his dinner, unable to avert his eyes as he drools, tasting the first bite at the sight of its preparation by his owner.

I sliced away a streak of surface fat and let it flop-dangle to the side. Then I cut into the smoked meat and pulled off a slab the breadth of my hand. Even though it had spent much of the night as Ninth Street flotsam, it was still warm. The taste was rich and sweet; my body took it greedily into my stomach, where it braced me and set me to a wonderful feast of slicing and swallowing and slicing some more. I ate so much so fast it barely got chewed.

After several slices of meat, I commenced alternating meat with fat. The fat was a clear jelly held firm by a brown crust, melting into rich juice in my mouth that went down as meaty liquid.

Excitement about the unexamined portion of the bounty meddled at me while I ate. As soon as my stomach pains eased, I washed down my wonderful breakfast with water and set about examining the balance of my nighttime harvest.

Stuffed inside the whiskey crate, along with the two bottles, I found a store of shingle nails and a jar of boot buff. That pleased me as it meant I could give my brokens a good shine. Also in the crate was a little canvas satchel partially buried in the nails. I yanked it loose. The canvas was poked through with nail holes and before I could act, part of its contents spilled out, sending up a strong aroma with a warning message to take special care. I knew its nature before cradling the leaking sack in my hands. Someone had concealed a small amount of treasure inside the nail box. It was coffee!

Along with the rich odor came the smell of pecan shells, probably added to the coffee to stretch the grounds for longer use. But I didn't mind—it was coffee, a special treat so wonderful I could hardly believe my good fortune. There was little firewood, but I didn't require very much. I set about making a small fire on the kitchen stove—just enough to heat one kettle, knowing the smoke would go out the back chimney only. While waiting for the water to boil, I studied the rest of my newly gathered bounty.

A muslin-cloth sack contained a new pair of trousers with fresh suspenders, some old shirts, and a hair brush. I set them aside wondering if Extra might find use for them, though they looked small to me.

One canvas bag held papers with more writing on them than

I had ever seen, except in the Bible and other big books. Some of the papers appeared official, with important-looking print on the top about the government, Confederate States of America, Department of War, office of this-and-that, division of so-and-so. Some reminded me of the papers in Missus Pegram's private coffer by her bedside. There were lots of columns of numbers, with check marks added afterward in pencil. I took a wad from these piles and stuffed it in the oven where my coffee water was not yet at boil. The check marks and the columns of numbers disappeared in a blue flame.

Another canvas sack held a painted flower vase wrapped inside a petticoat. The vase did not survive the night and was broken at the top and cracked down the middle, despite the protective wrapping. It rattled while being unwrapped, and when I turned the jagged edge on end the contents spilled out. It was fancy jewelry. A fine pearl necklace and matching pearl ring tumbled to the tabletop. They each had a greenish hue that blended with fine white. The largest of the pearls was mounted in the ring, which appeared to be real gold. I put the necklace around my neck and slid the ring onto my thumb, the only finger it would fit, and continued to study my gathered treasure.

A box held a fancy churchgoing hat belonging to some mistress. It was small and pink in color, with a black lace veil that could drape down over the face or tuck up into a wedge at the top. I removed the blue ribbon from my hair, still there since Missus Pegram tied it ahead of Sunday services, and replaced it with the hat. I pulled the veil down over my eyes. It gave everything a crisscross look. Wearing the hat and pearl necklace, I studied my coffee water.

Almost ready.

I tucked the veil up into the wedge.

There was a smart leather grip with a metal clasp. I opened it and found that it had concealed hinges inside the leather so the top locked into a wide, open position. I knew right away it was a doctor's bag. I withdrew the first item that got my attention because it looked like a kitchen tool, a pouring strainer with a handle and a looped end covered over with cotton muslin for straining out dregs. I set it aside. There was a pair of heavy scooping instruments made of metal, and there were devices for gripping, devices for grabbing, and devices for plucking, drilling, and sawing.

I had never been to a doctor for any of my sicknesses. Once, when I accompanied Missus Pegram during a trip to see Doctor Toms, he would sometimes give me a quick look-over after he finished with her. He poked about at my neck with his large fingers and looked in my mouth with a stick. Then he gave me a pat on the back and said, "That's fine, child, that's fine." One time, when I was in the examining room with Missus Pegram to help her undress and re-dress, he put a cup to my chest that connected to his ears with a hose. He listened, and then with a kindly smile pronounced me fit.

"A fit-a-ninny young'un you are," he said, "just a regular little fit-a-ninny."

"Say 'thank you' to Doctor Toms," Missus told me, so I recited as instructed.

"Thank you, Doctor Toms." Afterward, I remained puzzled about what had just occurred and what its meaning may be.

This leather grip contained the same type of ear-trumpet device Doctor Toms used that day. I withdrew the odd tool from the bag. Imitating him, I put the ends into my ears and rested the cup on my chest. The result was sudden amazement. That sound was familiar to me. I had heard it before. Sometimes, while lying on my bucky-board bed at night, the beating rhythms of my heart would enter deep inside my ear when it was buried snug into the folds of my straw-tick blanket. But that sound was a distant beating, like a notice from afar. This sound was going into both ears through a clever instrument making a thunderous barrage with those same rhythms. I listened to the booming as it echoed, stopped, then boomed again inside me. It was a wondrous discovery. I closed my eyes and let it invade me. This was me—me—talking to myself. It conjured me into a spell, making me pretend I might understand the meaning and interpret it like an apostle of the gospels.

Beat-ah-beat. Beat-ah-beat. Beat-ah-beat. It spoke to me. *Beat-ah-beat. Beat-ah-beat.*

But the spell did not work. I could not understand its meaning, so I put the sounds of my heart to the words of Dr. Toms' redemption that day, and whispered along with my body's rhythms: "fit-a-ninny, fit-a-ninny, fit-a-ninny."

A great pain set in after I removed the plugs from my ears and let the ear-trumpet rest on my neck the way I had seen Dr. Toms wear it. The device had made my ears so sore I could think of nothing else. I rubbed at the insides with the tips of both little fingers. There was an odd feeling deep inside my hearing that scared me and I feared I may have used the device improperly—causing damage. Trying to fix the strangeness, I worked my jaw up, down, and around hoping to set everything back into its proper place. I was relieved when the pain eased up and finally went away.

I left the ear-trumpet where it hung upon my neck, resting atop the pearls; the cup at the end dangled nearly halfway down my body. I mused about my newfound decorations: church hat, fancy pearls, doctor device. What else might I find to add to my attire?

The bubbling hiss of the pot notified me the water was at boil. With no other means at hand, I scooped the precious coffee grounds into the doctor's strainer and poured the water as slowly as I could manage into the nearest container, which was one of Missus Pegram's small mixing bowls. I took care to soak the grounds through and through. The sifting liquid turned light brown at first, then dark brown, then it dyed and swirled around into a rich black, nearly the darkness of the boot buff sitting nearby. Like the ham, the smell invaded me before the taste was upon my lips.

The first sip was nothing but painful. It made me remember the habit Missus Pegram had at the breakfast table of conferring her blessing upon anything that was too hot to partake.

"Whoa. Hot as hello Pete!" she would loudly announce.

I did the same. "Whoa! Hot as hello Pete," I said, speaking to my coffee, plopping my lips up and down to cool the burn. I swirled the coffee around in the mixing bowl, letting the heat rise from it. A large chunk sloshed onto the tabletop, where it quickly ran down to the edge and dripped to the floor in a brown waterfall. It seeped into a crack between the floorboards and disappeared. Watching it, I wondered if Ole Missus Rat liked coffee. After a moment I took another sip. It was still overly hot, but I smacked my lips and sucked in a big breath to make the burn ease up, then swallowed. It was wonderful. I could taste the pecan shell but did not mind. It was coffee, and coffee was coffee. It had been a long time since the kitchen could boast of such fine morning aromas as bacon and coffee. If Missus Pegram were present, she would enjoy it with me and we would both drink in quiet pleasure. On that Monday morning I drank my coffee without her. The taste of it was rich and hot and wonderful.

During my nighttime adventures, I had picked up a burlap bag that held only a box. Withdrawing it now for the first time, I saw it was a wooden chest, medium in size. The bold words printed on top read "Property of the Confederate States of America." Underneath, written in a faded, scratchy pencil, were the words: "Captain Zollicoffer."

Except for "zero," which means cipher, I didn't know any

words that started with *Z,* and for a long time when first learning my letters with Missus Pegram, it was my favorite one. I liked the sound and feeling of "zzz," as it sang from the end of my tongue and bounced against my teeth. "Zzzuh!" I enjoyed making it say.

Below Captain Zollicoffer's name, in the same scratchy writing, there were war words about where he did his work: "Army so and so" and "Regiment this and that." There was no latch and the box opened easily.

Like the coffee earlier, another wonderful aroma struck me. And like the coffee, I knew its meaning before seeing it. It was tobacco. There were three large, sweet-smelling cigars of the type Master Pegram would call "Cubano." Also inside the box was a small pistol, a wad of paper letters held together with a purple ribbon, a clever little jar of tooth powder, and a tin drinking mug.

I held the box to my face and inhaled the rich odor of tobacco. The smell of it conjured me to thinking on the recent past when buggy-wagons loaded with bundles of freshly chopped or cured tobacco clogged the streets. Farms from all around sent their crop into town, while Charleston and Savannah sent it up by boat. "From Richmond to the World," read the fancy painted words on the wall of the Shockoe warehouse. "The Best Chew Is a Bright Chew," read another.

The three cigars had been jostled about and were showing tiny nicks to the wrapper leaf, but no serious damage had been done to their smoking value. I set them aside for safety.

The little jar of tooth powder looked to be carved from some animal's horn, maybe goat I fancied, or some exotic creature in Africa. Words on the side read "India Mint Tooth Powder," and there was a tiny pour spout. I tapped some of the yellow-white contents onto my palm; it was crusty, like pebble dust. I wet a fingertip on my tongue and dabbed at the little pile in my hand, which turned it into a paste, then I rubbed it to my teeth. The gummy mess had a flavor of green mint, but I didn't like it and quickly spit it into the kitchen bucket used for floor droppings. I washed the taste from my mouth with a gulp of coffee, which had reached the perfect warmth for drinking.

The ribbon-wrapped letters appeared written in a lady's hand and I felt sorry to have come across Captain Zollicoffer's personal items. Whoever he was, I did not care to worsen my deed by violating the private thoughts of his heart as well. I hoped he was alive, but feared otherwise as the odd ones seemed to only claim goods from those who were not around to protect their worldly possessions.

As for the pistol—it was much smaller than the shiny pistol Master Pegram packed into his satchel when heading off to war work and there were droplets of oily grease oozing up from the machine parts in the middle. The bone handle was the color of honey.

I had seen guns aplenty. They were always about. Nearly all the Butternut boys had musket-rifles when they marched past the house heading north to the war, or south to war. The officers had pistols and some of them were handsome things with pearly handles tucked into fine leather belt-pouches. I had never handled any and the only gun I ever really held was the old Pegram family musket, the long gun in the cellar's "memorial to antiquity." That one was longer and much older than the muskets carried by the Butternut. It was a heavy thing that took all my strength to tote downstairs on a Sunday afternoon when the house was getting some cleaning and clearing.

"Oh, Miss Francine, you can do it," Missus barked from behind me on the steps, toting an armful of worn-out cottons soon to become rags for cleaning. We had started to take in Butternut borders from time to time, so we were moving odds and ends from the upstairs guest room to become cellar storage. Master Pegram was already there nailing up a peg board for hanging the old gear.

"Welly, well. Look at our li'l ole pantry rat toting granddaddy's old musket," he said, enjoying the sight as I teetered down the cellar steps struggling to keep the long barrel balanced ahead of me.

"I declare, doesn't she just look the picture of a Boston Minuteman," said Missus Pegram.

"Mmmm-mmh! Why, you handle that old flintlock like a true colonial patriot. Maybe we should conscript you against the Yankees," he said.

Looking now at the pistol in Captain Zollicoffer's box vexed me. It made me glad Extra was not present because I knew he would take it for himself and I knew too that he would feel pleased about possessing it. I heard tell that some field hands might be allowed to hunt with their master, and take in a rabbit for their stew pot. But in Richmond, there was no such thing. And for Extra, I conjured that owning a stolen pistol could only come to trouble for him. Taking it by the handle, I carefully carried it to the pantry, tucked it into one of the empty apple barrels, and covered it with the burlap bag that held the Zollicoffer box. I closed the box containing the private letters tied with a purple ribbon and pushed it aside.

I did, however, help myself to the Captain's tin cup, which I used to transfer my coffee from the bowl. It had a well-worn handle that fit my fingers nicely

Braced by the coffee and ham breakfast, I returned to the unexamined bundles still arranged about the table and floor and quickly plumbed the contents of each, measuring their usefulness.

The effort turned up the following list of sundries both queer and natural:

○ a leather grip filled with ladies' petticoats, crinolines, bloomers, garters, and two pair of fancy shoes (much too large for me)

○ one muslin sack with two items: a sewing kit, containing mostly buttons but also one mostly used spool of brown stitching thread, and one new spool of blue knitting yarn

○ a metal-handled hand mirror (broken) tied to a matching comb and hair brush

○ one seed crate filled with a score of small leather-bound books, each not much bigger than my hand—the Bible being the only one I recognized for certain

○ a leather horse purse containing a clump of wrinkled Confederate money, some of which scattered across the tabletop and fell to the floor (I knew the bills to have no value)

○ a large burlap wrap, which unfolded multiple bric: a fancy blue glass perfume jar (broken during the night, which soaked the musty burlap making it smell oddly sweet); two fancy white bone smoking pipes (one broken); a fancy tin spittoon; and a fancy China bed pot (with a badly chipped rim)

○ an oil sack holding half a bushel of rotten sweet potatoes, which befouled my nostrils, so I quickly heaved it to the corner to join the chewed-up carcass bones of Ole Mister Rat

○ a fine beaded purse containing a pair of white gloves (one with a hole in the forefinger tip) and an assortment of lady's toiletries, including powder and hair-pins

That concluded the entire bounty.

Aside from the ham, coffee, and cigars, there was little among the stolen sundries that posed any use, except that I knew Master Pegram would be pleased with the two bottles of whiskey. If he didn't take them to Daddy's Little Farm when he arrived, they could be used as barter once the ham gave out.

I sipped more coffee, still warm and bracing to my insides. The giant eggshell was the queerest member of my bounty, its golden-colored speckles glimmering in the morning light. I knew Easter to be the next holiday. Perhaps it was to be the center of a showy Easter dinner at one of the rich homes on Grace Street, possibly Mistress Barksdale or Granberry or even Mistress Winder at her Main Street home.

The most exceptional item in the whole odd assortment was the pearl necklace. Real pearls have real value and all the mistresses of Richmond possessed them. Some wore short strings and some wore long strings that dangled to their exposed bosom-tops. They all fingered their pearls at different times during socials.

"Ohh, Ruth, so nice to see you," Mistress Barksdale would say, drawing out the words while clutching her pearls with a wide display of teeth.

"Ohh, Margaret, very well indeed," Missus Pegram would say in response, fingering her own more modest pearl drapery, as though Mistress Barksdale had asked after her health, which she had not.

That was their way when they were not overly acquainted or they were not on each other's list for socials and church meetings. Mistresses Pegram, Bartow, and Garland treated each other with familiarity. But when mistresses of the larger homes on Grace and Franklin were encountered, the streets and stores were filled with the sounds of "oohs" and "ohhs" while all parties stood about picking at their pearls and smiling big smiles.

"Why, Mistress Barksdale," I said aloud, fingering my own string of pearls, "why I do declare—that is such a lovely Easter egg. And so big."

"Oh, thank you, Miss Francine," I said playing both sides of my game.

Being recovered from my fever and feeling emboldened by a belly full of ham, I poured more coffee into Captain Zollicoffer's tin mug and lit one of the Cubanos in the stovetop fire. I had smoked only twice before—each time with Extra during our occasional get-togethers at the fence behind the privy—and thought it to be pleasurable. I drew on the Cubano, inhaling the rewarding aroma and blowing it out with satisfaction. It was wonderful.

With the heart trumpet and pearl necklace still around my neck, the pink hat still perched on my head, tin cup in one hand, and Cubano trailing smoke in the other hand—I ventured into the parlor like a grown-up proctor come to examine his slaves.

The full shine of morning flashed from the drape's borders, casting more than enough brightness to light every aspect of the room. Nothing in it had changed, which seemed odd. Somehow, I felt that I had changed, so why not the parlor? I had been a thief in the night, risked my own safety, made clever choices, and satisfied my hunger. Shouldn't the house understand and respond accordingly?

Though crooked, the four pictures of Paris, France, held steady above the fancy settee. It was still a pleasant afternoon for the ladies with parasols who strolled past the big church. The wide avenue still bustled with fancy buggies filled with happy couples and laughing children. The same men labored upon the same boats upon the still-flowing river, while overhead, strollers still looked down upon them with idle admiration. They were all unfazed by the changes at number 212 Ninth Street. But I was not certain about my least favorite picture. There was something new there that worried me. The rotund dandy in furs was still being served coffee by his adoring ladies

yet his face seemed to look out at me with a small but noticeable difference. One corner of his plump mouth turned up; one
eye in his long, disapproving face arched down. He seemed to
sneer at me, hurling scorn with his taunty pomp in objection to
my pearls, ear-trumpet, pink hat, coffee tin, and fine cigar. He
seemed to say, "There may be only one peacock in this house."
I never did enjoy that picture.

Below the four pictures, the China-head doll sat upon the
fancy red settee, her dress spread out proper, head tilted to one
side. She stared forward, blank and empty. I wondered if there
mayn't be more in those glassy eyes. It was a small change in
the sharp blue color of her eyes that glistened with new
knowledge and said to me: "Well, now! Look at you!"

I stoked on my cigar and blew streams of smoke into the
parlor. Staying clear of the entryway, I peeked past the drape's
edge to Ninth Street and beyond. Judging from the sun, I
calculated the time to be mid-morning, perhaps nine o'clock.
Directly across Ninth Street, the Basin Bottom Livery was a
darkened ruin. The odd ones of the night were nowhere to be
seen.

Standing there, I resumed my play of vanity. I tugged at my
pearls.

"Well, Mistress Barksdale, so nice to see you," I said, drawing
out the words as best I could, with a wide set of teeth.

"Ohh, Miss Francine," I answered, "I declare! How is that
lovely home of yours on Ninth Street?"

"Why Mistress Barksdale! It's fine, just fine. Do join us for
Easter dinner, won't you?"

"Oh, Miss Francine," I curtsied with appreciation. "Thank
you so very much. You always set such a lovely table."

I raced upstairs, where the front window had a superior view
of the street. There were no heavy drapes, just a lace curtain. I
stooped carefully to look at Richmond from that height. The

vista from the house, down the hill to the river, was a scene from the devil's lair. Hell and torment laid waste to nearly everything. Fires still raged to the east. Only to the northern oblique could I see buildings untouched by the blazes of the night and previous day. The Great House of Government stood upon its grand hill, completely spared.

I turned away from the ugliness and resumed my game. "Oh, Mistress Granberry, do come downstairs to the parlor. We'll be so much more comfortable there."

"Very well, Mistress Francine. Let's retire to the parlor."

Back in the parlor I let loose. I played the rolls of Missus Pegram, the fancy Mistresses Granberry and Barksdale, and myself; I pranced about smoking, sipping coffee, and pretending to serve sweets, then meats, then fine wine.

"Oh, Mistress Pegram, these meat biscuits are so buttery. Just wonderful."

"Thank you so much. My Miss Francine made them, of course. I declare. I just don't know what I would do without her."

"Why, Miss Francine, you must tell us, what is the wondrous secret? Is it the salt? How much salt do you put in your bread dough?"

"Oh! And that pecan fudge! Oh, so rich!"

"Oh, yes, indeed. I declare. Mmmm."

"Miss Francine, did you prepare that fudge, too?"

"Oh, yes. My Miss Francine did it all. She prepares the best pecan fudge in the whole capital city. Why even Mistress Lee has paid a calling just to sample it."

"Oh? How is Mistress Lee?"

"Well, she's fine. Has arthritis, you know. But she's fine. She stopped by last evening for tea and some of Miss Francine's fine sugar cookies."

"Ohh?"

"Oh, yes. President Davis loves those sugar cookies, too. I declare!"

I went on with my game, clutching my pearls, smoking, drinking my coffee, and waving my arms about the kitchen and parlor until I grew hoarse speaking in such high-pitched tones.

Then I turned to other ideas. I plopped down upon the fancy settee and spoke in a low tone, like a man.

"Good evening, Miss China-Head Doll. So nice to see you." I put the heart trumpet device to her chest and pretended to listen.

"Why, you certainly sound fine! Yes, ma'am, real fine. You are a just a little ole fit-a-ninny. And so cute, too, uh-hmmm." I patted the China-head doll, making her droop to one side. "Just a cute little ole fit-a-ninny. Why, bless your heart!"

My indulgences came to a sudden end when I heard a noise that had two parts, the first being a kind of a slamming sound of wood upon wood. I can only describe the second part of the noise as a quaking rattle. I could not place either as belonging to any regular event. It was not the slamming of any door or the solid plop of a footfall upon the steps either front or back. The first noise seemed to come from the kitchen but the second part had no clear location at all and seemed to belong to the very air I was breathing. I wondered if something had fallen from the sky.

The Thomas clock heard it, too. Silent since the day before, it delivered a single chime. It was a not a regular chime signifying time, but a reluctant, almost bashful tone that rang out one brief moment after the rattle shimmied through the house. Bashful or not, it was a chime nonetheless which I understood to be a toll of warning.

CHAPTER TWENTY-FIVE: MISS FRANCINE PEGRAM

It must have been as it was for the Butternut when the fated event that privately tormented their thoughts had finally come to challenge their publicly boasted grit. While sleeping, eating, at loiter, lollygagging under trees—the alarm sounded, hammering like a chisel upon their bones to muster for the dreaded moment. It's the Yankees. The Yankees are coming!

Everything stopped. I gulped a great measure of air. A silent chill took a grip upon me then spread quickly to grip the house, the street, the entire world. I listened as the night owl on the tree limb listens in the moonlight. If Ole Missus Rat had been scurrying in her cellar den, I believe I would have heard her pattering about. But there was nothing. The house was dead quiet.

Could it have been a harmless event, maybe a loose board falling from the roof or a rotten tree limb breaking free to slam the outside wall?

Numb and silent, I wondered if craning my neck forward would make a revealing noise. If I stood up, would the cushion springs coiled inside the fancy red settee betray me with telltale creaks? I waited. I knew the tones of footfall upon every floorboard in the house and could quickly conjure the location had there been anything. But there was nothing.

I slowly stood; my toes clutched the oaken floorboards for the firmest possible balance. The smoke from my cigar curled outward in the airless parlor. The pearl necklace around my neck rattled slightly against the ear trumpet. From the parlor I could see the fancy dining room and knew it to be clear of danger. The hallway was unaltered, my service chair remained untouched, the stairs appeared proper. From the middle of the hallway I craned my neck to peer upward to the second-floor landing but observed nothing out of the ordinary.

In the creaking passageway leading to the kitchen I craned my neck past the corner. Still nothing. I tread the boards lightly, but could not avoid making the one loose board squeak like a bird with such familiarity that I fancied it was needling me with ill laughter.

The kitchen was now the only unexplored room on the first floor. Before entering, I listened hard for anything that might explain the cause. The back door worried me the hardest. If the noise meant the rear entry was breached—the intruders, be they thieves or Yankees, would already be enjoying my assembled bounty—the whiskey in particular. Of course, a band of Yankees in the kitchen would be noisy, so it all added to nothing I could understand. I counted to three in my head then hurriedly rushed through the final steps to the kitchen.

Again, nothing. Everything was ordinary. My bounty was untouched; the back door remained closed. I could see the yard through the kitchen window, the garden and the privy beyond it. Nothing seemed put out of order.

I took a grateful breath, my first easy one since the strange noise rattled both me and the house. I stoked my cigar, drew a long haul on it, and blew a thin stream of smoke across the kitchen where I watched it fade from thick cloud into thin air. I fingered my pearls.

"Oh, thank you Lord," I said. " 'Twas some unknown something. 'Twas neither Yankee nor thief from the street come to invade the house. Thank you, Lord. Lordy, Lord. Thank you!"

I required a trip to the privy. I eyed the chamber pot with the chipped edge sitting on the kitchen table but decided against it. A walk to the privy would also allow me to view the Spotswood yard up close. I would be able to see who was about and make some inquiries into matters that be.

I studied the yard from the back-door window. The day was heavy with moisture; stubborn, mid-morning dew clung to the fresh weeds in the dilapidated garden with a weight that made them droop. The few remaining loblollies were smaller still and appeared caked over with a greasy smear, the ground-fall of smoke and ash delivered by the fires. A small chill passed under the door to my feet, which worsened my need to get to the privy. I curled my two big toes, making both of them crack with a pair of loud, satisfactory pops. The path to the privy looked clear and safe. I took a long haul on my Cubano then placed it upon a dish next to the coffee pot. I put Captain Zollicoffer's coffee tin next to that. I blew the smoke out in a thin stream. Then I stepped out to make the walk on the privy pathway.

The odor of burned Richmond was a bolt to my nostrils. The smell of the fires had been a heavy presence in the house, but now that I was outside, it was a shock how strong it was and how ugly. It wasn't just an odor of burned wood; it smelled of a horrible variety of charred everything. I wondered about the nails that held the boards together. What about mortar and metal? The list of ingredients in the stew of odors hammered at me: stables, houses, fancy French furniture, whole warehouses, tobacco, cotton, horses, dogs. Wide streaks of gray sky lined the west. Were they really clouds or were they layers of Richmond burned and ascended to heaven?

During the short walk, quick flashes of morning sun shown through the rising smoke and felt good as they warmed my face. Just as I pulled at the privy door, a smell of fresh honeysuckle rose through the bitterness.

As always, my legs dangled over the seat ledge, but it was the first time I noticed them being long enough for my toes to scrape the privy floorboards. A rusted nail protruded from one board and I worked it with my big toe. It wiggled a little, but it would not return deeper into the hole when jabbed down. A sow bug emerged from a nearby crack. It came halfway out, looking as though it were seeking explanation for the disturbance to his home caused by the idle work of my toe. I conjured a picture of his family sleeping under the board; if the disturbance were great, they could each roll up into a tiny ball, protected by a hard outer skin, and simply wait for the disturbance to pass. I stopped wiggling the nail. After a moment, the bug seemed relieved and disappeared back into the crack, returning to his home and family under the board. My feet were wet from the short walk through morning hay grass and coated over with greenish bran; I rubbed them together, knocking some off.

My legs were dirty and skinny. I wondered if they would grow wider at the hips like a real woman as they also grew longer. I could not imagine that really happening. Being longer now, they appeared skinnier than ever. The sight brought to mind Extra's vow to me. When I became a woman—we would be married. But with skinny legs and hips, I conjured I was still a girl.

The familiar oak branch drooped just beyond the ledge of the privy window, blossoming with soft greenery—but the fires had coated the fresh leaves and buds with an even fresher coat of ashen pallor. No birds gathered. Neither was there a sound of bees or other buzzing things despite the promise of spring, which normally sends up a noisy celebration of all things that fly.

Beyond the Spotswood fence, the hotel outbuildings were lonesome looking. All windows were dark, all pit-fire materials left where they lay. One black pot dangled from its spit, twisting slowly. I could not guess where everyone was. There was no indication inside or out that the main outbuilding sheltered anyone.

The balance of the day loomed. Perhaps Extra would return, or Master Pegram. If so, I would share my breakfast bounty with them. But I needed to clean the kitchen, which had become a comic torment from my unpacking. Nails, useless money, petticoats, a giant egg, and all the rest of my stolen bounty remained scattered about. Perhaps I would clean myself, too, if I could pump a bucket of water without drawing too much attention before returning to the house. And I could use the boot buff on my brokens.

I went to the well pump. A green serpent scurried from under the gooseneck handle. In three quick spurts of movement it came round to the sunshine, pausing upon the lip of the spigot. It was the length of my little finger. Its tongue flicked once then took a breath, making its green body heave with a replenishing sigh. I moved forward and it darted down the pump shaft and ran to another station of rest at the edge of the well platform, where it flicked its tongue and sighed again.

The water pump resisted movement at first, as it always did. My usual manner was to lean hard on the gooseneck with the help of my body weight to get it moving up and down properly, but I feared too much muscle would make it squeak loudly. I kept a sharp vigil in all directions, wondering if my noggin appeared like a bird's head when it darts about with caution. Nothing new or alarming appeared on any front, so I leaned into the handle, working it loose with only a little noisy objection from the rusty primer, until it bobbed up and down with ease.

The first few spurts loosened a filthy coat of fire ash, setting it floating inside the bucket. I stopped pumping to rinse it. The green serpent was gone, likely reconnoitered to the weedy grass.

Now with a rinsed bucket, and still no signs of any gathering attention, I commenced the whole effort a second time.

Being familiar with water toting, I know that two buckets are easier to manage because you can strike a balance. Oddly, a single bucket seems heavier because it is awkward. But wanting to make haste, and needing only one bucket, I pumped only one.

The presence of trouble was not immediately apparent. I backed my way into the kitchen, working at keeping the door open with one hand, straining to avoid spillage with the other. Stooped over, walking backwards one careful baby step at a time, I eyed the floor I knew so well, knowing when I was close enough upon the table to release my burden. Once there, I squared my feet and shoulders, gripped the bucket with both hands, braced, and spun about to hoist it to tabletop.

"Well, hello, Li'l Miss!" were his first words, garbled by a mouth full of ham. "I see your missus has evacked without you. I declare, you must be lonesome in this big ole house all by yourself."

The shock was great. It was the foul green-eyed Butternut called Lieutenant Dunnovant. He was sitting at the table—my table. Both elbows perched on the edge, both forearms pointed up casually, as though he were surrendering. One hand clutched a slab of ham, the fingers soaking with moistness of fat. The fingers of the opposite hand held the cigar I had left in a countertop dish, its smoke curled thickly behind him.

The alarm left me unable to control my labor, the bucket went flying with a clatter, its contents spilled against the wall and quickly gathered to a puddle that drained into the corridor. He slurped as he spoke, working at a half-chewed slab of ham still dangling from his lips, newly swollen with a great purple sore in one corner.

"It is so nice to see you again, Li'l Miss." He eyed me up and down. When the ham disappeared past his lips he put the cigar—my cigar—to them, took a long haul and sent the smoke swirling across the table filled with my gathered bounty. The purple sore on his lower lip was so large I conjured it may bust open. He was careful not to let the Cubano touch that part of his mouth. I could not imagine what sort of beating he must have taken since I last saw him. There were other bruises too, scrapes to his face and one eye slightly darkened. He was no longer wearing butternut gray, having apparently traded the smelly uniform for a garish set of bruises and somebody else's trousers. And he no longer smelled foul. Despite his goose-egg and darkened eye, he was shaved and washed.

"What a mighty fine table you set, Li'l Miss," he said, gesturing to the ham and coffee and—with special approval in his puffy face—to the two whiskey bottles. "I declare, it is truly fine!"

I wanted to run, but he was too close. I decided to wait for better timing.

His eyes settled upon the pearls around my neck.

"And I declare," he said, "you have arrived at your fine table wearing nothing but the finest jewels." He was getting set to reach for the necklace.

"What happened to your face?" I blurted, hoping to change his mind. He had not yet seen the pearl ring on my thumb. Holding my right hand to the side, I twisted the ring around my thumb so the pearl faced inward toward my palm. At first chance, I let it fall from my thumb into the pocket of my gingham.

"Well now," he said, "there is still a war going on. Ain't it so?" His eyes never let loose of me. I conjured he knew I was set to bolt for the back door if I saw a razor's slice of profit to the effort.

"Ya mean the Yankees did that to your lip? The Yankees are in

Richmond?"

"Well now, Li'l Miss, I didn't say that did I?"

I stared dumbly, waiting my chance.

"Sometimes to get what you want in this life, you just gotta take your licks." He took another draw from the Cubano.

"Most everybody left town. Afraid of the Yankees," I sputtered.

"Uhh-hmm."

"Did the Yankees start the fires?"

"Well now, Li'l Miss, if the Yankees ain't here yet, how could they be the ones what did that?"

I pretended to relax. "You mean we, I mean you, I mean the Butternut boys set the fires?"

"Well it won't Marse Robert himself. But I allow that must be it, on orders most like from Marse Jeff. His bureaus and the like. But it got out of hand most like. I can't imagine even government fools in their Sunday suits would do this to the capital city with intent." He kept a watch on the pearls and eyed me over with the goat face, the same way he did at the pump the previous morning. I knew he meant me no good. My skin twitched as I worked to invent some option for myself.

"Mister President Davis left town yesterday. I saw him myself when he departed church early. He cut a path up Ninth Street."

"Uhh-hmm? Is 'at a fact? Well now." He inhaled another ham slug. His tongue licked the rich grease that lingered on his lip, carefully avoiding the purple sore. Inside the swollen purple was a white ring, inside the white was a red center.

He took another long draw on the Cubano, leaning a smidgen closer to me as he did. He lowered his voice and spoke in a tone as though in confidence, "That's when he heard the news, most like."

"What news?"

"Why Li'l Miss, you know as good as anyone else." He smiled

at me the way masters and mistresses did sometimes, an airy kind of grin that told me I was doing something that met with approval. It was the same smile Doctor Toms gave me when he listened to my heart, the same as when Mistress Bartow thanked me for serving her more sweet potatoes. In this case, it was a smile that gave me a glint of hope. Maybe he would go easy on me. "If Richmond is afire," he went on, "and it is; if the Yankees are coming, and they are; then it only means one thing, Li'l Miss."

"What's that?"

"Why now, that's easy, Li'l Miss!" His smile grew bigger by a thin edge and even displayed some generosity.

"It is?"

"Sure. Go ahead," he encouraged. "Give it a try." I wasn't sure of his meaning. For a moment I thought he might be inviting me to make my planned bolt for the back door, which we both knew I was itchy to commence.

"It mean, uhh—"

"Hmm-hmm. Go ahead, Li'l Miss."

"Umm . . ."

"Uh-huh."

"Butternut lost!" I blurted loudly.

His face altered with such quickness it surprised me. His sassy grin fast disappeared. That was all right—it was not a real smile and it meant me no good. But the face that replaced it was startling. It was not a mean face. Nor was it angry. It was just different, suddenly altered, as though he were puzzled. It reminded me of the way a bird dog looks when a creature suddenly arrives in his view without prior warning, some squirrel or rabbit that he had neither heard nor smelled is suddenly right in front of him, mocking his existence.

I caught him off his guard and wondered what it would mean. My big toes pressed at the kitchen floorboards, flexing, getting into better position to hoist me into a hard bolt. I kept my face neutral so as not to give away my intentions, but my skin twitched with urgings and I worried he'd see me getting set. I shifted my weight to my right leg, the better to push off to the left—toward the door. Then, slowly, his face changed again and the sour smile returned.

"Well now, Li'l Miss. I guess that's the pure meaning of it, ain't it? You did cut right to the very core of the thing didn't ya?"

"Sah?"

"Ya summed it good, Li'l Miss."

"Sah?"

"Didn't I say you were a 'smart Li'l Miss.' I did tell you yesterday that you are smart. Didn't I?" I stared at his purple sore without answering. "I say, didn't I tell you so yesterday?"

"Sah?"

"That you are smart little miss. Didn't I tell you?"

"Yessah."

"Why just look at all this here. I do declare." He swallowed another chunk of ham and gestured at the table laden with stolen bounty, sputtering bits past his sore lip as he spoke with a full mouth. "We got ham and coffee and cigars and all kinds of doodads. Yes, ma'am! You were busy during the night. And look at this here. A big ole Easter egg. Did that egg take your fancy Li'l Miss?" He eyed the pearl necklace. "Yes, ma'am! You sure do have a taste for finery." Once again he was set to reach for the necklace.

"Watchu mean?"

"Mean about what?"

"That I cut to the core, sah? That Butternut done lost?"

"Oh, yes. Well 'course, the plain matter is, that's not exactly the way. Least, not just yet. As it stands now, Marse Robert is on the run. And a true run it is this time." He sighed and briefly looked away but quickly reconnoitered. It was my moment—lost.

"And the Yankees?" I asked.

"Well, now, Li'l Miss, if Marse Robert is on the run, then the Yankees must be chasing him, ain't they?"

"So they not coming to Richmond?"

"Oh my. Oh my, Li'l Miss. They're coming. They are coming sure enough. There's enough of 'em they can do it all. Yes ma'am! There's enough of 'em they can chase Marse Robert, and march into Richmond, and stoke their factories in their Cleveland-towns and their Baltimore-towns, and eat their fancy Boston beans all at the same time. Yes, ma'am! They can do it all."

"How many?"

"Well, now, Li'l Miss. You sure do have a way of cutting to the summed-up core, don't ya? I reckon that's my work now. Seeing about the 'how many.' Seeing and counting, and counting and seeing. That's what I'm doing. What'ja think of that?" I only puzzled at his words.

"Sah?"

"You ever hear of Major Mosby, Li'l Miss?"

"No, sah."

"Uh-huh. Well, no matter. That's what I'm doing. Seeing and counting, and counting and seeing."

"When they gonna get here?"

"Well, now, Li'l Miss, let's see. Unless I miss it wide, they were done hard marching before morning light. I reckon they commenced an easy walk into east Richmond by early morn." He took another chunk of ham and spewed more bits past his purple sore. "So . . . oh . . . well . . . I'd say they're due at the Capitol Building . . . coming in on an east-north-east oblique . . . uh . . ." He glanced at the ham, then back at me, and gave a small shrug. "Right now. Yes, ma'am. I'd say right about now.

They'll probably be on Capitol Hill any minute now."

He didn't seem fearful of the idea. He eyed me hard all over again with the billy-goat face and I understood that, having eaten, along with the timing of the Yankees, he was set to commence some new action. Just then, his greed got the best of all other urgings; his eyes wandered to study the pearls one last time. "Those truly are some mighty fine pearls, Li'l Miss. Yes, indeed, mighty fine."

I made my move.

I got as far as the back door and even had it partially opened before he was upon me, closing the door with an angry slam. If the main door had been open, if I had only the screen door to contend with, I would have been over the fence and into the Spotswood out-yard before he could've cleared the back stoop. But I was caught. He held me fast by the shoulders and took me back to the table, where he commenced "Li'l Miss-ing" me and "I declaring" me and "tut-tutting" me. He pushed aside some of my stolen bounty to create a space on the table then hoisted me to sit in the cleared out space, picking me up by the shoulders and plopping me down as if I were a Christmas goose at supper table. Without bumping the pink hat at all, he carefully removed the pearls from my neck and let them fall into the pocket of his trousers. Then he took the horn end of the ear trumpet and put it to my chest. He pretended to be a doctor and commenced a new manner.

"Well now, 'tick-tick.' " Then, "Well now, 'tock-tock,' " he said, pretending to listen to my heart rhythms. "You got purty light brown eyes, Li'l Miss. Didn't I say yesterday that you was purty?"

I knew I was in a bad way and I confess I lost all conjure for better options.

CHAPTER TWENTY-SIX:
MISS FRANCINE PEGRAM

There are words—but I cannot bring myself to say them. So I will use the words I can manage, to get at the meaning of it. He pleasured himself upon me as a man takes pleasure with a woman—first on the kitchen table, then again upstairs where he carried me under his arm like a scoop of Monday laundry and also where he ransacked Missus Pegram's chester drawers and Master Pegram's wardrobe in search of valuables. In the border's guest room where he found nothing else to his liking as being worth taking, he went at me again, talking nasty at me past his purple lip-sore the whole time until he finished.

Then he dragged me back to the kitchen. He squeezed me into a chair behind the table and slid the table hard against the wall so I was pinned tight between the wall at my back and the tabletop at my front. He opened one of the two whiskey bottles stolen during the night, lit the second of the three Cubanos after the first got smashed during what little fight I could summon, and plunked himself down next to me so I had no avenue of escape.

I hurt. I was sore everywhere. During one of his dog mounts, he slapped me a hard pop that knocked off the pink hat, making my noggin throb. Bones, flesh, muscle, soul, heart, head—it all ached. My arms were gone limp where he grabbed and squeezed down hard on me when I tried to run. Not that I couldn't still run if given the chance. I could. And I was still plotting my escape, despite my nakedness. But he knew that too, which is why he squeezed me into a tight spot at the table as he set about tending to his other appetite—whiskey.

The drunker he got—the more I thought of Captain Zollicoffer's pistol with the honey bone handle that lay hidden under a burlap bag in one of the pantry barrels. It was the one item in the house still undiscovered by the invader and, were he to find it, I knew he would take a keen interest.

In between eating more ham, smoking, and getting drunk on whiskey—he went at me on the tabletop one more time. This time, instead of talking nasty at me, he sang out with the Dixie song, keeping his musical pace while working on his pleasures. When he finished, he jammed me back into the chair—again squeezing me between table and wall where he had kept me handily confined.

He had been there all day and was even starting to sober up a bit when he decided to pack up just past dark. He corked up what was left of the whiskey and slid it into a leather sack beside the unopened bottle, along with the best pair of brass candle-holders in the house and a broken pocket watch taken from the Pegram bedside tables. The pearl necklace was still in his trousers' pocket. At the back door he paused and turned back for a final look. He ran his eyes around the room, studied me in the jammed-back chair, what remained of the ham scattered across the table, and the tormented mess of useless Butternut money, broken bric, pink hat, giant Easter egg, my gingham dress, and the devoured body of Ole Mister Rat, all of it laying about the befouled kitchen floor.

"I told you once 'bout keeping your business to yourself," he said just ahead of closing the door behind him. "Being a smart Li'l Miss, you'll figure that out. Secrets are best kept secret."

I wondered briefly if I might manage to fetch Captain Zollicoffer's pistol then chase him down and shoot him dead before he cleared the back fence.

"One more thing," he said. "Give my regards to Marse Robert next time he comes into the parlor."

Chapter Twenty-Seven:
Miss Francine Pegram

"Hello!"

It was a man's loud voice followed by knocking noises. I looked for Lieutenant Dunnovant to reenter the back door but it did not happen. He was gone, though I was uncertain how long he'd been departed. It was dark outside.

"Hello," it came again.

I slowly pushed the kitchen table away and stood; my arms and shoulders ached mightily where he held me down and gripped me to drag me from room to room. I tiptoed past the clutter of the kitchen floor and stepped into the corridor.

"Hello."

In the parlor, I peeped past the curtain, where I could make out great movements of men and horses in the night. I tiptoed to the entryway. The shadow of a man spilled through the window. The loud rap came again, followed by the man's voice again.

"Hello?"

I knew it was neither Master Pegram nor Extra. I stood behind the door.

"Hello. You inside there," the voice said, this time with impatience. "Hello, hello."

I was not thinking normal. No action other than the one I took came to mind. The front door latch snapped with its familiar clicking sound when I unlocked it and turned the knob to open the door.

A tall boy in a blue uniform stood on the porch. He seemed stunned. He just stared at me, like he'd never seen a slave girl before. He looked back at the street, then turned to me, then nervously looked back at the street again. He was not at all dirty. His face was smooth, clean, and very pale, coated over with blotches of baby's pink blush.

I didn't have to ask. I knew he was a Yankee. It's true, it's true, I thought. They're here. They're in Richmond. A Yankee is standing on the front porch! A real, live Yankee! He turned away from me to speak.

"Uh, miss, we're checking all the houses . . . door to door . . . for safety . . . making sure no regulars are concealed." I couldn't think why he would show me his back, unless that's the way all Yankees talk to each other.

"All right, Private. Go on to the next house over." It was a second voice that boomed orders from the street, orders that quickly sent the blushing, rosy-cheeked boy down the steps without looking back. I studied the other Yankee man as he approached the porch with a fire torch for seeing better in the sooty Richmond night. He stopped short of the first step.

"Listen, child, you all right?"

I did not answer. He was much older, not a boy at all but a grown man, round and heavy like Mistress Bartow except that he was quite short. And he was in possession of the biggest nose I had ever seen. Were it a wedge of pie, that nose would be called a generous slice. His uniform had a few markings of importance. Behind him, the street swarmed with activity— horses and wagons and Yankees moved everywhere with rapid purpose.

"Can you hear me child? Are you all right? Have you been hurt? Is your master at home? Do you require assistance?" He paused after each question as if considering what to do next. Still, I did not answer.

"Well, all right then," he said. "Listen, child. You know what this means, don't you, girl? It means you are freed of your master. You may go find your people. Do you understand what I am saying?"

A great charge of horses pulling a fire wagon galloped east. A buckboard laden with crates rumbled south led by a team of fresh, rough-and-ready bays. The many pillars of smoke arched slowly in the dull sky looking like black canals connecting the devil's home with heaven. There were no more orange flames. The fires were no more.

"Ya'll are Yankees!" I blurted to the short man with the pie-wedge nose in a frank manner as though I were announcing we're having potatoes for dinner.

"Yes, ma'am!" he responded in an equally frank manner, commencing a litany of "so and so Corps, so and so Division, so and so Brigade, so and so Pennsylvania Reserves." He made a gesture as though he planned to tip his hat, but did not follow through. "Well, I guess you're all right. Listen, child, you run along and put on some clothes. And by the way, I am sorry to have interrupted your medical practice."

I looked down at myself. Oh, Lord have mercy. I was naked. Except for the doctor's ear-trumpet—I was standing there in the doorway having a chat with a Yankee while dressed in my full, buck natural, just the way Lieutenant Dunnovant left me.

I closed the door, walked upstairs, pulled back Missus Pegram's fancy embroidered spread of Georgia cotton, hand-stitched in Charleston, and slid under the fine cotton top-sheet. I curled into a position surrounded by the posts of heavy maple rising from each corner of the bed like four guardian sentries.

CHAPTER TWENTY-EIGHT: EXTRA PETTIGREW

Before morning, the hill surrounding the Great House of Government turned into a camping ground—but it was not the Johnny boys moving in to pitch a blanket and call it a tent, or make a lean-to shelter with rescued boards. It was old folks and women. It was the ones who had not refugee'd south, the ones what lost their houses to the fires of the night—the fires that blazed right up to the edge of Bank Street south of the Great House before they quit, and right up to Ninth Street, just opposite the Pegram house before they quit in that direction.

They arrived upon the grounds of the Great House, each one toting a little something—a chair, a blanket, or a bucket—anything they saved on the run that won't burned or stolen.

After sunrise, they saw us eyeing them from the steps under Father Washington, and called out to us for help. Both River-james and I stepped in—digging out a pit-fire for one family, stacking up satchels to make seats for another. I carried one old man whose spindly legs hardly allowed him to stand. I toted him up the hill from Bank Street right to the steps of the Father Washington statue, where I sat him down easy in a rocking chair brung up behind me by his daughter. She thanked me with what little words she could manage, then sat down on an upturned cooking pot and commenced weeping so hard that I felt sorry for her. If I had a house what burned down, I reckoned I would also sit upon an upturned pot and weep like a baby.

By mid-morning, nearly all the open space around the Great

House was claimed by homesteaders staking out a small piece of safety. Me and Riverjames spent much of the day helping 'em, though we got separated doing it. They mostly had no money, as they ran from their homes without purses, even without britches in some cases. Even so, some gave me small compensations of kindness—useless Confed coins or a doodad of some sort.

One sad man with stoop shoulders who had rescued two rickety chairs and a small table asked me to help him get set up. I toted his salvage up the hill to a small plot of open ground, where I steadied the furniture so it didn't lean over too much against the hillside. He plopped down amid all the other weeping put-outs as though it were a fine parlor, as though there were nothing at all not right about it. He withdrew two small ivory smoking pipes from the breast pouch of his overalls, filled each with tobacco, lighted one, then handed me the other and gestured for me to sit in the other chair.

So I did.

I learned that man was a shop owner. He ran a small cobbler shop called Fourteenth Street Cobblery and had slept in the back room behind the shop since the war started. When the madness of the night came, he fled with nothing but his overalls that he was wearing, two chairs, one table, and two smoking pipes. He told me he stood aside and watched as persisters and Johnny deserters broke in to steal all the shoes he'd repaired just ahead of the shop burning to the ground. Afterward, he walked to the grounds of the Great House of Government, weighed down with his salvage.

It was the first time I ever sat at table with a white man. It didn't seem to bother that man at all that I was a slave. It was like he didn't see my blackness. We just sat there in the open, on the grounds of the Great House of Government on his salvaged chairs placed beside the salvaged table, and puffed away at a bowl of fine pipe tobacco that I knew had been sweetened with a delicate scent of rum.

All around us, the other put-outs also set up all manner of makeshift camps as best they could. One or two had a slave girl with 'em. But mostly they were all put-out citizens and none of 'em took any bother of me or my pipe-smoking cobbler companion.

After that man finished his bowl, he sighed, placed the pipe atop the little table, then leaned both elbows onto his knees. An unhappy baby cried loudly in the very next make-do, a gathering of people sitting on satchels not six feet downhill from us.

"Oh, me," he said. "Well, I guess that's it. There's nothing else to do." I was uncertain of his meaning.

"Sah, if you have no more tobacco, I have some in my pocket. I stole it from the Shockoe House." He cocked over at me with a thin smile.

"No. You keep what you have."

He reached into the pouch of his overalls and withdrew a small single-shot pistol, which he inserted into his mouth and pointed the tiny barrel toward the top of his head. When he pulled the trigger it made only a dim popping noise and didn't seem to do his noggin much harm at all. A second later, there came a small, misty cloud of red swirling outward from one ear. That's when he slumped in the chair looking sound asleep, but I knew he was dead.

I looked around. None of the other put-outs had seen it or even taken notice. I took a final haul from the rum-tinged tobacco, then placed the pipe on the little table next to the pipe he had been smoking.

"I is sorry, sah," I said, as I stood and moved away through the crowd.

As the morning wore on, the crowd of put-outs grew.

Some of 'em was so sorry they looked like no more than field hands, having left their burning houses with nothing more than the clothes on their backs, their white skin darkened over with soot, some hurt with everything from scraped knees and bloodied elbows to broke bones, which they held in makeshift slings with faces of terrible pain.

Confed bonds with the numbers "one, zed, zed, zed" blew along the grounds and got picked up by some for stuffing into the small pit-fires that dotted the grounds.

Different ones come along to take advantage. Hucksters and hawkers of all type appeared. They walked around the grounds of the Great House of Government as they worked the crowd trying to sell goods to people who needed just about everything to start over. They offered drinks of water and dried apples for sale. Some even had bread, which they waved about over their head calling out the price—one hundred Yankee dollars per loaf. There were lookers a'plenty, especially lookers at the waving bread—but mostly no takers, so the peddlers wandered off, leaving the miserable put-outs to their misery.

One huckster-man working the crowd did things different and had a lucky business to result. But this peddler was not selling. He was buying.

He was the oddest man I ever saw. He had a round, reddish face crowded with marks of the pox. Fat in the middle and wobbly at both top and bottom, he wore a dark suit. And he worked the crowd with a wooden satchel slung over his shoulder, a satchel bearing a pasted-up sign. I heard a man reading the words aloud as the peddler passed.

"Fine jewelry bought. Top prices. Union currency," he recited. Then he added, "I ain't got no jewelry. Wish I did, I'd sell it and buy me one them hundred-dollar loafs."

I sat on the ground and watched as that wobbly-man commenced outdoor shopkeeping with this one or that one. His wooden satchel had spindly legs that popped out from the sides, supporting it like a table, and a lid that opened from the top. He took a pocket watch from one man, examined it under cover of his satchel-desk, tucked it into a secret drawer inside, and gave the man a pair of Yankee paper monies. Once business concluded, he closed the satchel top, fingered at the legs until they popped back into place, hoisted the carrying strap over his shoulder, and mosied along to the next customer who held up cufflinks, a picture frame, or a hatpin for his consideration. Some tried to sell him eyeglasses or trouser belts yanked from their britches, but he paid them no mind.

The big news happened late morning, or just about midday. Everybody on the grounds of the Great House of Government knew it was coming. But when it came for real, they just stood there slack-jawed like they never really believed it.

It was the Yankees.

Lord-a-mighty there was lots of 'em. It seemed like there was none one minute, then a minute later there were thousands. They marched, walked, trotted, and rolled into town on every sort of wagon there is. It was like a morning storm of locusts swarming to the cornfield. And lots of 'em were black men in Yankee blue, which got the happy attention of all the slaves who emerged from everywhere to ballyhoo and yippie-yay. In two minutes' time it seemed like Yankees was everywhere. Officers called out orders and men in blue commenced running this way and that, up and down, back and forth, in and out.

That's when I spotted Riverjames again in the crowd, who was possessed of spiritual happiness.

"Time to say thankee to de Yankee," he pronounced after running up to me. Then, without looking back, he trotted off, bouncing and bobbing from Yankee to Yankee with a great smile of gratitude as he offered each of them a plug of fine chewing tobacco.

'T'wont but about ten minutes after they arrived on the hill o' put-outs that ole Stars and Bars was struck from atop the Great House of Government and replaced with Yankee stripes. The put-outs stared up at it with twisted lips, seeing it as just one more misery heaped upon all others. Many of 'em stood cryin' like babies while they eyeballed that Yankee flag.

But there won't no fightin'. Won't no Johnnies left to fight. And the put-outs had no will for nuthin' much 'cept weeping.

CHAPTER TWENTY-NINE:
EXTRA PETTIGREW

Well, 'twon't long before I got grabbed up by the Yankee fire brigade. An officer on horseback trotted halfway up the hill of the Great House of Government as he pointed to slaves at loiter.

"You there, boy, and you, and you, and you over there. You men come down and assemble on Bank Street."

At first I didn't know what to think. He called us "boy" but he also called us "men." I looked back and saw that Riverjames, who was under the columns of the Great House of Government, was not selected by the officer on horseback and was still happily occupied gifting Yankees with tobacco. Halfway up the hill, I could also see the dead man who invited me to smoke with him. He still sat slumped in his chair, but the other chair and table were gone, as were the two pipes. It made me grateful that I still had four dollars of good Yankee money and some stolen tobacco. If anyone knew I possessed it, I feared I would be rapidly relieved of it. I hastened down the hill to the meeting place where the officer on horseback gave us work orders.

"You men will go with this troop of volunteers here," he said pointing to a group of about forty black men in union blue. "You'll be issued pickaxes, or hoes, or whatever is needed to put out hot smolder and to prevent new fires. Understand?"

We nodded.

"And pull down walls that're in danger of toppling over. Understand?"

We nodded.

"Now, I know you're probably hungry. After your work today, Corporal Wadsworth here will see to it you get something to eat. We got plenty of food. And that'll be your pay for a day's work."

I studied Corporal Wadsworth and could not help but admire him. His blackness was deep and his crisp blue uniform bearing two yellow stripes on each shoulder was clean and made of fine cotton. When the officer pointed to him, he nodded at us with a proud smile and we all nodded back, proud to be working for a black man.

"Any questions?"

"Is we free?" one slave ventured timidly.

"Yes, you are," said the union officer on horseback. "Now get to work."

And so we did. We worked through the afternoon and into the night. During the work, I helped put out smoldering ruins at the Shockoe House, the very place where that commissary agent ordered me to help set the fires just one day prior.

Some of the two score black men in blue uniform were full of themselves, taking enjoyment at being put in charge of us slaves. One or two even bullied us good. But Corporal Wadsworth mostly called them off and kept things moving smoothly as we lined up on the street and moved inward with pickaxes to break apart any materials still serving as fuel for the fires.

"What kind of slave were you?" he asked me while laboring side by side in the charred ruins.

"Hotel porter," I said.

"You get beat much?"

"Sometimes."

"With a whip?"

"No. Mostly fist wallops upside the head. With a cane sometimes."

"How often?"

233

"Hard to say. It happened less as the Johnnies took to losing battles. But Master Pettigrew—he whup somebody near 'bout every week. I got my share."

"He ain't your master no more. You understand that, don't you?"

"Yes," I said, hesitating.

"Where's your people?"

"Ain't got none. Dead or sold off."

"What are you going to do now?"

"Don't know. Everything happening quick." He nodded as he worked his hoe in the hot ashes.

"Take ya time," he said, "a lot of change is coming. Most important, you ain't got to get beat no more."

I learned he was a free black from New York who worked in a print shop and had knowledge of his own people. His daddy was from a place called Trinidad and his granddaddy was from west Africa. His momma was from a place called Brooklyn City.

We worked our way toward one lone, giant wall still standing amid the rubble—all that was left of Trader's Bank, where Master Pettigrew did his finance work. Six stories high, it leaned teeter-totter against the sky, its open windows looking like a giant magic trick displaying a checkerboard pattern of stars. We tossed pitch-hooks through the upper windows, then let the ropes drape along for some distance until we stood half a block away, where we heaved and tugged and heaved and tugged until the wall came down, sending a wave of rumble and ash and soot rushing over us.

"You educated?" I asked Corporal Wadsworth when the storm cleared and we sat down in the middle of the block behind piles of rubble, where no white officer could see nearly fifty black men hiding to take a rest.

"Grade four."

"That why you got two stripes instead of one?"

"Sergeant took to me during training 'cause I have a way with helping people get over the hump. My men listen to me."

"I got a girl can read. She's real smart. She refugeed outta town with her mistress."

"How'd she learn?"

"Her mistress teach her. In secret."

"It's good she can read. But her mistress ain't her mistress no more," he said.

Telling Corporal Wadsworth about Missy Fran made me proud. I could see he was impressed. It made me want to find her and tell her about everything that happened to me since we departed at St. Paul's the previous morning. It seemed a hundred years had passed since. I missed her. I knew then that I loved her. And I was glad that we would soon be married.

Three boys bearing burlap satchels and buckets brought us dinner amid the darkened blocks of hot smolder. We received a half hunk of bread, a generous tin plate of white beans that had little chunks of fat, and we each got a small green apple.

After dinner, we labored into the night digging at the hot smolder with pickaxes. At one point we labored around what used to be the old Basin Bottom Livery directly opposite the Pegram house on Ninth Street. I paused to study it as I had on the morning of the previous day. Except for the soot that coated the clapboard, nothing about it had changed. Everything was shut down and drawn tight. I was glad Missy Fran evacuated with the Pegrams. It meant she was in a better place and she was spared the fire. The good news is that the house, too, was spared and would be there for them when they returned. That made the Pegrams among the luckiest.

When the officers finally let us go for the night, I was as tired as I have ever been in my life. A man on horseback trotted over to inspect our work. He asked us if we had a good dinner and we all said "yessah." Then he announced that we were all "dismissed." I dropped down and fell asleep with two other newly freed slaves on a patch of cleared dirt that used to be home to Trader's Bank, one of the tallest buildings in all Richmond.

CHAPTER THIRTY:
COMPSON WINDER

I rose early that Monday morning to tend to the horses. It was only then that I could see that the farmer's nearby house was a ramshackle mess. It even seemed a marvel that it remained standing. Only one of the two windows held glass; the walls appeared set to tumble and I could see that it consisted of no more than two small rooms.

Soon after, the others stumbled from the barn to wash at the farmer's well. They called to their host, but he was not in the house and soon emerged from the distant wood to join them at the well, where he introduced himself as Mister Virginius Lodwell. He was about as beat down a man as I have ever viewed. His sagging, sun-beat skin appeared dyed to the color of copper, but he was still in possession of moderate vigor and moved with a natural determination to continue putting one foot in front of the other. His sixty acre farm, which he managed himself, grew only cucumbers.

"No slaves?" asked Master Winder.

"No, sir, never did have one. Just me and my two sons. My wife's family had a house girl in the olden days. But they're all gone now."

"Why cucumbers?" Master Winder asked. "Why not money crops—tobacco, cotton, corn?"

"Pickle factory is nearby in City Point. It's just me now, so that makes it easier."

"Where's your wife, Mister Lodwell?"

"Died afore the war, taken by the fever. My oldest son was killed up at Sharpsburg. Last I heard, my other son is still nearby in Petersburg. I'm hoping he'll get back in time for plantin' this year." They all listened to his sad story while drinking from his well and dipping their handkerchiefs into the water bucket to wash their faces and necks.

"Get yourself a darkie," said Mistress Bartow, "that'll help you through the rough days."

"They cost money, ma'am. I ain't got much 'atall, as you can see." He gestured to his shabby farmhouse. "And I certainly ain't got money."

He apologized to them for having no food to offer. But he welcomed them to stay in the barn as long as necessary and offered the use of the well as much as they liked. He explained he had just walked to the main road before sunrise to see what could be learned—and came back with news from Petersburg that could be summed up in the same one word that applied to Richmond: evacuation. At first we thought he meant the citizens of Petersburg. But he did not. Master Cyrus Winder set us straight after we loaded up the wagon and resumed our journey south.

"Well, if the whole world is evacuating, where's everybody going?" Mistress Bartow asked as we bounced through the farmer's open cucumber field, taking a shortcut to the nearest road. "We can't all evacuate to the same place. There won't be enough room when we get there."

"That farmer wasn't referring to people like us," said Master Winder. "He wasn't talking about folks who live in Petersburg."

"Why, who was he referring to?"

"Soldiers. The Army of Virginia."

"You mean General Lee is evacuating his position at Petersburg?" the plump lady asked him in an irritated voice.

"Sounds like it," said Master Winder.

"Why now? It's been nearly a year," she complained. "Just last week the papers named Petersburg as 'the Three-Hundred-Day Battle.' Can't General Lee wait one more day, until we have all safely arrived at Ruth's farm in Roanoke Rapids?"

"Oh, Helen, General Lee doesn't know we're headed for Daddy's Little Farm," the skinny Mistress Pegram said. She was set to take further objection, but Master Winder cut her off.

"It's becoming clear now. His withdrawal from Petersburg is the reason for Richmond's own evacuation. He's on the run."

"General Lee on the run? Oh, poosh!" said the fat lady, dismissing the notion as something that simply does not happen.

"I'm afraid so."

"Well, he'll turn and fight," she whined in objection. "He always does."

"I don't know," Master Winder said. "He's never had to turn and fight without a government in place in Richmond. Jackson is gone. Stuart is gone. Now Richmond is gone and Grant is in charge. Things are different this time."

"Well, where's he going?"

"I do not know, but wherever he's going—we want to be going the other way," said Master Winder. On that note, I turned to him and nodded in agreement, a gesture they all noticed, which hushed them up but only temporarily. Again, it was the fat Mistress Bartow that persisted.

"Why the other way?" she asked. "We should certainly be safer in General Lee's shadow. He would do all in his power to see that no ill befalls us Richmond evacuees."

"Well, Helen," my master began, "you are familiar with the Mary Had a Little Lamb nursery rhyme—the one that says 'and everywhere that Mary went, the lamb was sure to follow.' "

She gave him a tilted look of puzzlement. "Oh, Cyrus, please! Don't talk in riddles, not at a time like this," Mistress Winder chided at her husband, patting his arm.

"Oh, it's not a riddle at all, my dear. You see, we don't want to be going the same way as General Lee because wherever he goes, it's Grant that's sure to follow. And we don't want to be in his way."

That shut her up. The plump lady had no response. All of us in the wagon were hushed by the thought that we could be in more danger as pilgrims bound for Roanoke Rapids than if we had simply hidden away inside our respective homes in Richmond. Because they refugeed, here we were, wedged between the running armies of General Lee and the chasing armies of General Grant. The idea of suffering as they had for the past day just to put themselves into greater risk of harm seemed a mean trick to 'em all and to me, too. It made me angry that I had to abandon my wife. But then, if we must all come to a bad end, it was better that she was not with me.

None of us had long to worry.

At the main road we were fast overwhelmed by a wave of Confederate soldiers marching west. A lieutenant on horseback gave us a hasty survey, then ordered a group of rag-tag men to relieve us of our horses and wagon, apologizing all the while as they put us all out by the path. The wagon quickly filled with so many walking wounded that I lost count at ten.

Two of the womenfolk wept loudly during the exchange, while the skinny Mistress Pegram just sat down on a log and looked on with a slack jaw and yellowed eyes at the whole passing event. As for poor old Master Winder, he became befuddled, making incoherent offers of money and gold and promises of future employment in his wagon factory if the soldiers would only leave us be. But his efforts made no difference to desperate, wounded men in need of horses and wheels.

"We're right sorry about this," one of 'em said as he physically pushed Master Winder aside. "Money won't do us much good, sir."

"You got any boots in them satchels?" another soldier called out from his seat in the floor of the wagon."

"Money will buy boots, Private," said my master, thinking he was still in a position to negotiate.

"That's dandy," praised another soldier, "we'll just hop over to the nearest cobbler shop and buy us all some fine new boots afore ole Useless Ulysses comes a runnin' up from behind tossing his whiskey bottles at us." His joke raised an immodest chuckle among the cramped rag-taggers squeezing into the wagon.

"I am sorry about this, sir," said one private as he climbed to the driver's position, grabbing the reins. Ya'll just go anywhere except west and ya'll be fine."

"Is it safe to go back to Richmond?" Master Winder inquired.

"No-o-o, sir," came the response as the private eyed me over in my red vest and top hat, "not right now. Ya'll be like peacocks in a yard full o'hound dogs if ya'll try that now. Give it a couple of days. Things'll quiet down after we're gone. Then you can head back to ole Richmond."

"Where's General Lee leading the army?"

"Well, we ain't supposed to say, but it ain't no military secret. Every Yankee chasing us knows it. We're going west to Amelia, following the Appomattox River."

He snapped the reins hard and gee'd the team. Both horses turned to hand me a worried look before breaking into a canter. I declare, it hurt my heart to lose those horses. I did so love 'em both.

"Well, we'll just have to walk back to that farmer's sad house," the plump Mistress Bartow said, while my Mistress Winder flapped her tiny hands and blubbered.

"Let's just leave the satchels for now," Master Winder said, still befuddled. Then he said, "Compson, hide the satchels in the bushes." That's when they all turned their attention to Mistress Pegram, who said nothing. She just sat on that log staring out at nothing.

"C'mon, Ruth," the plump one said, "we're walking back to that farmhouse." It took a while, but she finally managed to get the skinny Mistress Pegram to stand and we all walked back down the path and through the farmer's barren cucumber field. He was not home when we returned, and it was Mistress Bartow who entered the ramshackle house without invitation.

"I cannot spend two whole days in that barn with bats flitting about as we wait for the army to pass," she complained. "I declare, I am in sore need of a real chair for my delicate derriere." Too tired and too defeated to do otherwise, they all followed sheep-like into the house, while I remained at loiter in the yard. A moment later, Mistress Winder emerged pinching her overly big nostrils in an unladylike manner and waving at her face.

"Lord, Compson," she said to me, "it smells worse in there than it does in the barn." I couldn't imagine a way to make it any better for 'em, but I didn't have to. The plump Mistress Bartow found something to distract them all.

"Whoa, look at this," she announced, coming out to join Mistress Winder on the porch. "I found them in a wall cabinet. I declare. Why, it's dried codfish. Two of 'em. Two whole dried codfish." She held them to her nose and inhaled. "Mmm. Rich and salty," she said. "Where on Earth did he get these?"

"I declare," said my mistress, removing her fingers from her nose, "that Mister Lodwell did not speak truthfully about not possessing any nourishment to offer us."

"He's likely saving them for his son," said my master. "He's hoping his son will arrive from Petersburg now that the army is on the move."

"Well, won't his son be going west to Amelia along the Appomattox with everyone else? Just like that lieutenant told us?" asked the plump lady.

"It could be he may stop here along the way," said Master Winder, still eyeing the two brown slabs, each being weighed like gold ingots in Mistress Bartow's chubby hands.

"Well, he will just have to accept our money as payment," she said, handing one fish to Master Winder as she broke the other in half and presented the portion that contained the head to the still-silent Mistress Pegram. After Master Winder broke his in two and they all four ate half a codfish each, they sat down wherever they found it comfortable.

"I hope Farmer Lodwell doesn't shoot us for eating his boy's dinner," Master Winder said after a while.

"Oh, poosh. That old man can't shoot anyone," the plump lady argued back. "Why, we'll just have Compson let him know how we feel about that."

"I declare we are not familiar with such habits," said the Mistress Winder, her pink face powder now almost worn away, revealing a skin so blanched it seemed unlikely it had ever been exposed to sunshine. "It would be insult upon injury to have Compson thrash our poor host after we robbed his pantry," she said.

"Well, then, I shall thrash him," said Mistress Bartow. "Besides, when all this is concluded—saving the four of us will be a superior ticket for him when knocking at heaven's gate. Better for him than his good deed of saving two mangy codfish for a boy who may never show up."

"What about sacrificing one and maybe two sons to the Confederacy?" asked my master. But the plump lady had no response.

As the day wore on, they all took turns visiting the well and the woods to relieve themselves. I mostly napped in the barn while the rest of 'em sat uneasy in the damp house. We heard sounds of men marching in the distance and the occasional report of artillery explosions, but no one emerged from the wall of wood encircling the little farm. That was good. It meant that no one, neither blue nor gray, took any notice of this barren cucumber field, and that meant the war was passing us by.

It was past nightfall when the next event happened. I was awakened in the barn by a mysterious and profane whispering. When I opened my eyes, I was greeted by such a ghostly apparition hovering directly over me that it made me fear my time was come nigh. Then I saw it was the skinny Mistress Ruth Pegram. She was squatted in the hay, leaning into me, her eyes burning with a possessed spirit.

"Damn you, you damnable man," she whispered. She bared her lips and showed me her yellow teeth, one of 'em poking out at such an angle it looked like it must be painful. "You release him," she said in a soft voice that at the same time seemed to scream with nasty dread. "You release him . . . release him . . . release him . . . release him," she went on and on. I was not only startled by her behavior but also worried about her intentions: being, as she was, a white Richmond mistress; and being, as I was, a black slave; and being, as we were, alone in a barn.

"Mistress Pegram—" I began. But she would have none of it.

"You will not win," she hissed. "I will not let you. I will defeat you." Then she leaned in until her lips were right atop my eyes. "My name is Ruth," she said like a mean warning, "and you know I shall be ruthless with you to save my little boy."

It alarmed me so, I must have bumped her. I tried to sit up and I must have bumped her arm. She jumped up and switched over to shouting.

"Damn you, you damnable man. You will not kidnap my son from his rightful abode in heaven. The Lord may look the other way, but I will descend to the fires of hell to fight you! I will eat

rats to defeat you. And I will defeat you. I will endure your mis-
cegenating desires to defeat you. And I will defeat you. Jasper
. . . Jasper Garner . . . come to me . . . release him . . ."

On and on she went. When I stood up she raced from the
barn, past the house where, having heard the ruckus, the others
were emerging. Without stopping or speaking to any of them
she ran on into the barren cucumber field, where she stopped in
the middle distance and commenced howling in the moonlight—
raving about men and devils and babies and Yankees and rats.

We all gathered at the edge of the field to watch.

"What's happened to her?" asked Mistress Winder, staring in
disbelief.

"She's broke into madness," her husband mumbled.

"It must have been the dried codfish. Could it be? Oh, Cyrus, is that why that farmer has run off—because he's poisoned
us all?"

"No," said Master Winder, "that's the dementia. I've seen it
at Chimborazo. This war gets to be too much. People just break
down from it all." We watched for a while as she behaved oddly,
pacing up and down the plowed ruts of last year's cucumber
crop—walking, then racing, then dancing a nasty jig—all the
while flopping her arms, raving, howling, and hurling condem-
nation at people and sights unseen by us.

"Why, she has jumped with both feet into a mental wilderness," said Mistress Winder in a soft, lilting voice as though
reading poetry.

"Lunatic," the fat Mistress Bartow barked. "Why, the poor
thing is gone plumb cuckoo."

Master Winder sent me to fetch her, but she had no intention
of being moved. When I got halfway to her, she began to strip
down. First it was her shoes. Then her limp calico dress went
fluttering like a ghost in the darkness. Finally, her camisole and
all her unders came off with a toss to the ground. I turned

back. I simply had no appetite for fetching a naked white woman from a cucumber field at night, especially not when her shouting would likely bring down a whole brigade of soldiers any moment. Upon return, I kept my head bent down in showy display that I possessed no interest in eyeballing Mistress Pegram's nakedness.

"I'll go, Compson," Master Winder said when I rejoined 'em.

"You can't, Cyrus—why you don't even have your boots on," his wife warned.

"The field is dry enough now," he said. "Compson, go fetch the farmer's blanket from the house and have it ready when I bring her back.

"Yes-sah," I said.

"Be careful, Cyrus," his wife uttered limply.

I returned with the blanket before my wealthy master had gotten very far, walking slowly down one furrowed row in his stocking feet. As he drew near to Mistress Ruth Pegram she backed away—her gaunt frame of nakedness reflecting in the pale light of a quarter moon. For a few minutes it was a ridiculous cat and mouse. When master got close, talking as he walked, trying to calm her—she backed away until finally there was only the wall of woods at the opposite end of the open field. When she had no choice but to let master grab her or dart into the woods—she elected for the latter, disappearing into the darkness like some haunted apparition of the night. We heard Master Winder call at her twice to come out of the wilderness. When she did not emerge, he followed after.

It was not long after the two of them abandoned the open field for the wooded darkness that Mistress Marion Winder came down with a spell of her own. She cried and wrung her hands, pacing back and forth at the edge of the field until, after two minutes' time, she darted away through the cucumber field and soon enough, she too disappeared into the wood.

"Shall I follow?" I asked the fat Mistress Bartow after a moment of slack silence passed between the two of us.

"I think not," she said, which suited me fine. I knew she did not want to be left alone, and I did not want to go running through a thick wood in the darkness after my master and mistress and a crazy naked woman as the armies of General Grant pursued the armies of General Lee around the central Virginia countryside.

"There's nothing more to do except wait for morning."

"Yes, ma'am," I said.

She returned to the dilapidated house and I spent the balance of the night in the barn, pleased that I had not been accused of causing any of it to happen.

Chapter Thirty-One:
President Abraham Lincoln

Richmond!

I will soon visit the capital, the very seat of government directing this horrible war.

In truth, of all my privately indulged hopes during these four long years, I do confess I never indulged in fancy aforethought that the day would come allowing me to trod upon the streets of the rebellion's capital city. Now that it has, I say plainly—it is the finest, most inwardly serene and luxuriating happiness of all my days.

This war is concluded!

It is now certain that nothing less than full surrender of all Confederate troops is imminent. It is a great blessing provided at last by the heavenly Father. I shall say a prayer to Him expressing my deepest gratitude tomorrow while in that place—while in that city called *Richmond.*

★ ★ ★ ★ ★

THE FIRE:
DAY THREE
TUESDAY, APRIL 4, 1865

★ ★ ★ ★ ★

CHAPTER THIRTY-TWO:
MISS FRANCINE PEGRAM

I awoke, as always, at dawn.

At first I was uncertain of my location; I wasn't even certain I was awake. The bedding and unfamiliar shades of gray morning that filtered through the windows were strange. I had never awakened near a window. Except for two days prior, in the cellar with Missus Pegram, I had never awakened anywhere that I could remember except upon my bucky-board bed in the kitchen pantry.

The feather mattress was soft. The cottons, embroidered spread, and quilted cover were blessings of such comfort that I feared for a moment I had been taken by Jesus during the night.

I sat up, wondering if I mightn't be lying in my own coffin only to find I was actually in a place always forbidden to me— Missus Pegram's own bed. In the next moment, all the meanness of the previous day came rapidly back. And I knew I could wait for Master Pegram no longer. I needed to find Extra.

I rose, used Missus Pegram's chamber pot, washed in Missus Pegram's basin, then brushed my hair with her fancy ivory brush set, which she had failed to pack ahead of her hasty departure and which Lieutenant Dunnovant took no interest in.

Without making the bedding, I donned my other gingham, recently cleaned on the washboard without benefit of soap. I switched the pocket contents with the dress that still lay soiled among the tormented mess on the kitchen floor. My properties were all safe: pearl ring, pocket knife, undated street pass, and deed of my own transfer from Master Pettigrew to Master Pegram "for cause" over the back fence at the Spotswood Hotel in 1853.

I retrieved the boot buff from my harvest of thievery, sat on my step stool, and used a kitchen rag to polish my brokens. I strapped them to my feet, lacing them tight, which gave my feet a secure, snug comfort. I was proud of my shoes and always kept as smart a shine as possible upon them. Mistress Bartow frequently sang admiration at my care of them.

"Lordy, Lord, child," she would say, "I declare, those shoes never looked as good when they belonged to my Evelyn."

Then I breakfasted on what ham and coffee remained.

The view from the front steps of number 212 Ninth Street was of a ruined world. Everything to the east was thoroughly burned, as though plowed under in favor of some hateful crop of slag and ruin. It was as though Jesus drew a line, making all fires stop at Ninth Street. Yankees labored opposite the house, dragging flotsam of burned ruins into great mounds in the empty block.

Standing on the porch, I observed something I could never have guessed. Many of the Yankees at labor were black men in blue uniform. They were, as Mistress Bartow so often pronounced it, "as black as the ace of spades." But there were more of them than the number of all cards in a deck, and they labored hard at the cleanup, dragging out smoking planks of wood and stomping out smoldering piles of hot rubble.

I walked cautiously to the street's edge. It was as though Master Pettigrew's Basin Bottom Livery had never existed. I was pleased it hadn't stabled any horses for months; that meant none had perished. I wondered about Jules, the mute errand boy whom I'd last observed on Sunday morning hoping to catch a mongrel dog for his breakfast. But he was nowhere to be seen.

The farther I ventured from the steps, the more I could see.

To the north, the Yankees bustled in all directions like spring bees at the hive. They swarmed around the government buildings and the Great House of Government with much hurried activity. To the south, the view was different. Near the Tredegar factory, they acted more like soldiers, standing about in columns, their rifles at the ready.

My block, the one bordered by Ninth and Main—the entire block that included the Pegram house and the Spotswood Hotel, was spared. I held my breath and slowly walked north to Main Street in the morning sun, which felt good on my face, but the stink of blackened soot was a mean test that required forbearance.

At the hotel door, I was greeted with my first disappointment. Old Caesar was not at his post. That blunted me. Without him, I would need to make my introductions alone. I crossed Main Street and sat on a log in front of a rickety wee-wah fence that circled a rickety old house. I watched. Yankees went in and out of the hotel; more came out than went in, mostly walking to Ninth Street, where they turned north toward the buildings of government, and mostly their uniforms bore fancy decorations signaling their importance as captain or major and so forth. Just as with the Butternut, I conjured the important officer Yankees got more comforts, including hotel rooms.

They had a settled-in look. It was as though they had been in Richmond for many weeks, when in truth, they had arrived not even one full day prior.

I readied my story in case I was stopped by Master Pettigrew or some other who might find argument with my presence. I would say I bore a message from Missus Pegram that Extra was needed at St. Paul's for important work.

"Please, sah, is Extra's where 'bouts known at this hour, sah?" As to the nature of the work—I wouldn't know. Not knowing could be excused; not having an explanation at all could prove vexing. If necessary, I had the undated pass signed by Missus.

The morning chill nipped at me even as the sun rose to my left, its warmth slowly breaking through the morning cover of gray. The columns of pillowy smoke climbed from the burned district to mingle with the clouds. The foul odor of blackened char was a constant violation that everyone—Yankee and servant alike—was required to tolerate.

After a chunk of time, Old Caesar did not return. Having overstayed my time on the log, I heard from a mangy dog that I failed to observe on the porch of the dilapidated house behind me. He delivered a low-toned growl, and when our eyes met, he rose unsteadily with a curling-lip snarl, limped down the dilapidated stoop, and waddled my way as fast as he could, hissing and limping and snarling all the way.

As soon as he reached the fence gate, he stopped and commenced quivering and nipping at his own legs with yelping cries of pain, all the while trying to keep up a snarl in my direction. I saw that he was an aged rag-tag creature left behind to guard a rag-tag house. He regretted his charge from the stoop, as it had caused his legs to ache with the torments of age.

I felt sorry for him. But being afraid of dogs as I am, his message rang hard on me and I obeyed it. I backed away. I crossed Main Street walking backwards to keep a watch on the sad creature until I reached the other side. Then I turned and slipped into the Spotswood lobby, just as a pair of Yankees emerged. The second one held the door for me.

"Go ahead, child," he said. They both eyed me while exchanging a glint-eyed look of amusement.

The door closed with a heavy snap. I paused inside. The lobby slowly came into view as my eyes adjusted. Yankees milled about, some at loiter, some moving with purpose in both directions upon the staircase. There were men not wearing uniforms at all, but were instead dressed in fancy Sunday suits, toting fine leather grips.

Mister Cobb was behind the front desk—a small, pale man with spectacles who lived in a small room behind the first-floor office. I knew him mostly for his back-door trots. Sometimes when I was in the privy or at loiter near the back fence with Extra and the others, he would hasten from the Spotswood's rear porch to use the hotel guest privy. He always chose the single-seater. At no time, either going in or coming out, did he ever offer comment, unkind or otherwise, to any servant in the yard that I could recall. I approached the desk where he tended to various papers in between receiving room keys to be hung in a dark-wood cabinet behind him.

"Good mornin', Mistah Cobb, sah." I said. His lip curled a little, reminding me of the rag-tag dog whose snarling lip I just fled.

"Yes?" he said with a tone of distraction.

"Mistah Cobb, sah, Missus Pegram wish me to make inquiries upon Extra. He required at St. Paul's for some work. You seen him, sah?"

"No." was his only response.

A Yankee approached the desk to drop off a room key, which Mister Cobb took and hung in the cabinet. The Yankee departed but another quickly approached to ask if the dining room would be serving that evening.

"Five-thirty," Mister Cobb said. "Potatoes and beans. No greens yet. Bacon, if the ration gets through."

I held my ground for one last effort.

"She say de church work required by de Yankees, sir."

He gave me a quick second look. "Ask after him in the kitchen," he said, pointing a limp finger in the proper direction. I required no further invitation and departed his company with a scurry. I passed the arched entryway of the dining hall without a glance into the seating area, rounded a corner, and entered the swinging door of the kitchen.

Because there were so many Yankees buzzing about, I expected to see a hive of kitchen workers at labor with various breakfast preparations, as well as the early stages of supper. But it was not so. Two servants worked at the counters among the many pots and bowls. I knew them both. One was the ill-tempered slave-woman known as Cussin' Sally-Martha. The sight of the other gladdened my heart. It was ole Miss Edna, a hard worker, so old her face appeared carved in a withered chunk of coal. She had been the Spotswood indoor cook for more years than anyone could recall.

Sally-Martha was nearest to the kitchen entrance, laboring upon a generous pile of unripe, twisted white potatoes that appeared touched with blight. I conjured them stolen from a nearby farm cellar and delivered to the kitchen by the Yankees. Even in their state of green and brown dry-rot, they held promise and looked good to me.

"Hello, Sally-Martha," I said, announcing my presence. She paid no attention. I moved on to ole Edna, who I knew could neither hear nor see very well. She had no fire going yet in the large iron stove, but a nearby pile of kindling told me she was making ready to begin cooking. Three great bowls of beans were soaking in water nearby.

"Hello, Miss Edna," I said loudly. She turned slowly like an old tree and gazed down. Her eyes clouded with shimmering gray.

"Who tha?"

"It's me, Miss Francine. From the Pegram house behind the fire pit." She considered my words.

"Oh, yah. Miz Fran. How you do?" Her mouth barely moved as she spoke each group of words with its own separate breath. She wore a dark gingham dress that hung limp on her bones, covered with an apron that made an outline around her great drooping bosom. "De Yankee in town," she said matter-of-factly.

"Yes, Miss Edna. I know." Specks of white seemed to float inside her gray eyes.

"Dey livin' in de Spotswud."

"I know."

"Dat mean we free."

"Miss Edna, have you seen Extra?" I asked.

"Wha?"

"I said—have you seen Extra?"

"Extra?"

"Yes'm."

She weighed my question. Her shimmering gray eyes darted back and forth inside the sagging coal of her face. "Naw. Naw, Miz Fran. T'aint seen Extra." She paused as if laboring upon a thought, then added, "Naw. Naw t'ain seen. Nah since lass week."

"Thank you, Miss Edna." Disappointed, I turned away. I had seen Extra since she had.

I did not wish to speak with Sally-Martha but now I knew I must. I walked past her as though I had no mind to pose the same question to her, hoping that would tempt her voice. If it did not, I would be required to turn back. My plan worked.

"Lookin' fah ya man?" she said without turning from her jumble of potato.

I stopped. Her large bony hands skillfully worked a short knife on each tuber, first cutting the eyes, then quickly slicing the leathery skins. Each pass of the blade brushed close past her thumb but never touched anything unintended. The tubers' bumpy flesh had a bitter odor; the rinds mingled with juice and dirt on the counter. They were green on the underside and thickly wrinkled on the upper. The deep wrinkles in Sally-Martha's hands resembled the rough texture of the unpeeled tubers. A potato bug took shelter under a large curled slice of brown skin, his feelers waving about cautiously.

Nothing Sally-Martha ever said could be taken with trust. She was known to carry on with great rants endowed not only with wild curses, which made the men laugh and earned her the nickname, but also with tales farfetched and ghostly. Some of her stories told of having received visits from the devil much like Missus Pegram's own rants. Extra told me that on several occasions Master Pettigrew would confine her to a storeroom in the cellar to prevent her from upsetting guests and diners. I waited, hoping she would volunteer some additional comment, but her tongue remained silent, requiring me to speak to her.

"Do you know where Extra is?" I asked.

She did not look up from her peelings. The bug feelers under the large curler were gone, withdrawn to some safe harbor deeper within the pile of green and brown peelings.

"Sally-Martha. Where is Extra?" I spoke with as much command as I dare.

"Dat man ain't yo man." Her words were flat; she never stopped working the short knife. Her lips and nose squirmed and twisted as though some spot itched with torment. If it were my nose, I thought, I would scratch it even though my hands were soiled with tuber juice.

"We're going to be married soon," I said. She turned to me with knife in hand.

"Chile! You is never gonna marry dat man. Dat man not yo man. You hear me?"

"Yes, Sally-Martha, I hear."

"You put dat damn fool notion out yo mind."

"All right, Sally-Martha."

"Oh yes-s-s," she said, starting to commence a rant spell, holding the knife higher and slowly moving her hips. "Oh, my-y-y yess-s-s. Dat man ain't yo man. Oh, no-o-o-o. Ain't gonna be yo man. Oh, no, no-o-o-o." I braced for great waving, cussing, and even dancing about. But fortunately that did not follow. She stopped short and looked hard at me without speaking.

"Sally-Martha . . . I . . ."

"Hush, Miz Fran." It was ole Edna interrupting. "Miz Fran, come ovah hea." I left Sally-Martha to her tuber peelings and walked back to the stove and bowls of soaking beans.

"Yes, Miss Edna?"

"Miz Fran. Go hunt Extra. He in town. Sally-Martha see him. He in town. When yo find—yo boaf com bak to me."

"He didn't get sent to the ramparts?"

"Naw. He in town. Go find."

"All right. Do you know where to look Miss Edna?"

"Naw. But yo look. Yo can fin."

"Why do you want to talk to us both?"

"Hush. Yo fin. Then come. We all talk." She leaned to the counter with one hand to brace her aged body, her head moving back and forth as she tried to make her mostly blind eyes find me standing before her.

"All right, Miss Edna. I'll find Extra and we'll come back to you."

"Dat's good. Yo come."

"All right, Miss Edna." She turned back to her beans and wood kindling.

I walked softly behind Cussin' Sally-Martha to depart the kitchen, grateful she made no further comment. The hallway was calm. For a brief moment, no Yankees or other men were coming or going. I retraced my steps, passing the dining room, where I looked in with no more purpose than a casual glance. But what I beheld froze my brokens to the floor as lightning chills hammered at my bones.

It was Lieutenant Dunnovant!

He was sitting at a dining table with his back to me, still wearing his plain clothes from the previous day. His manner was slack, at rest. It was apparent he was a guest at the hotel, which meant the Yankees had no way of knowing he was a Butternut lieutenant. Should he turn around and behold me standing in the hallway, it would surely alter his composure in a manner I did not wish to encounter. I thought again of Captain Zollicoffer's pistol hidden in the pantry barrel and within one thinly peeled moment of time, I made ready to bolt. But I did not. Something else seized my attention.

Sitting opposite the Butternut officer who had violated me so meanly was the odd man I observed Sunday morning prowling the crowd at St. Paul's bearing a billboard notice for his jewel business; his face dented with pock scars, his large eyes holding no color at all, just black centers surrounded by white.

I wanted to run, but stopped again when I saw what that odd-looking man clutched in his short, stubby hands. It was a necklace, the very same string of smooth milky pearls with tints of green taken from my own neck the day before. He held it close, examining it, working each pearl past his bulging eyes. Mugs of coffee sat before the two men. They were discussing some point of business centering upon the necklace. I figured from the manner of their exchange that Lieutenant Dunnovant was selling the necklace and understood too that the odd-looking, jack-o'-lantern man was considering its purchase. The sale would likely finance the lieutenant's stay at the Spotswood and help him advance his Butternut assignment of "seeing and counting, counting and seeing," as he put it.

I had overextended my thin moment of sliced time in the corridor. The jack-o'-lantern man somehow felt my presence. Without any hint of movement, his puffy black eyes darted— and suddenly he was eyeing me dead-on. He held his glance a sufficient length of time so as to make curious the man who violated me in mind and body. The last thing I saw was Lieutenant Dunnovant's shoulders turning to get a view of what had drawn his companion's attention. But by the time he'd completed twisting 'round in his chair, there was nothing to see. I was gone.

I was down the corridor, past Mister Cobb's front desk, and out the front door with a bolt. I ran across Main Street up Ninth Street and didn't stop until reaching Franklin.

So, Lieutenant Dunnovant was still in Richmond and staying at the Spotswood. That meant he might be back to attack me again, which meant I could not return to the house until Master or Mistress Pegram returned, and it meant I would not be safe anywhere in or around the hotel, possibly not anywhere in all Richmond. I needed to find Extra to help me conjure the next step.

The Yankees mostly paid me no mind. They came and went on foot, horseback, and wagon. I passed Mistress Ashby's house and saw her familiar face peering from a window. She was not among Missus Pegram's regular social acquaintances, but I knew her from our visit of mourning after her colonel husband was killed during war duties and from the occasional chat-fests held upon the footpath. She stared at me a while but betrayed no sentiment in her strained eyes other than worry over what she saw parading in the street. Missus Pegram once commented she was never the same after her husband died.

On the north side of Franklin, I stopped across from Mistress Lee's house, where I received another shock making me wonder over the sudden change wrought upon the world. Standing on Mistress Lee's porch was a guard, a young Yankee soldier. He couldn't have been much older than me. The musket-rifle strapped over his shoulder pointed skyward in a smart fashion and his overly large blue uniform hung loosely on his body, making him look boyish and a little silly. But in addition to all that, just as with many of the others tending to the fires, he was "black as the ace of spades"!

It made me forget myself. I stood by a parked wagon opposite the Lee house for a long time just looking at that boy. He didn't move much. He just stared ahead, making me think he was only imitating the manner of a vidette more than he understood what real sentry duties might amount to. I guessed too that he was proud and a little bit afraid.

Others stared at him. Richmonders who had not evacuated were now venturing out in search of food or whatever goods of relief might be had, and they too paused to look at him with shock. After gawking for a moment, they mostly hurried on past the Lee house with considerable unhappiness. Two mistresses looking oddly orphaned without their servants in tow put handkerchiefs to their noses as they bustled past with discomfort. One passing mistress, who did have her house girl with her, hastened by but was required to stop with a case of the nerves and bark at the girl, who had paused at loiter directly in front of the boy to stare at him with a jaw gone slack.

"Ova," the mistress called in a husky voice, pretending to whisper. But the girl did not budge. "Ova, you come here this instant," the mistress pronounced at a full bark, which snapped the girl from her trance and sent her running to catch up. I wondered why I had never seen Ova or her mistress before, but figured that to be the way of a large city.

Made of fine brick, the Lee house was better than ours. I scanned the windows. There was no sign of life, no movement at all. I knew Mistress Lee was inside. Various mistresses at St. Paul's had said she was too ill to evacuate and that Doctor Toms was tending to her. But neither she nor any of her house help appeared to be about. The house was still and quiet, as though trying to hide the way a mouse does when caught in the open, hoping to go unseen in a room full of cats.

I moseyed west on Franklin Street, looking back at that sentry boy several times to make sure he was still there. Each time I glanced, he remained perched on the top step of Mistress Lee's porch, with a stiff neck staring straight ahead, looking like he felt fancy in that blue uniform too big for his skinny bones.

It was on Fifth Street near Grace that I viewed the day's second puzzle signifying a changed world. It was a flag. But this was not an ordinary flag, not the Butternut Stars and Bars. It was the Yankee flag. And it was flying right out in the open, attached to a porch pole angled out from a column of a fine, fancy house. I knew it to be the wrong flag because Missus pointed out the differences to me once when they were pictured side by side in the newspaper.

The mistress of the house was standing at the yard's edge waving, handing out greetings and blessings to the passing Yankees as though they were all her brothers come home from war. She wore a fresh dress with a calico print design, which Missus Pegram scorned when she saw it on display in Mister Gordon's Lady's Fashion Emporium as being overly "showy." But weeks later, when Mistress Lee was seen wearing the same dress, it became a "fine and charming change of pace."

I had seen the mistress of this Fifth Street house before but could not put a name to her face. Perhaps it was at St. Paul's or during a visit to Chimborazo to pet the wounded. She was buoyant with cheer, bouncing to her toes as she waved first one hand, then the other, then both at the same time.

"Welcome!" she said to a passing Yankee on horseback. "Thank you, sir!" she said firmly. The Yankee nodded his hat and trotted on.

"Good morning, soldier," she said to a single Yankee walking from the other direction, who was burdened with a drawer pulled from someone's desk.

"Good morning, ma'am," he said, giving a small tip of his

cap with one hand, while the other pressed the papers that filled the drawer to prevent them from flying away.

"Thank you for saving us. Welcome to Richmond," she said with a smile what was broad, happy, and gracious.

"Yes, ma'am," he said. He nodded and walked on, holding the drawer awkwardly in front of him. To the north on Grace Street, a large group of Yankee soldiers hurried east toward the buildings of government, some galloping on horseback, some on foot in a rapid march.

"Welcome! Welcome to Richmond, brave soldiers. Thank you, gentlemen," she shouted to them, waving. But none heard her. They rapidly disappeared to the east, sending up a dust cloud.

It was then her cheery countenance settled upon me, standing at the footpath where I stared up at her happy display.

"Why, hello, sweet-pea," she pronounced with a warm smile. "Isn't this a wonderful day?" But I said nothing. She stepped from her porch and walked to the gate where I stood.

"Hello," she said to me again. "You look familiar. Are you one of Dot's children?" I did not know anyone named Dot and shook my head.

"Are you with the McIntosh house?"

"Pegram," I said with a plain voice.

"Pegram? Pegram. Oh, yes, the Pegrams. Down on Ninth Street. How are they? Did they evacuate?" I nodded yes.

A sudden clap of noise rose from the corner at Grace Street, where soldiers, horses, and wagons gathered at some loud labor that took our attention. I could not tell if they were loading up or unloading their cargo. She turned back to me.

"Well, they'll return, sweet-pea," she said. "Don't worry, we're all Americans now. They'll return, sure enough. Don't you worry, sweet-pea, this city will be rebuilt and everything will be just fine from now on." I could not conjure why she would take such cheer from the arrival of the Yankees.

"Do you know where Master Pegram is?" I blurted.

"Well, no, sweet-pea. Didn't he evacuate with your Mistress Pegram? And anyway, he is no longer your master. But don't worry, he'll come 'round. They all will. We're all liberated now," she said, speaking almost like a preacher. She must have seen disappointment in my face.

"Sweet-pea, you see those soldiers yonder?" she asked.

"Yes'm."

"Well, they are our saviors. The war is over, honey. This nation is one again. You are no longer a slave. The South can call me scalawag all it wishes. It doesn't matter because you are liberated! I am liberated! Oh, isn't it glorious!" She clutched her hands to her breast, then turned and walked back to her porch, where she had a better view of Grace Street and commenced welcoming and waving at the soldiers all over again. I looked up at the Yankee flag fluttering from the porch pole.

"That's Old Glory, sweet-pea," she announced, having seen my study of it. "It's been hiding behind the hallway mirror for four long years. But it's out now." She rose to her tiptoes and shook the words from her throat. "And that's just where it's going to stay. Right here on this porch."

A Yankee on a great sorrel trotted behind me, heading south on Fifth Street sending up a small dust storm that swirled about my feet. His passage drew her attention and sent her into a state of rapturous glee, bouncing to her toes and waving with both hands.

"Bravo!" she shouted. "Thank you, kind sir. Welcome, liberators! Welcome to Richmond." He tipped his hat to her in a cloud of dust, which sent her clutching both hands to her bosom, her face devoured with pride.

I walked on.

I turned east on Grace Street toward the buildings of government. There was a great dustiness to the streets. The wagon-rut loblollies were mostly gone and turned to floating clouds of grit and gossamer. With the Yankees came a return of scattered horse-heap left unattended. Now, with the morning sun and the dry-bones of the streets, it added to the burned odor of soot, making the smell more labor for the nostrils.

I passed Mister Bee's Dry Goods & Grocer on Grace and noted much hubbub upon the broad front steps. Boards were nailed to the main door and across the wide windows, though I could see sharp points of broken glass behind them. The long, covered porch of the store was filled with a multitude of servants at loiter, lounging on crates and boxes. They paid me no mind as I passed, involved as they were in chattering, like birds on a limb, about being free. On and on they went about "freed-up" this and "freed-up" that, barely listening to what each other was saying. I scanned their faces for anyone I might approach about Extra, but did not recognize any.

Arriving at the front of St. Paul's, I was pleased to see that it too was spared of the fire. The sight of its front steps and tall columns were comforting. But there was little coming and going in the church itself and I saw no familiar face to whom I could post inquiry.

I decided to journey to Chimborazo.

If Extra was in town and did not come to me, he might be hurt. If so, he might be in the ward for wounded slaves. I had heard him speak of it, but during my visits with Missus Pegram to deliver flower bunches and pet the soldiers, we never stopped in that particular ward and I did not know its location.

Passing the grounds of the Great House, I saw it was covered with clusters of people huddled in camps and little makeshift tents. Everyone of them looked so hangdog I could not conjure what it was all about until halfway past the block, when it struck me dumb—they were the put-outs, the persisters, people displaced by the fire, white folks whose homes had burned, and many of them, I conjured, were the odd ones committing much of the thievery two nights past. They were everywhere on the rising hill, their little encampments and small pit-fires stretched right up to the base of the Great House of Government. Some had a variety of satchels and household bric, which they gathered protectively in private huddles. I saw cooking pots, oil lamps, and a painted portrait of Jesus on the cross that leaned against an oak tree. There were bits of furniture, salvaged, most likely, before the fire took their homes. A variety of chairs were littered about—some appeared taken straight from the dining table. And there was even a fancy curved-back seat with fine cushions that reminded me of our own Queen Anne chair. A man in a dirty suit sat upon it, shoulders in a stoop, arms limp, afflicted; his suffering eyes looked out at the world without looking at anything in particular. A woman on a stool sat next to him, her head buried in her crinolines gathered about her knees.

I walked on into the greatest concentration of Yankees that surrounded the hill of government. They buzzed everywhere around the buildings known to me as the "departments." Missus Pegram could list them with familiarity: "War Department," "Treasury," "Court Chambers," and so on.

Also buzzing about were the many gatherings of slaves, those who tended house, kitchen, stable, and grounds. They were at loiter and lollygagging in huddled groups everywhere; all without any passing Yankee seeming to care or even take notice. There were field hands, too, who had traveled in from the farms and plantations. They were easy enough to spot, as they were the most unkempt and wore the poorest clothing, many having little more than overall britches.

Just as with the others, the field hands spoke about being "freed-up," waving their arms and saying "you is free," "we is free," and so forth.

It took about three-quarters of an hour to reach Church Hill, which I passed quickly enough. On the other side came Chimborazo Hill, and atop that was the spreading ground of that vast place of awful suffering.

The approach to the hospital was a long dirt road and a short land bridge spanning a great gully. On this morning the undrained gully was swollen with water delivered by the rains of the previous week, which made the land bridge a muddy pass worsened by multitudes of Yankee wagon wheels churning the ruts into an impassable bog.

The going was so unpleasant, I thought of turning back. My feet sunk deep. The mud caked onto my newly polished brokens and oozed nearly past my ankles. Passing Yankees on horseback eyeballed me hard but none stopped, the mud being so thick it required them to keep a full gallop else their horses too would become wedged tight in the muck. I was set to abandon the trudge when a double-team dray halted nearby.

"Grab a-holt." The driver was a Yankee man hauling a load of crated goods up the hill. There was no room for me in the wagon, not even on the seat beside him as the crates occupied every available space.

"Just grab a-holt. Ain't got no room, girl. Just grab a-holt," he said. I sludged to the wagon's side, each foot making a sucking noise as it pulled from the mud. The right wheel had a fender-guard and beside it, a foot-tread. I put one foot on the tread, gripped the wagon with one hand and intertwined the other arm around the ropes securing the crates.

"Aw'ight. That's it. Hold on, girl," the driver said. I noticed he was short and chubby, though his nose could offer no comparison with that of the other portly Yankee who stood near the house on the previous night. He whipped the double-team and we lurched and lunged over the gully along the land bridge. Chunks of mud flew off the turning wheels, splattering my

gingham. Once up the hill and upon the grounds of Chimbo-
rozo the going eased up, the team snorted loudly, and the wet
mud fell away from hooves and wheels. I knocked my brokens
against the wagon sideboards, making the mud fall away in
large clumps.

"Gimme a shout," the driver barked, turning his head toward
me. "I'm delivering to main medical supply. Building sixteen.
You gimme a shout." I nodded, grateful that he made the team
walk easy after we arrived atop the grounds, allowing me to
eyeball everything. A solid-color flag of yellow flew from a pole,
the sign of what I knew to be soldiers in a state of suffering. Just
as in downtown Richmond, the Yankees were everywhere on the
hill and they were all in a state of busy movement. Wagons,
horses, men, soldiers, servants, and even children swarmed
about with hasty mission. I understood why the Yankees were in
Richmond—but Chimborazo, the site of Butternut misery and
suffering? It was a mystery. How did they even know about it?
And why did they wish to be here, too?

Bouncing along, perched on the foot-tread of the low-riding
dray, I paid close attention to all countenances. Extra's tallness
would make him easy to spot. All windows were open, revealing
much inside activity. There were men with ear trumpets. Plump
women with tightly tied hair buns bustled about with so many
armloads of rags that I fancied it must be wash day. Each building entrance had a gathering of men at loiter in all stages of
injury, though some did not appear wounded at all.

As the horse tails constantly switched at flies, we rattled
deeper into the grounds, passing ward after ward, but none
provided sign of Extra's tall carriage. I also kept an eye out for
Master Pegram. Had he been wounded, he too would have been
taken to Chimborazo. But still, I detected no familiar countenance. Finally the short driver heaved at the team and we
lurched to a stop.

"Main medical supply. Building sixteen," he announced. I stepped off and moved to the side. The arm that gripped the lash ropes was stinging. I gave it a good rubbing and scraped mud from my brokens on the split logs of a nearby pile of firewood. It was then I noticed the flies. They had been buzzing at us since the wagon first lurched onto the pathways in and around the ward buildings, but now that I had dismounted, the greatness of their number was ugly. Large and mean, they flocked around the buildings in great dark clouds. I felt a woeful pity for any man, Butternut or Yankee, who lay in a bed where such unrelenting torment hammered at them. I swatted at the flies who found me a worthy target until I moved farther from building sixteen, which eased their attentions.

The driver yelled some words and a pair of scraggly men with a wheel cart emerged to transfer the wagon's crated-up goods into the building. Judging from their sad condition, I guessed them to be wounded Butternut boys, but not wounded enough to be in a bed, or stationed at loiter in front of the many wards as so many others were.

The short, plump driver dismounted, lit a short, plump cigar, and commenced puffing away as he watched the two sorry men labor with the wheel cart as though supervising them. I hoped he could offer aid to my purpose.

The aroma of the cigar wafted over me and smelled good. At the rear of the wagon he turned away, unbuttoned his trousers, then let go with a yellow stream that splattered in the mud. Just as the stream was fading he ripped off a volley of gas with considerable volume, enough to draw a disinterested glance from the two scraggly workers.

He returned to puffing and pacing with a distraction, then wandered near me. "You working here?" he asked plainly. I shook my head no. "People? You got your people here?" Again I shook my head. "No work. No people. Why you want to be on this mud hill, girl?"

"I'm looking for Extra, sir," I blurted.

He paused puffing, removed the cigar from his mouth, and looked at me. "Looking?"

"Yessah."

"Looking for what?"

"Extra," I repeated.

"Extra what?"

"Dat's his name. Extra."

"Who's name?"

"The man I'm lookin' for."

"What kind of name is that?" I was uncertain how to relieve him of his confusion.

"That's who I'm looking for. Extra. That's his name. He might be here at Chimborazo."

A bolt of clarity came into his face. "Oh. A slave boy!" He grinned and wiped yellow cigar juice from his lip, then chuckled at me with eyes that enjoyed some sort of joke. "Well, that's a good name for a slave boy. Afterall, a slave is something 'extra' ain't it?" He chuckled more loudly. "Or maybe he was his Momma's 'extra.' " That made his chuckle turn into outright laughter. He showed teeth the color of sickly yellow with wide spaces between each of them.

"He work at de Spotswood Hotel. He a porter there. But he ain't there. Sometimes he loaned out to de tobacco business, sometimes to de war business."

He weighed my words. "Well, if your man ain't on his job at the hotel, he sure ain't working the warehouses."

"Sah?"

"You look at your city on the way up this hill, girl?"

"Yessah."

"Wha-chu see, girl?"

"Fires?" I said.

271

"Fires, indeed. Johnny sent all the tobacco to blazes. Mayo Bridge, too. As for the war, well, that's near 'bout over. Johnny's on the run from Petersburg is what I hear."

"Over?"

"Near 'bout. One thing's a certainty. It's over in this city o'ruin." He nodded at the burned area in the distance. "And if it's over in Richmond, why, it's near 'bout over everywhere."

"Yessah," I said.

"Where's that leave you?"

"Sah?"

"Well, there's no tobacco. There's no war. So your man could hardly be sent off to work either when both enterprises are put out of business."

"Yessah."

He resumed puffing his cigar and his attention strayed away from me. He considered the scraggly workers, who slowly moved the crates from wagon to building. Flies swarmed at them both, yet they did not object as forcefully as I would in the same situation.

There were no trees on Chimborazo. They'd all been cleared to make way for the many ward buildings, making it a mudhill of unnatural nakedness filled up with great ugliness on the outside and great suffering on the inside. From building sixteen, I could look down one row and see perhaps twenty ward buildings, ten on each side of the path, and every doorway had a variety of men at loiter, smoking and dozing—many with bodies absent arms and legs. Some limped about the mud on crutches; some wore little more than long-john rags, making it impossible to know the Yankees from the Butternut.

Halfway down the row, there was a gathering at the door of one building—a bunch of Yankees that retained their blue coats. In the middle of the group stood a man who'd been chopped off at opposite corners. With no right arm, nor left leg, he stood with one crutch tucked under his one arm as he leaned heavily on the opposite leg. I stared at him so long I felt bad about it and turned back to the short man. The scraggly workers toted their final load. They returned into building sixteen and closed the door behind them.

"Grab up," the short man said. He climbed up the wagon and seized the reins. "C'mon girl, grab up. Let's look for this Extra boy of yours on our way down this ugly hill-o'-mud."

"Yes-sah," I said, moving quick. It was what I hoped for. I climbed aboard again, this time sitting beside him on the buck-bench. He gripped his cigar in the corner of his mouth as he worked the double team into a turn and we headed deeper into Chimborazo's town of wards and suffering men.

"What's this Extra boy of yours look like?" he asked.

"He tall, sah."

"Tall is he?"

"Yessah."

"Anything else?"

"No, sah. He just tall."

"Welly, well. That's fine, I suppose. Tall ain't much. But with a name like 'Extra' we probably don't need much more'n that."

We commenced stopping at every other building and everywhere that wounded men were at loiter.

"Anyone know of a slave boy working here on loan. Tall. Goes by the name of Extra?" Mostly they just stared back with dumb eyes; the ones capable of it would shake their heads "no." Once in a while, one or two would hobble near the wagon hoping to buy or beg tobacco. Each time the short driver said he had none to spare, which I knew to be a lie. Besides the cigar he was puffing, he had at least one additional cigar tucked inside his coat pocket.

His tongue loosened during the mission. In between stops to make our inquiries about Extra, he talked a streak of blue. He had an odd way of speaking, in short bursts that came from the side of his mouth and not at all spoken with the proper, civil manners of Missus or Master Pegram. He was a sergeant in the Yankee medical corps. He told me his name, but it was mysteriously long and I did not understand it. He was from the city of Dancer in Europe, which is not in France. He told me how his own mother and father arrived by boat at the northern City of Jersey, strode from the boat right into town, where they bought a shop on Main Street with some cash, some barter, and something he called "promissory portion of future profits." I liked the sound of the words and repeated them back to him.

"Promissory portion of future profits."

"That's right," he nodded with approval. "It worked out good for 'em, too. They set up shop and were selling hardware, shodding horses, and bartering for dry goods within three days of walking off that boat. My momma and daddy are hard at work there right this minute. 'Jersey Shop of Sundries,' it's called. They're doing fine." He spoke with pride about his family. "The war has been good for business. I'll be back soon to help 'em out, just as soon as Bobby Lee stops his running and I get my discharge."

He went on about past wars. His father's father profited plenty from previous battles pitting Empire So-and-So against So-and-So Empire. He puffed and talked and talked and puffed all the way down the hill, pausing only to inquire about Extra with the various wounded men standing at loiter.

At one stop, we witnessed the performance of a man gone odd. It was the usual fly-swarmed gathering of wounded Yankees at loiter around a ward-building doorway. They met his questions about Extra by eyeballing each other, giving helpless shrugs, saying they never heard of anyone by that name, then asked for a handout of tobacco or rum. One of them, with a bloodied bandage around his neck and chest, asked if we had any news from Philadelphia.

"It's still there soldier," the driver yelled. "You'll be back soon enough."

"Yessir. Can't be too soon for me. True what we hearing on Petersburg?"

"True enough, soldier. Bobby Lee is on the run." With that, a scrawny fellow, who'd been sitting on a log amid the Yankees, rose from his sad, droopy haunches and commenced whining, wailing, and thrashing. His filthy long-johns hung from his stooped shoulders like a sack; his only other attire was the cap of his Butternut uniform. He wide eyes spelled a terror; he swung his arms about like a man out of control, but he was in such sorry health that each effort was a slow, pitiful struggle.

"Naw-w-w," he cried slowly, "naw-w-w," as he bucked about slapping at his sides, then "aieee, aieee," he wailed, staggering and tugging at his whiskers. He turned his attention to the Yankees and tried to strike at them—none were in any condition for fighting, but one with a thickly bandaged leg managed to square his position and bring his crutch around on the Butternut's backside, which sent the pitiful fellow into the mud with a belly flop. Even then his raving would not be silenced. He rolled over to one side and commenced shrieking and crying great sobs of remorse. "Nawww," he cried in between his loud weeping, "nawww, nawww, nawww."

The driver gee'd the double team and we lurched away from the scene, leaving the Butternut man crying in the mud amid the ravenous flies. The hapless Yankees stared down at him, scratching at themselves as they watched.

"Goddam," the driver cursed. "That's all there was yesterday morning. I been driving wagon-loads of goods and wounded men up and down this hill for twenty-four hours straight without relent. At first, that's all there was. They were all crying, trying to run, vowing to fight. Fight, fight, fight. That's all they talked about. Goddam, they're near 'bout dead. Ain't no fight left in them Johnny bodies. Most of the ones that got left here could barely get out of bed. 'Course, the spirit ain't dead. I even saw a Johnny boy with no legs dragging himself through Chimborazo mud to avoid capture." He spit yellow juice over the wagon side. "That'll all change soon enough. Their spirit'll break when Bobby Lee hangs. Ya gotta break the spirit," he said with hard tones at me, showing me yellow teeth with all the spaces separating them. "That's the secret to ending all appetite for fightin'. Breaking the spirit. It's the only way."

The double team needed no guidance. I could tell they had journeyed among the ward buildings enough times to find no surprise in it, except now they bridled objections at the frequent stops being made on my behalf.

Near the end of the downhill leg, the muddy path pulled away from the ward buildings and the blackened pitch of downtown Richmond came into full view. It was a sad sight in the mid-morning sun. The thick, dark columns of smoke were gone, but thin ghosts of smokey cloud lingered above the great piles of warehouse rubble. To the south I could see the river, and beyond it the smaller city of Manchester, which held steady without any sign of the war having visited. Beyond the western edge of Richmond, the great cemetery was visible on yet another hill in the distance, its many trees of holly shading the dead from the rising warmth of the day

We concluded the descent; the double team left the flies and mud behind and lurched back onto the dry dirt streets of Richmond, their bobbing heads showing satisfaction to be relieved of the strain the mud placed upon their legs. The short man's ministrations to my purpose had found no useful news.

We pulled onto Broad Street, one of the few paved over with cobblestones, setting up a fine clip-clopping sound. The driver waved at an oncoming wagon and we all skidded to a broadside stop, mid-street. It was a work wagon, much like the one I was riding on, except that its sideboards were painted in white and decorated with red lettering. The much-faded print was still easy enough to read the words: "Mrs. Semmes Boarding School for Virginia Ladies." But the wagon bore neither ladies nor crates. Instead, it carried five men sitting on stools, tightly holding on to the sideboards to avoid being tossed over as the wagon pulled to a quick stop. The driver and each man perched in the rear were smartly dressed in fresh suits and little hats with narrow brims that sat atop their heads instead of coming down around their ears. Four of them had ear trumpets hanging from their necks.

"Good morning, sirs," my driver said, skidding the double team to a full halt. He saluted the men, who all promptly returned the salute and sang out a chorus of "good mornings" in response.

"I can report to you that the storehouse is now fully stocked. Building sixteen, final delivery just completed."

"Very good, Sergeant," the wagon driver said. "Where're you bound now?"

"North. The turnpike. Reconnoiter at the Fredericksburg rail line. They're working to get the lines repaired out there. More shipments coming in near 'bout every hour."

"Did the chloroform survive delivery this time, Sergeant?" It was one of the riders wearing an ear trumpet.

"Yessir, Captain. Ether, too. Ain't no breakage to report, regardless of that mud. And there's plenty of opium, too. Just arrived this morning on shipment from Baltimore."

"Very good, Sergeant," the driver said. He was ready to salute and gee-up his team.

"Who's your friend, Sergeant?" one of the riders asked.

"War waif, sir. Picked her up on the hill. Looking for her fella. Thought maybe he's impressed on Chimborazo. But he ain't there." The men studied me and I noted their glancing faces indulged in some amusement.

"Well, he likely wouldn't be working anywhere," one said, hitting hard at the word "working." "Most of 'em are in the street celebrating."

"That's a fact," another rider with an ear trumpet said. "They are one happy group of people this morning." He tacked on a type of singsong whistle to his words and shook his head. The others joined in with a chorus of nods and smiles.

"They are that!" said another. "They are prancing and parading about in downtown Richmond like it's Saturday night in church. Hap-pee, Happy! Yessir!"

"Yessir!"

"Oh, yes!" another said, adding to the chorus.

"They are having themselves a regular party if you know what I mean, Sergeant," one of them spoke from the corner of his mouth with a wink. They all smiled broadly, their heads bobbing up and down, enjoying the private nature of their fun. My driver chuckled too, but I understood none of it.

" 'Course, some of 'em are being pressed to work," said the first one who inquired about me. "But it's doubtful your man is among them, now the fires are out. Not unless he has some skill that can be put to use."

"What's your man do?" another rider asked straight at me.

"Hotel porter, sah."

There was a moment of silence.

"Well, girl, you'd best check the hotels," he said. "Give him some time, he'll likely show up in a day or two."

That marked the end of the encounter. The driver of the boarding school wagon gee'd his team and it lurched east, headed for Chimborazo's mud. My driver gave them a quick salute, chopping at the air with his hand and gee'd the double team.

I turned to watch their departure. They all held onto their peculiar little hats with one hand to prevent them from flying off; they gripped the wagon sideboards with the other hand to avoid being spilled from their rickety stools. Their ear trumpets flopped about as they all struggled to keep balance. I wondered why they didn't they just sit on the floor of the wagon.

"Oh, those poor men," the driver said after they passed. "Oh, my, oh, my! Those poor men." He held the cigar in the corner of his mouth without puffing it. "Unh, unh, unh!" He looked down at his lap, shaking his head. "Never has this city witnessed passage of such a wagonfull of sadness as that one." I recalled the wagon of torment that stopped at the house Sunday morning, unable to imagine a wagon of sadness worse than that.

"Who were they?" I asked.

"Girl, you be grateful that no matter what travails you may be facing in the days to come, you will not be a patient in any ward, laying upon any bed on Chimborazo Hill on this day."

"They not dressed like soldiers," I ventured. He removed his cigar and sucked hard at his teeth, making a clicking sound.

"Well, they may not be dressed in full uniform like regular soldiers, but they are soldiers. They are captains. And girl, they are more than officers. They are surgeon doctors. Everyone of 'em." He looked at me straight on and spoke with the weight of the Sunday morning preacher. "And with five surgeon doctors headed for Chimborazo all at one time, with a storehouse full of chloroform and every ward filled up with the ailing—unh, unh, unh. It sure is a sad thing. The bone saws will be busier than ever before. By the end of this day the furnaces will be stoked hot, burning up piles of feet and arms and legs cut from them boys' bodies. Oh my goodness! Unh, unh, unh!" He looked away and slowly shook his head some more.

After that, he spoke little as we clip-clopped a few blocks west on the fine cobblestones of Broad Street. It was a part of

279

Richmond I had never seen, Missus Pegram never having any reason to bring me this far. Broad Street itself was the widest in all Richmond. We passed houses, buildings, and open fields. We passed a set of train tracks with rails curled in the air, looking to me like a giant man had twisted them into a lady's hairpin. Farther on there was a train engine, burned, without wheels, sitting plump and useless upon its bottom. If trains can die, this was a dead train. It looked like a giant black pig had dropped dead and been left to rot right where it spent its final breath.

We passed a building with grounds and front steps filled with great numbers of servants, mostly women and children. They were sitting and standing within the boundaries of the yard as though it were a thing apart, a different country, a private zone of safety. Many were eating, partaking of what looked to be bowls of soup. I twisted in my seat to study them as we passed. A few took note of me and returned the study.

The driver saw my interest and broke his silence.

"Church of Africa! For the freed-up," he said as though announcing the next song for the chorus. "Free Baptists!" he added. "Seeking refuge in the church! I'll tell you, times don't change much. That's just like olden days when the serfs and vassals headed straight for cathedral at first sign their lords and leaders were taking to arms over some challenge." I was uncertain of his meaning. Only after we had completely passed it did I turn back to the front of the wagon, where I noticed he was glancing my way.

" 'Course, times have changed in one respect," he said in a friendly tone. "They're the ones with sense enough to behave themselves, to get off the streets and stand aside. 'Cause most of the colored folks are out here on the streets prancing and parading." He shook his head with inner amusement. "Yes, ma'am!" he spoke loudly to the horses. "Prancing and parading." He glanced again at me and winked, puffing up the fire tip of his plump cigar.

A short while later the wagon reached Twelfth and Broad Streets, where the Great House of Government came into view on the southern side, serving as my landmark.

"I'll get out now, sah," I said.

"Very well." He tugged the double team to a halt. "Good luck to you."

"Thank you for your kindesses, sah," I said after stepping down. He nodded and gee'd at the team, and the wagon quickly passed.

Once again, I was alone upon the streets of Richmond.

CHAPTER THIRTY-THREE:
EXTRA PETTIGREW

We finished putting out the fires by mid-morning Tuesday, stopping only to be fed a breakfast of fine cornmeal bread and a generous hunk of fatback.

The Yankees worked hard getting things back to order as best they could. Big groups of 'em worked at putting out the fires. Others stood vidette in front of what buildings of government did not get taken down by the flames. Freed-up slaves took to 'em with keen interest. They followed, calling after 'em, thanking 'em, clapping, yahooing, and yippie-yi-yaying over 'em, which the Yankees seemed to tolerate fairly well and some even liked it fine, stopping to take bows and laugh among themselves at the gathered crowds of black men and women who stood on corners making celebration.

Corporal Wadsworth wrote out his name and address in New York City for me. I thanked him, but did not say I doubted I would ever visit him in a place so far away.

Being done with my work, and Tuesday being my first full day as a free man, I cast about for a way to find my own manner of celebration. I again spotted Riverjames in the crowd and we idly walked together a while as he happily bounced from Yankee to Yankee offering gifts of free tobacco. He never missed a black man wearing Union blue but neither did he cheat any white Yankee. He gifted any of them that wanted a chaw or a cigar or a handful of loose leaf. After he paid visits to all Yankee videttes posted around Father Jefferson's Great House of

Government we both wandered back to St. Paul's. I didn't much want to wander with him in that direction, but was grateful I did. 'Twas there I saw Mister Maxcy Pegram rushing from the church. He was in a fluster of head-turning, his feet bobbing upon each step, moving so fast he nearly tumbled before reaching the pathway.

"Oh, Extra," he said with a relieved manner when he saw me.

"Sah?" I said, "is you back?"

"Yes," he said. "I arrived this morning. Extra, where is Miss Francine?"

"Sah, she with you." His shoulders fell as he gazed at me.

"She's not with me. And she's not with Ruth." Then he asked, "What about Ruth? What about my wife, Mistress Pegram. Have you seen her?"

"Not since she come out of church two days ago," I said. Then I asked, "Sah, how you get back so quick from your little farm in Roanoke Rapids?"

"Extra, I just got back from Danville. I haven't been to the farm. I discovered this morning that my house has been pillaged. It looks like a goddamn Chinese slop jar. Miss Francine is not in the house as she is supposed to be and I am uncertain as to my own wife's fate." He sat down on the steps of St. Paul's and made a heaving gesture to the east. "This city is burned and the South is undone," he said, putting his head in his hands.

"I is right sorry, sah," Riverjames said, bobbing about at a hover nearby. He held up his burlap sack. "Would you like a cigar, sah." Mister Pegram ignored him.

"This is horrible, just horrible," he cried. "I knew it was coming. We all did. Why did I allow myself to be away from home when it happened?" He looked again at the burned char that commenced directly across Ninth Street. "Oh, me," he said, "my wife is somewhere on the road to Petersburg in the aftermath to all of this. Oh, it's simply unfathomable."

"Sah," I said, "may I ask you, sah—if Mistress Pegram on her way to the little farm down at Roanoke Rapids, why you say Missy Fran not with her?" Instead of speaking back to me, he pulled out a notepaper from his side pocket and handed it over. I took it and studied it, then handed it back, wondering if his worry and fret made him forget about the facts. "Sah, I can't read." He took the notepaper and read aloud.

"I have evacuated to the farm with Helen Bartow and the Winders . . . I anticipate arrival shortly after nightfall . . . a horse and buggy awaits you at the Winder's stable . . . make immediate effort to join us upon your safe return to Richmond where Francine awaits."

"Francine not with her missus?" I asked.

"No."

"And she not in the house, either?"

"No."

"The church?"

"No. I just looked," he said. "And I've been to the Winders' house. It's more ramshackle than my own. There's no buggy. And there's certainly no horse."

I remembered then seeing that fine wagon with the stout team of horses bearing what I thought was Mistress Pegram and others I did not recognize. That must have truly been Mistress Pegram. But if Missy Fran was left at home, I couldn't figure why she wouldn't answer when I knocked, unless she was afraid. Like Mister Pegram, I was worried now.

"Mister Pegram, sah, where you 'speck she is?" I asked.

"Extra. I do not know. She must have just run off." He rose from the church steps in a way that let me know he was more than just worried. He was angry, too. "Ya'll free to do whatever 'tis ya'll want now. Isn't that the way it is? Absquatulate or parade in the streets like dogs in heat." He looked at the nearby rubble-ruins that still smoldered. "Just look at that," he said, his lips set to a full quiver. "That fire has reduced us all to a city of shadows."

Still ignoring Riverjames, he pushed past me and walked to the corner, where he turned to walk south down Ninth Street toward his house, looking like a man on his way to a funeral and about to bust with a full attack of blubbering.

So Missy Fran did not refugee with her mistress. And she was not in the house on Ninth Street. I had to find her. Now that things had changed, maybe the time had come to marry before it was too late. Maybe we could get set up somewhere with me working as a free black. That's what all the slaves were talking about—where to work, where to live, how to make better times happen with real wages.

But even with things changing over, I still mightily feared coming across Master Pettigrew and having him know I was not off working the ramparts as he expected. But fear or not, I knew I had to go to the Spotswood to look for Missy Fran, and Riverjames agreed to help me.

We went to the hotel the back way, down Ninth Street and through the overgrown field behind the Pegram House, then over the fence into the out-yard. I could tell from the type of smoke just starting to come from the rear kitchen chimney that ole Miss Edna was at work, so, still wanting to avoid Master Pettigrew, I sent Riverjames inside to make my inquiries. He came back with the news.

"Sh-sh-she look for you," he said.

"Missy Fran is looking for me?"

"Tha-that's what she sa-sa-say. She say Miss Francine co-come this mo-monin'. She ask 'bout you. And heh-head off 'gain when they tell her you not on de ramparts." Before I could ask anymore of him, ole Miss Edna was calling for me from the back porch of the kitchen.

"Extra," she rasped as loudly as she could. "Extra, yo com

hea." I ventured from my hiding place inside the slave-quarters and walked into the open, to greet ole Miss Edna.

"Yes, Miss Edna," I said.

"Yo go fin Miz Fran. She lok for yo. Now yo lok for her, too. Yo go fin. Den yo both come hea. To me."

"Yes, all right, Miss Edna."

"Dat 'potent. Yo come. When yo fin, yo both come to me. Dat 'potent."

"Why's it important, Miss Edna?"

"Nev-mind dat!" she rasped loudly, jerking her ancient arm and causing loose flesh to shake about on her bones. "Yo do. Dat 'potent."

"All right, Miss Edna," I said. "As soon as I find Missy Fran, we'll come to see you."

"Yah. Dat fin. Yo do dat."

"Is she all right, Miss Edna?" I asked.

"Yah. She fin. Go. Yo fin Miz Fran," she said as she walked back into the hotel kitchen.

Riverjames helped me. We asked after Missy Fran at St. Paul's and looked around the crowd of put-outs camping on the grounds of the Great House of Government. I knew now, at least, that she was not harmed. She had asked after me in the Spotswood not long before we encountered Mister Maxcy Pegram. That meant she was near, which meant we'd eventually find each other. But as for looking, I didn't know what else to do. I was set to walk back to the house on Ninth Street to see if she had returned there when Sergeant Paxton observed me and approached, drunker than drunk. He had cast off his Johnny jacket and exchanged his Butternut pants for regular trousers.

"Well, if it ain't that big ole buck," he said teetering toward me. "How you doing, Extra?"

"Mornin', sah," both Riverjames and I intoned to him with reluctant voices.

"You send them niggers to that ape man in Washington City like I told ya?"

"Sah?" I said, hoping he would totter on past us both if I played dumb.

"What about that Colonel Gist? You ever find that red-headed prig?"

"No, sah."

"Just as well. He probably skeedaddled out of town. Ain't no point in fighting no more. Look at all this here," he said, eyeing the Yankees and gesturing at a pair of black men in blue uniform. "Ain't that a sorry sight?"

"Sah?"

"It is. It is one sorry sight for sore eyes. Just a goddam shame. Violation of nature. That's what it is, goddam violation of nature." He teetered and spit into the dirt, catching himself before he fell down. "Whatchu do with that wagon, boy?"

"Sold it, sah." His manner changed fast and I knew I had made a mistake.

"You sold that wagon and sorry old mule team?"

"Uh . . ."

He came in close to me. I could smell his whiskey breath. " 'Uh?' " he repeated, mocking me.

"Uh, yes-sah," I said.

"How much you get?" I decided there would be no value in dodging and no risk in speaking truthfully. With so many Yankees about and all the freed-up slaves celebrating, I doubted there was anything he could do to me.

"Four dollar Yankee," I told him. He reeled back, as though I'd just slapped him a good pop. After a moment he recovered.

"You got the four on you, boy?"

"Yes-sah."

"How old are you boy?"

"Sixteen."

"Sixteen." He rubbed his chin while he studied me. "You ever ride a woman boy?"

"Sah?"

"I say, you ever ride a woman?"

"Uh . . ."

"Naw!" he laughed, waving an arm and nearly losing his balance, "you ain't never." He got close to speak in confidence. "Listen, boy, I still got fifty-cent Yankee. You give me two of your four dollars and I'll see you get admitted to Screamersville. That's one place where people so drunk with whiskey and jubilation that blackness don't matter no more. I seen it for myself. Ace o'spades or jack o'diamonds. But it's because the war is over, so that ain't gonna last much longer. You gotta go now and you gotta have an escort. You split the four with me and I'll vouchsafe you into Screamersville. You can get drunk and spend the rest of the day in congress with a fine whore-woman."

"Uh . . ."

"Never mind 'uh,' boy! C'mon, let's go." I was uncertain. I wanted to find Missy Fran, but I do confess I had some fondness for his proposal. I turned to my friend.

"Riverjames, you want to go to whore-town?" I asked.

"No tha-tha-thanky, Extra. I got my wa-wa-work here. I got to say 'thankee to de Yankee.' It de work o'dah Lord. It specially de work o'dah Lord since de ta-ta-talkin' bush done picked me special for my special duties."

I smiled at him. It was a clever joke about the talking bush and the great laughter we shared two nights before under the statue of Father Washington. Sometimes Riverjames could surprise you, making you realize he wasn't so dumb after all.

"You behave yourself," I told him. "You stay out of trouble now."

"Ain't no trouble 'bout doin' the Lord's work," he said,

bouncing and smiling back at me.

It's true, I had never been to a whorehouse and there were times that I wished mightily that I could pay a visit to one. Now, with things changing over, money in my pocket and my days as a single man counting down to the day I would wed Missy Fran, I figured it to be an acceptable way to spend the afternoon. I nodded at the drunk Sergeant Paxton, who hastened to take the lead, wobbling the short distance to Byrd Alley and Screamersville whore-town, which lay concealed in the shadow of the Great House of Government.

At midday, the whore-town was bustling with business and the Yankees paid us no mind. They were in Screamersville for whiskey and women and didn't seem to mind much about me. Sergeant Paxton introduced me to a white whore-woman who took my money and led me into a tent pitched right in the middle of the Screamersville yard.

It was fine.

I don't know how he knew, but Master Pettigrew found me in whore-town. As before, I figured he wanted to whup me. But he didn't.

"Extra," he said, "can I speak with you?" I pulled on my long-johns. We walked to a side table and ordered grog drinks that turned my tongue with a sour taste—but I drank it down anyway. I much preferred the fine bourbon I got drunk on Sunday night in the bushes under the statue of Father Washington, but that was all long gone. The woman who served us was naked—a great black whore-woman with bosoms the size of over-ripened melons and big ole legs. Master Pettigrew looked her over good.

"Yes-sah?" I asked.

"Extra," he began, "this changes everything. Of course, you

already know that. I'll get right to my purpose in seeking you out, Extra. If you return to the hotel and work for me—I will pay you a wage and give you a room of your own."

"Sah?"

"That's right. A room of your own to live in—*inside* the hotel. Of course, it won't be a front room, or on an upper floor. But it will be your own."

"Sah."

"I need you, Extra. Ress-uh-ress; business is business. You're a good worker. And you've got some smarts. Of course, there's good reason for that. But, if you come work for me, I think you'll be happier."

"I dunno, sah."

He looked about at the various whore-women in various states of nakedness.

"Go ahead, celebrate. If I was you—I would." He again eyed the big girl that served us grog. "But after the celebrating is over—well, I think you'll find a lot of the freed-up negroes will have a rough time of it. True, they're now free from ownership. But they will not be free from necessities. Come work for me. You'll be better off."

It was right odd for me. There I was—sitting down at a table with my former master like an equal—negotiating over my own labors while surrounded by whores in the act of delivering their wares to groaning men who had paid the price.

"Sah, why you say there's a good reason for me having some smarts?" He stopped glancing away at whore-women and the men occupied with collecting their pleasures. He held a steady eye on me.

"Extra," he said after a pause, "I'm going to tell you something you do not know."

"Yes-sah?"

"Extra—you're mine."

"Sah?"

"You're mine, Extra. Mine."

"No, sah. Things done changed."

"No. I don't mean that. You're no longer my property. That has changed. But you're still mine. He tossed out more dead Latin that sounded like "my-uz-vizkus." "It means, you are of my own flesh and blood. And that will never change."

It took me a moment to understand what he was telling me. "Who my momma?" I asked, once it became clear.

"Eh?"

"Master Pettigrew, sah, if I your own flesh and blood, who my momma?"

"Extra, your race has been a burden to the white man for two centuries in this country. We have tried to do right by you. Now, for better or worse, things have changed. As a man of business, it is my duty to do what I must to survive. Ress-uh-ress. And I want to do the right thing by you. Come and work for me. And you won't have to call me 'master' any longer."

"Who my momma?" I demanded.

"Extra, I'm going to give you some advice. Sometimes it's best to let the past just stay in the past. That's where it belongs."

"Did I know my momma?" He leaned in, looking at me good and hard, and lost all interest in the whoring going on all around us.

"Extra, your momma was the whore-woman I sold off when whore-towns like this one popped up everywhere. Extra, Miss Avery-Ann was my concubine and she was your momma. I couldn't compete with places like this, and I needed the money, so I sold her off."

"Why nobody ever toll me she my momma?"

"I wouldn't let them. And they didn't want you to know that your momma was a whore-woman."

Well, I didn't know what to do. I didn't know whether I

should run away as fast as my feet could carry me—or go back to the Spotswood and work for him. I was glad when he told me to think about his offer and departed Screamersville. He even gave me two dollars Yankee, which he called "a gesture of goodwill." He said I could show up at the Spotswood whenever I wanted, whenever I finished whoring. He said I could just show up, get my own room, and go to work as hotel porter— but this time for real wages.

I felt right sick. I knew what it meant. After all, I was there the night she was born. I won't but four year old, but I raised her and kept her in clean unders when she a baby. Now I knew that she was more than I thought. She was more than just Missy Fran. She was what they call—half-sister. We had the same momma. Her daddy was her master, Mister Maxcy Pegram. My daddy was my master, Mister Mills P. Pettigrew. But we had the same momma—the concubine Miss Avery-Ann Pettigrew. That meant we couldn't get married. That's why Cussin' Sally-Martha didn't want me to find Missy Fran. That's what ole Miss Edna wanted to tell us. She wanted to tell us that we can't get married. We just can't. 'Cause Missy Fran was my sister.

CHAPTER THIRTY-FOUR:
MISS FRANCINE PEGRAM

I let my brokens carry me down Twelfth Street. Within one block of the Great House of Government I came to know what the surgeon-doctors were winking and smiling about. The slave and house servants were celebrating in the streets. When I first passed the area that morning, they were gathering on the corners, pooling their wits and talking about freedom. Now, it seemed every slave in Richmond was emptied from their houses, hotels, and kitchens to gather in larger groups. They cheered and, in general, made a festive ruckus everywhere I looked.

Women slaves paraded about with their bosom-tops on wide display as though they were mistresses at an evening social. Slave men laughed loudly, encouraging the women to mock their mistresses and masters.

"Fetch muh dinna, yo sweet tang," one man shouted, clapping his hands for a happy dancing woman, her prominent bosom waving about.

"Fetch it yo-sef," came the retort, as she pranced up and down waving her hips, her hands on her waist.

"Fetch muh apple pie, sweet tang." He clapped out a regular rhythm.

"Fetch it yo-sef," she said again, dancing.

"Fetch muh to-bak-ee."

Again, "Fetch it yo-sef."

"Fetch muh slippers, sweet tang."

"Fetch yo own damn slippers." With each chorus his clapping

grew louder, her smile grew wider, and all onlookers cooed and wowed with noisy approval. Then came the finale.

"I say, sweet tang, fetch muh whiskey." She stopped prancing and wiggling and turned to face the man.

"Ain't no whiskey to fetch to yo sorry sef. I done drank all de damn whiskey!" That sent up an uproar of happy approval from the crowd, which laughed and waved and nodded and clapped.

The many small and large gatherings blocked passageways and spilled onto the streets, blocking traffic in many places, forcing the Yankees to maneuver around them, which they did without objection.

Some slave men wondered noisily about their fate: "What-now?" . . . "What-nex?" . . . "Wha-choo-goan-do?" . . . and so forth. Some of them loudly proclaimed their gleeful vows: "Ain't gonna tote dis" . . . "Ain't gonna fetch dat" . . . "Ain't gonna do for de massa no mo."

The ones who chose not to dance or mill about sat on curbstones, porches, and doorways singing gospels. It was as if all of Richmond had turned into one great outdoor church assembly and everywhere there was song, talk, and loud banter about freedom. I watched the displays, wishing I could find Extra so that we too might celebrate the end of our own slavery.

On Twelfth Street just past the Great House of Government, the charred city commenced. Between there and the river lay only ruin. I crossed Bank Street, sensing that if my wanderings led me back to the house, at least a quick dinner of ham and coffee could be taken before I left again to continue my search.

Pinching my nose to block the foul odor of blackened slag, I saw yet another crowd of excited people coming toward me from down below, near the river. It was distant, but I could see it was not just another gathering of prancing slaves and servants. There were Yankees, important men in suits, servants, and even children. The time was not yet noon, but the cool of the morning had long departed and the heat of the day had commenced. Some men in the crowd removed their coats to drape upon their arms as they labored up the hill, through the burned city. Instead of turning, I crossed Main Street toward the gathering and met up with them south of Cary Street, even as more servants emerged from the charred ruins to join its outer edges, which consisted of a circle of Yankees-at-arms marching with formal airs. Within their own tight redoubt, a few fancy-dressed men kept up at a brisk clip. At the very center was a tall man with a rangy gait, wearing a top hat like the one Compson Winder wore. He held hands with a doll-faced little boy who struggled to keep up.

Dust whipped and swirled around the group as it grew in size. The front was kept open as soldiers gestured for all on-comers to move to the sides, which gave me a good view. A trio of field hands who emerged from the charred ruins shouted with excitement at the sight.

"Bres-de-Lord!" said one of the laborers, his large hands pressed to the side of his face. "It's Massa Lincomme hisself! He done come to Richmond!"

"Ju-bee-lo!" pronounced another, dancing a jig. "Dis de day o'jubelo!"

"He here! He here! Oh, Lordy, I see'um, I see'um!" praised the third with loud excitement. "I see'um wid my own eyes." They moved toward the advancing group, blending with the others as it continued to increase in size and excitement.

Different ones called out to him. "Massa Lincomme" . . . "Praise Jesus" . . . "Oh Lawd" . . . "You is de savya" . . . "Thank de aw-mighty" . . . "It's de salvation" . . . "Oh Massa Lin-comme."

The chorus of praise and whipped-up excitement continued until the group enveloped me at its very center. I did not maneuver to make it happen. I was standing stark-dumb in the middle of Twelfth Street and was obliged to either join up or get bumped by a multitude of elbows as they passed over me. As I posed no worry to the soldiers, they made no objection to my presence, so I took the option of walking next to the tall man and opposite the doll-faced boy, now retracing my steps back to the north.

I guessed the boy to be about my own age. He wore a fancy suit, a long black overcoat, and silk hat. A loose black ribbon adorned his neck. His face blushed the color of cherries as he took in the sights swirling about him; the rest of him bleached whiter than white as he huffed and puffed to keep up the pace. He clutched the tall man's forearm with affection and the fearful dependence of a suckling puppy. He looked at me and I smiled, which seemed to please him.

As for the tall man, he possessed all the proper attire to compose a gentlemanly appearance, but nonetheless he seemed disheveled in some general way. His shoes, I could clearly see, were in need of boot buff. I noted not only his height, made so by the awkward length of his springy legs, but also the unseemly length of his fingers, his arms, and even his neck, which was unshaven beneath his dark whiskers. One shoulder stooped below the other. His face was drawn, but content. There was a glint of ready happiness in his dark, sad eyes. They were eyes that appeared to look into the beyond, at things unseen.

As it moved north, the crowd became so large it could no longer keep a brisk pace. When the Great House of Government came into full view, with its grounds filled with the hangdog masses displaced by the fires, the group halted completely; one large servant was so overcome with excitability, he dropped to his knees directly in front of the crowd's center, clasping his hands in prayer. The soldiers stiffened as they watched to see his intentions.

"Oh, Massa Lincomme," he bawled, looking up at the tall

man. "I rather see you than Jesus hisself! You is more 'potent, sah!" The praying man blocked passage. The cherry-faced boy firmed his clutch upon the tall man's forearm. "Massa, we is saved," he continued. "You is de savya." The man gasped for air, bawling great tears that rolled down his huge, brawny face made dirty from hard labor and swollen with the fevers of jubilation.

The tall man loosened the boy's grip, extended his arm around the young one's shoulders, and leaned down to him. "Son, you need not fear these kind people," he said quietly.

He turned to the praying man as the crowd grew hushed. "You must not kneel to me. You must kneel only to the Lord," he said in firm tones. "It is the Lord who provides your liberty."

His words concluded, he again took the blushing boy's hand and resumed his stride uptown.

Looking for a reaction as they moved past him, the crowd eyeballed the kneeling man. He held to his position upon his knees, looking up, straining his neck with a pivot to watch as the tall man loped past him. He stopped bawling and turned silent, his eyes flushed with a touch of the spirit. I could hear his mumbling as we passed him by.

"Moses," the kneeling man whispered to himself with rapt tones of amazement. "Moses done come!"

The crowd soon grew so large it became unmanageable. One of the soldiers barked a command resulting in the others withdrawing long knives, which they attached to the business end of their musket-rifles. That rapidly made the crowd more somber, causing them to give the center extra leeway.

The tall man paused to regard the stately columns that ringed the Great House of Government before continuing north across Grace, Broad, Marshal, and Clay Streets. People who chose not to join the parade stood on porches and crates, staring with fixed wonder at the passing spectacle. Mistresses, masters, and slaves alike gawked long and hard; many held babies aloft to allow them a glimpse of the tall man. Shutters flew open to reveal waving handkerchiefs and faces both curious and contemptuous. One haughty mistress watched the parade from an upper-floor window, hands on her hips, face in such a tight scowl I imagined she mightn't be able to undo the expression of meanness once we had passed, leaving her fixed forever in a glower of hate.

I wondered if it mightn't be best for me to fall out, but my decision was made for me soon after we crossed Broad Street—the second time for me in a single morning. The gathering stopped at the Great White House of Mister President Davis, where the tall man, the boy, one soldier, and two other important-looking men entered the front door, which closed with an uncivil "whump" upon the crowd. The remaining soldiers took up positions of sentry, their musket-rifles held crossways over their chests.

"Glory be," whispered the crowd outside.

"Hallelujah," it said. "Massa Lincome hisself in de house."

"What dis mean?" . . . "What dis mean?" was a question repeatedly whispered by an old gray-haired servant whose eyes were white with blindness. Finally, someone answered in a loud whisper.

"It mean he talking 'bout us." That hushed the old blind man and sent everyone who heard the exchange into a temporary quiet. Many in the crowd stared at the house with church faces. Tears rolled down some, others gazed hard with wide-eyed adoration.

I scanned the crowd for Extra—but he was not there. Yet there was, amid the odd mix of master and slave, two faces familiar to me. One was a servant named Riverjames, who I knew to be one of Extra's fellow bonded-out men. The other familiar face was the jack-o'-lantern. His red face stood out in the crowd, higher than the rest, about half a block away. I conjured he was standing on his wooden satchel box. He slowly eyed the crowd back and forth, reminding me of the time I saw an old owl in the oak tree by the privy, looking patiently at the ground for a mouse or mole to come wandering past.

Riverjames was closer, near the front of the crowd, heavy in the middle and with graying hair but still in possession of long, powerful arms. His droopy eyes were filled with the spark of watery life. He was constantly in motion—even when sitting still he seemed to move about in some way, continually making adjustments to every crook of his body. Sometimes it would be a rolling glide of the shoulders; sometimes his very skin seemed to ripple with twitches, the way a horse can shake flies from his rump with a useful tremor. Most all the time, his head bobbed with motion as though to some music only he could hear.

The others made fun of him because he was raised a field hand and because he could not speak well. He sputtered and stumbled so badly over everything that it sent others into fits of laughter. They called him "Rah-Rah-River," to make fun.

"Why are you called Riverjames?" I asked him at the back fence the previous summer.

"Muh, muh, muh ole momma," he said. "I wuz bo-bo-boan on de boat on de James River." Another bonded man laughed with objection and mocked his manner of speaking.

"Dats one of your ole plantation cow biscuits—your momma didn't never set foot on no boat. She only worked the tobacky fields her whole life. What you say-say-say 'bout dat-dat-dat Rah-Rah-River!"

"Wo-wo-won't Momma's boat, wuz de-de-de master boat," vowed Riverjames. "He wuz takin' de ba-ba-backy to sale on de boat."

He was easy to take note of as he trotted about the gathering carrying a burlap sack, his shoulders bouncing, head bobbing, dutifully springing from Yankee to Yankee handing out plugs of chew tobacco from the burlap. I conjured the chew plugs came from one of the warehouses, a bounty Riverjames provided for himself in generous portion during the fires, most likely. I knew it was his way. He could not talk very well, but he was thoroughly churched. Instead of dancing and singing about freedom in the streets, he occupied himself by gifting the Yankees. Handing out tobacco chew was his way of saying his "thank-yous" for the blessings of Jesus.

I stood aside, watching him for a while. Riverjames took care not to intrude. If the Yankees were talking business or had a scowling face or some ugly manner—he passed them by. But if they had an easy manner toward slaves, which most all the Yankees did, he trotted right up to them to deliver his gift. Nearly all accepted. And nearly all of those who accepted commenced chewing right away—which quickly created a front line of blue uniforms happily jawing, slurping, and spitting tobacco dregs all over Marshal and Clay, the two streets surrounding Mister President Davis' Great White House.

As time passed, the crowd grew bigger. First it gathered only around the front door. Then it spilled all the way around, and within a short time it grew deeper in all directions. There were some masters and mistresses at loiter among the servants, but mostly the gathering was made up of slaves, and other curious people that Missus Pegram called "working whites," or "shop folk."

New arrivals of slaves wanting to know what was what were advised in hushed tones: "Massa Lincomme in de haus" . . . "He done come to Rishmun" . . . "Massa Lincomme" . . . "Massa Likum" . . . "Oh, Massa Linnkoam." It was a repeated whisper that passed among the crowd like a prayerful verse.

I worked my way through the crowd to a point near a wide willow tree at one corner of the Great White House and stood behind a pair of Yankee guards who had walked up Twelfth Street with the parade. They took no notice of me and carried on with their peculiar way of speaking about places familiar to each other. They spoke of Baltimore, which I had heard of, and other places I had not. They also talked of pairing with women, and named Richmond as a place where resolution of appetites of the flesh might be had as long the money lasted.

As Riverjames worked his way along, gifting the Yankees with tobacco, he eventually reached the two Yankees near me at the willow tree. They received his gift and commenced jaw-boning their chaw while maintaining their prattle over what the missus would call "fallen women." I stood just beyond them. It was then that Riverjames took notice of me, which I hoped for.

"Wha-wha-why, Miss Fran, wha-wha-whatchu doin' here? Didja see Massa Le-Le-Le-Lincomme? Ain't dis a great day? He here. He here. He here hisself. Ah seen him myself, ah done seen Father Abraham. It ju-ju-just a great day!" He went on making big gestures of wonderment and waving his burlap satchel. I knew it would be a while before he stopped, so I cut in on him.

"Riverjames, hush up," I said. I tugged him to concealment behind the willow. "Listen, I'm looking for Extra. Have you seen him?"

"Extra?"

"Yes. Extra. Extra! Riverjames, where is he? I haven't seen him since he was hired off Sunday morning to work the ramparts."

"Wha-wha-why Miss Fran—"

"Riverjames, if you know where Extra is, you must tell me."

"Miss Francine, I is sorry."

"Sorry about what Riverjames?"

"Uh, Miss Fran, I is sorry, I ain't sa-sa-seen Extra since last week at de Shockoe House." I sensed that maybe he was lying to me, but I had never known Riverjames to be untruthful about anything.

"You sure?"

"Yes, ma-ma-ma'm. I fih-fih-figa'd him working his porter job. De Yankees gonna need porters. This be go-go-good times for hotels. Ya-Ya-Yankees is everywhere."

I did not plan to weep, but I did. My disappointment could not be concealed and tears began to streak my face. Not knowing what to do for me, Riverjames dug into his burlap satchel, withdrew a generous tobacco plug, and curled it into my hand. While the satchel flopped open I saw it was filled with a pile of loose rolling tobacco mixed with chew plugs and many grand-looking cigars, allowing him to please the Yankees with a gift that fit any preference.

"Muh-Muh-Miss Fran, I is sorry. Don't cry," he pleaded. "Ta-ta times is gonna get better. Massa Lincomme in de house, Miss Fran." He pointed and looked with longing at the door of the Great White House. "Yes'm!" he said. "Massa Lincomme hisself!"

Squatting on a willow root, I let loose with a great sadness made the previous day by Lieutenant Dunnovant's violations. I kept my weeping as silent as I could, but I could not stop the tears. They flowed mightily. I needed comfort. And I wanted to find Extra to receive that comfort. Thinking my unhappiness to be his doing, Riverjames worried.

"Do-do-don't cry, Miss Fran. I is so-so-sorry. Extra be ba-ba-back soon. That much ah know. He be back."

He kneeled his large, powerful body down to my level on the willow root, putting his watery eyes directly in front of mine. For the first time, he spoke without a single stumble. "I go find him for ya," he said. "I do it, honey. I find Extra for ya."

He smiled and his words arrested my tears, at least for the moment.

Sitting on the willow root with Riverjames promising help and the jack-o'-lantern man standing in the crowd, I cleared away my wet face and commenced forging a plan. I worked it over in my head a couple of times until I had the details down good. Then I returned the plug of chewing tobacco to Riverjames.

"Doan you wannit?" he asked.

"No, thank you, Riverjames." He put it back in his satchel and withdrew a fine cigar.

"How 'bout dis? It mighty fine." It was indeed fine looking. It was in good condition, long and well wrapped; of the type Master Pegram would call a King Kohiba. I conjured lighting it and spending the rest of the afternoon sitting on that willow root, smoking and talking with Riverjames and waiting for the Tall Man to emerge from the Great White House of Mister Jeff Davis. But I did not. I signaled for Riverjames to lean in close and listen, which he did, stretching full wide between me and the two Yankees still talking about having their pleasures of the flesh with women. I told Riverjames my plan. Some elements of the strategy came to mind only as I spoke. Then I told him again. Then I made him repeat his part of it back to me. He did so and nodded with happy compliance.

"Ah do-do-do it for you, Miss Fran. You know I will."

I withdrew the pearl ring from my gingham pocket. Riverjames inhaled a noise. With one hand inside the satchel for protection from curious eyes in the crowd, I slipped the ring onto the cigar, pushing it until it tightened down on the fattest part. I held the cigar up for Riverjames, gripping it like a knife handle to conceal the special cigar band from all except him. He studied the round pearl and golden ring in the middle of the King Kohiba. His eyes grew wide. His mouth opened.

"Ah do it, Miss Fran. Yes, ma-ma-ma'am. I do it for ya." He carefully put the cigar bearing the pearl ring into his satchel.

303

"An doan worry none, Miss Fran. Dat funny lukkin' man be no-no-no trouble for me."

He rose and hastened to the rear of the crowd as I advised. In a short time I lost sight of him. The idle-minded Yankees standing nearby had changed over from talking about women to discussing war business. They made references to Petersburg busting loose and General Lee being on the run.

"I hope it's true this time," one said. "That cat musta used up his nine lives by now."

"Me, too. I don't wanna walk south no farther than Richmond. Baltimore's about as far south as I ever wanted to get. Now look at me."

"Yeah," said the first one. "I wish I was back in Baltimore now."

"Me, too. And I damn sure don't wanna go to Petersburg."

"Yeah. At least we ain't gettin' shot at, even if we are in Richmond."

I leaned from the willow root to peek past them. Pressing my cheek to the warm bark of the tree, I could spy the jack-o'-lantern man holding his post in the crowd. His matted orange-brown hair blew about his sunburned face and flopped atop his bald crown. *Perhaps he's the devil taking note of everyone present for future use,* I thought. If Lieutenant Dunnovant was secretly counting Yankees, this one might be the Prince of Evil—released from his domain of torment through some portal in the burned city to walk about Richmond tabulating everyone, whether Yankee or otherwise.

The sight and sound of a door opening at the Great White House quickly silenced the crowd and drew all faces. Once again it was followed by disappointment. It was only a Yankee emerging to bear message to the porch sentries. He spoke his words, turned, and retraced his steps. The front door slammed behind him with another "whump." When the crowd understood it meant nothing pertaining to the Tall Man, the chatter and clamor resumed, one small excited cluster at a time.

There was much weeping. Slaves wept. House servants wept. Field hands wept. Masters and mistresses wept. Some men I took to be former Butternut wept. The only group that did not make a contribution to the tears was the Yankees, who mostly stood about at loiter—talking, eyeing the crowd, and happily spitting their tobacco chew if they were among those fortunate enough to be visited by Riverjames and his burlap satchel.

An assembly of slave children turned choir sang a hymn directly opposite the front door of the Great White House.

What mistresses passed by did not tarry long; they came into the crowd and departed quickly, unhappy with the nature of the gathering but generally unable to suppress their curiosity. When they learned the gathering was formed because the Tall Man had taken up residence in Mister Davis' Great White House, most of them hustled away, elbowing servants aside while making breathy noises of scorn. I could tell that some of them wanted to see the Tall Man but did not want to be seen trying to do so. To conceal their desires, they held to one position for a time then scurried away with displays of disgust over the whole matter, only to settle upon another position in another part of the crowd before commencing the process all over again. When one small gathering of mistresses was joined by a newcomer, they called her name and commenced weeping anew at each other, burying their quivering lips into tiny handkerchiefs.

Finally, Riverjames came into view. He edged his way through the crowd from the south; his great bouncing head could not conceal abundant pride. He was on a mission, his smile wide with happiness as he took up position a short distance from jack-o'-lantern man and resumed gifting Yankees with tobacco plugs. He moved casually, edging closer to the jack-o'-lantern without showing any intent of approaching him directly. Once there, his great height was nearly equal to the odd man's own elevated tallness on his wooden satchel.

Then Riverjames spoke to him. From behind the willow, I could see his lips deliver the message, almost hear it with my own ears, having heard him repeat it as he worked the crowd.

"Care for some tobacky, sah?" he said. He waited for a response, but there was none. The jack-o'-lantern man ignored the invitation without bothering to remove his black eyes from the crowd. Riverjames spoke again. "Tobacky, sah?" Still no response. Undaunted, Riverjames leaned in close to one of those protruding ears pasted to the side of the pumpkin and whispered.

I felt a sharp flash of sun. The willow branches cast crisscrossing shadows. If I tilted my head forward—the sun glared straight in my eyes, a tilt back—they were shielded. I conjured the time to be noon, or just a few minutes after. My body sorely hurt from Lieutenant Dunnovant's violations, but I tried not to think about the pain of bruises and sore bones.

The jack-o'-lantern turned his puffy eyes toward Riverjames. I anticipated trouble. A moment passed before the swollen lips spoke. Another moment passed. The puffy lips spoke again. Riverjames withdrew the King Kohiba from his satchel and held it aloft, his large hand cupping the ring, concealing it from all eyes except those of the jack-o'-lantern, whose dark orbs fixed steady upon the sight. Before another moment could pass Riverjames returned the large cigar to his burlap satchel, which sparked an unhappy flinch to the sunburned face. It was quick, but it was enough. That odd-looking man wanted my pearl ring—and I knew it.

The swollen lips moved again as Riverjames listened, his posture arched in stiff labor with effort to hear every word and remember it long enough to pass it along to me. Riverjames nodded, gave a quick bounce that he intended to be a bow, turned toward the south, and maneuvered deeper into the crowd in the opposite direction from me and the willow tree—just as I instructed. He had done his job.

I sat on the willow root to await his return. After a short while, he made his bouncing way back, this time approaching from the north after working his way fully around the gathering. He kneeled beside me, talking excitedly.

"Mah, mah, Miss Fran—he know wha you talk'n 'bout!"

"What did he say, Riverjames?

"Miss Fran, he-he-he say—'yes'm'!"

"Yes what?"

"Yes'm. Yes, he got setch a 'ting. And he say he wa-wa-want do biznez wid you."

"Did he make an offer?"

"Yes. He sa-sa-say he pay twelf whole dolla Yankee for dat ring."

"Twelve?"

"Yes. No-no-no questions ask. Twelf dolla Yankee cash on de barrel-head!"

Someone emerged from the Great White House, which drew all attentions of those gathered, including Riverjames, but it was not the Tall One. It was only a Yankee soldier who ambled over to a grouping of other Yankees with no particular purpose. Seeing it did not portend anything important, the crowd resumed their murmuring of "hallelujahs."

"Oh, Miss Fran, ain't dis de-de-de wonda?" Riverjames said excitedly. "We is free. Free! And now Massa Lincomme hisself done come."

"What else did he say?" I asked.

"Who?"

"That man you showed the ring to."

"Oh. Tha-tha-that's all, Miss Fran." He shrugged, slow to remove his attentions from the house. "He just say he be-be-be at de church like you ask. Dats all."

I was figuring as fast as I could upon my next step. The sun was high in the sky. I conjured it had been about an hour since the Tall Man and his son entered the house. The day was becoming warmer with each passing minute; only a few clouds of puffy white dotted the sky over eastern Richmond in the direction of Chimborazo.

"Miss Fran. You is sma-sma-smart. Ah know you is. Extra always say so. Tell me, wha-wha-wahchu think Massa Lincomme gonna do?"

"I don't know, River."

He leaned in close to question me. "You think he go-go-gonna stay here. Stay to hep us?"

"I don't know, Riverjames."

"Dey gonna let us go-go-go our way. Work and sutch?"

"I don't know, Riverjames."

"Is the Butternut go-go-gone for good?"

"I don't know, Riverjames."

"What de Ya-Ya-Yankees do now?"

"Riverjames, please, I just don't know! There isn't any way to know. The whole world is tilted over."

He paused to regard me with his droopy, moist brown eyes. "Dats it," he said excitedly. "It do-do-done tilted. Now we got see if'n it keep on turning or tilt back d'other way." He gave up firing questions at me, nodding as though he understood everything. "Ah said you is sma-sma-smart. And you right. De whol wa-wa-world done tilt right over."

"Riverjames, I want you to help me one more time. Will you do that?"

"Miss Fran, I ha-ha-hep. You know ah will."

I explained only a small part of my plan to Riverjames. Afterward, I accepted one of his cigars as a gift, then said my goodbyes and left the gathering at Mister President Davis' Great

White House. I moved north, staying out of the view of the jack-o'-lantern until I was buried deep in the crowd and emerged on the other side. A short distance away I could hear the group at the front. It finished their "marching hallelujah" hymn and commenced another. This time, it was a spiritual I was familiar with:

> Go down Moses
> Way down in Egypt land
> Tell ole Pharaoh
> To let my people go
> When Israel was in Egypt land
> Let my people go
> Oppressed so hard they could not stand
> Let my people go

Once beyond the crowd to the north, I swung around, walking west for one block, then south, returning toward Broad Street. I quietly spoke the words to myself while crossing Broad Street for a third time in a single day.

> Thus spoke the Lord, bold Moses said
> If not, I'll smite your first born dead
> Let my people go.

Chapter Thirty-Five:
Miss Francine Pegram

Minutes later, I stood on Grace Street opposite St. Paul's, where I beheld yet another spectacle. The freed-up, celebrating slaves had organized a parade. Led by a group on horseback, it marched west on Grace Street. Some of the horses were beaten-down old nags and some were unhitched carriage horses; the men on horseback waved their hats about like happy fools on holiday. Former slave men blew flutes and boys banged upon box-crates as though they were drums. A man hoisting a walking stick topped with a large squash scurried back and forth like a Jimmy crab, waving his squash on a stick as though it were a magic ornament. Then came a group of men proudly wearing sash ribbons of no meaning that I could figure. Then a line of women arrived toting a banner with words that I could not read because they gripped it too loosely. Finally came the field hands—hundreds of them: young, old, tall, taller, dark, darker, thick, strong, mean, happy, dumb, heavy, skinny, wide, stooped, limping. They were mostly men but there were some women, too. They were sweating, broad-shouldered, child-like, manly, bearded, shaven, bald, opened-mouthed, flap-lipped, no teeth, big teeth, scarred-backs, and poked-out eyes. They had no ribbons to wear, no crates to bang upon nor magic ornaments to wave about. They just walked behind the noisy front lines looking somehow both sheepish and proud. Most wore the same bib-trousers they had on when they departed the fields that morning or the day before, and many were without shirt-tops.

I recognized some faces in the crowd as being the field hands I saw sitting in Extra's wagon Sunday morning. I followed along for a block, hoping to get to them to ask after Extra, but they were in the middle of the crowd and I couldn't manage it.

Once the last field hands marched west on Grace, a flurry of traffic returned to the streets. Yankees and horses and carriages had all waited with courtesy for the parade's passage. That too was an unusual sight—white men waiting for a great crowd of black men to pass was something new. But not everyone was patient. Some few mistresses and masters remained on the footpath, gawking with disgust, squinting in the dust, their lips folded into dumb contortions exposing yellow teeth as they eyed the parade disappearing to the west. Knowing the way mistresses think, I could easily conjure their fears: the Butternut fled, the city burned, the Yankees arrived, and now servants are openly parading in the streets. For them, it marked a world undone.

At St. Paul's, I settled upon the servant's bench under Minister Minningerode's preaching window. Since my wanderings that had begun just after dawn, it was the nearest I had come to the Ninth Street house. From there, I could see the Great House of Government with all the put-outs still camping on the grounds and the hustle of Yankees around all the buildings of government. In the few hours since I had first passed, the Yankees had taken on workaday airs. Farther south lay the open fields of the burned city, with its foul odor seeping into everything just as storm waters find their way into every wooden crack.

I felt inside my gingham. The gift of Riverjames' cigar had joined the pocket's contents. Still working on my plan and worrying over the possible outcomes I watched the narrow footpath for signs of the jack-o'-lantern's arrival. Not far from my bench a fresh dandelion burr sprouted from a crack between slate rocks. Missus Pegram called them weeds, "horrid little creepers." I didn't mind them, but she hated them. "I declare," she would say, "they would probably grow in the desert if you planted 'em there." But she said nothing about weeds when I plucked a bundle of yellow-faced dandelions the previous summer and we ate them for dinner, hairy leaves and all.

The noise of a passing wagon, laden with war cannon, roared past. I watched it lumber past me to the north as the driver made loud demands of his large, healthy, double team. That's when I saw him. He stood half a block away, at Ninth and Bank, waiting for that very same wagon to pass before crossing over toward me. The wagon left an eddy of dust in the air that appeared to single him out and make a run at him, intentionally swirling about his jack-o'-lantern head. He covered his eyes with a tiny hand in a feeble manner that did nothing to stop the dust eddy from having its vexing way upon his peculiar appearance. Clumps of fleshy hair flopped in the dirty wind. The legs beneath his giant-egg middle wobbled to find steadiness. He carried his wooden satchel over his shoulder.

After the cannon wagon lumbered past, he stepped from the curb, teetered across Ninth Street to the west, then tottered across Grace Street to the south. Watching his rickety gait approach stirred me with doubt. I worried of unimagined ways that my plan could go wrong.

"Lieutenant Dunnovant say he send regard, sir."

It was after his third round of pacing in front me that I spoke. I confined my attention to my brokens on his first pass. He checked his pocket watch on the second pass, wobbling back north as far as Grace Street before turning and waddling back to my servant's bench. I did not raise my gaze after speaking, but knew he was regarding me with those black eyes.

"You are Mister Dunnovant's girl?" he sputtered.

"He send his regard, sah," I repeated. Still, I did not look up.

"Will he arrive at this location?" he hissed. I did not answer. "Will you take me to your Master Dunnovant?" He made several drawn-out, muffled wheezes. "My child, does he wish me to send you back to him with a message?"

"He Butternut!" I blurted, looking up for the first time. "He a Johnny man!" I quickly lowered my gaze back to my brokens, but took a picture of his eyes with me. They were black with greed. But they also told me he suspected nothing. I was to him what I hoped to appear to be—a girl, a negress, pickaninny in loyal service to a white man.

"I think I understand," he hissed. "If he has been discovered since this morning, the armies of the north would not be overly hospitable of him or the nature of his business would they? Is he observing us now," he asked, "from some window or nearby carriage?" He glanced around the street.

"He Butternut, sah. He can't walk 'round Richmond no more."

"Very well, I think I understand. It is difficult for a man of his position to conduct business following this tide of invasion. But surely he knows that as a merchant, I answer only to the laws of trade and have little regard for these matters of regional passion."

"Yes-sah."

"So I ask again, child, does Mister Dunnovant wish me to send you back with a message?"

"He stay at the Spotswood, sah. Just like you."

"Yes. Does he wish me to meet him in his room. He is directly below me as I recall. On the third floor."

I made note of the information.

"Naw-sah. He not in dah room right now."

"Oh, very well. I grow tired of this foolishness. If he wishes me to increase the tendered offer made earlier to that giant, dumb nigger-boy, I will do it. As a gesture of my genuine interest, I raise the bid to fifteen." He was overtaken by a fit of wheezy coughing, then turned to hurl a body of yellow spittle to the street. I conjured him possessed of the consumption.

More noisy traffic on Ninth Street removed all possibility of talk. This time it was a group of mounted Yankees at quick trot going south toward the Tredegar manufactory, sending up so many boots and hooves I could hear them echoing through St. Paul's empty chamber of worship. A small gathering of servant-women emerged from a stoop to rally at curbside. They applauded the passing Yankees on horseback and shouted messages of "bress de Lord," "thank ya'll," and "bress all de Yankees." The jack-o'-lantern regarded them, pulling a handkerchief from his woolen vest to wipe the remaining spittle clinging to the corners of his small, quivering mouth. The handkerchief was coated over with yellow stains of sickness.

"Fools," he hissed, eyeing the servants as quiet returned to the street. "Do they truly believe the gods of the Pharaoh waged this war for their salvation from bondage? The marketplace of tyranny will never be denied."

"He say he figure it worth more, sah."

"Oh?" He dabbed at his swollen nostrils with the handkerchief.

"Sah?" I asked.

"Yes."

"He say, you see dat ring a purfect likeness to de necklace?"

"Yes," his hissed, "I made note of that. I also note it is unfortunate that Mister Dunnovant does not conduct his business all in one meeting. Yet, I cannot judge his decisions. Perhaps he does not because he cannot."

"Yes-sah, dat right."

"Well, the information you convey tells me you are indeed a genuine emissary of Mister Dunnovant."

A drunk Yankee ambling up Ninth Street stopped nearby to

stare at the physical oddness of the jack-o'-lantern. He eyed him from top to bottom, but the merchant of jewelry paid him no mind.

"Tell me, child, how is Mister Dunnovant to receive his payment for this item?" I did not answer. "Surely he does not expect me to give you money then await your return." Still, I did not respond. "My child, there is no intent to lessen Mister Dunnovant's honor in this arrangement, but even on these blighted, war-wasted streets, business is still business and assurances are still assurances. I must view the item before proffering any finances." Still I made no response.

He took measure of me.

"Very well, child. I know not how Mister Dunnovant intends to pursue this matter of business, but I will offer him twenty-five dollars for the ring, providing of course it is the one that comes attached to a very interesting cigar."

"He say he want foaty, sah."

"Oh?"

"That's what he say. He want foaty dollar Yankee." I gave a shrug as though I had no grasp of the number's meaning.

"Well, now, it took quite a while to arrive at the heart of the message didn't it child. He took another measure of me. "My child," he said finally. "I have been in this trade far too long to be duped by the oldest game ever waged upon a fool. I must see the merchandise before tendering the money. And it must be the same merchandise I beheld a short while ago. You may tell that to Mister Dunnovant."

"Yes-sah," I said. And then slowly I pulled the King Kohiba from my gingham pocket and held it aloft. "You mean de merchandise attached to a fine cigar jus like dis one?"

The cigar held no attached ring, which meant the plan had to work fast. I did see a quick flash of anger come over his red face, making the crater scars twitch. His arms were flimsy, but flimsy arms or no, I knew a swinging blow was about to befall me.

"Cigar, sah? Ca-ca-care for a cigar?" It was Riverjames. He had moved in quickly, his great body bouncing at the ready once he observed me withdraw my own cigar for display, his signal to step up quick. I returned my cigar to my gingham pocket. The one Riverjames held aloft bore a glistening ring of gold mounted with a lustrous green-white pearl looking like a treasure atop a treasure.

The dark eyes of the jack-o'-lantern fixed on the sight.

"Heh-heh-hello, Miss Fran," Riverjames said. "And go-go-good day to you, sah," he said to the merchant. "I is ah-ah-honored to speak wid you 'gain."

"Yes-s-s," the jack-o'-lantern's lips hissed absently.

"Ain't dis a wo-wo-wonderful day?" Riverjames continued. "Yes-sah! It just a wonderful da-da-day." He held the King Kohiba upright, rolling it with his fingertips. "And dat be a fine smo-smo-smoking cigar, sah."

"Yes-s-s," the jack-o'-lantern hissed again, his face pocks twitching, his small nostrils fanning out, emitting a thin stream of yellow ooze. He popped out the legs of his wood satchel, which reminded me of daddy longlegs. He opened the lid, sat down next to me and took the cigar from Riverjames. Using the lid of the satchel to conceal his actions, he removed the ring and examined it for a prolonged moment with an eye piece.

While he did so, both Riverjames and I ogled the contents of the box. The inside lid was adorned with small hooks that held many dangling items of color. There were necklaces and bracelets of green, red, brown, and yellow. The loose ones rattled and flapped about when he opened the top. I saw white pearls of various sizes and noted there were chain links of gold and silver.

Finally he snapped from his trance-like study of the ring. He rubbed away the ooze on his lip with the back of his tiny hand.

"Very well, child," he said. "You were true to your word. The merchandise does indeed meet my expectations. Yes. I will pay the forty dollars Mister Dunnovant asks."

The words shocked Riverjames, who watched the man dig into the breast pocket of his burly boat to withdraw a leather purse, and from that he pulled four folding papers of ten dollars each. The sight of it so excited Riverjames that I knew he was about to lose all steadiness.

"Riverjames," I barked trying to pull him back. "Our labor is now done. Mister Dunnovant want us to bring dat money back to him." It worked. Riverjames looked upon me with confusion. He had no idea what I was talking about or who Mister Dunnovant was.

The merchant held four pieces of money aloft.

"Take the money," I said to Riverjames. He did so as the merchant put the ring into a small drawer inside the case, closed the drawer, closed the lid, stood, and snapped the legs of his daddy longlegs satchel back into place.

"It is apparent, my child, why Mister Dunnovant puts his trust in your services," he said, swinging the wooden satchel to his backsides. "You have acquitted yourself very well." He took no interest in Riverjames, but studied me for a moment.

"Do you have family, child?"

"I free now, sah," I said.

"Yes, of course. What is your next occupation child?"

"Sah?"

"Your work. What will you do now, child?"

"My next work, sah?"

"Yes. You are now in Mister Dunnovant's employ. But you understand there are great changes taking place, do you not?"

"Change, sah?"

"Of course, change," he hissed. "What else might you believe

317

these public demonstrations of the chattel class constitute? You retired to bed last evening as property, you awakened this day at some liberty to pursue other options. 'Emancipated' as your chief of state calls it."

"Sah?"

"I am speaking of President Lincoln." With that, Riverjames could contain himself no longer. He let loose with a pent-up volley of bouncing whoops and whoopees as if a tightly bound spring inside him had bust.

"Oh, yes-sah! Massa Lincomme right here," Riverjames shouted. "He here. He here in ole Richmond. Yes-sah! It de great man hisself come to make us free." I noted that the words were so important to him that Riverjames did not stutter or stumble a single time. The merchant waited impatiently for the outburst to pass.

"What I mean to suggest child is that I could use the services of a spry-witted assistant such as yourself. I run a business. I travel quite a bit in pursuit of gems and finery. A young individual with your cleverness and—shall we say—exotic allure, could be a fair boon to my affairs." Riverjames was bouncing and waving excitedly. He leaned down to whisper loudly into my ear.

"Muh-Muh-Miss Fran, dat work he talkin' 'bout. He offer you a job!"

"I travel by train primarily. Washington City, Baltimore, Philadelphia, New York. Occasionally I take a carriage to a few, select smaller towns. You would travel with me, of course."

"Ba-Ba-Baltimore!" Riverjames shouted, unable to contain himself, bouncing and sputtering into my ear. "Dat man say he take you to Baltimore."

"I buy. I sell. Shops. Individuals. Investors. Ladies of considerable means." He paused to eye me over good. "You would accompany me, of course." His jack-o'-lantern face took on the veiled glare of the goat, making my stomach tighten as I recalled Lieutenant Dunnovant and Captain Zollicoffer's pistol.

"I is fine, sah," I said. "I hep Master Dunnovant. But I do hotel work, sah."

"It would mean quite a bit of progress for you. As my assistant you would require proper attire, even some finery."

"Dat mean nice dresses, Miss Francine," Riverjames barked, his head bobbing next to mine.

"And the lodging accommodations would surely be superior to your arrangements as chattel. I tend to avoid the public houses, preferring instead guest houses, country inns, city hotels."

"Like de Sposswud," Riverjames said. "De hotels in Ba-Ba-Baltimore even better."

"And bear in mind your diet will not suffer. I always partake of a generous breakfast."

"Coffee and ham-biscuit in de monin'!" Riverjames continued.

"Of course, child, work is work. Don't be persuaded otherwise. I spend long hours in search of finery where it can be had at reasonable prices. In that regard you could prove quite useful, just as you have proven so in service to Mister Dunnovant."

"Oh, Miss Fran, you ain't 'fraid o'wa-wa-work," Riverjames said with encouragement. I took his hand and squeezed it as hard as I could to settle him.

"There is even the occasional journey abroad by ship. I started my work in Europe many years ago in Amsterdam. I also do trade with shops among the English, the French."

"France! Muh-muh-Miss Fran. He say you visit France. Dat a whole world away! France! Oh my. Uhn, unh, unh." I turned to Riverjames where he was leaning down to me and put both hands on his shoulders, making him settle down. When he did,

I turned back to the merchant.

"I thank you, sah. But I is fine. I got work here, sah." The spittle bubbled at his lips. I ventured a way to settle his business with me—I would let on that I understood his full meaning. "And I got me a man here, sah. He a bonded man. He got good work. We going to get married now." The jack-o'-lantern face considered this new piece of information. Yellow spittle bubbled at the corners of his lips.

"Very well," he hissed unhappily. The goat face faded. He pushed past Riverjames with a sneer and waddled away south on Ninth Street, teetering so upon his spindly legs that it seemed he would take a tumble with each step. At Main Street he turned west, bound for the Spotswood most likely.

Riverjames watched him depart, his wide smile unchanged, his upper half bobbing, dancing to the music of his secret, simple world.

"Oh, Miss Fran!" Riverjames crowed. "You sho-sho-sure is a smart one. Dat was the smatist lil 'ole piece o'business ah ever did see. Yes'm. Oh Miss Francine! Foty dolla Yankee! Yes, ma'am!"

He handed me the four green slips. Each was labeled several times over with the number "ten." Front and back: "ten," "ten," "ten." There was also "ten dollars," "ten dollars," and "ten dollars." I conjured there must be so many dumb Yankees, the North was required to stamp the value of money enough times so it could never be misunderstood by anyone. On one side, on the left of each green slip was a small portrait of a man I recognized. I folded one slip and held it high.

"Riverjames, look at the portrait," I said. He leaned in close, studied it, and let go with another round of whoops.

"Lordy! Miss Fran, dat's Ma-Ma-Massa Lincomme hisself. His likeness on de very money you made. Lordy, o'lordy! Ain't dis a wunnaful day. Miss Fran, Massa Lincomme on de money and he in Richmond. He uptown on Clay Street dis very minute. We free and now you rich! O'lordy me, what else gonna happen on dis great day!" He bounced and whooped and danced to his private music, taking on so it made me happy to watch him. I held one of the four papers aloft.

"Take it, Riverjames," I said.

"What?"

"Take it."

"Oh, Miss Fran, dat yours. Da-da-dat's de money you make off'n dat funny lookin' merchant man."

"You heard me, River. It's yours. You made money today, too. Here." He slowly took the green slip, holding it with care, studying the small portrait of the bearded man I had walked beside just a short while earlier.

"Ten whole dolla Yankee?" he asked in a whisper. I nodded yes. "Miss Fran, I's very grateful." He leaned down as if to tell me some secret, his big, wet eyes glowing as he took a deep breath and whispered with the strength of a man in church offering praise: "Naw we is boaf rich!" he pronounced.

CHAPTER THIRTY-SIX:
MISS FRANCINE PEGRAM

The noon sun passed and arched to the west behind St. Paul's steeple. The Yankees remained at their business of coming-and-going; former slaves remained at loiter on all corners and stoops and in nearly every recess where at least one person could perch with a wagging tongue about being freed-up.

Those who marched west in the parade were now returning—many of them at a run, headed for the Great House of Government.

"Miss Fran, wha-wha-why dey running?" Riverjames asked, edging toward the north, getting ready to run.

"I don't know," I said, as we both watched scores of former field hands hasten past.

"Sa-sa-somethin' up."

"You may be right, Riverjames. Let's go." I had other plans for him and did not want to lose him in the crowd, so I took Riverjames' hand and we hastened to the grounds of the Great House of Government where the put-outs were camped. Once there, we saw the running crowd had gathered tightly around the big statue of Father Washington.

There was much excitement in the air. Yankees huddled on the porch of the Great House looking like a blue-robed chorus at an outdoor church. Field hands climbed trees. Richmond citizens elbowed each other for position. Many of the put-outs also gathered, leaving their hang-dog camps to join the close huddle around the giant statue.

Riverjames picked me up and cradled me in his arms like a baby as he worked his giant, nimble body through the crowd, right to the front line where he stood me up in front of him and we bore witness.

It was the Tall Man. This time, he was riding. He had departed the White House of Mister President Davis in a big four-wheel carriage, which had stopped next to the statue of Father Washington for him to make a speech to the gathered crowd.

We arrived late and I did not hear much of what he said, though I did hear the word "birthright" and knew that he too was speaking mostly to the gathering of former slaves about being freed-up. The crowd did not cheer or even nod their heads. They just listened quietly, which I took to be an even more powerful form of approval.

He finished his comments just moments after Riverjames and me arrived. The driver gee'd at the team, but he did it a moment too early, before the wagon occupants were ready, which sent the Tall Man flopping back into his seat before he could settle down proper. Yet he took it with good humor, even laughing with his companions about making a hard landing with his bottom.

Beside him sat the cherry-faced boy, who caught sight of me as the carriage pulled away and handed me a bashful smile. I smiled back and gave a timid wave.

"Miss Fran, wha-wha-where Massa Lincomme go?" Riverjames leaned down to ask. "He not leaving Richmond?"

"I think he is," I told him.

Riverjames didn't like the idea and neither did many others. Some called for him to come back as they ran after the carriage. The put-outs did little more than watch. The Yankees waved good-bye and clapped politely. But it was different for the newly freed slaves. They watched the Tall Man's departure with worried expressions, mumbling prayerful sentiments as they waved dirty hats or held their hands high as though receiving the very spirit of baptism.

Young black boys ran after the carriage and I knew Riverjames was set to join them. I knew I wouldn't be able to hold him long, so I did what needed to be done.

"Riverjames, I'm conjuring that you know something about Extra that you not lettin' on," I said. "Before you run off after that carriage, I want you to tell me what it is."

"Oh, Muh-Muh-Miss Fran. How you know I know? I didn't say nuthin'."

"Hush. Now listen, I gave you ten whole dollars Yankee money. Now you tell me where he is right now." I felt sorry about doing it, but I did what had to be done. I had to make him feel guilty about the money.

"Oh, Missy Fran." He turned away to eye the carriage making its way down the hill toward Bank Street.

"Is he dead?"

That snapped him back to me. "Oh, naw, Miss Fran. He-he-he ain't dead. He whoring. I sorry, Miss Francine. He oh-oh-off whoring."

"Where?"

"Reitch yonder, up Byrd Alley," he said with a pointed finger just before bolting away to chase after the carriage bearing the Tall Man away from Richmond.

I walked down the grounds of the Great House of Government, past the put-outs and back to Bank Street. Then I turned east, just past Wm. Byrd Livery and Stable, where a pair of big sleeping dogs picked up their heads and gave me a good looking over, but I pretended not to see them.

The wide door of the livery bore words deeply whittled into the wood in an irregular pattern that read "STONEWALL LIVES." Above that, in small freshly penciled letters, were the words "not no more."

I was uncertain exactly where Byrd Alley was, but figured it must be near Wm. Byrd Livery and Stable, where I saw a Yankee on horseback emerging from a nearly hidden corridor behind the livery entrance. He trotted to Bank Street, where he entered the back and forth traffic and disappeared east, in the same direction as the Tall Man's carriage. Muffled cheers from deeper within the hidden corridor followed his exit from the alleyway.

Walking to the corridor, I found an alleyway with an overhead sign, "Byrd Alley," and at the other end of the alley hung another sign, a board with the words "Welcome to Screamersville."

Approaching the entrance as a cat angles in upon a mouse hole, I craned my neck. More cheers came from within and a pair of Yankees smelling of grog emerged from the alley without taking notice of me. Another Yankee entered from the street, also without paying me any mind. I fell in behind him and followed him all the way down "Byrd Ally" as though we were both heading for Sunday communion.

The narrow passage emptied upon a wide, open space beyond the rear of the livery. It was a private space, concealed on all sides by the rear walls of other buildings, yet it was a public space at the same time. The ground was mostly dirt in the open middle area, but along the outer edges there were many nooks and crannies behind the buildings that had board flooring and even some cobblestone. Canopies made of sheets, supported by makeshift posts extended from cellar entrances to shelter tables, chairs, stools, crates, logs, and every other device that could be sat upon. A Yankee tent, pitched in the middle of the open area, stood next to a pit-fire smoldering with a fry pan that smelled of bacon. There were piles of firewood and stacks of musket rifles. Every imaginable type of satchel, grip, clutch, tote, and bedroll littered every available space.

And everywhere there were people.

They were at lollygag in every possible position of loiter that a body could assume. They were standing, sitting, and lying. And they were drunk. They were in every possible condition of drunkenness, from gay afternoon social to darkly unconscious. One group in a drunken stupor sang and swayed with such thick-tongued merriment their song was unrecognizable. Another group, stooping in a tight gathering near the fire pit, whooped and hollered over a game of card wagering. The ones who were dead to the world snored where they fell, even with their limbs flopped into loblollies of spilled beer and whiskey. One skinny young Yankee was folded into a windowsill, his stomach sickness soiling his chest, his eyelids open but only his eye-whites showing as though death had overtaken him. Others sat on the ground, on chairs, the back stoop, rear balcony, wood-bin, curled up in pushcarts, and even reclining upon the limbs of the one tree arching over the Yankee tent.

Standing at the end of Byrd Alley like a spectator, I scanned the length of that tree. It was oak, with one gnarled and knotty branch that extended toward a boisterous grog party upon a second-floor rear balcony. It was fit only for a sober monkey, yet two drunken Yankees balanced upon it, toeing a foothold as they edged their hazardous way toward that balcony where happy onlookers in the second-floor grog-shop urged them on with encouraging shouts of glee.

The yard was filled mostly with men, but there were women aplenty. Women servers tended the men in the makeshift grog-shops under the canopies and on the balconies. They poured gin and whiskey into every variety of cup and container one could conjure to hold liquid. Other women flitted and flirted about the entire yard, selling and pouring whiskey from jugs.

The women were mixed. Black women labored alongside women with pink bosoms, milky bare skin and hair of every shade from brown to cotton white.

And there was nakedness. I refer not just to the women, many of whom were stone-bare, buck-naked, prancing about serving grog while cooing over the men as though nothing at all were out of the ordinary. Women who were clothed allowed the happy exposure of their full, flopping bosoms without regard. But I refer to the men, too. Many of them strolled about peeled in full or in part without any visible worry. Yankee and slave alike lollygagged in various stages of disrobe, some with such devil-may-care airs that I was not certain I was seeing it proper.

Well.

A snake likely strikes prey more slowly than I moved. There were two options for me. Turn and reconnoiter to Bank Street, or hide. I preferred the first, but my body made the decision for me and chose the second. At a corner just inside the yard, a pushcart was parked against the rear wall of the livery and lay at rest on a tilt. I scurried into hiding under that cart so quickly that I slammed my head onto the axle, hitting with such force I wondered if I hadn't knocked myself cold and dreamed the whole, wild spectacle. But I was not asleep. The circus of carnal gluttony was no dream. From that hidey-hole, with my knees pulled up to my chest and my back pressed against the chilly stones of the livery wall, I observed all.

It was, of course, an out-yard of business—a great swarming enterprise. The grog was for sale, the women were for sale, and with Richmond sold to the Yankees, who now filled the streets in blue uniforms with pockets full of good greenback Yankee money, there were plenty of buyers of both.

I had heard Mistress Bartow prattle on during more than one evening about the "shocking" places of gambling that had sprung up in Richmond during the war years, where women pursued what she called their "wickedness." She complained that some slave women were getting rich following the Butternut and providing services to them. "I declare," she said time and again, "our wonderful city is turning into a municipality no better then the vile cities up north where the villainous go unchecked in every appetite."

Now I was hiding in one of those very places of "shock" that Mistress Bartow complained of with such frequency. Some women, having made a sale, delivered their wares immediately— upon a log or atop a grog table in brazen disregard of onlookers and appearing to me like animals. They reminded me of shaggy dogs who care not where they mate or who views their union, so long as the thing is done—street, alleyway, or open field.

It was, of course, exactly what Lieutenant Dunnovant had forced upon me exactly one day prior and I had no tolerance for the spectacle. After my head stopped throbbing from the painful whack, I planned a rapid exit.

Then my life stopped. After all the shocks delivered upon me over the past days, there was yet another blow to come. And this one struck the hardest.

The door flap of the tent tossed open with a loud, leathery pop, sending it flying to the roof where it held firm. Thick smoke flooded from the opening. I knew the occupants of the tent were all enjoying cigars. A plump, milky-skinned, full-naked woman emerged from the smoke, waddled a few steps, and squatted in the dirt to tend to her needs. That left me with a dead-on view of the tent's interior. From my hidey-hole under that cart, I watched the cigar smoke rolling past the edges of the leather-framed passageway. As the cloud thinned, it revealed bed cots, bedding, bedrolls, grog jugs, naked women, and naked men. And there was Extra. He reclined upon a cot, propped up like a king in a deep pile of bedding, naked, smoking a great cigar.

★ ★ ★ ★ ★

I bolted from my hidey-hole with disregard for all consequence. I cut and ran so fast I doubt anyone saw the flash of gingham bound from under the pushcart and race from Screamersville, from Byrd Alley, across Bank Street, past the Great House of Government, past St. Paul's, and south down Ninth Street to the Pegram house, where I raced up the front stoop, through the parlor, past my servant's chair, and into the kitchen still befouled with the leavings of my own crimes of nighttime theft and Lieutenant Dunnovant's defiling of me as though I were his own private Screamersville.

In the pantry, I yanked away the burlap sack at the bottom of the empty apple barrel and retrieved Captain Zollicoffer's pistol with the honey bone handle.

I knew that only moments had passed; yet it seemed more like days. I felt strange. I knew it was me; yet it seemed like I was someone else, and I was watching it happen—like I was still in that hidey-hole watching that spectacle of flesh—except that now I was watching myself and there was nothing that could be done to stop me. The whole time I was racing back to the house, I had a picture of something chasing me. But it wasn't Extra or even Lieutenant Dunnovant. It was that man in the wagon of torment who sought mercy for his suffering, the one I befriended with my eyes, who had no legs, whose body disappeared into the slush of blood and filth, and who died while I was pumping water.

I never broke stride.

After retrieving Captain Zollicoffer's pistol, I bolted from the back door, raced through the yard, past the dilapidated garden, past the leaning privy of Pegram, over the back fence, past the slave out-quarters, past the double-seat privy financed with the sale of my mother, and into the back door of the Spotswood Hotel.

No one stopped me. How could they? They would have to see me to stop me. I am a shadow, a mere black reflection cast upon the ground. I move unseen and silent.

I bounded the staircase to the third floor, down the corridor to number 315, the number, as the jack-o'-lantern said, directly below his own number 415. I knocked gently.

"Come in," spoke the voice of Lieutenant Dunnovant. It was not what I figured to hear. I conjured I would receive no answer or receive some inquiry of caution reflecting his job of "seeing and counting, counting and seeing." Something like "who's there?" or "what is it?" or "go away." Using both thumbs, I pulled back the hammer on Captain Zollicoffer's pistol until it clicked into place. I turned the knob and walked in as if I belonged there, as if I were toting boiled egg and warmed-up milk to Missus Pegram in the morning.

He was on the bed in a reclining position, reading a newspaper in his stocking feet, his own pistol hung in its holster from a bedstead post by his head. I walked right up to him.

"Well, if it isn't my smart Li'l Miss. I was just thinking of paying you another visit," he said, smiling, before he saw the contents of my hand.

I extended my arm bearing Captain Zollicoffer's pistol—and fired. He fast understood that he was in trouble. He reached for his own pistol but fell out of bed before he could manage to grip it. I had aimed for his chest, but missed. The bullet struck him in the neck. The blood poured from a generous hole like the heavy flow of water from the well faucet when the gooseneck handle is pumped good and hard.

Squeeek—swoosh; squeeek—swooosh.

His green eyes studied me before succumbing. His lips, still bearing the foul purple sore, moved and seemed to make words that looked like ". . . smart Li'l Miss."

I dropped Captain Zollicoffer's pistol and retraced my invisible steps just as fast as I arrived. I ran back to Ninth Street, then north to Broad. My destination was a place I saw that morning with the Yankee wagon driver from the City of Jersey. He had called it the "Church of Africa, for the freed-up."

That's where I went. That's where I ran after shooting and killing Lieutenant Dunnovant. And that's where, like everyone else within its borders, I found safe refuge.

After waiting in a long row that curled through the yard and then into the back door, I was given a bowl of soup—not very warm, and flavored only with a hint of ham-taste and one spoonful of rice. I ate it while sitting outdoors on a log in the presence of many others. Later, we received prayers while inside the church and we sang a hymn:

> While I draw this fleeting breath,
> when mine eyes shall close in death,
> when I soar to worlds unknown,
> see thee on thy judgment throne,
> Rock of Ages, cleft for me,
> Let me hide myself in thee.

During services I held the hymnbook in one hand, sharing it with the girl standing next to me who could not read but seemed to enjoy looking down at the page as though she could. With the other hand in the pocket of my gingham, I felt the reassuring touch of my treasured pocket knife, slavery bill of sale, slave street pass, and three ten-dollar paper bills of good Yankee money.

CHAPTER THIRTY-SEVEN:
EXTRA PETTIGREW

It was only a blur, a streaking mixture of shadow and light. But I knew it was Missy Fran running from the brothel after seeing me. I tipped my whore-woman twenty-five cents good Yankee money and departed as quickly as I could.

I was approaching St. Paul's when I saw Missy Fran cut past me again. This time, it appeared she had come from the Spotswood, and she was running north straight up the middle of Ninth Street like a horse in panic at full gallop. I broke into a run myself and called out to her, but she could not hear above the rowdy street noise. I declare, I had no idea that girl could run so fast.

CHAPTER THIRTY-EIGHT:
COMPSON WINDER

I heard the rumble of the damned at just about dawn and knew it was not the wind. And I knew that no animals made sound like that, not even when they're moving in large herds. While I was walking from the barn to that farmer's ramshackle house to awaken the plump Mistress Bartow, a big covy of crows lit out for the morning sky. They were perched in the trees at the other end of the cucumber field, and I knew it was not I who disturbed 'em. It was the noise of many men on the march that made them unhappy, and set them to their first flight of the new day.

I was uncertain how to wake Mistress Bartow. I didn't want to enter the house through the main door. If she was in that farmer's bed it might mean startling her in a way I did not care to experience. Instead, I went to the back window that had no glass and loudly whispered.

"Mistress Bartow," I said, keeping my head bent down in case she rose up to be displayed in the window while wearing only her unders. "Wake up, ma'am. Wake up, Mistress Bartow." Finally, after a second effort, the sound of snoring stopped.

"What is it, Compson?" she said from the other side of the wall.

"There're sounds coming from the wood, ma'am. It's getting closer."

"All right, Compson," she said as the springs in Farmer Lodwell's old bed squeaked loudly. "Go to the porch, I'll be right there."

"Yes'am."

As she waddled to the porch still buttoning her dress and wiping her face with a lady's handkerchief, there came more sounds. I was not born in service to Master Winder. I was sold to him almost thirty years earlier at Odd Fellows Hall when I was a teenager. But I knew his voice and the voice of Mistress Winder. And that's what I heard being carried on the wind from the woods. It was distant. We couldn't tell what was being said. But I knew it was them. They were talking loud about something. Then the talking switched over to shouting and the shouting switched over to wild excitement. That was followed by a volley of pops that I knew with certainty to be rifle fire. Afterward, the distant twitter of morning birds stopped.

"Compson," Mistress Bartow said, looking beyond the cucumber field, "what does this portend?"

"Ma'am, I just cannot be certain," I said. We both held our vigil from the porch, looking off in the direction where dust clouds rose in the morning light. Then we got our answer. Two men emerged from the wall of woods on the opposite side of the cucumber field. They were followed by ten more, then—hundreds. They stepped forward into visibility like ghosts appearing from nowhere, walking across the dried cucumber rows toward the house. And they were Yankees—every one.

"Good morning, ma'am," said the first one to reach the dilapidated porch. He cradled his long musket-rifle in the crook of both arms and leaned his weight onto one hip in a surly manner, although he did remove his cap to the plump lady.

"Mornin'," she said without meaning it.

I knew she did not like his manner. I knew that her one word greeting was the best she could muster and that she nearly choked on that. She certainly could not speak the word "good" to him, even if he did remove his cap.

"Did you by any chance get separated from three of your party during the evening, ma'am?" he asked.

"Yes. Cyrus and Marion Winder and Ruth Pegram." She spoke fast to conclude all communications with him as quickly as possible.

"Uh-huh. And they were with you and this fella here?" He eyeballed me from head to toe.

"Yes."

"Pardon me for saying so, ma'am, but the two of you don't much resemble a Virginia farm couple. May I ask—what is your business here?"

"We are Richmond refugees. Mister Lodwell is the farmer. This is his cucumber field. He has gone off in search of his son."

"Uh-huh."

Yankees continued to pour from the distant wood and many more gathered nearby to listen to our exchange. They looked us over as though we were oddities of nature. It was a curiosity I could understand. After all, I still wore my black top hat, red velvet vest, proper chauffeur jodhpur-trousers, and fine, high-top riding boots. And with her in her Sunday gray calico, no matter how worn and tatty it had become, she did not cut the natural figure of a farmer's wife any more than I cut that of a field hand.

"That's right, we are all from Richmond, civilians wishing to escape hostilities. Can you tell us if there has been a battle for Richmond?"

The soldier finished eyeing us. He put his cap back on his head. "Well, ma'am," he began, adjusting the grip on his musket-rifle, "I am sorry to tell you the news. I don't know what those three people thought they were doing hiding in them woods during the night. It's a mighty odd thing to be doing.

But women or no women, my men took 'em to be rebel videttes and shot 'em down. As for Richmond, we're hearing there ain't nothing left to fight over no more. We're hearing it's done burned down. All of it. The whole metropolis. Right down to the ground."

She collapsed on the spot into a weeping pile.

Except for the news they bore, the Yankees did us no harm and eventually passed on, moving in the same direction the Johnnies had fled the day before, toward Amelia along the Appomattox River. They just kept coming and coming—thousands of 'em. It was mid-morning before I began my own plan. First, I helped Mistress Bartow back to that old farmer's bed, where she plopped down wailing like a baby with the fever. I had no doubt about what needed to be done. Neither did I have any regret about leaving that plump woman alone in that ramshackle house. I had to get back to Richmond and to my wife as rapidly as I could. Hearing the news, I worried for her safety and needed to move fast. Taking Mistress Bartow with me would only slow me down. So I did what I had to do. I just left her there in that bed and walked off—slow and steady against the tide of Yankees, nodding and "yes-sahing" at 'em all the way across that cursed cucumber field where all the craziness started.

At the tree line, I picked the spot where the shots seemed to come, which was close to where they all entered the woods the night before. Sure enough—I found them about five hundred paces in—dead, all three of them. Each one of 'em had been shot bunches of times.

It wasn't difficult to piece the parts together. Once they found each other during the night, they were lost. Rather than wander about and risk getting more lost, they huddled together until morning in a little dug-out space behind a fallen tree. That's what Master Winder would make them do. He was a smart

man. You don't become a master wheelwright, own a fine business, and be a rich Virginia gentleman without also being smart.
It was his misfortune to be brought down by the craziness of
others. That's an aggravating matter for which even smart men
have not yet ciphered a solution.

With the Yankees still streaming past, I looked down at the
bodies. The cause of it all, the crazy Mistress Pegram, was
clothed in Master Winder's outer jacket and one of Mistress
Winder's petticoats. Propped on a log, her naked feet poked up
like a pair of cooked turkey legs on a serving plate. I couldn't be
sure about it, but I swear it appeared that woman had more
toes than people are supposed to possess. But it was all too ugly
and I didn't care to look overly close, just as I didn't care to
look at Mistress Winder's dead face, twisted as it was to put her
unnatural nose on exhibition, making those ill-formed nostrils
appear to be a fleshy pair of kitchen scoops.

My master must have gotten shot first. From the look of it,
he stood up to approach the Yankees and address them. While
trying, hoping to explain the situation, the women probably
panicked and commenced yelling and crying out, which was
just more craziness and likely caused a score of trigger-happy
Yankees to fire off. He fell forward onto his belly—toward the
Yankees, shot in the face and chest. The women were shot in
the back and head as they scrambled from their dug-out huddle
to flee. They fell on their sides while trying to escape in the opposite direction from Master Winder. I declare, each of them
dog-leg twisted bodies did betray such states of anguish that I
felt right sorry for all of 'em.

When no Yankee soldier was close upon me, I stooped down
to Master Winder's body and reached under the lining of his
long-johns—to the small of his back where he kept his money
purse. It was untouched. Had he been wearing his own jacket
and his fancy boots—it would have been a sure sign that he was

a man of means and those Yankees would have given his body a good going over. But in his current state, shoeless and shopworn—he truly looked like nothing special, which I knew to be the only reason his purse went unmolested.

I removed the wad of Union currency and the heavy pouch of gold coins. I put the wad of paper Yankee money in my trousers pocket and dropped the heavy gold coins down the hidden pocket inside my long-johns.

Afterward, I joined up with the Yankees and walked easy until we reached the main road where I bid them adieu.

"Au revoir, les messieurs," I said, exercising my French on 'em. "Merci et la bonne chance."

"Au revoir," "au revoir," and "adieu," some of them called back to me, waving.

"I am free, free," I said in a cheerful voice, pretending to be jubilant. "Je suis libre, libre!"

"Liberte . . . liberte," two Yankees called back, as if congratulating me and themselves, too.

Unbothered to be walking, I took the main road north to Richmond. With the Johnnies on the run, the war near about over, the whole world changing over for the better, and a great fortune tucked inside my long-johns—it was my plan to start a livery stable and become the richest darkie that city has ever seen.

I walked on into the afternoon before meeting with a new challenge.

"My-oh-my! You sure are a fancy-lookin' one," he said to me.

"Yes-sah," I said, looking up at the white man on horseback riding south on the main road. I knew his old nag was likely stolen from some Butternut along the road from Richmond, because she was beat down and starving. I figured him to be a Yankee on the run—skipping out from his military duties.

"Where'd you get that Abe Lincoln hat and that red vest," he asked.

"Got 'em in Richmond."

"What'd you do in that terrible city?"

"Stable master for a rich man. He dead now. Yankees shot him down by accident on a farm near Colonial Heights."

"How much you want for that red vest boy?"

"Dunno."

"How 'bout one dollar."

"That be fine." I took off the vest and handed it up to him in exchange for the dollar.

"How much you want for that big hat?"

"Dunno."

"How 'bout one dollar."

"That be fine." Again we made the exchange.

"How much you want for them fancy riding boots?"

"Can't sell them, sah. I gotta have 'em to walk back to Richmond."

"What for? Ain't nothing there. I just come from there. It done burned down."

"Sorry, sah. I can't sell my boots."

"Five dollars."

"Tell you what, sah. I'll trade you my boots for this horse and give you back your two dollars."

"This old nag? She ain't much, but she worth more'n that."

"Well, that's my offer, sah."

He rubbed his fuzzy chin whiskers. "It'll mean walking for me," he said, eyeing me hard. "What you in such a big hurry to get back to Richmond for? Ain't nothing there. I told ya. It done burned down."

"I got work to do, sah. And ridin' will get me there quicker."

He rubbed his whiskers some more. "Well, all right," he said, "it's a deal." I sat down on a rock and pulled off my fancy high top riding boots, taking care not to let the gold coins inside my long-johns make any clinking noises. He dismounted, took off his union boots, and tossed them at me. He pulled on my boots, got up, and walked off without another word, looking like a fool wearing my black felt top hat, red vest, and thigh-high riders.

I contemplated putting on his Yankee boots, but the sight of that man's backsides ambling south in my clothes made me want to bust with laughter, so I hastened to depart before I irritated him with my own merriment indulged at his expense. I tied the laces together, straddled them around the nag's neck, and resumed my journey north to Richmond and to my wife— but now in my stocking feet and on horseback.

Turns out, that old nag was as determined as I was to see the whole thing through. She not only got me back to Richmond but found reserve to pick up a little strength along the way, like she knew something was up and wanted to learn what it was. I grew fond of her and spoke to her real nice, which she liked. Twice I leaned back in the saddle and rubbed her head and neck with my stocking feet. She liked that. It must have looked right odd to passers. But that was fine. Before we got back, I had named her Lucky and decided to nurse her over to a better life. She deserved the respect of a real horseman.

Those Yankee men were mostly right—a lot of the city did burn, but not all of it. Everything west of Ninth Street survived, which meant the Winder house and stable had survived. It stunk, too. I could smell it before reaching it. But that was fine. I didn't care. Nothing much about Richmond ever did smell very good to me.

Yankee engineers had slapped together what they called a pontoon floater across the James to replace the Mayo Bridge burned down by skedaddling Johnny Rebs. I guess they burned it so the Yankees wouldn't chase 'em. That struck me as stupid, 'cause it's Richmond the Yankees wanted, not all them broke-down Johnnies too skinny to fight.

I liked that wobbly bridge. It was smart, just a bunch of floating rafts all hooked up together, but it worked fine. I can't help but respect smart things and smart people, too, no matter who they are.

But not all Yankees were overly gifted with cleverness. They let me pass over their pontoons without posing inquiry of me. If they'd known I was in possession of more money than any of 'em dare dream in ten-score lifetimes—things would be different. They'd be all over me like flies on horse-heap. They saw I was a black man in my stocking feet riding a beat-down ole nag and they just waved me on across the river like I was just another darkie in a long line of useless, beat-down, freed-up slaves with nothing better to do than head for downtown, burned-up Richmond. I waved back at 'em. But inside, I was having me a good laugh.

Riding up Ninth Street I saw that Pegram girl they called Miss Francine. She was running north with a crowd toward the big statehouse. I called out—but she couldn't hear me over the street noise. She would want to know that her Mistress Pegram was dead—shot down by Yankees near Colonial Heights along with my own master and mistress. But I couldn't chase her down. And neither was I inclined to stop at the Pegram house to pass on my news. I had to get back to the Winder home—to get to my wife.

And by the grace of God, I found her safe in our room behind the stable, but everything else had been filched to a totality. She related how everything got robbed by white persisters—silverware, china, curtains, knick-knacks, old dueling pistols. I inspected the main house and saw it with my own eyes. It was picked clean as a week-old dog's bone. Even the statue of a praying naked lady in the garden was toted off by roving mobs of riff-raff white folks. Thankfully, they had left my wife un-troubled.

My intention was to take possession of the other horse and buggy in the Winder stable, but it too was stolen.

I rested a while and recounted details of the last two days to my wife while Lucky got watered and fed what was left of the hay. I told her of my plans to open a stable, possibly north of town where the Yankees could avail themselves during their comings and goings between Richmond and Washington City in the months to come. She was not overly taken with the idea. But when I showed her riches fit for the Sheik of Araby that I bore in my long-johns, she changed up and decided it was a fine idea. The Winders had no children. Now—with both of them lying dead next to crazy Mistress Pegram, and with what seemed like every slave in the entire state of Virginia roaming free on the streets of Richmond—there would be no challenge to my plans.

I put my wife on Lucky and walked beside 'em, heading north, slow and easy.

Lordy me. Lord-o'lordy me. I did say a quiet prayer to express my gratitude to Jesus for the blessings wrought by his divine intervention. After a while, I laughed. I just couldn't help myself. I laughed out loud, good and hard, with my head thrown back like a gospel singer in the choir. Both Lucky and my wife looked at me with puzzlement as if to ask, "What in the world have you got happening inside your head?"

CHAPTER THIRTY-NINE:
PRESIDENT ABRAHAM LINCOLN

It was quite peculiar.

It may have been the most remarkable day of my administration, at least from my humble viewpoint—yet there were no reporters present to record it. It is understandable that not a single newspaper man met us at the landing for the walk up the hill, for the journey was generally held in confidence. Yet, neither did any arrive for the carriage ride down the hill in the early afternoon—although by that time, the secret of my presence in the conquered city was far more public than my security men wished it to be. Indeed, I cannot recall any other time when I was received by such a crowd in such a heightened state of fervor.

That oversight on the part of our practitioners of the First Amendment can be explained only by those engaged in the philosophical study of supreme irony. Reporters never failed to preside over the most insignificant development at any affair of any bureau under my supervision. Yet they were absent from Richmond City on that great day. To me, that is an unparalleled demonstration of the comedic sense of justice possessed by the laughing gods of fate that rule us all.

The date of April fourth was notable for another reason to celebrate. It was Tad's twelfth birthday. We had a celebration planned—but in seeing my own excitement, he overlooked the forthcoming festivities with ease and implored that, instead, he be allowed to accompany me. I was pleased Mary had departed

City Point to return to the White House the previous Saturday. If she were present, she would not have permitted the lad to join me.

The river boat was too big for the Richmond wharf, so we transferred to a barge near the city and arrived earlier than anticipated on the morning of the fourth around eleven a.m. at a place named Rocketts. The planned security supplement was not present due to our premature arrival.

"We must be delayed, Mr. President. We await a carriage for your safety," they told me.

"Where is the carriage?" I asked with impatience, unable to remove my gaze from the burned silhouette of a defeated city cast against the morning sky.

"We are early, Mr. President. It will arrive shortly, sir. We cannot go without additional security. There is the danger of snipers, sir."

I accepted the admonishment. I waited. I watched the charred streets leading down to the boat landing as a child watches a puppet show with great wonder. There were Negroes present, laboring to clear debris felled during the destruction. They glanced occasionally with curiosity at our odd vessel, which did not receive or discharge passengers or exhibit any obvious point of business or purpose in being there. And there were stragglers at loiter—drunkards no doubt who appeared to have endured the night atop a massive stone amid the shoreline's protruding riprap. But there was no carriage. Such is the disappointment and womb-like isolation of being president.

After some delay that I determined to be more than generous—I could tolerate the delay no longer.

"Gentlemen," I pronounced. "There are security men aboard this barge. We shall walk."

"But Mr. President . . . you cannot sir . . . this is Richmond . . . you are not safe . . . it is the rebellion's capital."

"Shoulder your arms and make yourselves ready. I am going ashore." It amused me privately to see them hastily scramble at their madcap preparations. I do believe they were as worried on behalf of their own fate as they were genuinely cautious of my own.

I was the first to step over. I hoisted Tad afterward. His eyes grew wide to look down and see the dark waters of the James River lapping just two feet below his toes. Following us came Admiral Porter, two of his adjutants, Mr. Charles Coffin, and a half dozen marine sailors who quickly took the lead.

The nearest group of Negroes took notice immediately, which frightened Tad and made him grip my hand. For most of the walk through Richmond, he was as tight upon me as though solidly attached at my hip.

It was not long, just two blocks as I recall, before there was much excitement among the growing crowd. There were many more Negroes than anyone realized. They rapidly emerged from burned buildings and debris fields to follow our path with encouraging shouts and gleeful acknowledgment. By the time we reached the Virginia statehouse they had formed such a large gathering that the marines felt obliged to fix bayonets to discourage anyone from seeking greater proximity.

Tad's hand grew tighter upon mine, and I did pause to speak a quiet word of reassurance to him and to one Negro who dropped to his knees in fitful exaltation. Were it not for the propriety of my office, I say plainly that I would have knelt to the ground and wept alongside him, for I too felt exalted. It was a moment like no other.

I paused to admire President Tom Jefferson's classical Greek statehouse design, which I would have enjoyed touring in addition to my visit at the Confederate White House, but I did not divert our walk, which occupied perhaps twenty blissful minutes.

As it happened, even the brief stay in President Davis' house was a satisfying one. Aside from holding a meeting with General Weitzel and other officers of the occupation—where I was mostly distracted in mind—I also sat upon President Davis' chair and looked at his desk as I took a glass of water while feeling the support of his solid desktop at my elbow. It was then I said my prayer of gratitude to the heavenly Father. I did also indulge in a private moment of self-congratulation that it was I resting at the Davis desk in Richmond—rather than him resting at the Lincoln desk in Washington.

The blessed carriage made its tardy arrival at the Confederate White House and soon bore us away. There was a brief stop, again in the shadow of President Tom Jefferson's statehouse, where I said a few words under the towering statue of President Washington, this time not just to the gathered Negroes but also to a crowd of displaced, burned-out Richmonders looking about as hard-worn and haggard a group of people as I have ever seen.

Because there were no reporters present, these words comprise a reasonable paraphrase of my spontaneous remarks as best I can recall:

My friends, take heart that upon this day the Lord has provided salvation for us all. I speak not only of salvation for those freed from bondage, but also for those of you chained by the convictions of your past. You, too, are freed by these momentous developments that bring an end to national calamity and binds our country's wounds.

This war, we now know, will soon be over. And when it is, all men—Negro and white man alike—may rest in the confidence that right really has made might. But know also, that our might holds no malice, and bears only charity for those who fought to deny the natural birthright of Negroes, and in so denying—split us asunder.

Should we falter in our mission to heal this great nation, many future generations will also be made shadows in these flames of Richmond, every bit as much as we have all been shadows in the fire of this hateful war.

And know too, that with the end of this war—the horrible shedding of so much American blood—is nearing its own merciful conclusion.

With the grace of God, we shall be one again.

Afterward I called upon the house of my friend General George Pickett, who made it his business to fight for the South. He was not home. His wife answered the door and I left word with her that I paid a friendly calling.

During our return voyage to City Point, Tad thanked me and told me the visit to Richmond was the finest birthday present he ever had. I smiled and nodded in the affirmative when he inquired if he might still have birthday cake upon our return.

CHAPTER FORTY:
MISS FRANCINE PEGRAM

Later that night, two lines were formed that separated the girls from the boys in what they called the nave, then each group marched in different directions. I got sent with the other girls into a narrow back corridor of the church made even more pinched for walking room by a long row of scrimpy bed cots. Each cot had a thin mattress stuffed with real cotton, topped by a tiny pillow and overlaid with one frowzy woolen blanket. After we said more prayers, the candles were blown out and we were told to go to sleep.

I slid my brokens under the cot and curled into a tight bundle as the sad events of the last three days revisited me over and over in the dark. Again and again the man in the wagon of torment sought mercy, Missus Pegram left me to burn in the fires, the China-head doll spoke to me during my sickness, Lieutenant Dunnovant took his dog pleasures upon me, and the Tall Man paraded up Twelfth Street amid a great jubilation of slaves. And again and again, it all occurred while Extra was not working the ramparts, but in town—whoring.

★ ★ ★ ★ ★

AFTER THE WAR

★ ★ ★ ★ ★

Chapter Forty-One:
Miss Francine Pegram

I called that church home for nearly one full year. It's where we ate morning bread, had evening soup, and, after singing and praying, got sent off every night to our scrimpy bed cots. Pastor Burkett was a young man, not much more than twenty years of age. But he was kindly to the "war orphans," as he named us, and explained that he had no choice but to put the ones who stayed on for any chunk of time into some manner of "earn your keep." The mostly useless few boys did mostly toting and fetching. The girls mostly got put to making stitching repairs, cleaning, and kitchen labors, which is where I landed until Pastor learned I could read. That got me moved over to helping write up "reconnect notices," as he called them—letters the Sunday worshippers wanted for mailing to the lost and sold off.

Over the months, I made many trips from the church in the company of others, including Pastor Burkett, to run errands for shopping and food barter. But during the winter, I made two journeys on my own that were like a healing tonic for me because they helped end visions that haunted me each night— visions that prevented me from sleeping, no matter how tired. After those two trips, I was able to drop into my nighttime slumbers without seeing and reseeing the wagon of torment, the fires, Lieutenant Dunnovant, the jack-o'-lantern man, and Extra whoring.

The first trip was an errand, early on a Saturday morning, to buy a bag of root turnips from a former slave who'd set up a roadside stand near the Great House of Government. It was bitter cold and Richmond was covered with a layer of fresh snow. But I didn't mind. As I have said, running errands in the grand city of Richmond has always been one of my private joys. I wore two pairs of socks with my brokens and wrapped my frowzy woolen blanket tight around my tummy for warmth.

On the way, I gave thought to walking past the Pegram house. But instead, I took the straightest path, as instructed by Pastor Burkett, and promptly bought the turnips for church dinner. On return, I can only explain it by saying that curiosity and boldness won me over. Instead of walking the straightest path back to church, I went trudging down the familiar Ninth Street hill, being pleased along the way to look back and see only my own prints trailing behind me in the snow. Once opposite the Pegram house, I paused to give it a study.

Having learned various facts from different ones in the days and weeks after the fire, I knew Missus was dead. It was mostly Pastor Burkett who related news events as they became known, always taking care to pass on any ugliness with a soft manner, including the gossip news about my momma and Extra's momma being the same.

While looking at number 212 Ninth Street, I reached under the woolen blanket to feel my three notes of good Yankee money weighted down in the pocket of my gingham where I kept them anchored with a string to my granddaddy's knife. Then I rubbed my tummy, knowing that my secretly kept money was going be a boon to me soon enough.

The house was the same, yet not the same. It appeared closed down and I doubted former Master Pegram was home. But I had no desire to know where he might be, even though I had conjured the secret truth—that he was my daddy. Watching it made me remember a time in the middle of the war, also in the snow, when I spied a litter of orphaned puppies in the empty lot behind the house. They were different shades of splotchy brown, probably bird dogs. They were not helpless newborns, but neither were they old enough to be on their own, fending for themselves in the hard cold. Most likely their momma was dead. No momma dog I ever heard of would abandon her pups, so I conjured she must have been killed somehow, maybe butchered by starving slaves or Butternut soldiers. For about five days running, I kept a sharp watch. During every trip to the privy and every short chance I got to peek from the upstairs rear window I would look out, hoping to spot them.

They were a curiosity because of the hard differences between their looks and their ways. They were clumsy little piglet dogs in need of a good petting. Yet they did not behave like puppies; they behaved like wild creatures. They crawled with caution among the debris piles and snow loblollies the way Ole Mister Rat once crawled in the cellar's "useless memorial to antiquity." I saw them trying to hunt birds, but being puppies they were clumsy and not very good at it. I did see one successfully pounce upon a mouse. But at that moment, his brothers began a rough fight to take it away from him, which allowed the terrified little creature to escape in the tussle.

"Don't you dare touch them dogs, Miss Francine," Missus Pegram warned. "They are wild and most likely nasty with the sickness. You just stay out of their business. Nature will make do with them," she said.

She was right. Nature did make do. After a few days they dwindled from five to two. And then I saw them no more.

Walking home with my bag of turnips, I knew it had been the right thing to do. It made me feel better to see that house again with a new understanding, and to know that my life behind those walls was done for good, and that nature did not "make do" with me like it made do with the puppies.

Two days after my visit to the Pegram house, and mostly

because I had become his most reliable war ophan, Pastor Burkett sent me out again. This time it was by wagon to Danville Station to pick up two former slave girls arriving by train who were making their way to their daddy who'd escaped during the war to a town called Albany. They were now planning to reconnect as a family. I was to pick them up at the station and bring them back to church for a few days of religion and good feeding before we sent them on farther north. When it was called out to me that the wagon had arrived and was waiting out front on Broad Street, I again bundled in my woolen blanket to keep my tummy good and warm, and trudged out into the snow.

Extra was driving the wagon.

It was the first time I'd seen him since that day in April, though I knew from news reports that he was still at the Spotswood and working for his former master. We didn't talk much at first. Then, while stopped in traffic, he looked over at me and spoke with a voice I'd never before heard come from him. It was the voice of a fully grown man.

"Missy Fran, I just want to say, I sorry."

"I know, Extra."

"Things got crazy during them odd days."

"I know, Extra."

"I thought you was refugeed south with your Missus Pegram. Then, when I found out you was still in town, well . . ."

"I know, Extra."

When traffic cleared up, Extra gee'd the team and we lurched forward, talking more freely over the noise of a rowdy Richmond very much on the mend, with great crowds of Yankees moving about everywhere with important business.

"Your ole missus dead," he said. I nodded. "You learn Mister Pegram your daddy yet?"

I felt the pocket knife under my blanket coat.

"Yes, Extra. I know."

"He working for the Yankees now. They sending him out to help 'em rebuild." I nodded. "Yankees figured that funny-looking merchant-man killed Mister Lootinunt in three-fifteen. That all we know about that." I nodded, though I wondered if he didn't know more about the shooting of Lieutenant Dunnovant than he was saying. "Father Lincoln dead, too. Riverjames told me ya'll saw him that day he come to town." He hesitated, and looked away. "I wish I seen him, too. I been right sorry every since that I missed him." I nodded. He looked sorrowfully at my tummy. "You all right at the church?" I nodded yet again. "I stayed on at the Spotswood," he told me. "I got my own room now. It's on the back side. I get better food. I get paid some little bit, too."

"What do you call him?" I asked.

"I mostly just call him 'sir.' He don't want me to call him 'father.' " He studied my tummy again. "When you goan have your baby?" he asked.

"Not sure," I said. "Maybe next month. Maybe a little longer. Pastor Burkett is kind to me about it. He says he's going to summon the midwife when my time comes." He nodded. "Extra," I said, "why didn't you tell me who my daddy was?"

"Same reason I didn't tell you 'bout your momma's slave work at the Spotswood. Same reason nobody told me she was my momma, too. They didn't want me to know she was a, well, you know . . ."

"Yes, I know, Extra. Did Mister Pettigrew tell you where our momma got sold off to?"

"Missy Fran, I asked and asked. He only say she on the middle neck."

"What town?"

"Dunno, Missy Fran. He just say she sold to a man who worked both land and water. So she off in the country,

355

somewhere near water. Maybe on the Rappahannock, or what they call the Chesapeake Sea. But we ain't heard nothing from her, not even since the Yankees took over. You thinking to reconnect if she alive?"

I was pleased that we were arriving at Danville Station, which gave me good reason not to respond to his question. The train chugged up in a timely fashion and we picked up the two girls. They were twins, only nine years old, and, I guessed, just as terrified of what was happening to them as I was that first day when left alone in the house on Ninth Street. Having a job to do with those girls, I couldn't tarry when we arrived back at the church on Broad Street. But I did want to make an offer to my brother.

"Extra, Pastor Burkett has me working some with different ones, teaching them to read. If you come to services, I could make introductions to Pastor and teach you some reading too after Sunday church."

"That be fine," he said, smiling his big smile at me.

That night, I fell into a quick sleep without visitation from my demons born during the "odd days," as Extra called them. But with the coming of first sunlight, the black dog returned to my dreams just ahead of the new day.

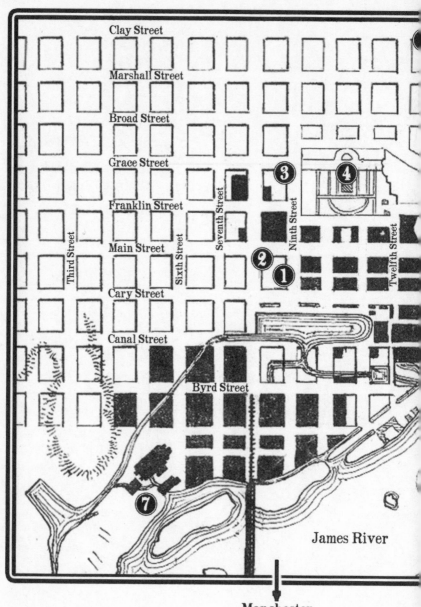

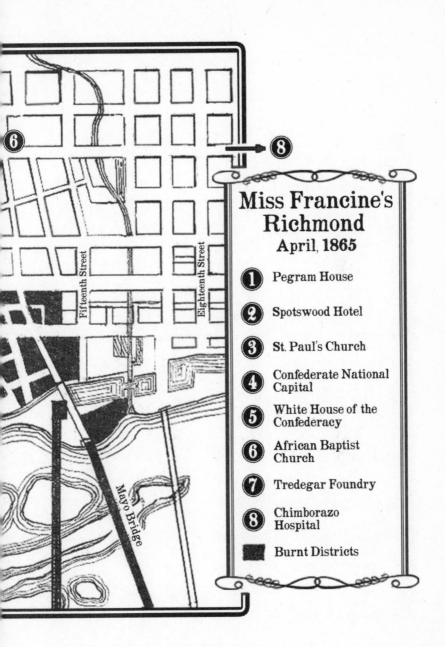

Miss Francine's Richmond
April, 1865

1. Pegram House
2. Spotswood Hotel
3. St. Paul's Church
4. Confederate National Capital
5. White House of the Confederacy
6. African Baptist Church
7. Tredegar Foundry
8. Chimborazo Hospital

■ Burnt Districts

NOTE TO THE READER

While couched in real events, the story of Miss Francine is fiction. Effort has been made to accurately depict authentic history surrounding the evacuation, looting, burning, Union occupation, and visit to Richmond by President Lincoln, although I have taken creative license where necessary.

Many locations in the novel are factual and remain standing today, including the White House of the Confederacy, St. Paul's Episcopal Church, and the Virginia Capitol, which served as capitol of the Confederacy and was based on a design by Thomas Jefferson. Chimborazo Hill is now the site of a medical museum and, along with the remains of Tredegar Iron Works, is managed by the National Parks Service. Hollywood Cemetery, mentioned only in passing in the novel, is a vast outdoor artisanal work of wrought iron and sculpted quarry stone that overlooks the James River and is the final resting place of two U.S. presidents, Jefferson Davis, twenty-five Confederate generals, and eighteen thousand Confederate soldiers. The "Lee house" had been rented by the general to serve primarily as his family's war residence and is now privately owned. Though fictionalized in the novel, there was a Spotswood Hotel that survived the war only to be destroyed in another fire on December 25, 1870. City Point was annexed by Hopewell, Virginia, in 1923.

For her support and tireless reading of the manuscript countless times, and loving it more each time, my deep appreciation to my wife, Lisa Weiss.

For his help and encouragement along the way, much gratitude to my friend Charles Salzberg.

For their professional guidance, I am indebted to the terrific Five Star team: Tiffany Schofield, Nivette Jackaway, Tracey Matthews, and Hazel Rumney.

My thanks also to Annie Bergen, Midori Takagi, Julie Jansen, Deborah Brodie, Jenny Cooley, New York Writers Workshop, Virginia Historical Society, Library of Virginia, the Museum of the Confederacy, the National Parks Service and St. Paul's Episcopal Church.

From among the great volume of materials available on the Civil War, I must single out three books in particular: *Richmond Burning, The Last Days of the Confederate Capital,* by Nelson Lankford; *The Fall of Richmond,* by Rembert W. Patrick; and *Rearing Wolves to Our Own Destruction, Slavery in Richmond, Virginia, 1782–1865,* by Midori Takagi.

ABOUT THE AUTHOR

Gray Basnight is a native of Richmond, Virginia, and a great-grandson of the Confederate secessionist movement.

For almost three decades, he worked in New York City in broadcast news as writer, editor, producer, reporter, and newscaster.

His first novel, *The Cop with the Pink Pistol,* received a starred review in *Library Journal* and was singled out as "Debut of the Month."

For more information, see the author's website: graybasnight .com.